THE RITORNELLO GAME

ALSO BY RHONDA CHANDLER

The Fires of Autumn

(Historical Fiction)

THE RITORNELLO GAME

RHONDA CHANDLER

STAIRCASE
BOOKS

THE RITORNELLO GAME

Cover design by Kristen Langefeld

ISBN 978-1-7325797-3-6 (paperback)

ISBN 978-1-7325797-4-3 (large print)

ISBN 978-1-7325797-5-0 (ebook)

Published by Staircase Books

Staircase Books

1111 S. Lincoln Ave. #465

O'Fallon, IL 62269-9998

United States of America

1

___

An Unexpected Enclave

Professor Mark Newlin pushed the door of his class-room open on a late August morning, the first day of the semester, and realized three things. First, the room was already filled with students. Second, he did not recognize the young man who was sitting at the front of the room where Jennifer, his student assistant, should be. Third, the books and papers he carried were slipping from his grasp.

He made a desperate grab for the books, caught his foot on the leg of a chair, and stumbled. One file folder fell, opening wide. Thirty-five copies of his course syllabus, *History 332: The Rise and Fall of Nations*, spread like a paper fan across the floor.

He used to have a quip in his repertoire that would cover embarrassments such as this, but he couldn't remember it. Instead, he found himself muttering "Thank you" to the students nearest the door who scrambled to pick up what he had dropped. He made his way to the front of the classroom, feeling stupidly awkward, and deposited his materials on the small table next to the heavy oak podium.

All the students appeared to be watching him intently and he hadn't begun to speak yet. Shouldn't they still be chattering amongst themselves, reluctant as usual to give up the social excitement of a new semester for the academic work of it? But no. They were looking at him.

He thought of the odd pattern of scars that made shaving such a delicate operation, especially the deeper scar close to his right ear. His face grew warm. Were they staring at that? Or did they notice that his clothes hung loosely on him, as he had discovered just this morning?

He cleared his throat. "Since my syllabus seems eager to be in your hands, I won't hold it back. Let's get these passed out."

He held out the file folder and nodded at the student perched on Jennifer's stool. Jennifer had long hair. This young man didn't have any, on the top of his head at least. A short, thick beard rounded his face from cheek to cheek. He reached for the file eagerly, and immediately took up his stance at the head of the first row of desks, thumbing through the papers as he counted off the number needed for that row. One of those small academic rituals that had the surprising effect of comforting Mark Newlin for just a moment.

But he was disappointed in himself. This lame beginning was not how he wanted to open this class. He paged needlessly through his own notes to cover his frustration.

He had meant to begin with the concise story of a kingdom from its beginning to its end. Then he would ask the students to guess which kingdom it was. He would follow it with another example, followed by another guess. This would engage the students' interest, and not twenty minutes into the topic they would find their thoughts broadening, reaching for understanding.

It was a part of the opening day that he always looked forward to. The moment he could sense the students making the topic their own. Today he planned to use the Carolingian Franks, followed by the Macedonians. He sent a quick check to that inner part of himself where his storytelling energy resided. Could he still do it?

Empty.

A breath of fear wafted out of the hollow place. He shut a mental door on it. So . . . he would do his planned opening on Thursday. What now?

The unknown assistant placed the file folder on the table and took his seat again. *Why didn't he know the student's name?* Mark had seen him before, surely. He felt too foolish, too tired, to ask him.

Mark cleared his throat one more time, looked out at the rows of expectant faces, and made a desperate effort to pull thoughts from the air.

"We've all been to the movies to see adventure stories that relate the clash of two forces, two peoples, two kingdoms, resulting in the inevitable defeat and fall of one or the other of them. From Troy to Rome to Stalingrad to the fictitious Gondor. Such topics are of great interest to the historian and to each person on earth. Because wherever we come from on this planet, our home country is at some point in its life span, and that should matter a great deal to us."

The sea of faces was still watching him closely. No one whispered casually to a neighbor. No one shifted in a seat. Whether it was due to his scars or his words, he would use that attention.

He took a deep breath. It didn't feel like enough. Fear seeped from behind the closed mental door. He took another breath.

"Dramatic though the fall of a people can be, predictable though it might be, what we might find astonishing is how some peoples rise at all."

Could they hear him in the back of the room?

"The study of the growth of strength, the fusing of identity and purpose, is fascinating. Historians, just like doctors, study a people like a baby, and see if they have the factors necessary to thrive.

"Of course, you can ask what it means to thrive, and I would have to introduce you to another group of arguing historians and sociologists striving to answer that."

Several smiles. But they looked strained. Polite. Worried.

"Thrive is a word with varying definitions." He was saying the words slowly. Too slowly.

Was he speaking loud enough? Was this boring them?

Suddenly he could not see their eyes.

Where did they go?

He couldn't hear himself.

Was he still speaking?

He had the strange sense of something off to his right moving quickly.

HE WAS STARING at a white acoustic-paneled ceiling with lights embedded in it. One of the light panels was directly, uncomfortably, above him. He blinked.

The classroom ceiling.

Why was he staring at the classroom ceiling?

A fringe of heads formed a circle around him.

Who?

Students?

I'm still in class!

The hard tile floor was pressing against his back and head. He blinked again. He tried a long, slow breath.

He didn't feel like moving, but he had to. He raised his right hand and gingerly touched his forehead. A murmur traveled around the fringe of heads.

His glasses. Where were his glasses?

He let his arm slide back down to his side. He had strength for nothing. He closed his eyes again.

His mind felt blank. Fuzzy. Confused.

Just rest. Just wait.

For what?

He felt more of his mind return to him. Like the way computers imitate the brain—running through a check of all their programs, all their systems.

Breathing. Check.

Heart. Check. Rate? Can't tell.

Temperature. A little chilly. Clammy. Check.

Mental powers. He answered the questions automatically. He had heard them asked so many times since the accident that they were memorized.

Mark Newlin

Professor of History, Gold College, Illinois

42 years old

Married? Was. Was married. No. Don't ask that!

All the mental circuits came rapidly back online, as if someone were racing from room to room in the house of his mind throwing every light switch on.

And he saw her again. Beloved Amy. Motionless. Crushed in the seat next to him. One arm extending from the mass of twisted metal.

Shut the lights off! Don't look!

In his helpless position, he had nowhere to run from the memory. Hot tears leaked from his eyes and made their way down the new map of his face. He felt wetness in his ears.

That decided it. He was not going to move from this place ever again. No matter how hard the floor was. He would stay. They could bury him right here.

"Professor Newlin? Mark? Mark?"

He opened his eyes. The fringe of heads parted, then were eclipsed by the gray hair and dark beard of Jerry Waite, chairman of the department. An unmistakable face.

"I'm here." Mark said it so quietly he wasn't sure if anyone heard it.

Jerry knelt by his side and let out a sigh that sounded like relief. "I've called the paramedics. They should be here soon. You'll be okay, Mark. You'll be as right as rain."

Right as rain? Jerry never talked like that.

Jerry turned to the students and raised his voice. "Class is over. You can go now. Check your campus email for further instructions."

At that moment, as the hard floor seemed to locate every bone and bruise on his body, Mark knew he would not be using his favorite class opening on Thursday either.

TWO DARK-HAIRED PARAMEDICS the size of defensive linemen eased him from the classroom floor and onto the bed they had brought with them. One of them slid a blood pressure cuff on his arm and inflated it. Mark kept his eyes on the ceiling as the cuff tightened. He had never enjoyed the sight of medical paraphernalia and the last months had made him hate it even more.

His thoughts whined like a petulant child, which didn't help matters. He tried to muster more patience while they shone lights in his eyes, and ears, and mouth, and even up his nose, put a thermometer in his mouth, and felt his wrist for a pulse.

"He seems to be in no immediate danger," one of them said. "His vital signs are stabilizing and are what we would expect after syncope. But we recommend taking him to the hospital overnight for further evaluation and treatment, considering what you said he's been through lately."

They were talking to Jerry and not to him. As if Jerry were his father and he was not yet eight years old.

"Whatever you think best," said Jerry.

He took a deep breath, calling his own voice into action. "No."

They turned to stare at him as if the dead had spoken. Jerry. The two burly paramedics. The student who had passed out the syllabus, whose name he still didn't know.

He tilted his head to look straight at Jerry. "I'm not going back to the hospital."

Jerry frowned, one hand pulling at the hair on his chin. The nervous habit that had been his for as long as Mark had known him.

"We can let him rest here for a few minutes," said the other paramedic, "while we start our paperwork, then do another check of his vitals."

Jerry nodded. "All right." But he was staring at Mark with all the evidence of someone thinking hard. He took a long, slow breath before he opened his mouth again.

"You can't be alone," Jerry said. "You know that. Not after this. And this isn't the first time."

He saw something else in Jerry's eyes, the guilt that he could not bear to see. Mark didn't answer and looked back up at the ceiling. Thankfully, he was no longer directly under the light panel.

What did this embarrassing little episode mean? Was it a continuation of the horrors of this past summer, or something entirely new?

"How is he? How is our Professor Newlin?" A voice—male, gravelly and ingratiatingly wheezy—intruded.

Stanwick. *Shouldn't he be in class right now?*

"Oh, poor Mark!" a woman exclaimed. Vicki, Jerry's secretary. A woman he could never feel comfortable around.

He felt like a zoo animal people had come to gawk at. Never before had he considered how the monkeys felt, gazing through the glass at all those staring faces. *A thousand apologies, monkeys.*

Stanwick made a show of trying to grasp his hand. Mark let him.

"This is awful. We can't let anything more happen to you. You're the pride of the department!" The handshake was too vigorous and Mark was relieved when Stanwick released him.

Vicki leaned across him and took the glasses someone was holding out. She bent over him and speared the frames over his ears, while snapping her gum. He smelled spearmint. He hated spearmint.

"What's this about the hospital?" She took up the theme. "Of course you're going, Mark! You have to!"

She turned to the paramedics. "He's going to the hospital. Take it from me. He's going."

"Are you his wife?" one of them asked.

Vicki sniffed. "I'm the department secretary, and I can sign whatever papers you need."

"Vicki, please." Jerry sounded weary. "Professor Newlin can make his own choice."

"I'm not going," Mark repeated.

"Then that's decided," Jerry said quickly. "We'll take it from there."

The paramedics moved toward him then and Vicki had to back up. A blood pressure cuff tightened around his arm again.

Interminable. That was the word for this. An embarrassment threatening to last as long as a session of the UN General Assembly.

He could be angry, but he was too completely weary to summon any emotion for long. He wanted to sleep.

A clipboard appeared in front of him. "You'll need to sign these forms, sir. They say we recommended EMS transport to the ER for further evaluation. And that you refused medical transport to the ER."

He signed, feeling like a rebel, then laid back on the pillow, energy spent.

"We'll need the bed back," said the clipboard-holder, too close to his head.

"There's a sofa in my office," said Jerry. "Could you put him there?"

Mark closed his eyes and let the weariness take him. Voices blurred together under the rumble of the wheels, the sensation of moving, a sudden jerk, a bump, then moving again.

In the halls he could hear the sounds of classes underway. Professors laying the foundations for another semester of instruction. The familiar rhythm of life.

A deep, resonant voice announced, "Any student who repeats the nonsense that medieval man thought the earth was flat will automatically fail this class." That would be Luedders, he thought, as the voice faded away behind him.

The gurney swung wide and paused near the open door of a classroom situated near the elevator. He could hear Tulia Cardoso's accented voice raised in lecture style.

"The Brazilian poor need to have an address. More than just a roof over one's head is a place with a street name and number. A place to receive mail. Without this, they are hampered economically."

Tulia always like starting her semester with detailed specifics.

The elevator doors opened. The gurney started moving again. Tulia's lecture was abruptly silenced by the closing doors and the elevator's hum. The slight musty smell of the history department elevator filled his nose. He kept his eyes closed.

The bed came to a final stop in a slightly darkened room. He opened his eyes. Jerry's office. The fluorescent light above his small fish tank. The hum of the pump, bubbling away. Jerry's favorite silver dollar fish swooping through their own private ten-gallon lake.

The paramedics lowered the bed a little, and Mark rolled onto the worn, orange vinyl sofa. Someone tucked a throw pillow under his head and spread an afghan over him. The fringe tickled his chin. He knew the afghan. Myra, Jerry's wife, had made it some years ago, and had made a matching one for the Newlins in Amy's favorite colors.

"Your glasses are here on the table next to you, sir." An unfamiliar voice.

He couldn't remember them being removed. But he murmured thanks anyway. He could no longer attempt to open his eyes. He heard equipment being closed, latched, shifted, removed. The click of a light extinguished. The sound of voices moving away from him. The gurgling of the aquarium. The door closed, and he was finally, gratefully, alone.

HE SLEPT FOR A LONG TIME. When he awoke and fumbled for his glasses, they were ready for him. Someone must have been watching through the glass door panel. The door opened and the whole gang filed in. Jerry, Vicki, Stanwick, Luedders, Tulia. And the mystery student holding a lunch tray, his faded gray T-shirt out of place in the middle of an army of professors. Thank goodness the others had classes to teach. This was enough. The room was crowded, and he felt claustrophobic.

"I hope you all have a place to sit down," he said, "because if you keep standing this is going to look too much like the sentencing of a prisoner."

Someone laughed. Chairs were dragged in from the outer office. Jerry took his usual seat behind his desk. Luedders reached out to shake Mark's hand. "So sorry, Newlin."

Jerry waved toward the food-bearer. "Mark, this is your new student assistant, Sean Merritt. I haven't been able to formally introduce you because of some sudden changes. Jennifer asked for special leave. Her mother's ill in Ohio. Sean has extra credentials that will fit your needs better this year, so I thought he would work out well for you."

"Glad to meet you, Sean," Mark said, from force of habit. He sat up slowly and slid his feet down to the floor.

Sean held out the tray to him. "I hope it wasn't the sight of me that brought on your collapse, sir."

Mark couldn't help but smile at that. He took the tray. It had the look of the cafeteria—a sheet of plastic molded into sections filled with chicken on bun, potato salad, cole slaw, and a large chocolate chip cookie. His stomach wasn't sure what it felt right now, about food or anything else. He supposed he should eat a little something.

"We tried it, Mark," Jerry began tentatively. "You wanted to start the new semester as normal, and it didn't work."

"You should have gone to the hospital," said Vicki, in her loud, strident voice.

"Vicki." Jerry's tone carried deliberate patience. "I'll need the day's drop-add numbers before you go home. It might take some time. Registrar's office will be slow today."

"Not if I worked there." She frowned at her boss, then left, with the air of a misunderstood martyr who would be proved right someday. In his heart, Mark was afraid she was right.

"Maybe you should have gone," Jerry continued, "but it was your choice to make. Dr. Matheson is on campus today doing sports physicals. He dropped by in time to chat with the paramedics. He plans to stop by your house later this afternoon."

Mark waited for more, but nothing more came. He looked around at his colleagues and swallowed a bite of chicken sandwich. "I'm sorry. I hope this mess doesn't cause more work for any of you."

Luedders had already picked up his section of Western Civilization. Stanwick had greedily snatched his Voices of History course. He had resented Mark's teaching of it ever since it appeared in the course catalog. And Jerry hadn't given Mark any new advisees this term, which meant the people in this room had more than their fair share.

Tulia flashed brilliant white teeth. "Don't even think about that, Mark."

Luedders stared at the floor saying nothing.

Mark looked up at Jerry. "My classes could just start a week late, right? I could pull in the missing hours with weekend projects. These guys wouldn't have to do anything more, would they? I'll rest a week longer then pick up where I should have today."

No one was joining him in his optimism. In fact they looked more serious with every word he said. He lowered his sandwich and looked intently at Jerry. "What's going on? Something is. You don't assemble a cabal like this for the fun of it."

Jerry picked up a pen and began to draw on his blotter, without looking at Mark. "I've been talking to the dean and the provost for a while. About you. We've agreed that you should—no, change that—you *must* take the semester off. You'll get your sabbatical early. Maybe part of it. Maybe all. That's up to you."

Jerry stared down at whatever his pen was industriously doing on the blotter. Behind him, the silvery fish swam nervously back and forth in their tank. "Your doctors thought you could use some months to heal up, and it looks like they were right. I know you had other ideas for it, but the truth is, you need a sabbatical now, for healing."

Mark didn't know if he was relieved or angry. "So I'm to sit at home and just, what?"

The faculty handbook used the term "a compassionate paid sabbatical." But to be sentenced to his home, to rooms without Amy's presence in them, and without classes and preps to distract him, well, it would choke him. Already did. He couldn't think of a worse torment.

Jerry looked around the room. His glance met knowing looks in the others' eyes. "Dr. Matheson also told us that brain injuries can make long-range planning or even any planning difficult. So, if you will allow, we decided to make some plans for you."

"It doesn't involve Patti does it? She's had to do too much already."

"No, not your sister Patti. I remembered your concern there. Something else. We've all been discussing this, and we think we found something restful. Maybe even enjoyable for you."

So they had all agreed on whatever it was. Jerry had the weight of the college behind him. He wasn't going to risk Mark saying no. He had let Mark have his way about the hospital, but Mark knew he wouldn't be able to oppose this plan, whatever it was, without great effort. And he had no energy for effort.

"What's your idea?" he asked, making his voice as neutral as possible.

Jerry seemed encouraged by this. "We have arranged for you to spend some weeks—"

"Months, really," put in Tulia.

"—at a beautiful hotel on the Mississippi River. A bed and breakfast, but they take long-term guests and have a chef who operates a full restaurant for dinner. It's called Riverview House, in Ashington Mills, Illinois."

He had heard of Ashington Mills. Had never been

there. Had been thinking more of Paris lately. "You want me to go into a home up the river?"

"Bed and breakfast," said Tulia with a laugh. "You know what those are!"

"It's historical," said Luedders in his deep, slow voice. "You'll like it."

Stanwick thrust a brochure under his nose. It looked worn from much handling and had a crease in the wrong place. He took the brochure and opened it carefully.

Riverview House
An historic mansion with a breathtaking view of the
Mississippi
First-class dining
Nine elegantly furnished guest rooms

"Well?" asked Jerry.

He felt numb. He forced the words to come out. "It looks like a nice place. 'Breathtaking view of the Mississippi.'"

Jerry relaxed. Visibly. "Good. They can host you from now until December 11. You'll see the seasons change along the river. It will be beautiful."

December 11? That was months from now. Would he take that long to heal? Were his colleagues aware of more than he was? He nodded his head slowly. Something more was coming. He was sure of it.

"The college will pick up the cost," Jerry said. "The college wants to do this."

That was it. He knew what was coming next.

"We owe you this—"

He held up his hand to stop the words. "Don't. No more of that." He couldn't go there himself.

Jerry closed his mouth and swallowed. An awkward silence settled on them all. Tulia, thank God, broke it.

"There's more, Mark. Tell him, Jerry! It's the best part."

"We're sending you with an assistant. Someone to drive for you, haul the bags, and maybe even help you with your research. You know, type things into your computer until Dr. Matheson feels you can look at screens again. Sean, here, is not currently taking classes, so he can keep you company for the whole semester and help you with whatever you need."

Mark turned to Sean. "Those are your special credentials? Hauling bags? Typing notes?"

Sean grinned. "I've also done a bit of unofficial nursing."

Oh.

He tried to educate the rush of humiliation that rose in him before it could completely take hold. He wasn't well. He wasn't strong. Instead of denying it, he might as well admit it and save everyone a lot of grief. Honestly, by fainting he had scared himself as much as he had scared them. And he was grateful no one had brought up his embarrassment at the faculty picnic Sunday afternoon, when some sort of weak spell had suddenly taken hold of him, and he had dropped his food plate on the shoes of the provost's wife.

Now it was his turn to look around the room and meet all the gazes. His head hurt. His eyes pricked, and he blinked hard several times.

They were all waiting.

Hoping.

Hoping for something good for him. Jerry, Tulia, Luedders, this Sean Merritt, Stanwick. Well, ignore Stanwick. His hopes probably lay in a different direction.

Mark looked back at Jerry as he spoke.

"The college is being very gracious," he said.

"So are you," Jerry replied.

He wished Jerry hadn't said it.

2
____

Oil and Rain

MARK TRIED NOT to feel resentful the next morning as he stood in the driveway of his campus house on Professor's Row, watching Sean load things into the trunk of the old Honda for him. Suitcases, of necessity. Book bag and laptop from force of habit. The problem with resentful feelings was that, in complete honesty, there was no one whom he could fairly resent.

Sean—packing for him last night, asking interested questions about the bookcases that lined his living room walls, sleeping on the sofa in that same living room, fixing his breakfast this morning, refraining from comment on the mostly empty cabinets and refrigerator—was taking great care to treat him with dignity and respect.

Matheson had come by yesterday afternoon to give

him another look-over, a pep talk, and the phone number of a doctor he knew in Ashington Mills with an appointment already booked.

Jerry and Myra Waite had come over earlier this morning for a quick, awkward goodbye. Everyone was clearly trying to do their best for him.

"This looks like a great car. Must be fun to drive," said Sean, slamming the trunk lid down.

It was the only car he had left in the garage. "You'll soon find out," he said, passing over the keys. He grimaced at the tone his own voice carried. Resentful. No doubt.

Sean seemed not to notice, but took the keys cheerfully and climbed into the driver's seat. Mark climbed in and shut his own door. At least he could do that much for himself.

Still. He felt less strong than he had yesterday morning. Or was it the same and his focus on the class had obscured it? That would account for the collapse.

He buckled his seat belt with a firm click.

Sean was looking at him. "Ready?"

He waved his hand. "Let's go."

And just like that they were off, driving away from the row of professors' housing, away from the college property and the town of Marlonburg, and out onto the two-lane highway that ran through corn and soybean fields on its way to the interstate. On to who knew what.

"You're not a bad driver," Mark said.

"Thanks. It *is* a great car. How old is it?"

"Twelve years. Still feels like new. It will probably outlast me." Now *that* sounded maudlin. What could anyone say in response to that?

"Well, maybe," said Sean. "But it won't lecture quite so well."

Mark gave a short laugh. "You're going easy on a crabby, trying man."

"Injury makes everyone crabby. I remember the talk you gave to new students last fall. You weren't crabby then."

"You were a new student last fall?"

"New to Gold College."

"Why Gold?" He had asked dozens of students the same question over the years and felt relief at the normality of it.

"It just felt right. I like the campus. I've never been to a small private college before."

Mark gave him a curious look. "You've been to other colleges?"

"A community college in northern Illinois. Illinois State. Southern Illinois University."

"Carbondale?"

"For architecture. The Edwardsville campus for a short stab at biology."

"What did you do at Illinois State?"

"Computer Science, Public Relations, sang in a choir, did some acting with an improvisation group."

"Then what?" Mark felt better asking the questions, prying into someone else's life instead of his own.

"Worked at a company in Bloomington for a few months, doing the janitor thing. A girl in the office had just graduated from Gold College and said she loved it. So I thought I'd come down and see it."

They had reached the interstate. After the long curl of

the on-ramp, they were headed north. North then west, all the way to the border.

Which sounded more adventurous than the Illinois border really was. Except to Jerry. American History was his life's study.

Jerry would know the history behind every inch of the Illinois border. In kindness, Jerry was probably sending Mark to a place he would love to go himself. Mark would remember that. After a week he would email Jerry and thank him properly. Right now, he was just trying to breathe normally.

"How fast do you want me to drive, sir?"

"No more than three over the limit. To allow for traffic flow."

"Got it." Sean programmed the cruise control.

They were skimming across wide, open places, the ocean of green that Mark had felt the awe of, when, as a young boy from Arizona, he had stayed with his Illinois grandparents for the first time. Now, he felt tight and tense.

Sean's voice broke into his thoughts. "You should probably drink some water now, sir."

"What?"

"It's been a half hour since you had any fluids. You're still healing from a concussion, among other things. Your brain and tissues need lots of fluid to carry out the work of healing."

Mark took the water bottle out of the cup holder and took a long drink, longer than he felt like at the moment. "Are you always going to boss me like that?"

Sean grinned—a slightly goofy grin. "Yes, sir. But only about your health."

They settled into their drive, and Mark found himself watching cars. Not absently like someone out for leisurely enjoyment, but like an air traffic controller who needed to know each one's exact location.

It was barely mid-morning. A Wednesday. Not a heavy traffic time for this part of the state, evidently. But there was a semi coming down the ramp to join them. It would be in their lane. Soon.

"Do you see that?" he said too loudly. Pointing.

"Yes, sir." Sean moved into the left lane giving the semi lots of room.

Mark felt his heart pounding. Muscles tight. They were coming up on a white SUV. He opened his mouth to say something when he heard the tick of the blinker, and Sean pulled into the other lane to pass the car.

Sean was a careful driver, doing just fine. So, why couldn't he just sit back and relax a little?

"Can I ask you a question, sir? Is this your first road trip since—"

"Yes," he said abruptly. He took another drink of water.

Sean kept glancing at him. Little glances with alarm in them.

Alarm. That is how the students were looking at him yesterday. With alarm. *God, help me. I'm a mess.*

Sean broke into his thoughts. "Do you want to talk about the accident? I mean, as your assistant, should I know?"

"Do you want to talk about why you can't settle down

and choose a college major you can stick with?" It sounded harsh. Too harsh.

"No. Well. Maybe. But not now."

"Ditto."

He stared out the passenger window at the green and golden-brown foliage going by. The farmhouses and barns scattered in the distance. The occasional row of trees. Railroad tracks that ran alongside the road.

He hated this. This tight, angry, snapping dog that lived inside him now. Hated inflicting it on other people. Especially a poor student assistant who was stuck in a car with him. Was saddled with him for months and no doubt regretted it already. How much was the college paying this Sean Merritt to stick with him?

Miles went by. And more miles. He forced himself to look for mile markers and count farmhouses instead of cars.

Sean cleared his throat. "Could I ask you why you chose your field of history?"

Safe ground. An olive branch, though it should have been Mark's to extend.

Mark turned away from the window and hoped civil behavior and an honest answer would count as an apology.

"My grandfather's influence."

"He was a history professor?"

"A farmer. He caught me digging up his windbreak one night."

"Sir?"

Mark took a deep breath and made himself talk like a normal human being, saying the words that had been used before, in front of classes of students even, by the Mark who once had been.

"I stayed with my grandparents every summer on their farm near Mattoon. My grandpa told lots of stories. Not small stories about people making mistakes, but big stories about struggle and triumph, how things came to be, and what had disappeared.

"Once he told me about the town of Circleville, Illinois and how it had completely disappeared from the map. Gone. Vanished. Plowed under. I couldn't get the story out of my mind. I thought maybe I could find it. Find Circleville."

"How old were you then?"

"About nine. For some reason I thought it was underneath the windbreak. So one night with a shovel and a flashlight, I started digging between the trees. Grandpa walked across the field to see what I was doing when I should have been getting ready to go to bed.

"There I am digging underneath these huge trees, and he tells me that Circleville was west of us, not even in the same county. I must have looked really disappointed, as foolish as I felt, because he gave me a pat on the shoulder and asked, 'But what *did* you find?'

"We shone flashlights on the piles of dirt, and he said, 'I will tell you what you have discovered.' And he told me the story of the man who planted the windbreak, a man who had—"

With a shock, Mark stopped speaking.

He had told this story so often, so automatically, that he had forgotten where the words would take him until he was already there.

"A man who ended up doing great things," he finished halfheartedly, and stared out the window.

The image of his grandfather took over in his mind. He could still see him, kneeling down and running his thick, knobby fingers through one of the dirt piles Mark had made near the outstretched boughs of an old, and incredibly tall, Douglas fir.

What you've found, Mark, is the work of a man who had lost everything.

What do you mean by everything?

His wife and his young daughter both died of cholera. He lost his job because he was taking care of them. After that, he roamed the country half-starved before my own grandfather took him on as a hired hand.

Mark remembered sticking his fingers into the dirt and feeling its coolness fall through them. Fireflies scooted around them as Grandpa continued his story.

One of the first things this hired man did was to plant this windbreak. No trees on our farm ever flourished like these trees. Do you know why?

He hadn't known.

Because that man planted his heart with every single tree and watered them with his tears. That's what you uncovered, Mark. The man's heart. The man's story. And that is quite a discovery.

They picked up the tools and went back to the house. Later, over bedtime cookies and milk, all Mark's questions spilled out.

What happened to the man? How long did he work on this farm? Did he ever get another family? Was he okay? Did he come back and visit the trees?

And he had been surprised to learn that after several years on the farm, during which the man had become more of a friend than a hired hand, he had married again, had five children, and became a type of forester for the state of Illinois, traveling the state and examining the woodlands.

But how could he do that, Grandpa? After hurting so bad?

Because love heals life, son. It always does and always will. Love is the gift from the Good Lord to this troubled earth. My grandpa's friendship helped heal him. The friendship of neighbors healed him. Their love for him. His love for them. His love for the land. It all worked together to heal.

Mark reached for his water bottle and unscrewed the cap. He found himself suddenly angry at the memory. Angry at the story. Wanting to argue with his grandfather.

No, Grandpa. The man couldn't have healed like that. Some things hurt so bad that you will never get over them.

He felt close to weeping again, and he didn't want to have to explain the tears to Sean. But he reached inside his mind and shut a door. Closed it firmly on that hymn-singing, praying, believing-everything-his-grandpa-said part of himself.

With that, he had an odd sensation of digging in the dark, still trying to find a place that didn't exist anymore. He shivered.

Sean was being patiently silent.

Mark cleared his throat and skipped to the summary of things he had learned from his grandfather. Things he still agreed with anyway. His teaching, storytelling voice came out automatically.

"I learned from my grandfather that all history is an

intertwining of the stories of people, millions upon millions of them. Some as thin as a thread, others as fat as a cable, but all woven together. He showed me that people matter. What they do matters. Their existence matters. That's why I can't help studying it."

Sean was listening closely, he could tell. Nevertheless there was only silence when he finished.

"Lecture number 217," Mark added after a while, trying to make a small joke.

"It's a good one," said Sean, checking his side mirror and flicking the blinker on before passing a car. "I think if I felt that way about any of the things I studied, I would stick with them."

"Not with nursing?" he asked. "Caring for people's health?"

"I do care about that. But I'm not very scientific, so I haven't advanced much beyond the basics of a caregiver. Did you know Professor Sorenson who just retired?"

"Sorenson in the math department? You took care of him? Half the math majors were afraid of him."

"He told me once that I was fairly decent at my job. So don't worry." A quick grin. "But, well. I don't know. Something in me, some engine inside that should provide all the energy or drive for a career, for any career, never seemed to turn on."

"You sound like an auto mechanic."

"I've tried that too." Another grin.

"So, I'm not taking you away from your studies at Gold?"

"Not at all. I'm still trying to decide what to focus on."

He took another drink of water to show Sean how repentant and obedient he was being.

"So what do your parents think of all your different fields of study?"

There was a slight pause. "They're dead, sir."

The words knocked the wind out of him. When he found his breath again, he said, "How long ago?"

"Over ten years for my mom."

He couldn't think about this. Not what it meant to the young man driving his car. His own cup of pain was so full, if he contemplated the pain of others, he would just come completely apart. But how could he ignore so great a grief?

"I'm sorry," he said. Sincerely.

Sean turned on the blinker again. They were passing a school bus filled with boys wearing blue soccer jerseys.

Now it was time for him to be brave. Sean had already done it. He could at least be honest with him.

He took a deep breath. "Well, maybe it's best you know. Amy and I were going to Paris this summer." The words came more slowly than he had intended. Like from a distant place.

"I needed to do research in Charlemagne's world, sites in Germany and France. We planned to start and end the trip with Paris. Everything we had ever wanted to see and do in Paris. We picked out this hotel in the Latin Quarter —Hotel du College de France."

The name still sounded like magic on his lips. Sad magic. Amy had been so excited.

"It's near the Sorbonne and Notre Dame. We booked a balcony room on a top floor. We planned to eat our way through a list of Paris restaurants and cafés before heading to Aachen and the real work of the trip.

"We were just a week away from going when an opportunity came up for Gold College. They were given a time slot at a business-in-education conference in Peoria. One that drew corporations wanting to invest in colleges like ours.

"Jerry Waite dreams of establishing a yearly lecture series at Gold College. A series that would cover all aspects of history and society, and draw great lecturers and great attention to Gold, especially to the history department. The Peoria conference was the perfect place to secure funding for it. Unfortunately, no one was available to go.

"Jerry's daughter was getting married. Luedders was presenting papers in London. Tulia was with family in Brazil. A strep outbreak kept others home. The provost had broken his ankle. We were like the cast in a comedy show where something was happening to everyone.

"The president and his development guy were already schmoozing someone else in New York. Jerry didn't want Stanwick to do it, so he begged me to make a presentation, attend receptions, all that.

"Amy and I figured that if we left early in the morning from the conference, we could get to O'Hare and catch the second leg of our flight to Paris. It would be tight, but we could do it.

"As it turned out, the conference went well. I gave presentations. People listened favorably. But I couldn't pin down a sponsor for Jerry's lectures. No matter how hard I tried." His throat felt dry. He took another sip of water.

"Amy and I dealt with our disappointment by ordering a dinner as close to the French style as we could get in the middle of Illinois."

He saw her sitting opposite him again, as real as life. The candles. The white tablecloth. Holding her fork out to him, a mushroom laced in cream sauce balanced on its tines. *Taste this, Mark! The next mushrooms we eat will be French!*

The click of a blinker pulled him from his memory. Sean was passing a gray minivan with a Wisconsin license plate. Mark rubbed his eyes and took a deep breath. "The next morning, well. An oily section of road. A light rain. A semi that lost control. And even Paris didn't matter anymore."

And it didn't.

At this moment, he hated Paris. Hated Aachen. Hated his research even, and didn't care in the least how Charlemagne's worldview had affected Europe for centuries. He even hated conferences, and the idea of history lectures, and semi-trucks, and rain, and every possible thing that had conspired to take Amy away from him.

He couldn't hold back the tears that came. Couldn't control them. And that was frightening.

"I am terribly sorry, sir."

Mark closed his eyes and held still. They had put Amy in a separate ambulance. He had protested, but no one answered him. They had already known what they couldn't yet tell him.

He wished for sleep. He wished for unconsciousness. But more than anything, he wished for the pain to go away and for Amy to offer him another taste of her dinner.

He remembered Sean's presence and took a handkerchief from his back pocket to wipe his face. "Sorry," he mumbled. They both had been using that word a lot, but he couldn't think of any better to say. The burden of embarrassment piled on top of everything else.

Sean was giving him quick glances. Eyes on the road. Eyes on him. Eyes on the road. Eyes on him. But with the sympathy was a look of analysis.

Fingers tapped on the steering wheel. "You know, my mom died when I was young. I didn't stop crying for a year. You've got even more going on. Outside of the tragedy, your brain has been injured. We forget that the brain is allowed to be an organ too and ache with hurt just like a broken leg or arm. Weeping is part of that—with or without the explanatory emotions."

Sean interrupted himself. "By the way, Dr. Matheson met with me too and gave me sheets of instructions for you. You told him about headaches?"

Mark took a drink from his water bottle before answering. "Strange headaches. Like my nose is pinching through to the back of my head. Or the back of my head is trying to button itself on the front of my nose. And then the moles and earthworms get started."

"What do they do?"

"Crawl. From side to side and all over the top of my head."

"Wow. Didn't know about the moles. What caused the scar on your face?"

"Glass, maybe. The EMT said there was so much

material around that they couldn't know for certain what had done it." He was speaking of something that must have happened to someone else. In a different world. In a different life.

"Any pain still there?"

"Not really."

"The things you can't see sometimes hurt the worst."

He nodded slowly and stared out the window. He didn't want to talk about it anymore. "You ready for a pit stop?"

Sean discreetly, but definitely, acted the role of private nurse, walking him into the restroom, then ordering their meal to go.

"Dealing with waiters, even nice ones, takes more energy than you can afford right now," Sean said.

Mark didn't argue. They ate their hamburgers in the parking lot. They had been on the road over two hours, maybe three. He had lost track.

"How much longer?" He hadn't really paid much attention to their travel plans.

Mark expected Sean to pull out his phone and tap on it and consult some computer map. Instead, Sean looked at the bulky black watch on his arm.

"Maybe a half hour. The hotel doesn't serve lunch, so it's good we're getting this now. Do you want me to gas up the car too?"

Mark shook his head. "No, we can wait."

They wadded up their wrappers, drove by the trash can, and tossed them in. Then, up the ramp and back onto the interstate. Mark was still tired, but part of him felt better. He resolved not to play traffic controller again.

He drummed his fingers on the arm rest. "So what instructions did Matheson give you about me?"

"About what you'd expect. Lots of rest. Good food. Fluids, of course. Relax. Stare at the river, that view they brag about. Then, we'll start some exercises, go for walks, build strength. For your brain's sake, he wants you to avoid looking at screens, whether phones, television, or computer."

"Fine with me. I get nauseous just trying to check my email."

"I can continue to do that for you, sir, but only when you ask me to. There are exercises for your brain too."

This sounded odd. "Physical ones?"

"Yep. We'll start when you feel more rested. But the brain can help itself now too. Pull its frontal lobe into higher action, or something like that." Sean glanced at him. "It means doing some math."

"After my testimony to the importance of history you want me to cross academic disciplines? Or is this the Sorenson effect?"

The grin was back.

"Just counting backwards by sevens."

He tried doing it in his head, but he felt like his brain was trying to shoulder its way through mud. Maybe later. Now it was time to ask a question that had plagued him. He felt a bit foolish asking it, but he couldn't remember. Someone should have told him, shouldn't they? Or did they think he already knew the answer?

"Did I hit my head again when I fell?"

Sean shook his head. "I was able to grab you in time. One of the girls was wearing a jacket because of the air conditioning, so we tucked that under your head. It made a decent pillow."

So matter of fact. So casual about something that seemed so monumental to him. But Sean, as some kind of nurse aide, probably saw this sort of stuff all the time. Probably had been watching for it, on Jerry's instructions.

"You notice everything then?" He tried to say it light-heartedly.

"No, sir. I've missed some big things that I really wish I hadn't."

"Well, I think you've already earned your keep," he said.

Sean laughed.

Large green interstate signs declared the city of Ashington Mills was almost upon them. Sean took the second exit. The road wound through some straggled clumps of old trees, past an isolated farm where a dog barked concern at their passing. Then it climbed a hill and leveled out alongside brick warehouses pierced by worn smokestacks. All the markings of an old industrial riverfront. Obviously the tired side of Ashington Mills.

Mark suddenly felt uneasy. "Look," he said. "We can try this place, but I'm not really sure about it. For Jerry's sake, I'll give it a week or two. He's the one who really wanted to come here, I'm sure of that."

"And after that?"

"We could keep going."

"Colorado?"

"Sure," Mark replied, ignoring his road fear for the moment. "Why not? Or Idaho."

"British Columbia would be great."

"Or the top of Alaska that is white on all the maps."
That had been a little kid dream.

"Kamchatka!" cried Sean.

"Kamchatka?"

"You said to keep going."

It was silly for a moment, pure escapism, but as they
passed faded signs on an old brewery building, Mark felt
heaviness close in on him again.

"I'm not sure after that," he said, looking out the
window. "What if we just see what comes?"

"I can do that," said Sean. "I'm actually very good at
that."

3

———

Riverview House

MARK WAS LOOKING out his window at the businesses they were passing—tax accountant, computer repair, hair salon—when he heard the blinker. Sean slowed the car and turned left toward the river. A long drive curved up from the street, and there it was, almost in a world of its own. Riverview House.

The thing was huge—a fortress of tan ridged stone against the backdrop of hazy, blue sky. Three—or was it four—floors. He had an impression of numerous turrets, windows, and balconies bursting out everywhere, all topped with red roof tile and verdigris.

A long, deep porch started at the front door, ran across one side of the house and disappeared around the corner. In the parking lot that spread out in front of the house, four scattered cars and a pickup truck slept in the sun. A dark-haired man was on his knees, weeding a flower bed that bordered the lot.

Sean pulled the Honda into a parking space close to the porch and turned off the engine. He stared out the window frozen in thought.

"What do you think?" Mark asked.

After a few moments, Sean replied, "Big. Bigger than in the brochure. What do you think of it?"

It looked like it could swallow a person alive, but that was hardly the opinion to give voice to now, since they had to stay at the place. Mark took a deep breath. "Impressive. I've never seen a house like that before. Very individual looking."

"Richardson Romanesque Revival."

"Is that what it is? How did you know? Oh wait, that semester in Carbondale?"

"The brochure." Sean was giving him the diagnostic look again. "Let's get you checked in. I'll come back afterwards, and get all our stuff."

Mark opened the door and stepped out slowly. The air smelled different. More humid. Was he smelling the river? The five steps up to the broad porch he could handle. That was good news.

Sean leaped ahead of him to grab the doorknob and pushed the wide wooden door open. They entered a short tunnel of a hallway covered with gleaming wood paneling. Beyond was a large open area. Mark could see the edge of a fireplace with black smoke streaks staining the wall above it. Was this historical effect or bad housekeeping?

He caught glimpses of dark wood and floral carpets through the doorways on their left. A massive staircase to their right blocked the view of the other side of the house. The whole setting had a feel of being pretentious and gracious at the same time. Probably the statement of some nineteenth-century tycoon who had known what he was worth and thought it right to show it.

A wooden alcove tucked into the bend of the staircase housed a check-in counter. A period lamp glowed in brass and green. Mark gave a quick peek over the counter down to the desk below. A twenty-first-century computer idled there.

Sean pounded the small bell that sat on the counter. Rather fiercely, Mark thought. He gave him a questioning look.

"They shouldn't keep you standing here," Sean whispered loudly.

A man came around the far side of the staircase. Serious of face, dark eyes behind black-framed glasses, neatly trimmed dark hair. No smile.

"I'm sorry to have kept you waiting," he said in a tone that carried no apology. He stepped behind the counter and touched a computer key. "Do you have a reservation?"

"I believe so," Mark replied. "Mark Newlin. Gold College."

The man looked up quickly and studied his face. "The professor? Your secretary Vicki told us all about you."

Great. "She's not my secretary." He had to say it, then felt foolish afterwards.

A conversational stalemate ensued. His fault. His to break it. "But the college told you I was coming."

The black glasses bent over the computer screen. "Yes, sir, and we hope you will find your stay with us restful and enjoyable." An obviously rehearsed, insincere response.

"Thank you."

"The college has requested one of our large suites for you and your attendant. We have two available. One on the second floor and one on the third. Which would you prefer? The one on the third floor has by far the best view—"

"Second floor," said Sean. "His health."

"But we do have an elevator so the floor choice shouldn't matter." The hotel clerk glanced at Mark, question in his eyes. "I told my wife—she manages the housekeeping here—that the third-floor suite should always be filled first."

"Is this your house?" Mark asked. He didn't know what made him say it. Something in the man's attitude was definitely proprietorial.

"It might as well be. I know it better than the owner. I am Todd Channon. I run Riverview House. And the third floor suite is our best."

Mark felt suddenly tired. *Did the floor choice matter?* He didn't know. He would vote with Sean. He owed the guy. "What he said," Mark answered. "Second floor."

Todd Channon gave out a sigh and tapped on his computer. "Second floor it is. Two sets of keys?"

"Yes, please," said Mark.

Todd pulled a receipt from his printer and handed it to Mark, along with the keys. The keys were real, two per ring. He pointed to one marked with a black dot. "That is the front door key. I lock the front door at ten o'clock every night so you'll need your own key after that. The other is to your room."

He led them through several large old doorways until they turned a corner and came into a hallway which was decidedly modern. The elevator doors were right in front of them.

"Was this, this elevator corridor, once part of the servants' portion of the house?" Mark didn't know why he was asking.

Todd Channon nodded proudly. "Yes, it was. This part of the house was extensively remodeled, but all the guest rooms are historical and original to the main house." He poked at the lit circle on the wall to summon the elevator.

"My great-great-grandfather built this house. My wife Stephanie is the head of housekeeping and sees to all guest needs. If you have any questions, you can ask either of us."

"Thank you," Mark answered.

Sean was saying nothing. His eyes were on the elevator doors in front of them. All his cheerful openness seemed to have disappeared the moment they stepped through the doors of Riverview. Maybe something in Todd Channon's attitude was getting on his nerves.

As they rode the short distance to the second floor, Todd continued his speech. "Our restaurant is the pride of Ashington Mills. Dining tables are offered to our staying guests first, of course. You will need to let us know by three in the afternoon if you will be dining in. If you forget or change your plans, let our hostess know and a dinner can be brought to your room."

The elevator door slid open, and they stepped out

onto the second floor. Mark saw a long inviting hallway with a warm wood floor. A deep burgundy patterned rug ran down it, beckoning.

They did not go down the hallway. Instead, Todd turned toward the central staircase. At the top of the stairs was a door, which he unlocked, then stepped back to allow them to enter.

"Should I hold a table for the two of you tonight for dinner?"

Mark looked at Sean.

"You need to rest," said Sean. "Maybe tomorrow."

Mark turned back to Todd. "Could we have dinner in the room tonight?"

"Certainly. Six o'clock?" Todd stood in the doorway. Polite, but definitely ready to go.

"That would be fine. Thank you."

Mark heard his footsteps hurry down the stairs.

"Sir, I'll get our luggage now." Sean looked like he wanted to say more, give some sort of nagging health instruction, but was holding back.

"Fine," Mark said simply. "I'll be here."

It was good to have a few moments alone. He set the keys and the receipt on a small table, and sank down on the bed.

The room was certainly spacious. Perhaps it had been the owner's bedroom once. Between the bed and the fire-place, the floor was littered with ornately-carved furniture pieces, furniture which had meant comfort a hundred years ago, but meant comfort no longer. Some chairs had thin wood arches for backs, giving nothing whatever to lean against.

That would make an interesting study: the history of comfort in America. He'd have to suggest it to Jerry Waite sometime.

The large windows were draped in a dark orange color, which seemed to clash with the salmon bedspread.

At the far corner, the suite ended in a rounded tower area. He remembered seeing towers from the outside. Here, narrow windows, one after the other, rose from floor to ceiling. Here, too, sat an inviting armchair, one that turned gently on its base to let a person enjoy the whole view. Mark pulled a lace curtain aside and looked out.

The tower was at the extreme front corner of the whole building with a view to the side garden and the trees beyond. Yes, there was the river. He could turn the chair to face it and the view would be pleasant. He looked around the other way and could see the parking lot, his Honda Accord, and Sean, grasping several bags, slamming the trunk with his elbow.

Mark went back into the main room and around the bed to two doors. One turned out to be the door to the bathroom. The other led him into a much smaller room— a bed, table, chest of drawers, one chair, and one large window that looked out on the side gardens and the river.

"Professor?" Sean's voice came from the main room. Anxious.

"In here," he called.

Sean came through the door carrying his suitcase and a book bag.

"You've got a better view of the river," Mark told him. "And more comfortable furniture. Jerry's office sofa beats anything in that other room. Don't suppose you'd trade?"

The grin was back. "Not a chance. Besides, this is dorm room size. Very cozy. Not fit for a professor."

"All right, all right." Mark went back through to his side. He supposed he should unpack. What if they stayed only two weeks? That would be enough to show gratitude for the college's generosity. Then: out of here. But to where? And, realistically, on whose budget?

He chose a chest of drawers with a wood-framed mirror and put his things in the drawers. Beyond the fireplace, another door proved to be the closet. Mark shoved his suitcase, laptop, and book satchel in it.

He felt very tired. It was afternoon—universal nap time for small children and all weary people. He kicked off his shoes, placed his glasses on the minute bedside table, peeled back the salmon bedcover, and crawled in.

THE CLICK of a door latch wakened him. Sean had opened the door to the hallway and a young Hispanic woman pushed a steel cart bearing covered dishes into the room.

"Six o'clock," said Sean. "Dinner time."

Mark blinked and reached for his glasses. Where could they set those big trays? All the tables were too small.

The dazed, blurry feeling did not clear away when Mark put his glasses on.

"I hope you enjoy your meal," the girl said. Her voice was welcoming and friendly, everything Todd Channon's had not been. "When you are finished, just put everything back on the cart and put it out into the hallway, under the large mirror."

He cleared the sleep from his throat. "Thank you."

"You are very welcome." She left them to it.

Mark washed his face in the bathroom then went to the tower. "There's not enough room in here for us to eat. The table's not big enough to hold anything."

He could hear the whine in his voice and was disgusted with himself.

"You sit in the tower," said Sean. "I prefer the floor."

"Modern hotels at least have a desk in every room."

"We could ask Todd Channon to bring you a desk."

Mark started to reply, then forgot what he was going to say. Did he want a desk? He didn't know. Dr. Mark Newlin, Professor of History would have wanted a desk. That Dr. Newlin would be up to his ears in research notes and publishing deadlines and clear purpose.

After the accident, the deadlines had turned into maybes and the purpose seemed not so clear. He felt like a child, seated on the edge of a merry-go-round, spinning, holding tight. Then his hands were empty, and there was nothing to hold onto anymore. And he was flying somewhere between the merry-go-round and the hard, packed earth.

"Sit here," said Sean, pointing at the armchair in the tower.

He obeyed.

His plate fit just right on the small table, and the food looked amazingly good. A piece of crispy chicken rolled into a barrel shape, rice and mushrooms on the side, green salad with orange and fennel, and a dinner roll that looked fresh from the oven. All the things that life with Amy had taught him to notice. It was a meal she would have loved.

"Nice river view?"

The words confused him for a moment, then he realized Sean was pointing toward the window.

"Um, yeah," he replied lamely.

He took a bite of chicken. It was perfectly crisped on the outside, oozing butter and herbs from its core. He gazed purposefully at the river as he swallowed. He should attempt to be a reasonable dinner companion.

"I think we've done the Mississippi a disservice." He felt himself retreating into his professor persona, but he didn't know what else to do. "We've made it work hard, built industries and factories as close as we dared, sent barges up and down it hauling everything, but we haven't let it just be beautiful. Like ... "

He couldn't bring himself to say Paris.

"Like other cities around the world." Amy had talked long about the beauty of the Seine when they were poring through Paris travel guides together.

He looked down at his plate. Several mushrooms were waiting. He wondered what to do about them. They stared up at him like a promise not kept.

"St. Louis lets part of it be beautiful," Sean offered. "The Arch and the park under it, at least. Although the water is bluer up here."

Mark corralled his thoughts. "It's pretty hard for other cities to beat the Arch." He pushed the mushrooms aside.

Sean's plate was completely empty, evidence of the male college student's rapid eating style. He stared at

Mark's full plate. "Make sure you eat. Matheson thought you weren't eating enough, and that would explain why you fainted."

Mark didn't want to discuss why he hadn't felt like eating lately. He resented Sean's comment. But he nodded to show he had heard.

A warning bell went off inside his head. Resentment calling to him again. Resentment was a frightening hole to dig yourself into. It called to him daily, ready to press the shovel into his hands. He worked hard not to answer, but feared that one day he would just fall in.

Sean kept on. "I didn't pay much attention when the hostess told me what the food was. Do you know what we're eating?"

Mark cleared his throat. "Chicken Kiev. Nobody does it much anymore. Everyone is pushing for their own unique cuisine." Amy was addicted to cooking shows. Had been. Had been addicted to cooking shows.

He poked at the last orange in his salad bowl. "If you want to see the river view, you should pull up a chair over here. Can't see that much from the floor."

"Nah, that's all right. I like the floor better."

Mark tried to eat enough so his plate would escape notice. It felt absurd. Forty-eight hours ago, he had not been aware of Sean's existence. Now here they were, in a strange town, in a strange house, eating dinner together.

From what Sean had said so far, it seemed he was trying to find a life. Mark didn't want the life that had been forced on him. They were two unlikely fellow travelers trying to find themselves on a road trip that had already come to a stop. This was a theme Luedders would wax morosely eloquent about. Luedders liked that sort of thing.

"There's dessert," said Sean. "Something they call River Pie."

Mark stacked his plates, relieved that Sean didn't insist on inspecting them. "That sounds odd."

"Well, there are odd ducks everywhere, especially on a river, I suppose."

Sean lifted the last lid from each tray and handed his plate to him, then crawled back to his place on the floor. Mark studied the pie as Amy had taught him. Coconut, nuts, chocolate chunks, and raisins poked out from the sides. A caramel sauce drizzled over it and pooled around it.

"Looks like a chunk of river debris," he said aloud.

Sean nodded. "Tastes better than the river though."

The meal was more food than Mark had eaten in a long time and his stomach felt it. Sean gathered up all the dishes, and rolled the cart out into the hall.

"Just like a classy hotel you see in old movies," he said when he returned. "I think I'll flop in bed and read for a while. You okay?"

"I'm okay," Mark replied.

He stayed in the tower for hours, watching the light change as the sunset approached, deepened, and faded. The closing off of the day. He used to like sunsets. Now they were the precursor to the hardest time of his existence. Night.

He had tried watching movies, comedians on the Internet, anything that would keep his mind from turning in on itself in the dark hours. But it took only a minute for the light from the screens to hurt his head. And the headaches and dizziness that resulted lasted for days.

Trying to read a physical book was no better. The brain protested the rows of print—and the visual exertion of looking up audiobooks.

What did it matter? He was trying to fill a hole in himself with shovelfuls of air.

Outside, the light disappeared, and he went to turn the bedside lamp on. He heard Sean moving around in his room next door, drawers opening and closing. Footsteps walked across the floor above his head. Todd Channon must have rented the third floor suite after all. Footsteps and voices sounded on the stairs outside his room. Women's voices suddenly louder as they passed by his door. One wondering if she had packed her sunscreen at all because it wasn't in her blue bag.

He put on pajama pants and a T-shirt and got into bed. Then got right back out.

Sean had left a water glass on the nightstand. He went to fill it from the bathroom tap, avoiding a direct glance into the mirror, then crawled back in bed. The pale blue numbers on the bedside clock said 9:42 p.m.

He wasn't tired enough or awake enough for anything.

He wanted to think about Amy. Not about the accident. About her.

But the accident wouldn't let him.

Instead his mind plunged again into a vortex of horrific fragments. The shock of the impact. The sound of crunching metal. The total bewilderment. The red cab of a trailer truck pressed into their windshield. The man by the side of the car. A paunchy man with a sagging chin and a large mole next to one eye, but a voice rich with concern. Mark could barely move, barely breathe.

I can't get her out, he said, over and over.

I've called the police. The paramedics are coming, said the paunchy man.

I have to get her out, he said.

You'll be okay. You're going to be okay, the man said.

Later, the ambulance door had closed, shutting him in, shutting Amy out. *Where is she? Where's Amy?* He could still feel the panic. Could always feel the panic.

She's going in the other ambulance. Don't worry. We're going to the same hospital. A blood pressure cord had dropped across his face. Then the siren started up, piercing his head.

He opened his eyes and stared up at the ceiling, forcing himself out of that nightmare and back into this gray world of sorrow.

She used to cuddle her pillow right next to his shoulder and rest her arm across his chest while they slept. When his snoring would catch for a moment and his breathing would halt, she would shake him awake. *I don't want you leaving me,* she would say.

He began to sob, wildly.

I don't know how to live without you, Amy. I can't even teach anymore. I'm a visitor in the life we used to have.

The storm passed. He took a deep breath, wiped his face with the front of his shirt, threw the covers back, and got out of bed. He picked up his glasses and looked at the electric clock.

10:37 p.m.

He felt spent. Hollow. Dizzy. And his head throbbed.

He walked slowly over to the tower, bare feet on the carpet, sank down into the chair, pulled the lacy curtain aside, and looked out.

The river was dark. Water and trees blurred together in the black of night. He looked away from the river and down the Riverview House drive toward the town.

Security lights shone out from different angles of the house. Light poles in old-fashioned style stood at regular intervals lining the drive and parking lot, illuminating broad circles at their feet. A cat sauntered across the parking lot, in and out of the pools of light, the only thing moving in the scene, until another motion caught his eye.

On the drive a woman came into view, walking slowly but steadily toward the house. She was tall with dark hair piled on top of her head, and wore a long, flowing dress of pale blue. She bent slightly as she climbed the hill of the driveway, arms folded tightly, hands on her upper arms, like a person who was trying to protect themselves from the cold. A cold that the month of August couldn't draw up if it tried. The cat, under a light pole, stopped to watch as the woman came slowly on.

She mounted the porch steps, deliberately, as if carrying a heavy weight, then disappeared out of sight under the roof. He thought he heard a door open and close in the distance, but there came no sound of footsteps on the stairs.

On the water, a light swung back and forth, purposefully stabbing through the darkness. A group of barges headed upriver, making sure of the channel markers in the dark.

Mark looked back toward the town. No one in the

drive. Nothing but cars in the lot—more than there had been this afternoon. A solitary car drove down the street in the distance, a short blip of white light then red between the trees.

He paced slowly back and forth for a while, walking from the tower to the room door, hoping his mind would fall asleep on its own. No luck. He tried doing push-ups. He could only complete three before all the aches inside of him objected.

A wave of frustrated anger rolled over him. He felt like lashing out at something.

On sudden impulse, he got his laptop out of the closet and jerked it open, turning his head away from the whirl of lights as it started up. When it calmed, he selected several keys, a series of directions he could give almost without looking. *Select File—Delete—Empty Trash.* Then folded the thing shut with a smack.

"There you go," he said, defiantly.

He paced again until he finally began to get tired, but he couldn't crawl back in that bed. Thoughts of Amy were too fresh there.

He grabbed his pillow and a small blanket from the footboard, and lay down next to the chair in the tower area. Flat on his back made him remember the classroom floor. No. He sat up and propped his pillow on a piece of wall between two windows, then leaned back against it. What was that numbers exercise he was supposed to do? Counting backwards by sevens?

100. 93. 86. 79 . . .

He forced his way down the number line until he

reached two. What now? Desperate for sleep, he cast around in his mind and grabbed a higher number. 2748.

Slowly, methodically, he worked his way down. He was still awake when he reached number four.

All right then. Higher.

14,968. *Take that!* 14,961. 14,954 . . .

He was startled awake by a thrumming engine and an unearthly screeching and grinding. After a few seconds he recognized the sound. A garbage truck. A prosaic, yet strangely comforting sound. The gathering of trash, the necessary cleaning up that said normal life went on. Gentle, pale light was falling through the windows.

He had made it through another night.

He gathered his pillow and blanket and groggily went over to the bed. The mattress and sheets felt wonderful after the floor. He rolled onto his left side, his arm around a second pillow, and gratefully fell asleep.

4

———

Your Secret Is Safe with Me

"I NEED to teach you some card games. Something you can play whenever you want to."

Sean was avoiding the use of the word "solitaire." And his offer held a hint that he must have been aware of Mark's struggle last night.

"Sure," Mark said, without enthusiasm. He took a swig of orange juice.

Sean had brought in their breakfast trays by himself this time. Mark was sitting up in bed, tray on his lap, feeling dizzy, and trying not to show it. His brain was paying for last night's distress.

Sean sat on the middle of the carpeted floor, tray in front of him, plate in his hand, and was already halfway through his spinach omelet. He pointed his fork at the omelet on Mark's plate.

"There's vitamins and protein in that. You need all of it. Matheson's orders. Take all the time you want. Just eat it all."

Mark had a sudden impulse to hurl the tray at him. He took a bite of toast instead.

Sean watched him, new uncertainty in his eyes. Had he guessed Mark's thoughts? Mark felt ashamed.

"I'll make you a deal, Professor," Sean said carefully. "You boss me around for anything college-related, and I'll boss you around about your health. Just consider my role that of a pesky little brother." He paused. "Besides, the college is counting on me to do a good job by you."

What an awful responsibility. Ball and chain with guilt attached. Mark didn't like to think of that kind of weight shackled to anyone. And he hated the idea of *being* the shackled weight.

"Fair swap," he said. "And a bite of omelet to close the deal." He cut a big chunk with his fork and stuck it in his mouth.

Sean nodded and bent to his food again.

While they ate, Sean gave him news of Riverview House. The dining room was at this moment half filled with breakfast eaters. Several out-of-state families getting their last vacation in before the school year started for them.

Sean had also picked up some brochures of the immediate area, including a map of the town for Mark's perusal. Those could wait. Mark didn't feel like getting out of bed.

Sean also mentioned a classic hamburger place he wanted to try. He suggested getting some burgers for lunch.

"Does that count as health food?" Mark asked wryly.

"I'll surround it with fruits and vegetables. You'll have so many vitamins you won't know what to do with them. By the way, should we reserve a place for dinner here tonight?"

Mark really didn't feel up to it, but he had just promised to let Sean be the health boss. "What do you think?"

The analytical eye was on him again. Mark ignored it and finished his omelet while he waited for Sean's verdict.

"I think you could take another day just resting in the room if you want. Stay in your jams. Don't shave. I'll bring you lunch, and snacks, and a newspaper, or anything you want to read. You can stare at the river, stare at the parking lot. Play cards."

"You mean, lie around while you stuff me silly?"

"A few more pounds would be good for you."

"Look who's talking, wire-weight."

Sean actually laughed. "That's my runner look. I eat like a horse."

"You run?"

"Four miles already this morning. You were sleeping."

Mark crunched his toast, then looked at the next bite more closely. "That strawberry jam tastes homemade."

"Really?"

"Yeah. Amy made jam every year. The kind you freeze. There's nothing like it."

"Maybe she would have liked this place."

Mark couldn't answer.

"Hey, I have a plan," said Sean. "We could build up your strength, and then you could start running. Start running regularly by December."

Mark shook his head. "No running. I'm more of a walker. I'd rather walk five miles than run one."

"All right. Five miles. Walking. By December. Deal?"

Could he do it? Five miles was a long way. And he was still so shaky. But, what else would there be to do in this place?

"How about this?" he countered. "You read five books of your choice on any aspect of history, and I'll train for your five miles and do it. I can check out books from any college library in the state for you. Five miles for five books. Both by December. Deal?" He imitated Sean's manner.

Sean responded with a surprisingly broad grin. "Deal."

MARK FOLLOWED Sean's plan for the day. He went back to sleep after breakfast and dozed off and on until his dizziness lifted and his headache faded. Relieved at feeling better, he went to sit in the tower chair and watched the parking lot steadily empty. Departing guests rolled suitcases out to their cars, heaved them into trunks, slammed car doors, and drove down the hill back to their normal lives.

Sean had all the energy Mark lacked and kept himself busy finding things to do—filling the car with gas, washing it afterwards, searching out the classic burger place—reporting on all this over a lunch of hamburgers and strawberry-spinach smoothies.

After lunch, Mark lay on his bed, nestled his tender head into an acceptable position, and stared at the swirls of plaster on the ceiling. He could almost make out a map of France in them. One ridge of plaster looked to be the right angle for the Pyrenees Mountains. That stand-alone swoop could be Paris, but that would put the English Channel too far away. Also, the western land arm of France that reached out to Brest was decidedly too skinny. If France insisted on being on his ceiling, it would have to look more accurate.

The sound of vacuuming came from somewhere down the hall. Doors opened and shut. He heard the hum of the elevator motor. Voices in intense conversation caught his ear, voices that stopped outside his door. A male voice, speaking low, and a distraught woman.

"Do we have to put up with this?" asked the woman.

Mark could not hear the answer.

"They'll take over the house again," said the woman. "They always do. And they don't have to come this soon. Why can't they stay with your dad?"

The man murmured a response, but Mark couldn't make it out.

The woman was quieter the next time she spoke. "All right, then ask Elizabeth to deal with them, so I won't have to."

More quiet words passed. Mark thought he caught a few. Then the woman spoke in a shakier voice.

"I don't think we can depend on that, Todd."

Had she begun to cry? Mark sat up in bed, alarmed. Footsteps sounded on the stairs and the conversation passed away.

He sank back onto the pillows. What had he heard? Unhappiness. Distress. The usual result of dissatisfying human relationships. Whatever the cause, it was clear that some very unwelcome guests were expected at Riverview.

Well, he wasn't the manager, just one of the many guests that came in and out of the house each year. He looked up and found a group of plaster swirls that formed a passable Ireland.

A while later Sean came in with a shopping bag.

"Found a half-price bookstore and bought these. And the public library is not too far away."

"What's in here?" Mark asked, reaching into the sack.

"History magazines, travel magazines. Some classic Agatha Christie mysteries. Some Dorothy Sayers too. Doesn't this house just make you want to read a mystery?"

"The right setting you mean? Brooding, waiting?"

"Yeah."

"No," said Mark.

"C'mon." Sean lowered his voice. "Don't you think a crime could have been committed in this house?"

Mark gave him a quelling look and hated himself immediately for doing it. *What was he turning into?*

Sean fell silent and dumped the bag of books out on

the bed. The poor guy needed some excitement. A nurse-maid's job was a boring one. Mark felt ashamed of himself.

"All right. I'll give you this. There *is* something unsettling going on here." He told Sean about the conversation he had overheard.

Sean listened attentively. "You couldn't hear anything Todd said?"

"Only a few words. He said 'first base.' Or 'cross first base,' or 'cross base first,' or something like that. He said more, but that's all I heard because it sounded like they were going up the stairs."

Sean stared down at the pile of books, lost in thought. Mark picked up a history magazine and thumbed through it. It held several articles on European battles and another about archeological discoveries involving ancient weaponry.

After a few moments, his brain began to protest against all the tiny words on the printed page. That uneasy feeling that always preceded the dull aches, which would grow in intensity if he didn't listen to it.

He closed the magazine and went over to the tower to look out. The gardener was working in the flower bed that lined the driveway, gloved hands deftly pulling out plants trying to root themselves where they didn't belong.

Mark didn't want to tell Sean, but the mysteries didn't tempt him at all. People died in them. It was one thing to puzzle over a theoretical death as a study of human motivation and wickedness. But not when death was too close, too real.

In a mystery, you closed the book and the pain was over. The only memory left was the thrill of the puzzle. Real death? You can barely breathe.

He turned away from the tower. The sound of water running in the bathroom told him where Sean was. He fished through the pile of books left on the bed and pulled out one that looked like number games.

Kakuro for Starters: A Beginner's Guide to Cross Sum Puzzles.

He flipped the book open. The squares were big, the ink pale. Maybe it wouldn't hurt too much to learn and do it, whatever it was. He could rest his eyes between each entry. The same brain that was sensitive to so many things was at the same time as restless as a caged lion. He had to do something.

Well, if these puzzles involved counting backwards, he was already an expert. He got a pencil from his satchel and settled himself in the tower chair. Mark was in the middle of the third puzzle when Sean opened the door to another rolling cart pushed by the same young woman from the kitchen. A T-shirt and flannel pajama pants were not appropriate attire for meeting anyone, but Mark was determined to be more civil than he had been yesterday.

"Thank you very much. I'm afraid I don't know your name."

She moved the cart so that he could reach for his tray without getting up. "I'm Felicitas. I go to Ashington College. My father is the gardener here."

Mark nodded toward the window. "He does nice work."

She smiled then. Brilliantly. "Thank you. I will tell him you said so."

There was still a smile on her face when she closed the door behind her. Now that was a smile that could power a heart, thought Mark. Somewhere, no doubt, there was a college man who lived for that smile.

"Pepper Steak," Sean announced. "Garlic Mashed Potatoes. Sautéed Brussels Sprouts with Bacon. French Roll. Dessert will wait and be a surprise." He said this as proudly as if he had made it himself.

"It smells amazing," said Mark. For some reason, he felt ready to eat. More ready than he had been for the lunchtime burger. Something inside him definitely felt better.

"Does everybody eat this?" Mark asked, slicing into a piece of steak. "Everyone in the dining room gets the same thing?"

"I think there are six different entrées each night. Chef's Choice and some others. I ask for Chef's Choice each time. Sorry. I probably should have checked with you."

Mark shook his head. It didn't matter. He took a bite of steak and his fork faltered in the air.

So good. So *very* good.

Sean was looking at him. "What do you think of the steak?"

Mark cut another piece. "I think I better not ask how much the college is paying for this."

"For Chocolate Torte with Cherries Mascarpone?"

"I definitely will not ask."

•   •   •

AFTER DINNER, Sean made good his promise and taught Mark several solitaire games with a deck of cards he had bought that afternoon as well. A few easy games, a few hard ones. Then Sean took the mystery books to his own room and settled in. Mark sat in the tower working on number puzzles by the light of the small table lamp, making sure to look up often.

The sun set and the sky darkened. A car went down the drive toward town, its taillights glowing red. The night deepened. Another towboat searched for channel markers along the river, beams of light flicking up and down the bank. Time passed. He was thankful for the puzzles, for something to occupy his mind and make him tired.

He was trying to recall if a run of six unique numbers adding up to twenty-three could possibly contain a nine, when he saw her again—the tall woman, dark hair pulled up as before—walking up the drive from town. Tonight her long sleeveless dress was red, but there was something so weary about her demeanor. He could almost visualize a burden on her shoulders, pressing her down, working against every step.

The front door opened and closed, but no footsteps came up the stairs. If the woman was a guest, she would have to come up these stairs or take the elevator. Where did she go?

Mark put down his pencil, took off his glasses, and rubbed his eyes. Tomorrow he would get up in the morning, and shave and shower like a normal person. Explore the house a little. Find a different spot for staring at the river. Maybe go for a short stroll in the evening.

What was tomorrow? Friday? A weekend crowd would come. Perhaps even the unwanted guests. He fell asleep wondering about the unwanted guests.

It was late morning the next day before he was ready to go anywhere. By that time guests were checking out and vacuum cleaners were starting up as if they had just come into season. Not a good time to explore the lower house.

At Sean's suggestion, they climbed into the car, and Sean drove—very carefully, Mark noticed—down the drive and to the left, into an Ashington Mills Mark had not yet seen. Sean pointed out all the things he had already discovered.

The city square was a broad lawn of green grass complete with a fountain, monument, and a border of tall trees. Mark liked it at once. Businesses fronted it on all four sides: a few restaurants, a coffee shop, something called Bar on the Square, a used bookstore next to other shops, an accounting firm, and two lawyers' offices.

As they waited for a red light, Mark studied a sign with black and gold lettering which read *Baker & Stow, Attorneys*. He wondered how many generations of Bakers and Stows had proudly carried on their legal profession on this square?

The light changed and in a minute the steel framework of a river bridge appeared. Two bridges arched across the Mississippi from Ashington Mills. Sean negotiated several side streets and found the entrance to the westbound bridge.

They drove over it and into the northeast corner of

Missouri, which seemed empty compared to the Illinois side. Except for a tall observation tower. Mark spoke without thinking.

"I bet we could get a great view of the river from the top of that tower."

Of course, he couldn't. He would get partway up and faint and feel like the most foolish idiot in the world. "Well, I mean you could," he added lamely.

Sean, thankfully, did not tell him he was an idiot. Instead, he shrugged his shoulders. "It would be a cool view. But, I don't like heights."

"You don't? Like how high?"

Sean pulled off the road into an overlook area, next to a picnic table. He tapped on the steering wheel, but there was a quirky smile on his face. "Let's just say, I was glad Dr. Waite had already given you the first floor instead of the fourth floor classroom when I signed on."

"Well, that's all right," said Mark. "He saved us both from a view of the maintenance shed."

"Dr. Waite said it was a classroom you used to like before they added on to the building. He made sure your favorite podium was in it too."

Was it friendship or guilt behind Jerry Waite's actions? And would Mark always be asking himself this question? Wondering about the reason behind every action of his old friend? That would make for a wearying existence for both of them.

"Is that why you voted for the second floor room at Riverview House and not the third?"

"Well," Sean looked awkward. "Somewhat, sir. It's just a habit I have. Don't think too much about it."

Mark remembered Todd Channon pushing them to take the third floor. That must have been what made Sean bristle. He felt instantly protective of his hardworking assistant. "Don't give it another thought. Your secret is safe with me."

They found the entrance to the eastbound bridge and drove back. From the middle of the bridge, Mark could see the red rooftop of Riverview House reaching high into the air, dominating the skyline off to his right.

Sean drove east until the main four-lane road, with all its traffic lights and businesses, evaporated into farmland and restored prairie. They turned around and chose a different route back through the city. A parallel road, a quieter road, which led block-by-block past a modern high school, then progressively back in time past older schools and homes, until they were in neighborhoods with brick streets and broad well-kept lawns from a hundred years ago. Sean slowed the car so they could look.

Thick, old trees lined this avenue, massive trees full of branches green-rich with leaves. Broken slabs of sidewalks testified to the stealthy work of their roots. Their towering presence hushed the air.

Behind these stood century-old houses, each one unique, the pride and beauties of a past day. The evidence of a history that took you out of yourself and made you marvel at what had come before you.

Sean stopped the car at the curb of a white house, with tall, majestic pillars and black-shuttered windows. In Mark's mind, the house represented one story in a city filled with stories, all woven together to be the history of human endeavor in Ashington Mills. He glanced at his assistant. Was Sean thinking of the mysteries that could have happened here?

"I'm hungry," said Sean.

THEY PARKED the car at a diner not too far down the street from Riverview House. The diner was shaped in a long stainless steel rectangle, imitating a dining car from the romanticized era of American train travel.

"Another classic, right?" he teased Sean as they slid into the worn turquoise booth. "Think they'll serve something up to the caliber of dinners we've been having?"

"Not by a long shot," said Sean. "Call it a cultural study."

Mark picked up a menu. "All right. I'll study a BLT on toast, cheesy fries, and a chocolate shake."

Sean's eyebrows went up. "That will bring your weight back."

"I'll be walking soon, right? Miles and miles," he answered flippantly, tucking the menu back in its chrome holder. It felt good not to be an invalid for a while.

Sean ordered a barn-sized cheeseburger with everything on it, plus the fries, which must have been too much. "I really don't want to go back to the house yet," he said, "but I think I better lie on my bed and groan awhile."

Midafternoon. He could do with a nap himself.

He offered to drive, but Sean wouldn't give up the wheel even though he looked a little greenish. Parking lot to porch went safely, but they were hampered in their need to get upstairs by a woman whose ivory leather luggage completely filled the entry hall. She was expensively dressed and leaned both arms on the check-in counter as if she owned it. Todd Channon looked trapped behind it, strangely on the defensive, staring at the computer screen, tapping glumly at the keys.

"I want the room I always have." The woman rapped quietly but firmly on the counter with every other word, gold bracelets rattling with each rap. "Why won't you give it to me?"

"It's reserved for paying guests, Aunt Fia," said Todd, keeping his eyes on the screen and not meeting hers. "You are family, and you won't tell me how long you are staying."

"That's because I don't know how long I'll be here. I need to talk to Ernie in person, and he hasn't come yet."

Sean poked Mark's shoulder. "Let's go round the back," he whispered.

They went back out on the porch, down the stairs, and around the side to a pleasant rear porch, which had a broader river view, Mark noted, than his narrow tower window. The day was warm, but the porch was shaded. He felt like sitting and resting there a while. He was about to suggest it when he caught sight of Sean's face. The guy looked truly sick. After all Sean had done for him, it was only right that he see him safely upstairs.

They entered the back of the large central room, ducked into the elevator corridor, and pushed the call button. The woman was still arguing in the entryway. Some phrases carried with special emphasis.

"Play-acting as some high-and-mighty manager! You'll be thrown out soon, you'll see!"

Sean stared at the floor. Mark began to wonder if he would make it to their room, when the elevator door mercifully opened. A young woman came out, a stack of folded sheets in her arms. She nodded politely to them as they stepped in. While the elevator door began to close, he saw her freeze, listening intently, a look of horror on her face.

Sean went to his room without another word. Mark took off his shoes and laid down on top of the salmon-colored bedspread and studied the swirls of plaster on the ceiling. He found his imagined map and tried to place Germany in it, but none of the little plaster ridges would cooperate. They insisted on making mountains in the north where the mountains wouldn't be.

He gave up the map, took off his glasses, and tucked his pillow into a comfortable position. The murmur of angry voices still came up from below. He covered his head with the other pillow and began to count backwards by sevens. From two thousand.

SEAN WAS STRETCHED out on his bed when Mark checked on him. His nursemaid had no intention of going down for dinner.

"I'm never eating again. There must have been something wrong with that burger." Sean lifted the pillow that covered his face and peered out at Mark. "You feel strong enough? Our table's still reserved."

"I'm strong enough," Mark replied, trying not to be irritated at the question.

It was his own fault it had to be asked anyway. He

hadn't been taking care of himself, and it was time he admitted that. Without Amy's presence, food had lost much of its appeal, its meaning. So he didn't think about it much.

But with Sean thinking of food all the time, Mark had eaten more in the last three days than he had in weeks. And he was honestly feeling stronger.

He went back to his room and wondered how to dress for dinner. The food at this restaurant was of the highest quality and customers could be expected to dress to match. Yet, Riverview House catered to all sorts of travelers and vacationers. Not all of them would pack ties and suit coats with their river sandals. He decided on navy blue slacks and a light blue button-down shirt. No tie. If they sent him back upstairs, they sent him upstairs.

The doors to the dining room were closed when Mark came down and a sign announced they would open at 5:30. He went out to the back porch he had admired earlier. There was not as much shade as before with the sun dropping to the west, but he found a chair tucked back against the stone wall of the house.

He lowered himself into it and stared out at the river. It wasn't in Europe, but it was one of the most famous rivers on the globe. School children around the world located the Mississippi River on their maps just as American children learned their rivers: the Thames, Rhine, Volga, Nile, Ganges, Zambezi. Could those children tell on their maps that a man on the east bank of the Mississippi was rolling up his sleeves in order to catch more of the early evening breeze? He could imagine a teacher somewhere saying,

Can you find the river? Can you find the bridge? Do you see the man?

Tulia Cardoso at the college called him a history romantic for the way he imagined things. Tulia's specialty was economics, along with her South American history. Luedders was all Europe, Ancient and Medieval. Jerry loved the New World.

Then there was Stanwick. He wasn't sure what Stanwick's compass needle pointed to. Unless it was trailing after Mark Newlin. Over the last years it seemed like he couldn't turn around anywhere without seeing Stanwick waiting behind him. Wanting to present at the same conferences, attend the same seminars, teach the same classes. Mark was more imaginative than competitive. But Stanwick's pushy insistence took a lot of the joy from his work.

Enough about Stanwick.

Itimu was fresh from Kenya and had a take on African History other colleges envied. Another university had made him an offer at the same time Gold did. But he had chosen Gold.

And this summer, Jerry, the dean, and a small committee had been interviewing professors from Seoul and Yokohama for a new Asian History position. All in all, Gold College covered it as best as a small college could do. Better than most small colleges.

He imagined his colleagues in their classrooms or offices, working away, advising the students from his list, picking up the extra hours of classes he was meant to teach. It didn't feel good.

The door to the house opened abruptly and a man

stepped over the threshold pulling the door shut behind him. The resulting sound was almost a slam. The man seemed about ten years older than Mark, fleshier around the face, like a drinking man. He wore tan pants and a rumpled tweed sport coat, looking more like a college professor than Mark did at the moment. It was not an outfit one could enjoy wearing outdoors in this late summer heat.

The man strode to the porch railing and bent slightly to rest his hands on it. He stared across the green lawn, walkways, shrubberies, and stone statues, past the flower beds to the silent river. One hand turned into a fist and thumped the railing, slowly and firmly, over and over. The sign of pent-up frustration looking for release.

Mark had just seen that same motion. *Where?* The woman in the foyer, with the bracelets, the one that had been arguing with Todd.

A sudden bellow of rage shattered the quiet afternoon. The gardener, packing up his tools for the day, jolted upright.

Mark had been saved from the full force of the voice by the lucky chance of sitting behind it. The man struck his fist once more against the railing, violently this time, then wheeled around. He caught sight of Mark, and it was his turn to look startled. He recovered quickly, but did not apologize.

"You're a guest here?" The question came out half angry, half embarrassed.

"For a while, yes," Mark replied.

"Enjoy the view," the man said, then stalked past him and into the house.

Mark shook his head. Was *anyone* in this place happy? Or even civil? Perhaps Todd Channon had just refused this man a room. Riverview House was turning out to be an odd spot for a rest cure. Had he seen one person smile? The young woman who had brought their dinner. Felicitas. She had smiled.

He got up and walked across the porch, down the steps, and across the grass to where the gardener was placing the last of his tools into a small wheelbarrow.

"Good afternoon," he said.

The man looked up, and Mark held out his hand.

"I'm Mark Newlin, staying here for awhile."

The gardener struggled out of his gloves, then shook Mark's hand. "George Juarez."

"Your plantings are beautiful. So many colors and textures. My wife would have loved them."

"Gracias. Thank you!" He was smiling like Felicitas, broad and brilliant. A welcoming sight. "And where is your wife?"

"She's dead now." It was someone else saying the words. Someone who also hit him in the stomach.

George made the sign of the cross, touching his own head and heart, then shoulder to shoulder. "I am very sorry."

"So am I."

This time George reached out for Mark's hand. Mark shook it again.

"The grounds look very nice," he said, glancing across the lawn. He wanted to say more, but no words presented themselves. He nodded a farewell and strolled slowly back to the house.

He didn't feel like eating, but if he went back up to his room he would feel more trapped up there than he did down here. And Sean would, between his own groans, start the concerned nurse act.

He might as well be alone in a crowd of people.

5

———

A Lonely Guilt

WHEN MYRA WAITE returned home from shopping at the farm store just outside of Marlonburg, Jerry's car was already in the garage. She put her bags down on the kitchen counter and went to the foot of the stairs to listen. All was quiet.

"Jerry?" she called.

No answer. She climbed the stairs to his study.

Jerry was sitting in his desk chair motionless, staring at the portrait of their laughing Katie in her wedding dress. Her new husband was laughing too, his hand stretched out and grasping hers. It was a beautiful picture, reflecting the joy of an amazing day.

But Jerry was not thinking of the joy of that day. Myra

knew that from the expression on his face. He was thinking of the phone call that came later, while the parents of the bride were cleaning up from the reception, packing presents into the car, putting leftover cake into containers. All the happy bustle. Until Jerry's cell phone buzzed.

His face had gone rigid as he listened to the dean's voice on the line. "No. No, she can't be."

The desperate tone, spoken as a plea, would stay in her ears forever.

Along with the words he spoke to her when the call had ended.

"There's been an accident, Myra. And Amy—Amy didn't make it."

Myra rubbed her nose, sniffed, and slid into the armchair, a chair she often sat in to keep Jerry company when he had work to do in the evenings. She knew he was aware of her. But, minutes went by and he said nothing.

"What's on your mind, Jer?" she asked quietly.

Jerry took a deep breath. "I should never have asked Mark to go to the conference. It wasn't that important. I should have just shelved the whole lecture idea. He didn't have time to do it, but he felt he had to, because he was a friend." He started to say more, but shook his head instead. His eyes were wet and tears filled hers too as she watched him struggle.

"You didn't cause the accident," Myra said gently. "You know this. The truck driver lost control coming down the interstate ramp. The road was oily from an earlier accident. That tragedy brought on another. And that is the truth about what happened."

Jerry didn't answer, probably didn't even hear her. But at least his gaze dropped from the wedding picture to the shelves below it.

Myra tried again. "Amy texted me from the conference, remember? They had fun there. She was proud of Mark's presentations and thought Gold College gained respect and attention because of them. She said it was a wonderful send-off for their trip to Europe. And that's the truth too."

He wasn't listening.

"Please, don't do this, Jerry. The grief is bad enough. Don't punish yourself for something you didn't do."

He started to shuffle papers around on his desk. Aimlessly, it seemed.

She didn't know what to say, and he was not looking at her.

She attempted something new, a change of subject, and tried to put on a brighter voice for it.

"Your sister called today. She said they bought tickets for Bermuda using part of the inheritance from your Aunt Louise. She wanted to know if you had decided what to do with your part of the money. I told her you were considering buying a convertible, since Louise loved cars, and she always wanted to show you her latest."

The desk papers were being sorted energetically now. "I don't know what I'm going to do yet."

Myra knew that the loss of a friendly great-aunt was not a cheering topic, but Louise had lived a full and happy life, and died reading the newspaper on her porch on a lovely spring afternoon in her ninety-second year. And she had left each one of her nieces and nephews twenty-five thousand dollars. Still, maybe Myra shouldn't have brought it up.

"Okay, Jer," she said softly.

She thought about the money. Twenty-five thousand dollars could buy several of the historical lectures that Jerry dreamed about. But several wasn't enough, not for the vision Jerry had for them, a vision he had talked about for so long that it was hers too. Three weeks in January, every January. Two lectures each day. Interim classes could be timed around them, so that every student could take part. It would be an academic, cultural, and community event like nothing ever seen yet in their part of the world.

He spun around, suddenly, in his desk chair and looked straight at her. "Did I do the right thing, sending him away like this?"

Of course he meant Mark.

"Is he as okay as he could be?" Myra asked.

"I don't know. Maybe. He needed to go somewhere to rest, and Matheson said I should make the decision for him. I've tried to make it right, Myra. Done everything I could to make it right."

"Then it wasn't the wrong thing."

He dropped his gaze and turned back to his desk again. She left the chair and came to stand behind him, wrapping her arms around his neck and resting her cheek on his bristly hair. "Let's just watch things week by week, okay? Mark knows you mean good for him. And Sean Merritt did do wonders for Sorenson. He'll be able to help Mark too."

Jerry said nothing more. Not for a long while. Not even when Myra kissed the top of his head and went back downstairs to put the butter in the refrigerator.

6

———

A Family Gathers

THE DINING ROOM doors at Riverview House stood open now. As Mark approached, the hostess looked up and smiled at him. "Good evening. Do you have a reservation?"

She was tall, and her dark hair was piled on top of her head. The long flowing sleeveless dress was a shimmery gold tonight. Her manner welcoming and professional. So different from the forlornness that surrounded her when she walked up the drive late at night. He must have shown surprise to see her. A questioning look appeared in her eyes.

"Yes," he said quickly. "I'm sorry. For a moment you looked like someone I had seen before. Yes, I'm a staying guest. Room—" He couldn't remember the number. He pointed in the general direction of his room. "Second floor, corner room with the tower windows."

She checked the papers before her. "Mr. Mark Newlin?"

"Yes."

"Will Mr. Merritt be joining you?"

"Not tonight."

The professional smile was back. "I'm Rebecca Powell." She picked up a menu card from the stand in front of her. "Follow me and I'll take you to your table."

In what had once been a manorial dining room, Riverview House management had arranged tables of varying sizes, all draped in pristine, white cloths, to accommodate about forty diners at one time. He was seated at a small table for two, which had been tucked into a nook next to a large window looking out onto the gardens.

Though it was early, half the room was filled. Mostly older couples, whose dress and manner showed them to be people of means. Almost all the men wore suit coats; the women had gold and pearls draped around their necks.

Exactly how much was the college shelling out for this? He would rather have had the money in a raise.

As he looked around, he caught sight of a woman standing in a doorway across the room from him. A server in black pants and white shirt pushed past her, a tray of water glasses in hand. The woman stepped aside then resumed her place studying the dining room. She was wearing a straight black sleeveless dress. Amy had one like it.

The woman's long brown curly hair was pulled half back, her eyes dark and serious. She glanced at him and as their eyes met, her expression became sorrowful, the kind of sorrow with sympathy in it. Embarrassed, he dropped his eyes quickly and studied the menu card Rebecca Powell had left with him. *Good grief! What had the irrepressible Vicki told the people here?*

A server, a young woman looking to be college-age, stopped at his table and set a goblet filled with ice water by his plate. "What else would you like to drink, sir?"

"Nothing at the moment, thank you." She moved on, her blond ponytail swishing behind her, and he examined the menu card again.

ELIZABETH CHANNON SPENT most weekend nights standing near the door that divided the dining room from the professional kitchen at Riverview House. It was a duty that came after a full week's work of teaching, but she didn't mind. The role gave her opportunity to watch. And she couldn't keep from watching. Looking for the moment when he would return.

Tonight the dining room was filled. The Egans were celebrating their anniversary with a few friends. She also recognized other long-time residents of Ashington Mills, regular patrons. Staying guests occupied another group of tables. A family from Virginia. A couple working their way up the Mississippi River from south to north. A professor from downstate who had just lost his wife in a horrible car crash. Her eyes were naturally drawn to his table, and she had to keep herself from it. At another table, a former student smiled her way, a gifted tenor. He and his girlfriend looked especially self-conscious, and she wondered if this were an engagement dinner. Rebecca entered from the main hall, menus in hand. A group of people followed in her wake toward the last open table.

Elizabeth stepped back into the kitchen. "Jim, table ten—party of four."

"I'm on it!" Jim walked briskly past her into the dining room, the gracious welcome of a good server already on his face.

She held the door for Felicitas, who was balancing a tray filled with drinks, then stepped back to watch again. Everything seemed to be going well.

Elizabeth focused on the doorway. If she could just see him walk through that door again, like she had seen him do so many times in past years. That was what she wanted most in life now. Just to see him again. To know he was happy. And safe.

David had been concerned for her. Scared. *What if he never comes back, Liz? Can you live with that?* She had no answer. Years had passed since David's death, and she was still watching.

As she stared at the doorway, allowing hope to pretend for a moment, someone did walk in. Someone she recognized. Someone who walked straight to the professor's table and sat down. Elizabeth's heart sank.

Mark couldn't decide what to eat. Sean usually just brought him things. Should it be this hard? Was struggling with choice another sign of an injured brain, or was he just more tired than he realized? He sighed, adjusted his glasses, and looked closely at the menu card.

"I told Nick he should use larger print for his menus."

A woman dropped into the chair across the table from him. She positioned a bright gold purse on the windowsill as if she were settling in to stay. It was the woman who had argued with Todd Channon that afternoon. Someone from the family that owned the house. Someone who was very used to getting her own way.

Rebecca Powell instantly appeared by the table. "I'm so sorry, Mr. Newlin." Then turning to the woman, bending lower and speaking in an urgent tone, she said, "Fia, you can't sit here."

Fia did not bother to lower her voice. "Of course I can. You said all the other tables are full. This is an empty seat, so I am here. Bring me a gin and tonic."

"Fia, please," Rebecca was pleading now. "We can serve you in one of the sitting rooms. Please don't make a scene."

Fia smiled coolly as one who knew she controlled the world. "I'm not making a scene, Rebecca. You are. And I will not balance a plate on my knees or get crumbs in my lap. I will sit and eat at a civilized table."

Mark couldn't stand this argument, or the distress on Rebecca's face. "It's all right, Ms. Powell. She can eat with me."

Rebecca gave him a look that managed to convey both gratitude and pity at once. "Gin and tonic," she said dryly, glaring at Fia before she turned away.

Fia gave a laugh, the ring of the victor in it.

Mark steeled himself and held out his hand. "We

should meet each other properly if we're going to dine together. I'm Mark Newlin."

Fia reached across and took it, her hand cool and hard with many rings. "Sophia Channon. I've had other names, but I always return to the original. It's the only one that lasts. Call me Fia."

"Thank you, Fia." Well, she could be civil enough. Now for this blasted menu again. One word stood out, and he chose it. Just in time. The blond, pony-tailed server was back, ready for the order.

"Anything with chicken in it," Fia said. Mark realized she had no menu card and held his out to her. She waved it away. "A green salad too."

The server remained mute, but looked questioningly at him.

"The risotto, please." He handed the menu to her, glad to be done with it. Without a word the server left. And he was left, with Fia.

He took a deep breath and prepared himself for an uphill evening of conversational attempts. "Do you have the menu memorized?" he asked. "I suppose you might, being one of the family." Not the best opener, but so what.

She shrugged, took her purse from the ledge, and poked through it, as if to check for something particular in it. She closed it with a snap and set it back on the ledge.

Amy had often told him, *People just tell you things, Mark. They see you and just start talking about all the big and little things on their minds. You have a face that makes people want to tell you things.*

Probably not Fia. And probably not tonight. And that

was for the best. It would take all the energy he had to keep the social niceties going.

She eyed him with annoyance. Perhaps she was regretting her rash choice of a dinner partner. Perhaps she was thinking "no clean, crumb-less lap is worth this." He hoped so.

"No one can memorize Nick's menus," she said, with an air of one talking to someone beneath her station. "He changes them all the time, practicing for his own restaurant someday."

"His own restaurant? Isn't this his own?"

"Not hardly. This is the family home. Nick would prefer some swank place in downtown Chicago with his name in lights above the door and his signature scrawled across every menu."

"He's good. His food is delicious. I hope he gets it."

Fia shook her head. "Oh, he won't get it. He's counting on family money that will never come to him. Betting on the wrong horse is Nick."

She spoke like a leading lady in a 1940s black-and-white mystery movie. She had the jewelry, the styled hair, the hard, closed face, and the look of riches. All she needed was a long cigarette in a jeweled holder to look the part. Her words had the taste of gossip, of "dishing the dirt" as the saying went, and they had a slimy feel.

The blond server returned, plopped down a short, clear glass in front of Fia, and immediately left without looking at either of them.

Fia reached for it at once and took a large gulp. She eyed him again over the rim of her glass. "You're not from here, are you?"

"No. I teach at a college downstate."

"I didn't know anything was down there."

"Thousands of people, growing crops, feeding the world, that's all."

It was his stock answer for comments like that, and he still liked it.

"Oh," Fia leaned forward, clutching her drink. "Oh, you're the ailing history professor."

He winced at this.

"The maid told me all about you. You were in a car accident. Wife died and all that."

And all that.

He didn't have the energy for this. Not in any part of his being did he have the energy for this. There should be a rule in life, that when you were wounded, bleeding from your soul's core, all the crazies would stay away and let you be. But there wasn't one.

Fia went on. "My oldest brother died that way. Left the biggest mess behind him."

He didn't want to hear about the mess. He took a drink of his water. Then another. How much longer would he have to endure this woman's company?

He stared out the window at the neat brick and stone walkways, the ornamental grasses clustered near black lampposts. The good work of George Juarez.

"You have a skilled gardener."

She looked startled. "Me? Oh. You mean the grounds? I have no idea what they do around here. It's a miracle it looks halfway decent."

A movement near the kitchen door caught his eye. The woman in black was staring at him again, worriedly.

Boldly he met her gaze, and, since Fia was looking away fussing with her napkin, he made quick eating motions, waving an imaginary fork in front of his mouth. The woman nodded and stepped back into the kitchen, the oak-paneled door closing behind her.

ELIZABETH FELT amazed by what she saw. The professor was working to make the best out of an impossible situation with Fia. A familiar task that usually fell to Elizabeth. But there he was, this total stranger, conversing politely, graciously, and she admired him for it.

But she knew from experience what uphill work it was, and when he made the desperate hand motion, she knew what he meant and why. It wasn't a complaint; it was a subtle cry for help. Things were getting tough at his table and the arrival of food, which always gave diners something new to focus on, would be welcome.

"Kelly, two house salads for table four right away. Priority."

"But there's only one ordered," Kelly protested, frowning.

"There's two now. One is gratis. But both are *top* priority."

"Here, Kelly." Felicitas was already at the salad station, her hands moving quickly. "I've got them about ready for you."

IN THE DINING ROOM, Mark carried on valiantly. "Where do you live, Ms. Channon?"

"New York, of course."

"What brings you back to Ashington Mills?"

"Family business." Her mouth shut tight like a clam.

He gazed out the window. A light breeze was making the tall grasses move gracefully back and forth. He could see a piece of the river in the distance beyond them. Fia checked the contents of her purse yet again. Was this a nervous habit?

Their server reappeared with two salad dishes and placed one in front of each of them. With relief, Mark picked up his fork and dove in.

It was very good. Mixed field greens, romaine, toasted almonds. That was probably goat cheese. And the dressing was light and slightly sweet.

"What's in the dressing?" he asked, one second before remembering who his dinner partner was.

Rebecca Powell was passing by their table and must have heard. "It's a vanilla vinaigrette."

"Thank you."

She did not linger but moved on. Fia poked vigorously at her salad dish, ignoring everything else.

The other woman was back at the kitchen door surveying the crowded dining room. He nodded his thanks to her, discreetly waving his fork, and was surprised by a sudden smile, a lovely smile. Something in her eyes made him think that she understood about his disagreeable table-mate.

Felicitas was serving the other half of the room, sharing her own generous smile. Their own server reappeared, tight-lipped and silent, and set down plates in front of both of them. His was piled high with risotto and topped with roasted mushrooms and parsley. The smell was amazing.

He took a bite and felt his tongue rejoice. If Fia would only remain silent while they ate, he might get some enjoyment out of this meal.

"Damn," she said.

He was not going to be so lucky.

"Damn," she said again, poking at her plate with her fork. "How could Nick put cheese sauce on this chicken? He's utterly ruined it."

Mark felt a mood come over him. A mood he couldn't hold back any longer. What Amy called his ornery, thumb-in-overall-straps, sassy-boy mood.

"Are you sure your curse didn't do that?" he asked.

If looks could pierce. "What are you talking about, Mr. Newlin?"

"You have damned your food twice, Ms. Channon. It's twice-cursed. You might have had a chance with the rice pilaf after one damn, but now?" He looked at her sadly. "The whole thing's a loss."

She stared at him warily. Confusion peeping out from the back of pride. In the end, she let out a laugh. "Do you never get angry, Mr. Newlin? Or do you stay cool and suave like Rhett Butler, not giving a damn yourself?"

She sounded playful, as playful as a hungry cat.

"I have never been accused of being suave, Ms. Channon, and yes, I do get angry. But, if I imitate Rhett Butler in not giving a damn, it is because I, a mere mortal, do not have a damn to give."

She stared at him, frowning.

"In other words, I'm damn-less," he said, giving her a

quirky smile. "And, also, being mortal as well, so are you. Which means your chicken is safe to eat. So's the pilaf."

He forked another bite of risotto, chewed it, and thought of Sean, missing this exquisite taste.

Fia was actually eating her food again, but as one who was allowing herself to be amused.

"Since you have some knowledge of history, Mr. Newlin, allow me to tell you something of this town's past, the *mortals* who lived here. If you had grown up in Ashington Mills, the name Channon would have meant a great deal to you. You would have been aware of everything the Channons thought and did. And you would have begged God to let the Channons look your way."

"Like the lords of old Europe," he said, trying not to react to such blatant arrogance.

She corrected him. "Like the dukes and princes." She leaned closer across the table, rings glinting in the light of the small lamp between them. "The Channons were worth millions when a million was worth something. We went to Harvard, Yale, and Oxford, and they were glad to have us."

He could tell that she was making the college point to show her family's superiority over his own profession and collegiate situation. It was annoying, but he had run into this before. He ignored the comment, like always.

Fia wasn't finished. "The grandson of the man who started the fortune built this house that you are staying in and dining in. For generations the people of Ashington Mills longed to see the inside of this house."

Her words stopped abruptly as she looked around the dining room. He couldn't restrain his imagination. What was she seeing? The end of glory? Commoners filling the rooms that were her family's alone when she was a child. Commoners dropping their napkins and crumbs on what was once her floor.

He felt sorry for her. Her pride blinded her and made her an unwelcome trial to those around her. But, to put it poetically, the place that once knew her, knew her no more. An awful feeling that he could understand. He couldn't help being interested in the fall of the Channon dynasty. What it had been, compared to what it was now.

She pointed to the wall opposite them, where honey oak paneling rose from the floor until a wallpaper of gold and red took over, reaching up to the ceiling. "My great-grandfather brought that wallpaper from France. The gold you see in it is real gold."

He looked again with open admiration at the work of the craftsmen who had done it, so engrossed in the story that the words just slipped out. "What happened to the family, Ms. Channon? Fia, I mean. What caused the loss of their fortune?"

She turned a glare on him that made him feel like a simpleton. "*Nothing* has happened to the Channons, Mr. Newlin. They have not lost one bit of their fortune. The Channon fortune is as great as it ever was."

Something didn't set right. Was she lying? Or had she exaggerated the glory days? Why would such a wealthy family have to rent out their home to travelers?

"Then who is the head of the family now? Just a question that any student of history might ask, of course," he added quickly.

"My eldest brother John Christoph Channon was until his death. His son would be now."

Would be? She was hiding something. Fia was choosing her words very carefully.

"And where is his son now?" He had a feeling the son was not Todd. Todd didn't have the confidence of a man with millions backing him up. She was slow to answer, so he rephrased the question.

"Where is the heir now?"

The cool hardness was back in her eyes, along with disdain she had inherited from her forebears. And yet, she answered him.

"We do not know."

She patted her mouth with her napkin and ate the rest of the pilaf.

Two PIECES of apple tart were set before them by their silent server. Fia showed no interest in any further conversation. So, as Mark ate his, he thought about what she had said.

Did her "we do not know" mean anything more serious than not knowing where the heir was at the moment? Was this heir aloof and distant, keeping himself and his millions away from the rest of the family? He wondered if Jerry Waite back at the college knew anything of the Channons of Ashington Mills, Illinois.

A sudden burst of loud music broke the hum of dining room conversation. Someone was playing a piano—no, *commanding* a piano—and with dominating talent. Mark, like the other patrons, raised his head looking around for the person or explanation behind the music. Not Fia.

"Ernie!" There was desperation in her cry.

She tossed her napkin onto the table, grabbed her purse, and hurried between the tables and chairs to the door, almost blindsiding Felicitas holding a dessert tray.

The piano music continued. Loud. Yes, the performer was definitely a person of great talent. And Ernie, if it was Ernie, was playing something that sounded a lot like Mozart, or Bach. Mark wasn't up on the finer points of classical composers.

Some guests looked annoyed at the sound. Others had looks of amazement, as if something wonderful was happening, and by lucky chance they were a part of it.

Rebecca Powell closed the double doors of the dining room, muffling the sound. From the look on her face, this was evidently not planned. Mark's server re-appeared.

"Are you through with that, sir?"

"You're talking more now?" he said with a smile.

"Now that Fia's gone, yes. I never say anything around her. For what you say will definitely be used against you— and against Todd and Stephanie. Stephanie's my sister."

"And you are?"

"Kelly. Did you want anything else?"

"Nothing, thanks.

He stood up as she gathered the dishes, and lowered his voice.

"Kelly, who's Ernie?"

Kelly made a face. "Another member of Todd's crazy family. An uncle, I think."

So Ernie was possibly Fia's brother. She had

mentioned "family business." Since Kelly was talking now, he'd try one more question.

"Which of the family owns this house?"

Kelly placed the rest of the silverware on the stack of dessert plates, then grabbed the napkins and tucked them between. "That would be Baiss, Todd's cousin." She pronounced it with a "z" sound, like maze. And for a moment he was confused.

"Baze? Not Base, as in 'First Base'?"

"No, B-A-I-S-S. Like Baze. But you can pronounce it anyway you want."

"Is he here tonight?" The moment after he asked the question, he realized how foolish it sounded. If Baiss were here, Fia, of course, would have known and not been so cryptic in mentioning his whereabouts.

Kelly appeared to see nothing wrong in the question. She shrugged her shoulders. "Who knows?"

She hefted the dishes into her arms and made ready to leave. He held out a ten dollar bill, feeling like a detective paying an informer. "Thanks for dinner tonight."

"Thank you." She snared the ten between her fingers, then wove her way between the tables to the kitchen door.

He left the dining room and walked out into the large central hall with the fireplace and the majestic staircase. The music flowed from the doorway to a room that, Mark realized, was directly under his own. His feet followed the music, and he joined the knot of people peering into the formal parlor.

It was a beautiful room with ivory floral carpet, its windows creating a broad bay toward the front of the house. Angled in front of this bay stood a gloss black grand piano. The top was propped up, and a gray-haired man in a black suit sat at the keys, pounding out the music.

The performer seemed oblivious to everything and everyone—including Fia, who stood just beyond the piano, staring out the window towards the parking lot. She did not look happy.

Mark glanced around. The angry man in tweed, who had spoken to him on the back porch before dinner, was in the corner helping himself to a drink. This looked like the set-up of a happy gathering.

He couldn't help thinking that Ernie's music not only announced his arrival, but also kept his family from talking to him when he didn't want them to. Fia clearly looked frustrated. Was the alpha dog making himself known?

Ernie struck the keys again. Mark's brain protested against the loud sound and he turned away.

He didn't want to wait for the elevator. His room was just at the top of this flight of stairs. He could rest on the landing if he needed to. Todd was behind his counter again, checking in a late arrival.

Mark took the first three approach stairs slowly, then turned onto the main run of the staircase when a voice called out behind him.

"Mr. Newlin!" It was the curly-haired woman who had been standing by the kitchen door. He did not want to be caught just now. He wanted to escape to his room. It had been a trying dinner, and he actually felt more up to Fia's spite than this woman's sympathetic looks.

But she had started up the stairs after him, and he had no choice. He kept his hand on the railing and turned.

"Mr. Newlin, I want to thank you for your help this evening." There was that smile again. He could not miss the kindness in it.

"Fia is my sister, and she can be very difficult. I don't know what Rebecca would have done with her. No one can handle Fia."

"You're welcome." He glanced toward the parlor door and couldn't help thinking that Ernie knew exactly how to handle Fia.

He felt awkward standing on the stairs, but the woman hadn't made a move to leave. She seemed stuck staring at the parlor door.

"How many are you—Channons, I mean?" He wondered if he had phrased that clearly, but she seemed to know what he meant.

"There were six of us. Three boys, three girls. Fia's the oldest of the girls."

"And the other man in the room? Is he a brother?"

"That's Will. Yes. John, the oldest, died in a car accident some years back." She said these last words carefully, and he had the distinct feeling that she was remembering the reason that had brought him here. And, that she had something more she wanted to say, but didn't know quite how to say it.

She held out her hand. "Forgive me. I should have introduced myself. I'm Elizabeth Channon. I teach choir at the high school."

That would be the high school he and Sean had driven by just this morning. And it struck him that a choir teacher was an odd occupation for a person who belonged to a family of millionaires.

"Mark Newlin," he said, shaking her hand, which felt more human than Fia's. "But you knew that."

He could have said good night after that and thanks, but it was his turn to pause. Should he ask her about the heir—if he was truly missing or just temporarily misplaced? He had a feeling that she might tell him.

He opened his mouth to begin when the front door opened and shut beneath them. A common enough occurrence with diners coming in and out, but it was Todd's involuntary yelp that drew his attention.

Mark looked over the banister and down into the entry hall. A woman had entered, pulling a black suitcase behind her. She wore black pants and a black blouse of some kind. Her hair was also completely black. But there was something in her manner, some darkness beyond the dark colors of her apparel that put one on one's guard. Todd looked nervous, wary.

The woman stopped at the counter below and said something to the manager that no one could hear, thanks to Ernie.

Elizabeth looked over the railing also, her curly brown hair falling across her shoulder. She was gripping the banister in both hands.

"Oh, God," she said quietly.

And it sounded rather like a prayer.

7
———

The Sticking Point

"W HAT IS GOING ON DOWN THERE?" asked Sean.

Mark's "faithful assistant," as he had mentally dubbed him, was lying on his own bed, leaning against a pile of pillows, cracker in one hand, a Lord Peter Wimsey mystery in the other.

Mark dropped down into the one chair in Sean's room. "You can hear that, can you?"

"Who couldn't?"

"Well, what you and your groaning stomach missed was a drama worthy of Shakespeare. The play's still going on. I just left early."

Sean's brow creased. "What do you mean?"

Mark removed one of Sean's socks from underneath him on the chair and tossed it onto a small pile of clothes at the foot of the bed. He settled himself more comfortably in the chair. Leaned back and took a deep breath.

"Imagine a posh restaurant—yes, we could call it posh —filled with well-to-do if not downright wealthy diners, and then the Channons descend. All of the older living Channons, if I count right. There's Fia, who invaded my table. Ernie, who wants the whole world to know he is a piano virtuoso. Will, who was probably on his fifth or sixth drink judging from the way the scotch was running down the outside of his glass instead of inside it. And Elizabeth, who feels the need to apologize for them. Oh, and one unnamed woman, who just showed up like a dark curse."

Sean's eyes widened. The book dropped from his hand. Cracker crumbs showed in his open mouth.

"And that's not all," Mark went on. "The family member who owns the house and all the money is missing. And I get the feeling a number of them want it—the money, that is. Especially Nick, our chef, who according to Fia, would like to open a restaurant in Chicago."

"You mean *missing*, missing? Completely? Police search and all that?"

"I don't know. Fia was being cryptic. But I did find out his name. Kelly, my server, told me. Baiss." Mark spelled it out for him. "Todd and the woman on the stairs must have been speaking of Baiss Channon, not baseball."

Sean picked at the folds in his blanket. His face showed he was doing some hard thinking. Probably wondering what Lord Peter Wimsey would do. "Are all those Channons staying in this house tonight?"

"Fia and the dark curse are. They both showed up

with suitcases. Elizabeth teaches at the high school, so I would imagine she has a place of her own. I have no guesses when it comes to Ernie and Will."

The piano playing beneath them came to a crashing stop.

They both held their breath and listened. Then Mark got up and walked through their suite to the outer door. Sean followed. Mark opened the door a crack.

Voices came up the stairwell. Angry and strident.

"That's Fia," he whispered to Sean.

Pleading. That would be Todd.

Slurry bluster. Will's.

A new voice. A woman's voice, carefully controlled and playful, yet totally without humor. A mocking, malicious voice. Fia evidently had not cornered the market on spite.

Sean whispered. "The dark curse?"

"Could be," he whispered back.

They could hear recorded violin music coming from the dining room. Rebecca Powell might have turned it up to cover the argument. The Channons were still in the parlor right below them.

Mark shut the door.

"It's coming up the air vents," said Sean. "Man, you're never going to sleep in here with that going on."

"Well, it's early yet. Maybe they'll quit. You know, get sore throats."

Sean looked doubtful.

Mark changed the subject. "How's the stomach?"

"Better, I think. I'm out of ginger though."

"Want me to get you some?"

Sean looked alarmed. "Not until you can walk fifteen

minutes with no ill effects. I've got my crackers. I'll be fine." The analytic look. "Have you driven since—?"

"Once or twice." It hadn't gone well. His head had hurt so badly that he had turned around after a few blocks and gone home. "Okay, we can get everything you need tomorrow, if you're up for it."

"I'll be up for it."

Fia's voice rose below them. Sharp, pointed. Almost hysterical.

"We can't stay here," said Sean. "Not if they carry on like this. You're supposed to be resting. What if we leave tomorrow?"

"Believe it or not, I feel bad for Todd. He's doing his best, then his family comes and destroys everything for him." He wondered what they should do, but felt no energy to plan anything. "How about we give it two weeks?"

"The college thinks we're staying until December." Sean groaned.

December. It felt like forever away from this muggy August night. What on earth had possessed Jerry and the administration to plan such a thing? The answer came instantly to mind. He only had to look in the mirror.

"Um . . . we'll see. Are you sure you have enough crackers? I can get some from the kitchen for you."

"No. I'm fine. I've got plenty."

He followed Sean back to his room and watched him sink down onto his bed again. "You need to select your cheeseburgers with better care." Mark put on the stern professor look.

"I thought I was supposed to do all the health

nagging around here." Sean looked impy. "So when are we going to go over your history research notes, Professor?"

Mark grabbed a pillow from the chair and threw it at Sean's head. The pillow met its target. That was satisfying. Mark ducked into his own room and shut the door before Sean threw it back.

Even though it was early, Mark changed into his pajama pants and T-shirt. He picked up the number puzzle book and settled himself in the tower armchair again. It was still light outside, but dull enough indoors that he needed the lamp on. The Channon voices talked below him, and though there was nothing harmonious in the sound, at least it was not as loud as the piano had been.

He paused in his puzzle and looked out the window. Several cars were heading down the drive back to town. Were they diners who had left early because of the argument?

He missed Amy. He wanted to talk about all this with her. Curl up together and think it through. The sadness of loss descended on him again. The heavy grayness of grief with fear in its folds.

He bent to his puzzle, forcing himself to concentrate. A five-square run of seventeen could not hold a number eight, so the eight must be over here instead. He wrote it in the box.

Somewhere around nine thirty the voices stopped. Above him, on the third floor, a door slammed. He kept working, thankful for the addictive nature of the puzzles, but often looked up to rest his brain.

Finally, he was too sleepy to go on. Night had already fallen. Or risen.

At one faculty picnic, the English professors debated if night poetically fell, or if it actually rose from the ground. The philosophy professors had taken sides on whether darkness was a presence or an absence. The artists talked of mixing black with any color for shadows, and the emotional impact darkness had on works of art. It was a beautiful example of how specialization shaped thought.

His grandpa would simply say, "Come with me, Mark. Let's go sit on the back porch and watch night come." And they would sit on the porch swing and gaze at the shadows creeping over the fields, tucking in the corn and soybeans, bringing much-wanted coolness, forcing all things to rest. He and Amy would do that too, whenever they found themselves with a view that had room to watch the night come.

He stretched and shifted in his chair. The river lay dark and empty in the night. He looked toward town. A solitary figure was coming up the drive, and the street lamps caught the shimmery gold of her dress. Rebecca Powell.

The clock read 10:48. He turned off his lamp and went to the bathroom to fill his water glass, then lay down on his bed, thinking about the Channons.

Was the Channon heir truly missing? Was that what the family argument was about? Kelly, his server, when he had asked her if Baiss Channon were here, had answered, "Who knows?"

Could she have meant it in the sense of *I don't care and*

no one else would either? He was almost sure she had meant *who could possibly know*? Or *no one knows*.

How could they not know?

Was there a mystery around the missing Baiss Channon? Or had Sean infected Mark with the mystery virus?

He turned off his bed lamp and rolled onto his side. Tonight, at least, he was ready to sleep first. The crack under the other bedroom door showed that Sean's light was still on.

MARK WOKE ABRUPTLY. Sean was standing by the door to the hall, fully dressed.

"What is it? What's wrong?" His heart started racing.

"They're at it again."

Raised voices, somewhere out in the hallway, he guessed.

Mark sat up, rubbed his face, and looked around. Light was already coming in through the curtain edges. "What time is it?"

Sean handed him his glasses. "Nine o'clock. They've been going on for fifteen minutes, and I can't stand it anymore. Let's get out of here."

Mark threw back the covers and climbed out of bed, then stood still listening. He walked over to the door. Didn't need to open it this time. The yelling was coming down from the floor above.

"Who is it?" Sean asked.

"That's Fia." More than likely she was shouting down the stairwell, her words all too clear.

"You have done nothing! I lost my home, and you don't care! And you're lying about the money. You need it too, and you know it!"

A child starting crying in the room above Mark. Heavy footsteps. The door above opened. Another voice, entreated, "Please, please. You're scaring the kids."

"This isn't your house!" Fia cried.

The door slammed.

"You're right about one thing, Fia." A sharp, cold male voice called up from the floor below them. "Nobody cares. And why do you need money? Don't tell me you've gambled it away?"

Fia screamed something unintelligible.

He heard the sound of a glass breaking. Thumping increased on the floor upstairs, like someone running back and forth. The cry of a frightened child.

He made sure the door was locked, then caught sight of Sean's pale face. Sean hadn't moved. Was watching him. The terror of the crying child was on his face.

Mark grabbed his shoulder and shook it, trying to pull him back to his normal self. "Hey, you all right? We'll get out of here. Find another place to get breakfast. Are you ready to go? Yes? Give me a few minutes, okay?"

Sean went to his room without answering. Mark hurried through his shower and shave. He dressed quickly, pausing only to look over the papers Todd had given them the day they arrived. One of them made him stop and think. He folded it carefully and put them all back in the top drawer.

The corridor and stairway were empty when Mark

and Sean stepped out of their room. Mark led the way downstairs, not wanting to stand and wait for the elevator.

Todd was at his desk behind the counter typing furiously. He did not look happy. He stopped typing as they approached, a silent question on his face.

"Just going out for breakfast," said Mark.

Was that a flicker of relief in Todd's eye?

"I've called the lawyer about this disturbance. Mr. Baker will be here soon."

"The lawyer?" Mark was surprised. "Not the police?"

Todd looked horrified. "You don't call the police on the Channons."

Mark repeated Todd's words to Sean as they walked down the porch steps, into the muggy late-summer morning. "'You don't call the police on the Channons.' Do you suppose that's family policy or town policy?"

"I don't know."

Sean's words were terse. Mark looked at him. Something about the argument had gotten deeply under his skin. Mark punched his arm. "C'mon. You'll feel better after breakfast."

They were headed down the drive, Sean at the wheel of the Honda, when a black BMW pulled in and sped past them towards the house.

"What do you bet that's Mr. Baker now?" Mark asked.

Sean didn't answer, just shook his head slowly, eyes glued to the road.

THE ATMOSPHERE of Pancake Sal's was a direct contrast to

the atmosphere they had left behind at Riverview. An open room with polished wood floors greeted them. A server guided them to a bright orange table. Light, happy jazz played in the background. Pancake Sal, or Salvatore, was a tall Italian man who wore a black and white striped apron and strode through the café smiling and chatting with customers. And the smell of coffee and cinnamon and warm butter was everywhere.

A flourish of white chalk across a black chalkboard wall announced: *Sal's Original Pancakes.* It was followed by more pancake varieties than Mark had ever seen before.

Sean chose the Original and Cinnamon Sugar, Mark chose Buttermilk and Apple Fritter. Followed by Italian coffee, of course.

Sean sipped his coffee slowly. He had eaten some of the pancakes, but hadn't finished them. His stomach could still be upset. The minutes went by, and Mark realized they were both wondering what to do next.

There was no reason, and absolutely no desire, to return to Riverview House at the moment. But a line of people stood on the sidewalk outside the door, waiting for Sal's pancakes, ready to pounce on this table once Mark drank the last of his cappuccino.

"What if we walk a bit?" he suggested.

Sean's eyebrows lifted. "Do you feel up to it?"

"Sure. We can just stroll." *Like the French do.* He wasn't sure where the thought came from, but it brought sadness with it. The echo of loss. He mentally shook himself.

"But first," he stood up with purpose, "I need to take a quick break. Coffee goes right through me."

When he returned, Sean said, "Okay. We can stroll."

. . .

THEY HEADED from the side street, where Pancake Sal reigned, toward the city square. Mark was taken with that large swath of green park in the center of the old downtown. He felt like walking all the way around it. Could he?

He mentioned it to Sean, casually, avoiding the health question. The walk would be the equivalent of four long blocks. Not far for someone who ran four miles each morning, but far for an "ailing professor." Fia's face came unbidden to his mind. He pushed it away.

They crossed the street at the light and turned west, the morning sun on their backs, and wandered down the row of shops and businesses that sat on the south side of the square. Historic stone shells, their windows and doors surrounded with strips of white marble, embellished with brass doorknobs and brass lanterns—yet, inside were yarn shops, title companies, dry cleaners, computer stores. Ashington Mills lived with its past and its present at the same time, as all cities do.

One sign seemed to fit both past and present. The pleasing light gray stone facade of *Baker and Stow*. Baker. The lawyer that had sped up the drive to mediate for the fighting Channons. He noticed Sean staring at the lawyer's office too.

Mark stopped walking and turned to face Sean. "We're in an odd spot, Sean. And unfortunately the spot is filled with Channons. Both of us can think of better places to be. So, what should we do?"

"We should go somewhere else. This is not what I

thought it was going to be, and I know it isn't what Dr. Waite or any of the others expected."

"I wouldn't mind leaving. But there is an unfortunate sticking point."

"What do you mean?"

"You didn't taste that risotto last night."

Mark hoped for a grin, but it didn't come. "Okay, but before I tell you, I want you to know that I am as frustrated as you are. Truly."

"Why? What is it?"

"For reasons I don't care to explore right now, Jerry hasn't told us the full truth about this arrangement. Gold College isn't paying for all this at Riverview. Jerry is."

Sean looked bewildered. "Are you sure?"

Mark nodded. "I looked at the bill more closely this morning. Those last four credit card digits are not the ones on the History Department's card. They are Jerry's. I'm absolutely sure." He cleared his throat. "A year ago Amy and I took a short vacation with the Waites. We got our receipts mixed up once, and I noticed how similar Jerry's last four digits were to the ones on Amy's card. There's no doubt."

"But if we leave early, that would save Dr. Waite money."

"Ideally, yes. Except for the other words marked on the bill: *Special rate. Prepaid. No Refund.*"

Mark felt the frustration swell inside of him. "I don't know what Jerry was thinking to commit to all this. But I'm sure he thought it would be a better, happier place than it is."

"You mean we're stuck here," Sean said sullenly. "For months."

"In a way, yes. I think Dr. Waite was being overly generous." And probably destroying his savings account at the same time, which made Mark feel sick and angry. He wondered if Myra knew about this, or if Jerry had been acting solo. *How could Jerry be so foolish?*

Sean jammed his hands in the pockets of his jeans.

"We could do day trips, if you're up for it," Mark offered. "Galena. Dubuque. Wisconsin."

"Yes, but what do we do when we come back? That house is like a nightmare come to life. How can anybody get stronger or heal in the middle of all that?"

"There has to be some crisis brewing," said Mark, "Some *thing* that would make them all return to the old family homestead. It's obviously not for love. It must be for money. Fia yelled as much this morning. Money they want and can't get."

He glanced at Sean to see if he was having any luck igniting the sleuth-spirit in him. Maybe there was a spark of something. Maybe not.

"So, we have this family puzzle in our laps," he went on. "We might as well play at solving it. We could start by following the money. Who has it? Who wants it?

"First: Who needs money? According to Ernie, Fia does, because of her gambling. According to Fia, Ernie does, for reasons unclear. Nick wants money to open a restaurant in Chicago, if we can believe Fia."

Sean dove in. "Perhaps Todd? That talk on the stairs you overheard? What if the hotel has to close soon because they're running out of money? That could explain the 'No Refund' policy."

Mark agreed. "Definitely Todd. Behind that haughty front is the cringing look of a hunted animal. Which makes these arguments even worse for Todd and Nick. Their own family is driving away their paying customers."

They had come to the end of the first block and waited for the signal light to cross the street, one of the main thoroughfares in Ashington Mills. Mark realized he was feeling tired.

When they turned onto the next row of shops, Mark walked even slower and hoped Sean wouldn't notice. He kept talking. "Last night, Fia claimed that the Channon fortune is as great as it ever was."

"So, who's got the money?" asked Sean.

"Presumably, this heir—this Baiss Channon."

They were walking by a beautiful building, and the sight of it made all the Channon questions slide from Mark's mind. A three-story, gray stone courthouse topped with a glistening white dome towered before them. More of the white marble this city loved formed the steps up to the entry. Three arches graced the entrance to the courthouse and across the top of these, tall letters were carved into more white marble.

Mark stopped and stared up at them, backing toward the street to be able to see them all.

Sean glanced up. "What is it?"

Mark pointed at the inscription. *For I, the Lord, love justice.* The attribution was written artfully in Roman numerals, chapter and verse, from the ancient book of Isaiah.

"Inspiration to a lot of lawyers and hope to half their clients," said Mark. "Dread to the other half, I would imagine. I've never seen anything like this."

Sean studied the inscription. "Do you think that any courthouse in the country enacts justice perfectly?"

The question surprised Mark. "Perfectly? You're using that word for human beings? You have to even ask the question? How old are you?"

Sean actually laughed. Which was a good sign. "I didn't mean to say 'perfectly.' It just slipped out."

"Of course, real justice is the only hope for a democracy. For any country."

Sean continued to gaze up at the inscription. "Okay, what about this? Don't you think that when people cry for justice, they redefine it to mean good for them and bad for their enemies? Even if they are the ones who have done wrong? Who believes that true justice would ever take a price from them?"

Now that was a real question.

For a fleeting moment, Mark could see Sean at the front of a history classroom, making the students laugh with some joke, then driving them to think more deeply with the next sentence. Yet, what if this wasn't theoretical? What if there was something more on his faithful assistant's mind, something from the tragedies of his own past?

Mark tried to answer gently. "Victims cry for justice. Perpetrators usually don't."

"Unless they are going for revenge."

Something in Sean's tone was a little unsettling. Mark

tried not to stare at him. "How just do you think revenge could be?"

Sean shrugged. "The person who wants it always thinks it is."

"Which makes actual justice less likely."

After a moment, Sean said, "True."

Mark stared up at the inscription again. There was something so impartial about it. Something fearful, yet hope-filled at the same time. The kind of thing you had to stop and revere. The kind of thing that didn't come from human beings.

He was also getting a crick in his neck from looking up.

Sean made no comment when Mark cut back across the park instead of completing the square. Nor when he paused and sat down by the fountain and watched the water spray for a while. Mark was grateful. But he sat too long to escape Sean's professional concern.

"How are you feeling now?" Sean asked, after tossing some pennies in the fountain.

"I'm feeling like I might grow a short beard like yours. Mark touched the side of his face. "To cover up this scar until it can heal more. I don't know if people are looking at me or at the scar when they talk."

Sean studied him. "That could be a good idea."

Mark stretched himself, then stood, and led the way across the rest of the green to where his car waited on the side street. A dozen people stood on the sidewalk still waiting for pancakes from Sal.

Mark paused with his hand on the car door handle and looked across the roof at Sean. "What if we find out more about the Channons? Knowledge brings protection, as they say."

"Who says?"

"Well, Luedders."

Sean took a deep breath. "All right, sir," he said politely. "Where do you want to go?"

"A place where we can uncover the context of what we are seeing. When you understand context, you're ready to deal with the rest. Without context, you're a lost man." He wasn't sure Sean was following what he was saying, so he got to the point. "What about the college library?"

"The library?"

"A professor's natural habitat."

Sean raised an eyebrow. "You did the 'natural habitat' line."

"I did the natural habitat line. Just get in the car."

8

———————

Going Exploring

THE RESEARCH LIBRARIAN at the Ashington College library showed no surprise when he introduced himself as a professor from Gold College and asked for materials on the Channons of Ashington Mills. Mark wondered how common a request this was. Perhaps Fia was right about the amount of attention her family drew in this community. Perhaps they were the local Kennedys.

He wondered if a Channon had ever been governor of Illinois, then laughed to himself. Because of his academic specialization, he knew every king of England, every tsar of Russia, and every leader of the Holy Roman Empire of the Germanic Nation, but could only name a few of the governors of his home state. Jerry Waite would be appalled.

The librarian, a tall, brisk, gray-haired woman, with a pair of reading glasses in her hand, led them to a local history room replete with long wooden study tables, trays of magazines, microfiche machines presumably loaded with old newspapers, and shelves of books. Several computers hummed on a counter along one wall.

Mark felt a small pulse of excitement. He was going exploring.

"Now, you must remember, Professor Newlin," the librarian said, waving her glasses at him, "that before 1917, the Channon family name was Bachen. Leonard Bachen, the same man who built Riverview House, had the family name changed during the First World War.

"You might find this helpful to start." She pointed at a shelf of books positioned in the center of one of the long tables. "We have books of reprinted newspaper articles grouped by topic, and since the Channons built our music building for us, the first book printed was devoted to a history of their family. It's the brown book on the end."

"Thank you. Thank you very much." He meant it sincerely. This would keep him from being tempted to face down a glowing screen.

"Certainly. Let me know if you need anything else. It looks like your assistant has already found the magazines." She left the room to them.

On this late summer weekend, they were the only two occupants. He took a seat at the table, pulled the Channon book out of its holder, and opened it on the table in front of him.

Sean sat down in the seat opposite with a short stack

of magazines. "What are we looking for? The truth about the Channons?"

"That would be ideal, but not likely."

"What do you mean? I thought that was why we were here."

"A historian is very slow to assign truth. But what we can get is context, a framework for understanding. Then we fit what we observe about the family into it."

Mark turned to the title page. *A History of the Channons of Ashington Mills, Illinois.* He flipped more pages and began to skim.

The earliest Bachen, an orchestra member named Augustus, also had a talent for business. He came from Germany and took employment with the famous Cornelius Vanderbilt. After some years learning from the Commodore, he headed west, ready to demonstrate his own energetic, entrepreneurial skills.

His name appeared among the early founders of Ashington Mills, sometime in the 1840s.

The Bachen name popped up in conjunction with a flour mill, then a saw mill. As the years progressed they became involved, now as Channons, in industrial machinery, "agribusiness," and even electronics. If there was something to make, the Channons made it. If there was money to be made, the Channons made it.

The Channons' history intertwined with the country's history. Their conservatism steadied them when the stock market crashed. During the Great Depression, they dropped wages instead of laying off workers, running their factories at a loss, trying to make sure that each of their men had some money coming in each day—a move that was highly criticized or praised, depending on who was writing the copy. It was a noble effort, surely, along with their support of soup kitchens. They had tried to take care of the poor of the city.

That made Mark think. Nobility could have been part of the Channon character once. Surely not this morning. But not every Channon had acted like this. He shared these thoughts with Sean, who listened soberly, but did not respond.

Mark turned back to the newspaper book. Channons had died in the influenza epidemic, in both World Wars, in Korea and Vietnam. Had the rest of the family died out? Had it all come down to these Channons in Riverview House?

Sean held out a magazine to him. "Hey, look at this." It was a glossy, two-page photo spread. Sean tapped a picture. Mark recognized Fia, a younger, smiling Fia, standing next to a man in a tuxedo.

Sophia Channon marries Victor Gaff.

Mark glanced at the date line. About ten years ago.

Gaff. One of the names that didn't last. Mark looked more closely at the man. He looked confident, as one used to possessing riches. Used to possessing. Fia and Victor. That would have been quite a match.

Mark went back to his book. He read about Channon births and Channon funerals. Saw pictures of Channons opening factories and, yes, even closing some of them. And there were photos of Riverview House being constructed. He shared these with Sean. That sparked his interest.

Another theme appeared in the Channon family. They

loved music. Obsessively. Their forebears had played in orchestras in Europe. The New World Channons endowed orchestras in Illinois and also performed with them. That would explain Ernie. And Elizabeth's choir directing too.

The Leonard Bachen who built Riverview House adored the music of the Baroque era. Purcell and Bach and Vivaldi. He also was a composer. As were some of his children.

Mark pulled a notebook and pen out of his pocket and sketched out a quick family tree, a habit he had developed years ago. He was glad to see that the action stressed his brain only a little. He wouldn't take many notes. Just focus on the Channons pertinent to Riverview House.

AUGUSTUS BACHEN (IMMIGRATED from Germany)

1st generation born in US: Friedrich Bachen

2nd generation: Leonard Bachen (later Channon), built Riverview House

3rd generation: Carl Channon

4th generation: John Channon, Senior, married Nora Bearden in 1953

5th generation: John and Nora's Children:

John (1955), Ernest (1957), Sophia (1959), Wilhelm (?), Juliane (?)

HE COULD NOT FIND a reference to Elizabeth yet. Maybe Elizabeth used her middle name. Maybe she was Juliane. Then who was the Dark Curse?

Next question, what about the 6th generation? *Whose son is Todd? Whose son is Nick?*

Mark sat back and took off his glasses. He rubbed his eyes. Pressure was growing in his head: it pushed at the back and pinched behind his nose. *That's no good.* Also, his eyes were having trouble following the lines. He had only skimmed as far as 1970, but he would have to stop.

He looked over at Sean, sprawled in a chair like he was at the beach, flipping through a magazine. "Did you find anything else?" he asked.

"Some."

Mark got up and walked around to Sean's side of the table to see the magazines and papers he had spread out. There was a picture of Todd and Stephanie Channon at the proud opening of Riverview House Bed and Breakfast.

Stephanie. She was Todd's wife and also the woman in the elevator who had heard the argument between Todd and Fia with such horror. No wonder. She had recognized the opening salvos of the war she feared.

Another picture showed Nick Powell, chef, in the kitchen. He was a man with dark thinning hair, dressed in the double-breasted white of the professional chef, and looking very proud.

"Powell? Is Rebecca his sister?"

"Wife," said Sean, pointing. *Chicago-trained chef assisted by his wife Rebecca.*

There was no picture of Rebecca.

A woman in another picture was entertaining the Greek ambassador in New York City. The caption read, "Juliane Channon Powell, one of the Wealthy Channons of Ashington Mills, Illinois." She had black hair, and a long, thin, uncompromising face, with a look of malicious playfulness in her eyes. The ambassador appeared to be laughing at something she said.

"The Dark Curse?" asked Sean.

"Undoubtedly. That would make Nick, our talented chef, the son of the Dark Curse. And Todd and Nick are cousins."

What a lovely mother-in-law Juliane Powell would make too. A thought of Rebecca and her nightly walks flashed through his mind. Where was she coming from?

Another picture seemed happier. Mark read the caption out loud. "John Christoph Channon, heir to the Channon millions, weds Barbara Charlotte Kingsley of Chicago." He looked closely at the faces—the bride and groom coming arm-in-arm out of the church—wondering if they had been happy. There was just that hint of uncertainty on the bride's face. He pointed this out to Sean.

Sean was holding a folded magazine, one finger tucked in it, marking its place. "I don't think you want to see this last one. I don't even want to see it."

"Why not?"

"It's a car accident. John Channon's."

"Is it bad?" He felt his heart pound harder. But he knew the answer. Fia had told him.

Sean spoke slowly. "He died."

Mark took a deep breath. His brain stirred with memory. Little mole claws began to tighten around his head. "Maybe later."

Sean nodded and laid the magazine down, closed. "You ready to eat again?"

He checked his watch. One forty. Time for a break.

They got some chicken wings at a mall on the east side of town, following this with more coffee. Before they left the mall, Mark picked up another book of number puzzles.

As he waited at the register, he had a sudden thought. Was Sean okay for money? How was he handling all these meals out? Was the college paying him enough to cover all this? And how to bring it up in a way that didn't embarrass him?

Mark had been rushed out of Gold College with the barest of explanations. In all fairness, maybe they had explained things to him. Maybe his health had kept him from paying attention.

Sean was idly spinning a display of bookmarks when Mark got the courage to ask. "Hey, are you okay for money? I don't know how prompt the college is on giving you what you need, and living on the road isn't cheap."

"I've got enough. I'm okay." Sean gave the display another whirl.

When they climbed back into the car, Sean didn't turn the engine on right away. Dark clouds were rolling in. A summer thunderstorm was threatening. Mark forced himself to say what neither of them wanted to hear. "I could use a nap. You ready to go back?"

Sean twisted the key in the ignition. "You haven't had a chance to take your vitamins either." He put the blinker on and pulled into the street, when the rain started. As the wipers swished, he said, "I still wish we could go to Colorado right now." He shook his head mournfully. "Oh, Dr. Waite."

9

Satie and Gin

THE RAINSTORM WAS INTENSE, and short. By the time they pulled into the wet parking lot at Riverview House, the storm was over.

Mark closed the car door and walked toward the house. Sean headed down a brick walkway toward George Juarez, who was hammering something inside the gazebo.

"I'm just going to see what George is doing," Sean called out.

The storm had left steamy, humid air in its wake. Mark went up the porch steps and reached for the doorknob on that curiously broad door, wondering what the climate inside the house would be.

Todd Channon was at his desk in the hallway. He

looked up with pathetic eagerness at the sound of the door closing.

"Good afternoon, Mr. Newlin. I hope you've enjoyed your day so far."

"I have, thank you. We went to Pancake Sal's, the college library, and the city park." He felt like a child reporting on his field trip. "You have a beautiful courthouse."

"Thank you. It's an amazing structure. Architects come from all over the country to study it."

Mark noticed the pride with which Todd said this. It was as if he had built the courthouse himself. Of course, maybe he had. Or, rather, his family had.

"Will you be dining in tonight, sir? One or two?"

"Two." He would bring Sean with him to dinner even if he had to wrestle him for it. There was no way Mark was going to risk an evening with Fia again.

"Very good. We have a special concert tonight in the main hall after dinner. I think you'll find it enjoyable." He sounded accommodating and hopeful.

"Thank you. I'm sure I will."

Todd bent to his work again, and Mark passed the desk and turned toward the stairs. The house was fairly quiet. The vacuum cleaners had completed their work for the day. The doors to the dining room were closed. From the direction of the kitchen came the muffled murmur of voices, interspersed with occasional metallic sounds. Cooks at work.

It felt like a Saturday afternoon might be expected to feel in a guest house. More importantly, there was no sign of Fia and the gang.

As he began to climb the main flight of steps, the sound of a gentle piano introduced itself. His first reaction was to lean over the banister to peek at Todd. The Riverview House manager was going about his computer work unruffled and calm.

All right. This was an expected piano. Maybe even a desired piano. So it wouldn't be Ernie.

Also, the piano music wasn't coming from that big living room parlor; it was coming from the opposite side of the house, from a corner he hadn't seen yet. And there was a tone, a something in the melody, that made him feel he had to stop and listen.

This was not Ernie's style. That was all domineering show, music that commanded you to listen.

This music invited you. Called you tenderly. It didn't demand your attention; it pulled at your soul.

He stepped across and down the other three stairs. He was on the dining room side of the house now. The piano was coming from a corner room, one that the long porch must wrap itself around. He approached cautiously and poked his head through the deep doorway.

This room was smaller, half the size of the big parlor. It had a polished, honey-colored wood floor warmed by a Persian rug, light cream walls, and comfortable, welcoming sofas. In the corner of the room far to his right, a piano stood at an angle, a small studio piano, and he could just see the side of the performer. It was Elizabeth.

At that same moment, something told her she was being watched. She stopped playing immediately and reached to close the book.

Mark felt terrible. His presence had stopped the

enchanting music. He came all the way into the room, with apology on his lips, when she said, "Oh, it's you." There was relief in her voice.

"Please forgive me. I didn't mean to interrupt. The piece you were playing was just beautiful. What was it?"

She closed the book so he could see the title. SATIE in large black letters. "A Gymnopédie. And the acoustics in this room are perfect for it. This was one of David's favorites."

She must have seen the question on his face. "My fiancé. I lost him in a car accident like yours. Except—I wasn't with him."

That explained the sympathy he kept seeing in her eyes yesterday.

"It was a few months after my brother John was killed, so David's death went unnoticed by my family. Actually, I don't think they even knew he existed." She slid the music book into a black bag that waited beside the piano. "Speaking of family, I understand you saw some of the family dynamics today. I apologize for that."

"If you are referring to their actions last night and this morning, then yes. I've seen the movie trailer version. Did you have the full reel after we left?"

She smiled grimly. "Something like that. Todd called to tell me that the lawyer was on his way, and he wanted me to come too. I came, but it was a show worth missing. But you didn't come to Ashington Mills for that. Here, please sit." She pointed at a sofa with a view to the front porch and took a chair opposite.

He sat down. Something in her manner suggested that she had said all she wanted to about her family. It felt important to apologize for them, but now she had finished, right when he could think of many questions to ask her. An awkward moment threatened until he thought of something to say.

"So tell me, what can we look forward to hearing at the concert tonight?"

She brightened at this. "We"ll start with a Bach piece —that's tradition for this household—then have some Liszt. You'll hear some film tunes. Some of my students— my juniors and seniors—are going to perform a few numbers that they did last spring. It's good experience. They're pursuing vocal scholarships and every performance counts. And they have a showstopping ending planned."

He couldn't wait to hear it and told her so. But, he really wanted to know what the Channons had discussed this morning. How could he ask without looking like a salivating rumormonger? What had Luedders once called historians? Purveyors of the truth of old gossip.

Ah, well, he should just leave and take his required nap. He opened his mouth to begin a polite farewell when someone else made their entrance, and he saw the alarm in Elizabeth's eyes.

Juliane Channon Powell, aka the Dark Curse, strode into the middle of the room followed by Fia. Juliane looked pointedly at Elizabeth, then at Mark, then back at Elizabeth.

Fia whispered loudly in her ear. "It's that sick professor."

A knowing look bloomed on Juliane's face. "Well, well,

little sister. Are you searching for amusement among Todd's guests? I thought this was a respectable house."

Elizabeth's face reddened.

Juliane turned to Mark. "You will have to forgive her or accommodate her as you wish, but I must warn you that she's been sitting on the shelf way too long."

"She's spoilt," put in Fia. She leaned on Juliane's shoulder and waved a finger at him as she said this. Will wasn't the only drinker in the family.

Fia and Juliane must have come from wherever rich people in Ashington Mills went to get soused when they didn't like what their lawyer told them. He guessed Elizabeth was an easy target for her angry sisters.

"I've been married three times," Fia bragged, clumsily digging through her purse. "Julie's only done it twice."

"Ernie has you beat," said Juliane. "Four times and he's looking again. But poor little Bessie." Juliane bent over Elizabeth's chair and pulled her red fingernails through strands of Elizabeth's hair, twisting the curls around her fingers. "No one wants her."

Elizabeth paled, and went still as stone.

Fia interrupted this with a cackle and a whoop. "Will! I've forgotten. How many times has Will been married?"

"Twice," said Juliane, her fingers tightening around Elizabeth's hair.

Fia turned to stare at her. "What about that woman from Dubuque?"

"She doesn't count."

They both howled with laughter at this and took a long time catching their breath. In her laughter, Juliane released Elizabeth's hair, and Elizabeth quickly moved away from her and went to the piano to grab her purse and music bag.

Mark was furious.

Furious at the scene.

And furious at the part he was being forced to play in it.

Watch, Amy. Thumbs in overall straps.

He stood up, ignored the cackling women, and used his fully authoritative professor voice.

"And now, Ms. Channon, if we could continue our conversation. The doctor thinks the piano lessons would be good therapy and wants me to start as soon as I can, but it depends on your schedule of course."

He pulled a small notebook and pen from his pocket and hurriedly turned the page where he had been taking library notes about the Channons.

"What was the name of the book you said I should get?"

She stared at him, blinking for a moment, then opened the piano bench. "You don't have to get it. I have one here." She pulled out a faded green book and began to thumb through it. "Did you study piano before?"

"Yes, about five years."

"Do you remember your notes and rhythm?"

"I think so. Mrs. Williams used to beat the counts out on my head. But the doctor wouldn't recommend doing that now."

"Of course not," said Elizabeth.

Fia and Juliane were watching, suspicious, but it didn't take them long to look bored.

"What about this one?" Elizabeth handed him the book opened to a piece that spread across two pages.

Intrada. By whom? Christoph Graupner.

"There's a lot of white space here. That's good." He felt like a little boy again, but made himself stay in the role, on the slim chance Fia and Juliane would find themselves feeling like idiots.

Elizabeth took the book back and positioned it on the music rack in a brisk, professional manner. "Here. Let me play it for you. See if you like it."

She had played only two lines of it when Juliane and Fia made a great show of leaving, drowning out part of the music. Laughing as they went up the stairs. The kind of laughter that appears to be at another's expense, but carries the tones of masquerade, of show. Empty of substance.

Elizabeth played to the end without taking any of the repeats. She turned to look up at him.

"You don't really mean to go through with this, do you?" she said quietly.

"Of course I do. A lady's honor is at stake. And I promise I will practice my fingers off."

Some of her blush came back, and he felt awful. He hadn't meant to remind her of her sisters' insults. Best to leave that subject quickly, by introducing a different one.

"Elizabeth, may I ask—who is Baiss Channon? Is there some mystery about him?"

She got up from the bench, marked the place in the book, closed it, and handed it to him, but remained standing by the keyboard. When she did speak, the words came sadly and low.

"Baiss ran away from home when he was sixteen years old. No one has seen him since."

A runaway? He hadn't expected this. "How long ago?"

"He would be thirty years old this December."

"He would? Does that mean—I'm sorry—does that mean he's dead?"

"There's disagreement in the family over that." She gave him a rueful glance as she put her purse over her arm and grasped her music bag. "One of the dramatic scenes you missed this morning."

"But what do you think?" He would bet that Elizabeth's opinion carried more truth in it than anyone else's.

She took a deep breath. "I think he's still alive. So does Mr. Baker, our lawyer, though he wouldn't say why."

Mark waved his arm, indicating the room and the house beyond. "Then how does all this stay running?"

"Through an allowance of the trustees. The board of the trust fund manages the money and oversees Riverview House."

"Waiting for Baiss to return?"

She nodded slowly. "Though there was a strong demand this morning to sell the house and divide up the proceeds."

It was an odd situation, but it explained the anxious, erratic behavior of some members of the family.

"If Baker won't say, what makes *you* think he's still alive?"

She looked directly at him then. "Hope."

10

____

A Child's Handwriting

A GLANCE out the tower window showed Mark that Sean was working with George. They had left the gazebo and were pounding wooden poles into the damp front lawn, George holding the pole, Sean swinging the mallet. Mark was surprised, but glad. It was good for Sean to get out and do something active, other than following Mark around, watching to make sure he didn't fall over again.

He tossed the piano book on the bed and lay down next to it. The pillow felt good under his head. He was exhausted, and there wasn't much time left before dinner to rest. It had been an unsettling day filled with unsettling people—unsettling Channons.

He kept seeing Elizabeth's face when her sisters came in. Kept hearing the cries of the small child upstairs during the argument on the stairwell. Felt the fear tensing Sean's shoulder, when Mark tried to shake him out of it. The cause of all this? A generation of Channons, acting the way they had always acted in their home, and oblivious to the people who occupied it now.

Uppermost in his mind was the thought of a sixteen-year-old boy on his own, alone.

What had made Baiss run? His parents? John and Barbara. He had seen their wedding picture in the newspaper today, but couldn't decide if they had looked genuinely happy or not. John was dead; where was Barbara now?

He stared at his plaster map on the ceiling, thinking of Fia and Juliane. Spite pretending to be playful. The sight of Juliane's slow fingers in Elizabeth's hair made his stomach turn. Throw in Ernie's controlling pomposity and Will's smoldering anger and you've got a toxic family mix.

Mark had known the Channons less than a week and would gladly leave them behind. Who wouldn't?

Had anyone gone after Baiss? Hunted for him? The police?

Todd Channon's voice came back to him. *You don't call the police on the Channons.*

He sat up and rubbed his forehead. He had to stop thinking about this.

To distract himself, he paged through the piano book Elizabeth had given him and found the piece she had selected. *What had a moment's impulse signed him up for? Intrada.* Maybe he could start working on it tomorrow while the vacuum cleaners were going. They could drown him out so no one would hear him play.

An F-sharp was circled in pencil on the page. So was a crescendo. Numbers written above certain notes provided helpful fingering. He flipped to the front cover and looked inside. The name hit him like a bolt.

Baiss Channon

It was a child's handwriting. Not a teenager, or even a preteen. A child's bulgy, unrefined letters carefully done in blue ballpoint pen. Maybe someone five or six years old. Yet, astonishingly, working on the pieces in this book, a book designed for good students at least twice his age.

Baiss must have been a child prodigy in a family mad about music. Gifted in a way that most people could only dream of.

And he was out there somewhere in this big, wide world.

A runaway.

Mark gazed at the book in his lap. Baiss had turned these pages, propped them open, must have practiced on the same piano in the same parlor, since his book had been in that bench.

Now Mark was holding it. Mark was going to have lessons on the same piano Baiss had used. The book was here, but the owner was missing.

Mark, I found this book.

Amy's voice filled his mind, and a memory came flooding back, sharp and clear as if it had just happened.

It had been one night, about four years ago. He and Amy had been hosting Gold College's new crop of freshmen history majors. Twenty-seven students had packed their college row home, shy with the newness of their college experience, eager to sample the array of Amy's homemade cakes, making their grown-up choices of coffee and tea.

In the midst of them all, Amy sliced cake, handed out napkins, wiped up spills, all while asking students about their hometowns, their families, their work, the dorms, their roommates. It was so like Amy. The cake and coffee night tradition had been her idea to begin with. She loved people with food and hospitality.

After the evening was over, he and Amy cleaned up. Luedders dropped by to see how things had gone, but really to snag a piece of caramel pecan cake. Mark was wiping down counters in the kitchen, listening to Luedders' groans of culinary delight, when Amy came in holding a book.

"I found this, Mark. Someone must have left it behind."

It was a plain black book, a journal, pocket-sized. He opened the front cover. A name was scrawled on the flyleaf. *Doug Hardbeck.* And under it, a drawn map and a series of musical notes, all artistically rendered.

"Yes, he was here tonight, that tall kid with the bushy red hair. He's in my Western Civ. class," he said. "I can take it to him Monday."

"But that's three days from now. What if he doesn't remember where he lost it? This looks important."

"He'll learn a good lesson then," put in Luedders between mouthfuls.

But the concern in Amy's eyes wouldn't go away. "I just think of how uneasy he must feel, hoping at any moment it will turn up, spending hours and days like that, feeling like a piece of him is missing. He could be frantic about it."

Mark didn't look at Luedders, only at Amy. He tossed his dish towel on the counter, and, leaving Luedders with the cake, they walked toward the residence halls on campus. They'd only gone partway when they came across several students near the path, bent over, hunting through the grass using the flashlights on their cell phones.

Amy called out. "Doug?"

One head popped up immediately.

"Are you looking for this?"

Mark could still see the relief on the young man's face as he hurried towards them and claimed his treasure. It was as if they had handed him back a piece of his soul. Amy had been right.

He could also still feel the sensation of his arm around Amy as they walked back home.

Amy had been a person-finding book-returner.

This all had nothing to do with Baiss Channon, of course.

And yet, somehow it did.

Mark looked at the name inside the piano book again. Who was this Baiss who had scrawled his name so proudly? How was he living his days now? Was he missing a piece of his soul? He wouldn't be missing this piano book. Mark was sure Baiss had gone on to something much more difficult by the time he turned sixteen.

He sighed, set the book down on the bed, and walked over to the tower to pull back the curtains and look at the river. No barges came into view at the moment, just a long stretch of empty water.

Truth be told, even though he tried to be upbeat for Sean's sake, Mark hated being here. Hated this crazy, strange, uncomfortable house. Hated Jerry Waite's guilty, misguided generosity. Hated this purgatory of life without Amy.

With a sickening sadness, he knew, even as he fought against knowing, that the sensation of his arm around Amy would, now and forever, remain a memory.

But Baiss could still be alive.

Elizabeth hoped so. That lawyer Baker thought he was. Which might be more than hope.

Wouldn't it be great if we could find him, Amy? If we could find Baiss and give him his book back?

It was a pleasant thought. And utterly ridiculous.

Mark had an injured brain, an injured body. Could barely read, let alone drive. And he had no idea where to start.

11

———

A Conflict of Interests

ONE LOOK at Sean's face and Mark realized this was not going to be an easy sell.

"I can't eat in the dining room. I only have blue jeans."

Why hadn't Sean mentioned this before? "Fine. I'll loan you a shirt and tie. That will dress you up enough."

"I have a shirt," Sean mumbled.

"Then go put it on and come back and pick out a tie."

"With blue jeans?"

"You'll look like a hip Nashville musician."

"No, I won't," Sean said, but he left for his room anyway.

Mark fumed with frustration as he tied his own tie, checking himself in the mirror. It had been a long, thoroughly exhausting day in every way. He had only been able to close his eyes for twenty minutes before being awakened by Sean, who in a rare moment of thoughtlessness, had begun singing in the shower, belting out "Come Fly With Me" with full lungs.

After Mark had said they would be eating here, Sean had come up with three different places that he would rather go. But the reservations had already been made; they were being counted on for dinner. There had been just that note of gratitude in Todd's voice when he said they would be there that made Mark reluctant to let him down.

Amy used to tease that he was a softie at heart. "If your students only knew," she'd say, putting her arms around him and giving him a soft kiss.

He pressed his fingers to his eyes, but his cheeks were already wet. He wiped them with a handkerchief, then stuck it in his back pocket. After arranging a few ties on the bed for Sean to choose from, he went to wait in the tower area.

Cars came up the drive, slowly and steadily, carefully selecting places in the rapidly-filling lot. Occupants emerged with the same care, not moving too quickly in the heat. The banner staked to the lawn advertised the concert tonight at eight p.m. He hoped there would be a good crowd for it, for Elizabeth's sake.

"Is the green one okay?" Sean stood there in dark jeans, a white button-down shirt, and Mark's solid green silk tie. Worn loafers on his feet.

"Fine. Let's go."

They were seated by Rebecca Powell at the same table

as last night, but this time Sean had the view of the kitchen door instead of him. A few eyebrows had been raised at Sean's attire, but nothing had been said.

"Nashville musicians are always high class," Mark whispered across the table.

They pored over their menu cards. Nick had gone all out tonight. Entrées ranged from Swordfish Champignon to Kentucky Burgoo.

"What'll you have?" Mark asked.

Sean looked like he was trying to decipher code. "I don't know."

"Let's have it all."

"What?"

"Appetizers through dessert. Let's order one of every-thing." He would make sure tonight's dinner, at least, went on his credit card and not Jerry's.

"All right."

Kelly set down the water glasses and pulled out her pad and pen with a smile. "What would you like to eat tonight, gentlemen?"

Mark led it off. "I"ll start with the Corn Cakes."

"Rib Bits," said Sean.

"The Carrot, Leek, and Chestnut Soup," he said.

"With Cheese Truffles," added Sean.

He couldn't help but smile. Sean was getting into the spirit of the thing.

"Pear, Endive and Boursin Salad."

Sean wanted the swordfish.

"Roast Duck," he announced for himself firmly.

"You're getting duck?" Sean was grinning again.

He put on an attitude he had seen Pim Montgomery,

head of the music department, do once. "There are times when only the duck will do." He turned back to Kelly. "With the Wild Rice, please."

"New Potatoes," put in Sean. "Cornmeal Rolls, and Lemon Cream Cake."

"Make my rolls Parker House, and I will close with Chocolate Zabaglione."

Kelly wrote quickly, then took the menu cards and left.

"Think we overwhelmed her?" asked Sean.

"No." Mark shook his head. "Sometimes she doesn't talk much."

He took a long drink of water. "I bet George Juarez appreciated the help with the banner."

"George is a good guy. He's got some family in Denver. He said they could even put us up for a few days, show us around."

Mark wasn't sure what to say.

"I told him we were here for the long haul," Sean added. "Only leaving for weekends, maybe, and that would be a bit too far."

"Yeah, it would be. Well, while you were swinging your mallet, I signed up for piano lessons."

Sean looked suitably astonished. "You did? With who?"

"Elizabeth. I'll tell you how it all came about when we get back upstairs. She loaned me a piano book and guess who it belongs to?"

"Carl Sandburg?"

He ignored this attempt at humor. "Baiss. Baiss Channon. And I think I want to find him. You know, so I can give his book back." He tried to say it lightly.

Sean spluttered into his water glass, then set it down, half-choking. It took awhile for the coughing to subside. "Why?" he asked hoarsely, when he could talk again. And that one word seemed filled with exasperation. Along with the opinion that Sean thought Mark was out of his mind.

"To put it simply," Mark replied, "I can't stand to think of him out there when all this is his."

"What do you mean *out there?* He's—he's probably on the Riviera somewhere. He could be a spoiled brat buying diamond yachts and parking them off-shore at Monaco, and here you are spending all your concern for nothing."

"Maybe. I've thought of that. But he was a teenager when he left, and I think something drove him away."

"So why hasn't he come back?" Sean was almost demanding.

Mark kept his voice calm. "That's what we need to find out."

"We? That's a tall order for a nurse, even one who reads mystery books, which I have now decided firmly to renounce."

Mark swallowed down his own frustration, frustration rising from the knowledge that he needed help to do what he wanted to do. That he needed help for anything.

"Look, you're my assistant. Paid for the duration. Some of those five history books you promised me could be read on the Channons. We might find clues."

Sean stared out the window. "No, sir. I'd rather not."

"The history of Ashington Mills then."

"No." Sean leaned closer and spoke in a low, firm voice. "We're not here for the Channons. We're here for you." He sat back in his chair again and gave a quick glance around, shaking his head. "We should never have come to this place. These people are like poison."

"I know." Mark watched him, waiting, wondering again what Sean might have heard this morning. Wondering how to ask him.

Kelly appeared and dropped off a plate of rib bits in front of him and one of corn cakes in front of Sean before whirling off, her long, blond ponytail swishing behind her. They exchanged plates. Sean picked up a rib and took a bite. Mark picked up a fork.

"What do you plan to do?" said Sean around his chewing.

"Wipe the sauce off your beard. We're not in the cafeteria." Mark tried to say it teasingly, but it came out flat.

Sean picked up his napkin and wiped. "All right. What will you do?"

"Ask questions. Lots of questions. Every person in this family has to be sitting on a pile of secrets. We listen to what they tell us and to what they don't. The library has information that we haven't tapped yet." Mark paused. "I'll need you for the intense reading and the heavy computer work."

Sean looked doubtful. "What if there's no crisis at all? What if he's just not returning phone calls?"

Mark gave up and ate the corn cake. He tried to focus on the food and let the disagreement leave his mind. Badgering Sean wouldn't help anyway. A badgered accomplice was no accomplice at all. He wanted Sean with his heart in the game, because without him, Mark wouldn't get very far. He didn't have the energy to do this on his own. Couldn't even walk four blocks without needing to sit down. And even a short look at a computer screen had lasting repercussions.

Mark finished the corn cake just as Kelly brought their salads. He and Sean continued to eat in silence.

Waiting for the duck, Mark attempted a neutral topic of conversation.

"You bought a book at the last bookstore we were at. Was that history book number one for our deal? What was it about?" He sounded too professorial, too official for the friendship that had developed between him and his faithful assistant. It felt like a step backwards for both of them. Judging from the atmosphere at the table, they both felt it.

"The Medici family."

The Channons of Florence, he thought, but did not say it out loud.

They ate their duck and swordfish quietly. When the double doors opened to admit more diners, he heard the scraping of chairs and commotion in the central hall. They would be setting up for the evening concert.

"I think I'll stay for the concert tonight," Mark said. "Elizabeth arranged the program."

Sean wasn't paying attention. Instead, his eye was following Kelly admiringly as she served tables near theirs. He smiled especially at her when she brought the zabaglione and lemon cake. And on his face was a look Mark had seen on countless faces during his years working with college students. *And it was ever thus with man.*

Mark moved his spoon slowly through the creamy

chocolate—the final master's touch on a dinner that had been a work of art from start to finish. He hoped he could meet Nick Powell soon and shake his hand.

Sean inhaled his cake in his usual style, then rolled up his napkin neatly. Mark finished his last bite and checked his watch. Almost eight o'clock.

Kelly came by to collect the dishes, and as she approached, Mark saw it: Sean's face lit up in friendly admiration, while—after a glance that took in all of Sean's attire—hers closed down tight in overt disdain. She even pivoted toward Mark, giving Sean a sense of the shoulder. A slap in the face without any words spoken. Mark watched the light fade from Sean's face.

"Will there be anything else, Mr. Newlin?" Kelly asked. She turned on the smile for him.

"No, nothing," he replied, setting his napkin on the table and reaching for his wallet. Sadness swept over him as he pulled out his credit card and handed it to her.

Sean left while Mark waited for Kelly to come back with his card.

THE STAGE HAD BEEN SET in front of the huge fireplace in the main entrance hall. Chairs surrounded it in arcs, their backs to the massive staircase. The occasional sofas remained, lining the short bits of wall between doorways. He perched at the end of one of these next to a tall grandfather clock, the uncommitted concert-goer, not sure how long he would stay.

Still, he was glad to see that most of the audience was

more enthusiastic. Many looked like parents of students eager to see their children perform. Others he recognized as fellow diners.

Elizabeth, looking elegant in long, formal black, arranged some sheets of music on a stand near the piano. The door to the Channon study across the hall opened, and teenaged faces peeked out. High-spirited. Ready and waiting. A refreshing change from the usual atmosphere of Riverview House.

The grandfather clock chimed eight times. As if on cue, the high school students poured out of the study and began to clap, drawing everyone's applause and attention. Then Elizabeth sat down at the piano bench and began to play. Within seconds the room hushed, listening.

The piece was complicated, energetic, and precise. He had no idea what it could be, but the music spoke to him, lifting his spirits. While he was listening, a man sat down on the other end of his sofa—a black-suited, gray-haired man with a tanned face and a whiff of cologne. An imperious look was in his blue eyes, the look of a hunter pointing out prey. Ernie. Or as the world must know him —Ernest Channon. After the brother and sister interchanges Mark had already witnessed, he couldn't help but think of him as Ernie.

Elizabeth finished, and Mark clapped along with everyone else. Ernie did not. She stood up, said something about the piece, then sat down again.

Mark leaned over to the man next to him on the sofa. "I didn't catch that. What was the name of that piece?"

Ernie barely glanced at him. "Bach. Just a Sinfonia." He flicked his fingers as if brushing away a gnat.

Mark nodded and sat back to listen to Elizabeth's next offering. The piano sounded dark and throaty at first, then the music made dramatic leaps, increasing in speed. Technical and quick, yet filled with humor, which Elizabeth brought out expertly. He had heard something like it on the old Bugs Bunny cartoons that had been his father's favorites. The audience appeared to enjoy it too. They tilted forward, mouths opened slightly, all attention, ready to catch every joke the piano told. Mark loved it.

He was glad to see that most of the chairs were filled. People stood along the walls, and Sean was among the wall-standers too.

It had been a Hungarian Rhapsody by Liszt. Ernie didn't join the applause this time either. He shook his head. "It's a crime to showcase the inferior talents of the Channons. Gives the world a sorry view of the family."

Mark didn't think of hesitating. "How can you say that? Her performance was brilliant!"

The imperious eye turned completely in his direction, but nothing more was said.

It was a moment of decision.

Ernie's behavior had been consistently repulsive to Mark. But in order to be able to ask Ernie about Baiss at some future date, Mark had to establish some sort of civil connection with the man. He hated the insult to Elizabeth's performance, but forced himself to hold out his hand. "I haven't had the opportunity to meet you yet. I'm Mark Newlin."

The man glanced at his hand and looked away. "Ernest Channon. I don't shake hands. Never risk an injury. Keep them strong for performance."

Mark lowered his hand. He caught Sean's eye from across the room. There was a question in it. Mark shrugged and turned back toward the stage.

Next, Elizabeth accompanied a girl with curly, red hair, who sang a classical love song with intense emotion. The song was not to Mark's taste, but the girl had a beautiful soprano voice. Ernie's expression blended imperious with bored, and he continued to protect his hands by not clapping.

A few more students sang solos with Elizabeth, followed by some interesting vocal duets. Then a quartet performed a song from *The Mikado,* which Mark recognized. Gold College's Music Department had done it just last year. Amy loved it. If only she could be sitting with him now, leaning against his shoulder, whispering expressions of delight in his ear.

The students performed in a way that would have made even a college proud, and Mark clapped vigorously. He didn't bother checking Ernie's response. Pride makes its own rules and Mark usually found them to be wrong.

Eight young men took their places across the front of the stage, barely concealing grins. They launched into a robust performance of "If I Were a Rich Man" from *Fiddler on the Roof,* which Mark found highly ironic, situated as they were in the middle of a wealthy Channon enclave. He glanced over in Sean's direction, but Sean had already left. On the final chorus the singers stomped around the stage, shaking their imaginary bellies, just like Tevye in the movie. It brought the house down.

A highly enjoyable evening was over. The students gathered in front and acknowledged the applause with rehearsed bows. Elizabeth looked pleased, and the audience clapped for her as well. The students filed off, and she stood alone by the piano.

"To close this evening, by special request, we have a performance by a famous concert pianist, a favorite in South America. Please welcome Ernest Channon." Ernie stood up and went forward, the expression on his face suddenly businesslike. Focused.

The timing was wrong. Mark could feel it. Elizabeth looked as if she knew it too. But her brother must have insisted on this. For what possible reason?

Ernie bent to the keys, fingers moving madly, his performance clearly much more difficult than anything they had heard tonight. Was he just trying to show up Elizabeth? Demean everything that had already been done? This clearly could not be in his best interests. Timing is everything in performance.

The audience tried to be polite, but their attention had already been given. Their blood was flowing; they were antsy and ready to go. Yet civilization has certain conventions. They were pinned like moths to a board, trying to appreciate something that took a great deal of energy to appreciate, and their energy was already spent.

Chairs were scraped. Coughs sounded. But the performer was in a world of his own. Not aware of his audience's needs or caring for them the smallest bit. Mark checked his watch. This complicated piece had gone on for six minutes and showed no sign of stopping. Some of the audience tried to discreetly sneak out the back.

Suddenly a woman's voice rang out over the music, and Mark saw Fia, standing halfway up the flight of stairs, drink in one hand, other hand on hip, shoulders back, in a pose that looked staged. He missed her first words, but there was no missing the next. "Play some jazz, Ernie! We're *dying* of boredom!"

The audience gasped in shocked embarrassment. Fia laughed, half-staggered down the remaining steps, and disappeared into the big parlor. But just before she did so, Mark thought he caught a glimpse of Juliane in the parlor doorway, a strangely exultant expression on her face. Had the Dark Curse been waiting in the wings?

Ernie stopped playing abruptly, his face a mask of iron. He stood up, jerked at his suit coat front, and left through the back door, shutting it firmly behind him.

The audience looked around for Elizabeth, like passengers on an airplane looking for the flight attendant when they unexpectedly hit heavy turbulence. *Tell us what this means. How to get out of this. Are we okay?*

Elizabeth strode to the center of the stage area and smiled at everyone. "Part of the magic of a live performance is that the unexpected often happens." Her voice was firm, yet soothing. "Well, tonight, it did. A sort of heckler and performer act, but I think Victor Borge does it better, don't you?"

Mark began to relax. *Well, how about that?* Elizabeth had her own version of thumb-in-overall-straps pluck. She didn't pause, but went rapidly on.

"I have to tell you that my most unexpected event in a performance occurred two years ago, during an afternoon show of *The Music Man*. Our student pianist had stomach complaints that day, and during the song 'Shipoopi,' volunteered what he had eaten for lunch directly onto the keyboard."

It was clearly a memory some of them shared. Hoots of laughter broke out, along with groans of remembrance. Elizabeth went on. "He continued to play in spite of it, and thereby earned Ashington Mills High School's first-ever Bravery in Performance Award."

Real laughter broke out at this.

When it had died down, she said, "Thank you all very much for coming. You've been a *wonderful* audience. Good night now." She dropped her head in a gracious bow, then stepped off to the side where students instantly crowded around her.

The room had been able to recover some of its joviality. People gathered their things and left murmuring. Mark went up the stairs slowly, holding the handrail all the way. Suddenly he realized he felt exhausted. Overwhelmed by all the events of the day, all the emotions of the day.

Was this open war between Fia and Ernie? How would Ernie retaliate? How frustrated Elizabeth must have been to have her students' performances used by her siblings for their own personal ends! And yet, she had been able to refocus the audience's attention back to where it should have been all along—on the students.

Sean's door was closed. Light came through the crack underneath. The green tie was laid out neatly on Mark's bed.

Mark got ready for bed in as little time as possible. He crawled under the hideous bedspread and was asleep in minutes, dreaming. Dreaming that Rebecca Powell came up the drive dragging Baiss Channon. But they couldn't enter the house. And no one heard them knocking because Ernie was gliding through the air playing jazz piano and swallowing money from a glass of gin and tonic. When Ernie sailed past Mark's bed, he noticed that the piano had wings like a duck.

12

A Gray Sunday

MARK WOKE UP EARLY, but stayed in bed, trying to relocate his imaginary map of Germany on the ceiling swirls, so he could add Denmark to it. He was also listening.

If he were a boy waking up in bed in this house, would he have heard angry voices? Would he have waited until it was safe to emerge from his room?

Baiss was the child of the only reasonably happy-looking couple in the library photos. Maybe Baiss *hadn't* been afraid to wake up. If the house had belonged to his parents, then presumably Ernie, Fia, Will, and Juliane wouldn't have been hanging around.

Then again, if his grandparents had still been alive, John and Barbara and Baiss might not have been living in this house at all, and when he ran away, it would have been from a different place. It would be important to know where Baiss had run from.

Mark took a deep breath and glanced at the clock. 6:38 a.m.

The soft light of this Sunday morning held beauty, but in the moment of turning his mind from the Channons to something as simple as morning light, the grayness of grief moved swiftly in. He felt again the haunting absence of Amy, that terrifying, fear-filled ache that threatened to crush him.

He had to get out of this room.

He got dressed and came down the stairs in time to hear the grandfather clock striking seven. All the chairs from the concert had been put away. Instead, buffet tables made a sort of spine down the center of the room, ready to receive whatever Nick Powell would give them.

Mark let himself out the back door and stepped into the shadows of the porch, a porch that had no idea the sun had risen on the other side of the house. He went down the steps and took the brick walkway to the edge of the lawn. Here, a wrought iron fence divided the manicured portion of the property from the wild grass and scrub trees that covered the steep slope down to the river.

The Mississippi flowed broad, silent, and steadily on, a gorgeous blue in the early light, unfazed by whatever drama the Channons chose to play out on its banks. The river was here before them. It would still be here after they were gone.

He decided to walk the full circuit of brick and gravel

paths through the gardens. Strolling speed. This could be a morning habit, a way to build up strength. He hated feeling weak.

He was taking the paths closest to the parking lot when a car pulled up. A figure got out, wearing the black and white serving uniform, and started walking down the sidewalk toward the house. Felicitas. He walked over to join her.

"You're here early. Didn't you work last night too?"

"Yes. I'm working the brunch this morning. It's a very good one. Are you coming in for it?"

"When does it open?"

"Eight o'clock."

"Do the cooks or any of you ever sleep?"

She laughed. "Tonight we will. Brunch is from eight until two, and then the kitchen closes until Tuesday morning."

"Do you work here almost every day?"

"Yes. It's hard to get all my studying in now that the semester has started, but I do it." They approached the kitchen entrance to the house.

"What degree are you working on?"

"Accounting."

"Sounds good. You can do a lot with accounting."

"I'd like to help my father with his gardening business." She dropped her voice, glancing at the kitchen windows. "He doesn't like me working here."

"He doesn't?"

She paused on the sidewalk, her face looking troubled. "You saw the concert last night? How it ended?"

"Yes."

She shook her head. "Sometimes I think the Channons delight in trying to hurt each other. And I know that some of the restaurant customers were glad to witness the family drama."

"That's unfortunate."

Felicitas gave a rueful smile, went up the steps, and disappeared inside.

Mark walked another slow lap around the gardens. The breeze was light and pleasant. A barge headed downstream on the river, its wheelhouse brilliant white in the sun.

So, Felicitas and George felt wary about the Channons, just like Sean did. Mark had to agree with them. Maybe Baiss had felt the same. Had he run before his father's tragic accident or after? Before he knew everything rested on him, or *after* he knew?

Clearly, Elizabeth was not like her older siblings. She must have loved this David of hers and real love has a way of reshaping a person. Amy's love had changed him. She had widened his heart and his life, leaving a hole nothing could fill. He rested his hands on the iron uprights of the tall fence and stared out at the flowing water as the breeze dried his face.

Can you see on your maps, children? The man weeping by the ancient river, weeping because his love is gone. Because she was taken from him and never again can he hold her in his arms.

~

When Mark walked back through the central hall, the brunch was already in full swing, a classy version of the all-you-can-eat. He was directed by Rebecca to his usual table and was glad to see that it was Felicitas who brought him his water, juice, and coffee.

He roamed around the buffet tables, plate in hand even though he didn't feel like eating. But that didn't matter. He had to get stronger. Collapsing wouldn't honor Amy. He knew she would be distressed beyond expression about his health.

Mark read the calligraphy above each tray. *Scrambled Eggs Hollandaise. Pastrami Hash. Rosemary Sausage in Pepper Gravy. Cheddar Grits. Butter Biscuits. Blackberry Kiwi Salad. Chocolate Pistachio French Toast. Bacon Brussels Sprouts. Baguettes.* A selection of cheeses with strawberries.

He filled his plate with eggs, sausage, a biscuit, and fruit, and took his seat. He sliced open the biscuit and laid a sausage in it with a dollop of the gravy. In spite of his lack of appetite, the result melted in his mouth.

Mark ate slowly and looked out the window. The morning sun glimmered across the garden flowers. The ornamental grasses swayed gently in the breeze. He could still catch a glimpse of the river at this angle.

Sean set down a plate and took a seat across from him. Mark held out his hand in greeting.

"You doing all right this morning?" Sean said as he shook it. The analytical eye was back. "Saw you down by the fence."

He couldn't talk about it. "The morning was just improved by Nick Powell's biscuit. What do you have there?"

"Grits, eggs and a baguette. For openers." Sean's tone was friendly, apologetic.

Mark smiled. Things felt easier again. "Did you run already?"

Sean nodded, his mouth full of grits. "Four and a half miles," he said, speaking around the grits. "What did you want to do today?"

"Haven't thought about much beyond this buffet. Did you know these eggs have lemon in them?"

After they had finished, they lingered a little over their coffee, not saying much. The brunch had drawn a fair amount of people, and someone would need their table soon. He thanked Rebecca as they left. Todd was at his desk, tucked in the corner of the stairwell, handing receipts to departing guests.

The phone rang as they entered their room, and Sean hurried to pick it up. "No, but he's right here. Who is calling, please? Patti?" Sean looked quizzically at him.

"My sister," he said reaching for the phone.

"Mark, are you all right?" Patti sounded anxious. "We just got back from vacation. Zach drove all night like usual. I've been trying to contact you, emailing and texting and everything. I sent you pictures of the boys playing on the beach, then I remembered you're not supposed to look at screens right now. I'm sorry. So I thought I'd call right away. How *are* you?"

Sean had left for his own room, probably to give him privacy. Mark sat down on the bed.

"Okay enough, I suppose. How did you find me?"

"You didn't answer your home phone, so I called your department at the college. I know it's a Sunday, but I happened to catch a lady named Vicki, who had come back to the office to get something she had forgotten. She told me everything. Oh, Mark!" Patti was close to tears.

Mark could imagine what Vicki had told her, could imagine how dramatically Vicki had told her. If Vicki were here, he would wring her neck. He tried to make his voice sound as normal and strong as possible.

"What did she say?"

"That you collapsed in the middle of class and refused to go to the hospital. And that you're at some long-term hotel on the river with an assistant to help you get well, and—"

He'd have to talk fast.

"I'm doing better, Patti, really. I didn't want to bother you on your vacation. I'm sorry I didn't tell you where I was going. It was the college's plan. I barely knew myself until it happened. Still trying to get used to the idea. And in truth, everything happened so fast. So let me catch you up.

"The guy who answered the phone is Sean, my assistant, provided by the college. He's waiting on me hand and foot. I can't breathe without him noticing. He also eats like a horse and is making sure I do the same. In fact, we just came from brunch."

Mark told her about the view, the size of the room, the college library. She told him about their vacation, about her youngest son learning to float in the ocean. Their conversation had become normal again, when Patti said, "Mark?"

"Yes?"

"Please take care of yourself. I don't want to lose you too."

It was the kind of line you hear in movies or read in novels as you consider the plight of people who don't really exist, enacting a drama you don't want to be in. Yet, here he was, right where he didn't want to be. But the love of a sister was in her voice, and it moved him. Reminded him that he was still tethered somewhere to life.

He promised.

After the phone call ended, he leaned back on the pillows, took off his glasses and rubbed his eyes. Patti had come to his aid immediately when she heard of the accident, leaving her two children with her husband in Indiana.

Patti was the one who had planned Amy's funeral. Who brought the flowers to Mark's hospital room. After the hospital had finally released him, Patti stayed with him another week, a week in which she sat by him on the sofa with a box of tissues as they watched the recording of the funeral. And then, torn between her brother and her family, who missed her dreadfully, she had gone back to Indianapolis.

The remaining weeks of summer had been horrible. Hours upon hours of grayness sitting alone in his living room. He didn't want to think about those days. He was in a better place now, even with Sean hounding him and the Channons throwing fits. Maybe *because* of that hounding and fit-throwing.

When did your feet ever feel like they touched solid ground again? When did this sickening flying-through-the-air feeling ever stop?

He didn't realize for a few moments that Sean had come in and was watching him. Sean spoke first.

"She sounded really worried. Should we check your email now? We haven't done it since we were packing at your house."

They hadn't done it because Mark hadn't wanted to. He rubbed his face quickly and sat up. "Yeah. Sure."

Sean reached for the laptop, settled himself on the floor, and flipped it open. "You've got seventy-eight emails waiting for you."

Mark leaned back into the pillows again. "Well, let's start. Give me the rundown."

Sean proved himself a very efficient assistant. He read down the list of senders while Mark stared at his ceiling map and called out "keep" or "delete." It took about five minutes to get the list down to the important ones—five of which were from Patti, and three from his mom and dad, all filled with concern for him. Sean read them out, then typed replies, introducing himself along with everything Mark said in response.

Tulia Cardoso wrote that things at the college were going fine, but that all his colleagues were deepening their appreciation for him, feeling the effects of his absence. She hoped the food was good and the view pleasant, and that he would forgive the exuberance of colleagues that were trying to do their best in a field in which they had no expertise. Also, her mother, a Brazilian chef, had just sent her another batch of recipes to try, and when Mark returned home she would fill his freezer with them.

"Wow," said Sean. "That food sounds great."

"She's a good cook. She and Amy used to get together and talk about nothing but food."

Luedders reported that Mark's house looked fine, and that they would forward his physical mail to him. Also, he hoped Mark would excuse them all for sending him up the river. Luedders' usual humor coming through.

Jerry Waite also asked how Mark was, as well as questions about his accommodations, how the trip had gone, and if he and Sean needed anything.

At last, only one email remained. "A fountain pen company?" Sean asked.

"Once you write with a good one, you'll never forget it."

"Did you bring yours with you? You could handwrite anything you wanted, and I could type it in for you. We could maybe start working on that research in a week or so? I think I remember where you filed it."

"Maybe." He answered carelessly, trying to find a plausible Norway among the plaster ridges.

Again he heard the click of Sean's typing. A pause. A few more agitated clicks followed by a longer pause. A pause one could feel.

"Professor?" A worried voice. "I don't know how to tell you this, but I can't find your research. I know where the folder used to be, but it's not there. All the files are gone."

Mark found a place on the ceiling where, with great imagination, you could envision Norway and Sweden reaching down to almost touch a rather abstract Denmark.

"I don't remember doing anything—"

"It wasn't you," Mark replied. His eyes searched the ceiling for a candidate for Iceland.

He heard the sound of the laptop being gently closed. Silence.

Noises from the rest of Riverview House filled the void. The hum of the elevator. Car doors slamming in the lot outside. The main house door opening and closing. Voices bubbling up from downstairs and the recorded violins in the background. But in their room, a pained silence held sway.

Sean finally broke it. "So, what if we take a drive and see what Ashington Mills looks like on a Sunday?" His voice was lighthearted, trying to mask its concern, and not succeeding.

At the moment, Mark felt he could stare at the ceiling for hours, but he knew he was giving Sean more to worry about. He sat up and swung his feet to the floor.

"All right," he said, avoiding Sean's gaze. "Let's get going. We can't be out too late though, because I have to get back and practice the piano."

THEY COULDN'T COME up with anything much to do, but Mark was honest enough to admit that it wasn't the town's fault. Dull eyes can't see what's in front of them.

Driving through the north of Ashington Mills, a part of the town he hadn't seen before, they came across a large park with an elaborately designed playground. Children zoomed down the slide, dodged the swings, and dug in the sandbox, while parents hovered protectively nearby, talking with other parents. He stared silently as kids in swimsuits squealed, running through the water spray at the splash pad. Families played catch; moms and dads pushed strollers. A little girl rode high on her dad's shoulders, her white sandals flopping against his chest with every step he took.

Mark was looking through a glass, at a life he and Amy had hoped for and never received. Another thing lost. Another thing that never came. That never would come now.

His face was wet again, but he didn't care. He continued to stare as the light changed and the park slid away from his view and the scene out the window became one of older houses. Then a donut shop. A dry cleaner. A dentist.

He used to love road trip movies with all their promise of exhilarating possibilities and unbridled newness. New country, new adventures. A chance to break away from an old life.

But, now, he desperately wanted his old life back. He was stuck in a road trip he couldn't get out of. Without Amy there was no place to anchor anyway. When he went back to Gold College, she wouldn't be there.

Did he even want to go back?

What if he waved his hand over a map, closed his eyes, and poked it with a finger? Then he could move to whatever generic town his finger happened to land on. He wiped his face with his hand.

Sean had turned into the grounds of Ashington College, and they were slowly moving through every part of the campus that could be reached by car. He stopped before a white block of a building, bright in the sun, with tall, white columns. Channon Hall—the music building the librarian had mentioned.

Fears gathered like barbarian hordes in Mark's mind. He shook himself, desperate to start a conversation. Any conversation. He said the first thing that came to mind. "So, why do you think the heir left?"

Sean seemed surprised at the question. "Is that really what you were thinking just now?"

"It's better than what I'm thinking right now. And besides," he pointed to the name on the building, "it seemed an appropriate time to bring it up."

Sean shook his head. "With a family like that, wouldn't you leave? I think the real question is, will he come back?"

Mark tried to imagine Baiss putting his finger on a map and blindly going somewhere. But, for some reason, the image didn't fit the character of the boy he had already built in his mind. "I don't know. I hope he does. If he gets his courage up. I hate to think of him out there somewhere, begging on an interstate ramp."

This would have driven Amy nuts. He could see her traveling all over the state, asking everyone on the side of the road if they were Baiss Channon.

Sean was idly tapping the steering wheel. He clearly didn't want to talk about anything Channon. Mark changed the subject.

"When do you think I should try to drive?"

"Maybe in a week or so," Sean replied, "if you take all your naps and up your fluid intake."

Mark shook his head. "You are tougher than Mrs. Baumgart."

"Who's Mrs. Baumgart?"

"My fourth grade teacher."

"What? She didn't let you drive either?"

Mark almost smiled. "Let's get back so I can practice my piano before any new guests check in."

13

The Dark Curse

THE MAIN FLOOR of Riverview House was deserted when Mark sneaked into the small parlor, piano book tucked under his arm. The room could not be closed by a door, so he resolved to play as quietly as possible.

He propped his music book up on the rack and opened it to the *Intrada*, then sat staring at it for a few moments, wondering how to begin. Most of the notes looked familiar, which was good. The rhythm didn't look too hard.

Hands separately, slowly. He could hear Mrs. Williams, his old piano teacher, say it in his mind. Left hand first was his own quirk. He liked to discover the supporting sounds first, then let the melody surprise him later. Mrs. Williams used to shake her head, but let him do it.

He stretched out his left hand. Thumb here, little finger there. *Here we go, Professor.* Quietly. Slowly. Ploddingly.

He made it reasonably well to the end of the first line. *Good thing that Ernie's not here. He'd have a heart attack listening to this.*

At the end of the second line, he stopped. Right hand's turn. Let's hear the melody.

For some reason, the melody touched him. It was happy, light, and triumphant all at the same time. Perhaps written for the entrance of someone the composer was happy to see, for it flowed with delight.

He had been at it for a quarter hour and was making progress when Juliane Channon Powell walked in with a vase of fresh flowers and placed them on the low polished oak table in front of the sofa. She had a soft look on her face as she considered their arrangement, a look he was surprised to see. It hardened as she turned to him.

"So, you're really doing this, are you?"

He looked over his shoulder at her. "Note by note, as you see. Or hear, rather."

She sat down on the sofa and studied him with a critical eye. "Fia called you 'the ailing professor.' Exactly how are you ailing?"

Piano practice was definitely over for the day. But maybe an opportunity had walked in. With any luck he might be able to get Juliane's view of her family, and perhaps shed light on some of the critical relationships that surrounded Baiss.

He closed the book and turned around on the bench to face her. "You are looking at a man without a spleen," he said lightly. "The doctors removed most of that after the accident. Which, I suppose, is convenient. Nothing to vent, as they say.

"Broken bones have healed, but are still sore. Concussion is taking its time. Stamina and strength are slowly returning, aided by your son's amazing culinary gifts."

She did not respond to the compliment to her son. Preferred to admire the rings on her own hand.

Mark tried to get her talking again. He nodded toward the vase. "The flowers are beautiful."

That same softening of expression as she glanced toward them. "Thank you." Quick as a flick it was gone. "Todd doesn't keep this place up very well," she said. "It was meant to be beautiful. Now it is merely 'historical.'"

"Todd and your son, did they grow up with Baiss Channon?"

A mocking look appeared on her face. The same one he had seen in the picture of her with the Greek ambassador. "You are interested in Baiss?"

"History professor with nothing much to do," he said, feigning apology. "Everything that has already happened is interesting to me and worth study."

She gave him a shrewd look. "Well, I bet you could find him before Ernie does."

This surprised him. "Ernie's looking?"

"He says he is, but not personally, I'm sure. The only thing Ernie does for himself is play the piano. And to answer your other question—no. Nick did not consort with Baiss. John would have had none of that. There was the occasional birthday party, to keep our father happy, but brother John usually avoided his relations." She smirked. "Which was fine with his relations."

"So, do you remember what Baiss was like? Have any idea or memory of him?"

She laughed. "He was a runt. The last of the litter. And the least."

Mark was confused. "I thought he was an only child."

"He was. But he was a long time coming. Nick is older. So is Todd. Fia's two girls were already in school before Barbara even got pregnant. And then when he was born, he was such a disappointment! Fat, slow little thing. Barbara did her best to hide her feelings about him, but when you're stuck with a slug, what do you do?"

He couldn't fathom this attitude toward a child, especially one's own kin. "I could not say."

But, what also caught him, was that Juliane was blurring a physical description of Baiss with an emotional one. A runt, by definition, was smaller and weaker, possibly slow, but never fat. Was she, without realizing it, saying that Baiss was in some way more vulnerable than the rest of the Channon cousins?

She cocked her head, looking as if she wanted to ask him a personal question, one which he did not want to hear, much less answer.

He spoke first. "When was the last time you saw your nephew Baiss?"

"I don't know. Maybe twenty years ago. Maybe less than that. I don't really remember when it was. He played the piano with an orchestra in Chicago, some big concerto. We had to go. Our father had died, and John controlled the Channon money. So we all had to dress up, file in, and watch that lump on the bench."

"Didn't he perform well?"

"He might have. I don't really know. You see, I hate the music. In fact, last night I bet Fia five hundred dollars that she couldn't make Ernie stop playing. Of course, first I made Ernie believe that he had to be the closing act for Elizabeth's concert. That was easy. He'll do anything I tell him. And of course, Elizabeth had no choice but to make room for him." She stroked the rings on her hand, looking satisfied. "I think Fia put on a better show than Ernie did."

No wonder Juliane's arrival had made Elizabeth shudder.

"I take it you're not close to Ernie."

She sobered and bent slightly forward, her dark eyes narrow. "Let me tell you this, professor. You know that concert night with Baiss in Chicago? The only thing, and I mean the *only* thing, that I enjoyed about watching Baiss perform was looking down the row and seeing Ernie dissolve with jealousy."

She leaned back against the sofa and studied him thoughtfully. "Something he'll never have to do while listening to you," she added.

SEAN AND MARK were in the car again, hunting for a place that would give them a decent dinner in a town that believed in putting its feet up to rest on a Sunday evening.

The conversation with Juliane was weighing on Mark's mind. He wanted to talk it over with Sean, but any discussion of the Channons was hit or miss with him. Mark wanted to bat ideas around, pore over events and implications, wonder aloud in conversation together, for as long as it took to find some sort of satisfaction.

It was something he and Jerry Waite could do, what had made them more friends than colleagues. Luedders also. And Amy always. They usually had some nightly topic to discuss.

He was surprised and encouraged when, after a long, quiet spell, Sean brought up the topic himself.

"You still think you can find him?"

"Baiss?"

"Yeah."

"I don't know. But I can't help trying to work it out. Study the known facts for cause and meaning. Call it the occupational hazard of an off-duty history professor, but there it is."

He told Sean about the conversation he had with Juliane and what she had gone on to say. "Ernie somehow hired a skip tracer to find Baiss, then went to the trustees for the money to pay him. The trustees agreed with him, although they insisted on handling the transaction with the guy themselves."

"What's a skip tracer?" asked Sean.

"Someone whose tactics are not usually on the up-and-up. They find people who don't want to be found."

Sean looked interested now. Maybe he was coming around. Mark hoped so.

"Did this skip tracer have any luck?"

"Couldn't find him, even though the guy was supposed to know his business."

"What actually do they do?"

"I can't tell you, specifically. Everyone's actions leave some sort of record, and these people know where to look. I found it interesting to learn that Juliane didn't seem to care. She doesn't need Baiss for anything. She just enjoys tormenting her siblings."

Sean pulled into the parking lot of a steak and buffet place and shut off the car. "So you've got this wealthy guy. There's a trust set up and running fine, and all his assets are managed for him. His family's waiting to get more money out of him, so he keeps a low profile. What's the mystery then?"

Mark could hear the stubbornness re-emerge in Sean's voice. He felt his own stubbornness rise in response.

"You're talking from an adult's point of view. Baiss was technically a child when he left. And I can't help but think, what did he know or fear that made him run?"

Sean looked away and drummed his fingers on the steering wheel. Clearly, Mark had used up all his assistant's willingness to deal with this topic. In a flash, he realized why.

Sean—on his own and working hard for his money—could have no real sympathy for a kid who had so much and just ran away from it.

Mark gave in. "All right. Let's just go eat. No more talk about Baiss Channon."

"Or any of them," said Sean.

"Agreed."

Later, when they returned to Riverview House, Mark decided to go to bed early. He was exhausted again, no surprise. And his concern for Baiss felt like a weight alongside the grief he always carried.

He dressed for bed and climbed in with his book of number puzzles. The piano book was on the nightstand. He reached for it and opened the cover to look at the wobbly letters of the name. Why did this childish scrawl get to him so much?

Mark didn't believe everything Juliane had said, very little of it actually. But he could imagine the loneliness and pressure put on such a child. He studied the hand-written name again, the uneven letters drifting downward by the time the writer got to the very last "n."

He closed the book, put it back on the table, and turned off the light. No matter what Sean said, Mark couldn't help but feel that Baiss, child or not, adult or not, wanted to be found. And he knew that Amy would have agreed with him.

14

———

The Worst Sort of Prank

"I BET you think I'm an evil, old bitch, don't you?"

The words were said rather proudly.

A week had run its course. Friday evening had come again. And Fia was sitting on the back porch, drink in hand, when Mark stepped out for some fresh air and a look at the view.

He took a chair near her and turned his gaze to the river. "Now, Fia, what makes you think that?"

"I saw your face when I yelled at Ernie last Saturday night." She was waiting for some sort of answer, some sort of rebuke that she could challenge in order to justify herself.

He didn't care to climb into that kind of hornet's nest.

"Why would you, a Channon, care what an ailing professor thinks?" he said lightly.

She took a sip of her drink and stared at the view alongside him. "A bad habit. My second husband was a professor."

"In what field?"

She scowled. "Music, of course. He married me to get money for a recording studio. When Papa wouldn't give it to him, he divorced me and accused me of all kinds of vile things. Papa paid to shut him up. So he opened his recording studio after all." She took a long drink. "He hated jazz. Now it's the only kind of music I like." She glanced at him, a smug look on her face.

"Touché to him?" he offered.

"And to Papa and the whole family."

"You look different," she said abruptly. "*Oh.* You're growing a beard. *Why?*" She put a certain amount of revulsion in the last word. The revulsion was in her look as well.

"Sean's influence." He wouldn't tell her that it also helped to cover the scars he couldn't bear to see. "I'm trying to imitate his spiffy look."

She shook her head and took a slurp of her drink.

Keep the conversation going, Mark. You might learn something.

But his mind was blank.

They watched the river for a few moments in silence. He was grateful for the evening breeze, bringing with it the sweet smell of garden flowers. Was that jasmine?

The lowering sun heated the porch. Soon it would be an uncomfortable place to sit. August had passed the reins to September, but September had plenty of its own warmth to play.

Fia broke the silence. "So, history professor, what are your politics? Republican or Democrat?"

Mark watched a hawk land in the arm of a dead tree along the riverbank. "A bit of both, I'm afraid. I find that the complexity of political opinions don't fit into neat, little boxes."

"That's a tactful answer," she said wryly.

"But a true one." He had the feeling he had dodged another argument. "What about you?"

Fia scowled again. "Neither. I was married to a politician once too. Now I get invitations to both parties' very expensive fund-raising dinners. I take great pleasure in tearing them into small pieces."

"Which political party did your former husband follow?" This was a minefield of a question, but it was out before Mark could call it back.

To his surprise, Fia answered calmly. "Oh, he wasn't for either party. Victor was for himself."

Victor Gaff, the one with Fia in the newspaper photo. Yes, he definitely looked the politician type.

She started up the conversation again, and there was something in her tone that said she just needed to talk to someone.

"What do you do with yourself here? Aren't you bored out of your mind?"

"Reading and walking, mostly." He had struggled more with the patience that healing required, than with boredom.

"I've been practicing my piano too," he added.

She wasn't interested in any of this. "You never answered my first question. Do you think I'm an evil, old bitch?"

What was he to do with that? He put on a mock professor air.

"You've used three words in an interesting way. The first one—*evil*—requires some definition. According to ancient wisdom, no one is good but God alone. So we have to let the opposite stand for all men. And, as a student of the past, I can vouch for the truth of that.

"The last word—*bitch*—refers to a member of the dog family." He leaned just slightly closer to her and blinked. "I see nothing canine in your appearance.

"That leaves the middle word—*old*. No sane man would ever discuss age when there is a woman involved. But I think you are too capable and energetic to be old."

She was staring as if not sure what to make of him. After a few moments she shook her head and took another gulp from the glass. She swirled the ice cubes and the small amount of liquid that remained, staring at the swirling, not looking at him.

"I'm a fighter, you know. I had to be in a family like mine. You never saw such bullies. Fighting back was the only way to stay alive."

This was unexpected. The curtain lifted on Channon family life. A curtain he needed lifted in order to understand Baiss. He wanted to keep her talking.

"So who was the worst bully? John, Ernie, or Will?"

"Don't forget Juliane."

"Okay. John, Ernie, Will, or Juliane. Who was the worst?"

"Whoever had you in their clutches. When I was ten, John tied me to a tree halfway down that slope to the river." She pointed. "It was snowing and cold, but he left me there. He said that if I told on him, I'd never get any money from him when he was in control. Then he went in to have dinner. When I didn't appear at the table, they sent the groundsman out to look for me."

Mark was horrified. "What did your parents do?"

"I told Papa what happened, and John denied everything. Papa chose to believe John over me." She swirled her ice cubes again. "And John made sure I never got any more of the Channon money after Papa died."

The evening sun picked out the lines on her face, and he wondered if inside every shrewish woman there stood a broken, little girl.

"So, what was Ernie like?"

She snorted and shook her head. "This will tell you. Juliane had a garden. It used to be over there." Fia pointed in a vague way off to the right. "She spent hours in it, growing rare flowers. It would have made me crazy, but she liked it. The newspaper came to take pictures. So did a gardening magazine. One night, Juliane and Ernie had some sort of argument, and Ernie got his motorcycle out and drove back and forth over the entire garden. Tore up every last flower."

He thought of the soft look on Juliane's face when she had brought the flowers into the small parlor. He could imagine the pain of seeing the torn garden. The irreplaceable hours of work. The destruction of beauty. The agony and anger. He felt it himself.

"And Will?"

"Will's a thief. He would take anything he wanted from you. He'd even steal from John."

"What did your mother and father do when all this was going on?" He remembered his own mother's stern face the time he was caught in a lie as a little boy. Retribution had been swift, sure, and painful.

"My mother 'kept to her room' as they write in the old novels. She was a professional invalid. Never had to be bothered with anything or anyone. My father didn't like any form of conflict. So he pretended it didn't exist."

The noise of diners arriving sounded in the hall behind them. The aroma of steak sizzling in butter wafted from the kitchen. Fia looked like she was going to take her glass and leave. But he had to ask her the most important question.

"Fia, what did you think of Baiss? What was he like as a boy?"

If she was surprised by his question, she didn't show it. "I barely saw him. I didn't live here then. I heard he played the piano all the time. That pleased John. John used to play the piano himself. Ernie was better than John in music. But, Baiss was better than Ernie. You can imagine the fun."

He could, but wouldn't call it fun.

Fia went on. "Juliane told me that Ernie pulled the worst sort of prank on Baiss. He told her about it later, probably had to gloat to someone."

She raised her hand to shield her eyes from the intense rays of the sun, and stood up.

He stood up with her. "What was it?" he asked. "What did he do?"

"Don't know. I think she was afraid to tell me. And it takes a lot to make Juliane afraid." She laughed, a *can-you-believe-that* kind of laugh.

It angered him. A young boy had been hurt somehow and his pain was a joke to the Channon siblings.

He looked directly in her eyes. "And yet you are all surprised that Baiss doesn't want to come back?"

The openness, such as it had been, vanished. Her face hardened and her eyes narrowed. He was, once again, a peasant. A peasant who had heard too much. His last question crossed the line. Channons could criticize each other, but no one else *dare* challenge them.

Fia stared at him, lips pressed tight. He had the feeling that she wished for a good retort, but couldn't think of one. She wheeled around and let the slam of the door do it for her.

Sean was sprawled out on his bed, reading a biography of Catherine de Medici, when Mark burst in. Sean looked up expectantly, marking his place with his finger.

Mark came right to the point. "Look. I know I've promised not to speak of the Channons—and I haven't, for almost a whole week. But something awful *did* happen to Baiss, something done by Ernie. Juliane told Fia it was a prank, but it unnerved *her*, if you can believe it, because she wouldn't tell Fia what it was. Presumably only Baiss, Ernie, and Juliane know."

Sean was listening quietly. It was a good thing, because Mark was angry.

"It would serve them right if he never came back! Let

them all drown in their debts!"

"So you don't want to find him anymore?"

Mark calmed himself and thought a moment. "I do. First, I have to make sure he's all right. Then I'd like to bring him back home and boot everyone else out."

His stomach tightened with sudden nausea, and he left Sean's room before the tears came.

He went to the tower room, sank down into the chair, and watched through blurred eyes as a barge slowly moved up the river. His mind worked to tease apart what his gut had just told him.

This wasn't just about bringing Baiss back. He wanted with all his heart to bring Amy back too. To have her read Baiss's name on the flyleaf of his book. To go charging off into the night to find the boy with him. Arm-in-arm. With him.

He tried to focus on the river, imagining himself inside the wheelhouse of that barge, directing it to push that heavy load in one direction while all the drainings of Minnesota, Wisconsin, Iowa, and upper Illinois were pushing back. The guy was making progress, slow and steady, but he was making it. Mark envied him.

He sat there long after the barge passed out of sight, staring at trees, at sky, at nothing. He felt the shift in the light as the sun dropped even lower towards the horizon.

He couldn't do this.

Oh, Amy.

He covered his face with his hands. The only good thing was that Amy was at peace. She was with God, a God he was not talking to right now, but she was with Him. Mark knew it.

He remembered the look on her face one night. He had been at a conference in Springfield, when a winter storm closed roads and slowed traffic to a crawl. He tried to call her, but his cell phone battery had died. Long after midnight, she met him at the garage door, wearing that fuzzy blue robe of hers, trying to hide her tears.

How tightly they had held each other then. How much they loved each other. They were together. Things were all right.

No more.

Grief whispered in his ear that nothing mattered now. Nothing at all.

Maybe grief can lie to a person.

Or was it despair that lied?

He wiped his face with his hand and stared resolutely out into the coming twilight, waiting. Hoping to see just one star, knowing it was too early.

After a time he felt stiff, felt the need to stand and stretch. As he stood up, something whirled in his head. He had wept too long. More than his injured brain could bear. He had wept himself dizzy. He clutched at the chair back to get his bearings. And of course, Sean chose this moment to come in.

"What if I order out for pizza tonight?" Sean asked. "I'll tell Rebecca to give our table away. She'll understand. You could just lie back and take it easy."

Mark almost answered with a nod, but stopped himself just in time. "All right," he said.

"We'll play cards too." Sean rattled on, but Mark could hear the concern behind the professional cheeriness. "I've never told you this, but I'm unbeatable at gin rummy."

15

———

Four Beautiful Notes

SATURDAY AFTERNOON. Mark started down the stairs a little before three o'clock for his first piano lesson with Elizabeth. He had been faithful in practicing his bit every day, speaking calmly to his brain as it dealt with the visual complexity of notes. Taking deep breaths and reminding it of all the things it was made to do. Inviting it to heal.

These were the internal struggles, known only to him. Listeners would only hear slow tones sounding on the keyboard.

Apparently Todd Channon had noticed his regular practice. The past two days when Mark had come down the stairs, piano book in hand, Todd had greeted him with, "The small parlor is free for you now, Mr. Newlin."

Today Todd was at his post by the stairwell as usual. A

few guests were milling around, gawking at the fixtures in the great hall, poking their heads into the old study. One toddler stepped into the fireplace to stare up the chimney before his mother grabbed him. No one else was taking Todd's attention though. Maybe Mark could risk a question.

Todd looked up from his computer as Mark approached. "We've put a sign up, reserving the small parlor for your lesson."

Mark was genuinely touched. "Why, thank you. Is Elizabeth here?"

"Not yet."

"Could I ask you a question then?"

"Certainly." Todd pushed his glasses up on his nose.

"To occupy myself, I've been studying the history of Ashington Mills and of your family at the library. You have quite a history."

"Thank you, sir."

"I hope you don't think it out-of-place, if I ask you something about your family."

The reserve thickened. He could feel it.

"You may ask."

"Thank you. It's a simple question really. What was your opinion of Baiss Channon? Did you know him well?"

For some reason Todd looked relieved. *What question had he been expecting?*

"Didn't know him that well. He's younger than me. But he was kind of a weird kid. Definitely not normal. I remember him sitting with a stack of presents at his birthday party each year, and having to sit and watch him open them all. Then Grandfather would insist on playing that ridiculous piano game."

"What game?"

A crash and the immediate sound of crying pulled Todd from his desk. The toddler, it appeared, had knocked over a planter. The manager of Riverview would be busy for awhile.

Mark went to the small parlor, set the book on the music rack, and looked inside the cover at that wobbly capital B. He flipped the pages to his *Intrada* and began to play slowly, hands together, working to focus his mind on the music he was trying to make, telling his brain to relax, forgetting everything else. When he finished the first two lines, he stopped.

"Very nice." Elizabeth set down her purse and some books on a sofa, then went to the doorway and flipped a small lever. A handle appeared, and she pulled on it. A tall pocket door emerged from the wall and slid across the open doorway.

"I wish I would have known about that door," Mark said. "It would have saved everyone else the grief of hearing me practice."

She answered with a smile and pulled up a chair next to the piano bench. She took a small notebook from her purse and sat down.

He was ten again. Mrs. Williams was at his side, and he, as usual, felt apologetic.

"I won't be confused with one of your gifted students."

"Nobody knows their gifts until they try them out. Besides, there are many reasons to learn how to play the piano. High performance is only one of them. Your reason is as valid as any of the others. Let me hear it again from the beginning."

He obeyed, trying to concentrate, but it was harder with someone watching so closely. When he had finished, she leaned in and deftly circled a few rests he had forgotten.

"Elizabeth, did you teach Baiss how to play the piano?"

She gave a sad smile. "I was his first teacher."

"How old was he?"

"Just four. He was playing with Barbara in this room, when he got bored with his toys. This piano had just arrived, so Barbara opened it up and let him play." Elizabeth leaned back in her chair. "He banged around a little bit, then started to pick out a melody and his whole face lit up."

"From a music book?"

She shook her head. "He made them up. He played another and another, for at least an hour. Barbara said he was transformed. And the music just seemed to pour from him.

"She asked me to teach him, but secretly, without John or Ernie knowing. They could be—well—obsessive, especially with music, and she just wanted him to enjoy it for a while. I was twelve at the time, but I had an excellent teacher and just passed on everything she taught me."

"How old was he when he used this book?"

"You won't believe this." A glow of happy pride was on her face. "He was five years old."

"That's incredible! Did you enjoy teaching him?" He

wanted to hear more of her opinion of Baiss. So far, it was very different than everyone else's.

Her smile was sincere. "Very much. We had such fun together. Baiss invented a game that we played every week. We had to hunt for the four most beautiful notes, four notes played consecutively that sounded like the most beautiful thing we had ever heard. Here, I'll show you what he chose when he first got this book."

She turned the pages to a small piece, a Largo by Corelli, and played the first four notes, slowly and evenly, letting each one sing out. Mark named them automatically in his mind as she played them. High A, down to the F, down to D, then up past the original A to the B-flat.

"That *is* beautiful." He meant it.

She leaned back in her chair again and the smile faded from her face. "I miss him. I worry about him so much."

"How long did you teach him?"

"About a year. Then John came home from a trip early and caught us in the middle of a lesson. I remember the look on his face. He was speechless with pride. But I thought it was pride in himself and what he had produced in a son, without much thought for Baiss. The look on the face that shows a selfish kind of satisfaction, you know? Baiss was happy because he was too young to tell the difference. Then, anyway."

She flipped the pages back to Mark's piece and pressed the book open. "I'm sorry," she said. "It's true. One shouldn't speak ill of the dead." She gave an apologetic smile.

"Because they aren't here to defend themselves?" he offered.

"Something like that, I suppose."

"That doesn't keep historians from taking a whack at them."

"No, I guess that can't be helped. Now," she pointed farther down the page, "let's look at the next section of the *Intrada.*"

Elizabeth was a good teacher, very good. In just a few short minutes, he had a vision of those next measures, what they meant to do in the heart and mind of the listener, as well as the nuts and bolts of their musicality. He saw the whole piece with new eyes, and his fingers were eager for more practice.

She penciled reminder notes in his book and closed it. Time to go. But he lingered.

"I'm just amazed at how much musical talent flows through your family." He wondered if the words sounded cheesy, or insincere, and hoped she would take them as he meant them.

She seemed to. "My father was a gifted pianist. He had a Steinway Grand in his bedroom and played every evening for hours after he came home from the office. Sometimes he let me watch him play. Always Baroque pieces, and almost always Bach.

"He revered Johann Sebastian Bach. I think the old family name *Bachen* haunted him. He had research done on our connection with Bach, but some missing birth certificates in the 1800s kept him from proving the link."

"That must have been frustrating."

"It was. But he named all his children after Bach's children anyway."

"Really? I'm not familiar with those names."

She gave him a half-embarrassed look and began to recite.

"John Christoph. Ernest Andreas. Sophia Henrietta—or Fia, as you know her. Wilhelm Friedemann."

"Will."

She nodded. "Then he started scrambling some of the names to get Juliane Regina and later Elizabeth Susanna."

Before Mark could open his mouth to comment, the door rattled and slid open swiftly, without a prior knock. A man stepped into the room, dressed in the white, double-breasted jacket and apron of the professional chef. Dark hair, receding hairline. It was the magazine photo of Nick Powell come to life. Mark could see the resemblance to Juliane instantly. The newcomer didn't even glance at him.

"Elizabeth, you're helping with dinner tonight, aren't you?" The same imperious tone his uncle Ernie used. No attempt to disguise it.

"Yes. Coming right now, Nick."

The chef disappeared, but the door remained open.

"Thank you for the lesson," Mark said. "I think the practicing is actually helping my brain find itself again."

"That's wonderful!"

"What do I owe you for today?"

"Let's not talk about that just yet."

"Next week, then?" Mark asked.

"I think that will work." She smiled, slung her purse

strap over one shoulder, and left in the direction of the kitchen.

Mark bent over the piano and picked out the first notes of the Corelli Largo. They were hauntingly beautiful.

What a game to play—the four most beautiful notes game! And what a different picture of Baiss Elizabeth had painted for him.

He rested his fingers on the keyboard and played the four Corelli notes again. A, F, and D, all progressing downward, then up and over to the B-flat.

For you, Amy.

He tucked his book under his arm and went back upstairs.

16

The Way the Sculptor Saw Him

DAYS WENT BY, and Mark was increasingly frustrated with his inability to move ahead in the search for Baiss Channon. One morning he was doing his promised exercising, walking around the lake in the center of the college campus. The library building stood at one end of the lake. Sean was inside, going through the stacks for more books to read.

During his third lap around, Mark decided it was time to cast the net wider, to reach for additional help. He pulled out his phone and pressed the familiar number. A light breeze was moving the water on the lake, and there was a new chill in it. Serious jacket weather was on the way.

"Gold College," said the bright voice. "How may I direct your call?"

"Music Department, please," Mark replied.

"Gold College Music, how may I help you?" The voice of a student worker.

"May I speak to Pim Montgomery, please, if he's free? It's Mark Newlin."

"Oh, hi, Dr. Newlin! It's Melanie from your Renaissance and Reformation class last year! Yes, he's free. I'll get him for you."

Mark waited. Two runners raced past him breathing heavily. Then the voice of Gold College's senior piano professor came on the line.

"Mark? How are you doing? They treating you well up there?"

"Just fine. I have a question for you, Pim. I need to tap into your knowledge of all things piano. What can you tell me about a pianist named Ernest Channon? From Ashington Mills, Illinois."

"I wasn't expecting that question." Pim chuckled, then took a deep breath. "Yes, I'm familiar with Ernest Channon. He actually performed here, probably a year or two before you came. He's technically brilliant, but very hard to work with. You know the Shigeru Kawai Grand we have in the auditorium? It was new that year, the result of some rather extravagant alumni gifts. It's a beautiful, beautiful instrument! Ernest could do nothing but complain. I think it was because the piano was unfamiliar to him. Turns out the piano is now more famous than he is."

"You mean, his career is not going well?"

"Oh, no. Sadly, no. He was all the rage for a while, then

his career just kind of evaporated. He might do the occasional tour of South America, but I don't think he does much any more."

"It evaporated?" This was interesting. "When was this?"

"Don't quite remember. I'd guess thirteen, fourteen years ago, or so. Outside of the fact that I couldn't stand the man, it really is a shame. He had world class talent, except for one thing."

"What was that?"

"No heart."

Mark could agree. "Do you know of a Baiss Channon?"

"The child prodigy? Ernest's nephew, right? Funny you should ask. Let me ask you this first. Have you ever heard of Lionel Davidson?"

"No."

"He graduated from Juilliard the same year I did. He teaches in Chicago. A genius. Just a pure, musical genius. Baiss studied with him for awhile. Davidson said Baiss was truly great, the best student he could ever hope to have in his lifetime. But his father was impossible. Always arguing, challenging, accusing, until Davidson couldn't take it anymore. He let Baiss go."

"You wouldn't know when this was, would you?"

"No, but I can ask him if you wish."

"Please. I know this sounds odd, but the place I'm spending my sabbatical is the original Channon family home. I've actually met Ernest Channon, and you know how it is, I can't help but be curious."

Pim chuckled again. "You've met him? Does he still have a cold handshake, you know, like a fish?"

"He doesn't shake hands anymore with anyone."

Pim laughed. "Well, he's not the only one to do that. Got a student now. I'll get back to you."

Mark slid his phone back in his pocket and looked around. He had done his five laps, but didn't feel like stopping. For some reason, Pim's information had been reassuring.

He pulled out the phone again and did something he had been putting off. He pressed the number for Jerry Waite.

"Hey, Mark." Apologetic. Hesitant.

Mark went right to the point of his call. "Did you know that the place you sent me to is the home of the Channon family? Channon Manufacturing, Channon Machine, Channon World, *those* Channons?"

"You're kidding!"

"I take it you know about them."

"Some. Haven't read much lately, but some years back they had all sorts of family tragedies."

"Did you know that the heir to the family fortune is missing?"

"No." It was spoken quietly. Jerry was very interested.

"I don't think it is in the news, and probably shouldn't be for the kid's sake, but his aunt couldn't contain herself at dinner one night and spilled the beans."

"Sounds like you're having quite a time."

Mark wasn't sure how to answer this. "I'd appreciate any other information you can find about him. His name is Baiss Channon, and he disappeared maybe fifteen or so years ago. Computer screens are still hard to look at. Sean could help, but he's not into this as much as I am. He's trying hard to be patient with my curiosity, but I hate to push him into reading about it. He is reading history though."

"You think you can claim him for the department?"

"We'll see. How are things in Marlonburg?"

"Oh, just puttering along."

Sean had come out of the library entrance and was walking across the lawn towards him.

"Gotta go, Jerry. Say hello to Myra for me. And thanks for checking into the Channons."

He pocketed the phone and went to meet Sean.

Sean greeted him with, "Do you feel tired?"

He shook his head. "Should I?"

"You went seven laps. I counted! Seven!"

"So, who's ahead? Books to miles, who's in the lead?"

Sean gave a wry grin. "I'll need a calculator or Sorenson to figure that out."

THAT EVENING MARK dined alone at Riverview House. He was getting stronger, and as a result, insisted that Sean take time off and just go somewhere without him.

Kelly, his usual server, had fallen into the habit of chatting with him from time to time. He learned that she was seven years younger than her sister Stephanie, Todd's wife, and was studying surface design at Ashington College. Oh, and she planned on making a lot of money someday.

But it was Sean who was on his mind as he gazed out the window at the trees in the distance, the new red and yellow of their leaves. What did Sean do all day? He ran. He read. He watched out for Mark's strength, water intake, and vitamins, and the naps Mark had recently given up. He played gin rummy with Mark most nights, and beat him most nights.

But, what else? What was Sean looking forward to, hoping for in life? Mark was ashamed of himself. He had given the absent Baiss Channon all his attention, and the very present Sean Merritt very little of it. And yet, Sean had given him so much.

He searched his memory for everything he knew about his faithful assistant. Sean had lost his parents and, therefore, his internal compass at a young age. Had somehow survived that to care for other people. He ran about five miles each day. He ate like a horse, but kept ginger and pretzels around for the times his stomach would rebel against him. He had a wide variety of interests, but hadn't been able to settle on any one of them.

There must be more. People were complex. Oh, yes. The secret Mark had promised to keep. Sean's fear of heights. He would not have been the kind of kid to climb trees in order to see over a fence, but since he was taller than Mark—over six feet—he wouldn't need to now.

Kelly interrupted his thoughts by setting down a plate of Portobello mushrooms stuffed with cream cheese and spinach, floating in a wine sauce he had forgotten the name of. She did not whirl away as usual. "The kitchen's all upset right now."

For a split second he imagined the ladles and carving

knives marching circles around the stove like some animated Disney movie. "Why is that, Kelly?" he answered politely.

"The Channons have made arrangements for a full formal party in October. They're going to invite a hundred guests."

He wondered who was behind this. "What's the occasion?"

"John Senior's birthday."

He couldn't hide his surprise. "His birthday? Hasn't he been dead for years?"

"Oh, yeah, but every several years they celebrate his birthday with a huge party. It's in his will or something. They're going to have rich people from all over the country." Her eyes glowed at the thought.

"So why is the kitchen upset?"

Rebecca Powell passed nearby, a stack of menu cards in her hand. Kelly pretended to rearrange the salt and pepper shakers on his table until Rebecca moved on.

"Because," she continued in a quiet voice, "the Channons haven't completely decided if Nick will be chosen to cater it or not. He's really mad. Loud mad, quiet mad, scary mad. He says it's everyone else's fault." She glanced in Rebecca's direction. "Sometimes I think he's unhinged."

She hurried off to the rest of her duties taking the pepper shaker with her.

Mark cut a bite of the mushroom and swirled it in sauce, considering what she said. Imagine a Channon birthday party for someone who had been dead for years, someone who left funds for it, presumably, in his will. It sounded like a very big deal. And it would be just like Juliane to stiff her own son.

After his meal, he climbed the stairs thinking about Sean, Baiss, John Senior, Nick, Juliane, and even Elizabeth. He felt sad, truly sad. Not grieving sad, just sad for people.

Sean met him at the door to his room. "How'd you like to do something funny for Dr. Waite?"

He didn't have the energy, but it would be good to do something for Sean. "Okay. What?"

"I came across this park on my morning run, and there's a statue of General George Rogers Clark in it. I could use your phone and take a picture of you and the general, and we could send it to Dr. Waite. He'd love it."

Mark wasn't sure about that, but Sean was so enthusiastic. How could he say no? "Sure."

"He'd probably frame it and hang it in his office."

"I bet."

Within five minutes they were in the car. Sean drove north through the square, past the entrance to the bridges, and into an older neighborhood. A part of town with corner bars and jumbled sidewalks. Was it imagination or did the people on the street have a hunted look? To live among houses and buildings that were torn and broken was like living with sadness. He shook his head.

"Something wrong?" asked Sean.

"What? Oh. No. Just thoughts, that's all."

Sean pointed to a break between the buildings where a spread of green crowned a bluff. "We're almost there, and I think we still have enough light."

They parked and walked across the grass, past the

playground, to the stone plinth where the solitary figure of General Clark towered high, his arms folded, as he gazed across the Mississippi and its river islands. Mark stood patiently by the base of the statue, assuming a slight professorial look, while Sean took his picture. At Sean's suggestion, he also crossed his arms in imitation of Clark.

Sean ran up to show him the result of his posing. "It's a little fuzzy after all. We'll need to come back in daylight to get a better shot."

Mark glanced at the cell phone screen. "Not bad." He put the phone back in his pocket. "For a guy who hates cell phones, you know how to work them pretty well."

Sean's grin reappeared, and Mark realized it had been awhile since he'd seen it.

"I was the designated picture taker at Illinois State. No one had to do selfies when I was around. I fell in love with photography and bought myself a real nice camera. It's back at the college. What do you think of the statue?"

Mark stepped back and looked up at it. "He looks confident. Like the British don't have a chance against these stubborn Illinois fighters."

"He looks determined," said Sean.

"Immovable."

"Stubborn."

"Arrogant," said Mark, then wondered at it.

"Tough."

"Tired."

"Complacent."

"Who's really to know? We're only seeing him the way the sculptor saw him." Mark checked the plaque on the base of the statue. "A sculptor who was working ninety-one years after Clark died, probably working from an old portrait. Definitely not from a personal knowledge of the man."

He stared back up at the face of the man who was the "Savior of Illinois" during the American Revolutionary War. Clark looked burdened. Weary. And was doing a great job of hiding it.

A thought struck him and he almost laughed: Maybe he was the one weary and burdened, not Clark.

He told Sean this. "No matter what we see, all we have is our own perceptions, our own experience and understanding. Those make up the camera lens that interprets everything. Human beings barely understand themselves at times, much less each other."

He studied the statue again. "That's how it is with all history. You get as close as you can; the rest of the understanding is God's."

"Is that what all historians say?"

"The honest ones do."

Mark kept looking at Clark's expression, wondering.

"What are you thinking now?" Sean asked.

Very well. Sean had asked.

"I'm thinking of what Baiss Channon would look like if he were up there, with only the impressions of his family to guide the sculptor. What expression would be on his face? And would it look anything at all like the real man?"

"But, nowadays, they're sure to have pictures of him."

Mark shook his head. "I asked Todd if there were any of him in the house, and he said no. And he didn't know where any could be."

"So the police had nothing to go on when they went looking for him?"

"Ah, remember what Todd told us? No one ever calls the police on the Channons, not even the Channons."

Sean stood there, staring out toward the river. "So, nobody looked for him? A guy disappears and no one looks for him? With all the money and privilege that he had? No one?"

Mark felt internally exhausted, yet wanted to calm and reassure Sean. But why? And of what?

He took a breath and continued. "I think the family doesn't want to admit to anyone outside of themselves that Baiss is missing. They've got to still be looking, I'm sure."

Mark would bet that some of the searchers only wanted Baiss because he was the door to money. Once they had what they wanted, they wouldn't care what happened to him. He could be lost forever, and they wouldn't care.

Mark wandered toward the brick path that lined the bluff-top, aware that Sean wasn't following him. The main channel of the river was hidden by a tree-filled island. This smaller channel, immediately below, had calmer waters. He caught the muffled sound of a powerboat returning to dock. He could see its tiny light as it edged closer to the island mooring.

Sean waited by the statue. Mark walked back and patted his shoulder. "Hey, have you had dinner yet? Let's go get something for you."

Less than an hour later, they were settled into a comfortable booth at a sports bar on the east end of town.

On a huge screen the St. Louis Cardinals were playing the Chicago Cubs at Wrigley Field. Mark didn't even have to look at the screen to know what was going on. All the bar patrons at the tables under the screen had definite opinions on every single player's performance. It was the seventh inning. The Cardinals were up by two runs.

Sean was staring down a pepperoni pizza with extra cheese. Mark had a smaller plate, a dessert called Cubbies' Dream. It was a frosted brownie decorated and cut in the shape of a pennant. He stabbed the tip of it with his fork and took a bite. Not fancy, but good.

Sean lifted a piece of the pizza to his mouth, all the cheese trying to decide if it should come too or stay on the pan, most of it somewhere in the middle. Chicago got a hit, and half the bar erupted in cheering.

"Is this too loud for your head?" Sean asked.

"It's okay," he said, taking another bite of brownie. Actually, it *was* too loud. He would probably end up paying for it, in headaches and sheer wonkiness. But it felt good to be around people who were energetically alive and cheering. You get warm standing near the fire.

He finished his brownie down to the crumbs.

"How was it?" asked Sean, mouth full of pizza.

"Not like Nick's, but good." He set down his fork. "Okay. Answer this question for me. I order this Cubbies' Dream dessert, right? Carefully made in the shape of a pennant. Now think. I just ate it."

Sean nodded, following.

"So tell me this. Is the owner of this place a Cubs fan or a Cardinals fan?"

It took Sean just a moment, then he started to laugh.

After the tension by the river, it was a good sound.

THEY STAYED LATE. Past the end of the game and through part of a Padres' game. But it felt good to do something like this.

"We'll need our keys tonight," Mark said, as the car turned onto Riverview House drive. "Todd will have already locked up. Hey. Wait! That's Rebecca." She was still dressed in her hostess attire. Perfect for an expensive dining room. A little odd for a late night walk.

Mark put his window down. "Rebecca! Can we give you a lift? I know it's not far, but there could be two thousand mosquitos between here and the front door."

Rebecca smiled. "Sure. Thanks." When she climbed in the back seat, Mark thought she looked tired. Very tired. He remembered the first night he had seen her walk slowly up the drive. That impression of weariness had been correct.

Once she was in and the door shut, he searched his mind for the right thing to say. He wanted to ask her where she had been. Why she was always out so late alone. If she was all right. But how to ask her?

Sean was quicker off the mark. "Hey, Rebecca, are you a Cubs fan or a Cardinals fan?"

"Milwaukee Brewers all the way," she said gamely.

"No! What?" cried Sean.

The resulting tumult took them the rest of the way to the front door.

17

———

Piercing the Night

ANOTHER SATURDAY DAWNED with more of fall in the air. Sean was at the wheel, driving them to the older, historic section of town where he parked the car on a brick side street off Green Avenue. They walked back to Green, dodging groups of people who had already staked out their territory with camping chairs. At last, they found an open piece of curb along the herringbone brick sidewalk. Mark looked admiringly at the proud, white-turreted house behind them. A black pole in the yard proclaimed that it had been built in 1895.

"I don't think I've ever watched a parade like this before," said Sean, bending his long legs and lowering himself to the ground.

Mark sat down and took a deep breath, pulling the

refreshing air into his lungs and savoring it. Just the right amount of warmth and chill to be invigorating. Autumn was here. "Really? No parades? Not even in high school? Where did you grow up?"

"Quite a few places. We traveled around a bit. Charleston, South Carolina. New York. Chicago. Rockford, here in Illinois. And more."

"You've lived in Chicago, and you root for the St. Louis Cardinals?"

"I'd be grateful if you wouldn't spread that around, sir." Sean delivered the line like a character out of a movie. Mark had to smile.

"Why are those kids carrying bags?" Sean asked.

"Every parade-goer knows that the people in the parade throw candy. Sometimes lots of it. Expect to get hit with Tootsie Rolls."

A siren pierced the air, announcing the parade's approach. The sound of it made him feel uneasy. He tried to shake off the feeling and peered down the street to see the front line of the parade a block distant.

"We had homecoming parades like this in Arizona, but I spent a lot of time watching Illinois parades in the summer with my grandparents. Patti did also, when she was old enough to come. High school bands use small town events for parade practice. So, if you wanted to, you could find a parade on almost any Saturday in the summer."

"What's in this parade?" Sean asked.

"School principals. Homecoming king and queen with their attendants. Floats from every class competing against each other. High school clubs. Class officers.

Cheerleaders. Oh, and the football team of course. Usually in jerseys and looking tough for the game—"

Mark's phone rang. The screen showed an incoming call from Pim Montgomery.

"Got to take this, Sean. It's the college. Save my curb for me, okay?"

He walked quickly down the side street behind them, away from the noise. "Pim? Thanks for calling back. What's the news?"

"Just heard back from my friend Lionel Davidson. We had a great time talking, but you don't want to hear that part. He says Baiss was thirteen years old when he took him on. Taught him until just after his sixteenth birthday."

So, this Davidson would have been the last teacher Baiss had before he ran away.

"What happened then? What made him stop teaching Baiss?"

"A big argument with Baiss's father. It was quite a blow-up. John Channon even threatened Davidson. Davidson says he's never been through anything like that in his whole career and never wants to again. He almost quit teaching."

"Did he say what the argument was about?"

"Apparently, the father wanted the son to be a superstar of superstars, so he was insisting that Baiss work on Bach's Goldberg Variations. That's a piece for a more mature artist, even among the gifted.

"Davidson wanted Baiss to wait five more years at least. You can damage young musicians by rushing them —even superstars need time to develop. The father would have none of that. Davidson picked a small section of the Variations hoping to get the father off his back, but it didn't work."

"Does Davidson know where Baiss went after leaving him?"

"No. Lionel swears no one else taught the boy in Chicago after he had him. It's a big city, I know, but the world of high caliber teachers is small. They know where everybody is and who's teaching who, just like major league baseball managers keep track of pitchers. He thought Baiss's father might have sent him to Europe to study."

Europe. That was a new thought. Mark kept thinking of Baiss being somewhere in the United States, but Europe? How do you find someone when they could be anywhere in the world?

"But Pim, if he were studying somewhere else, wouldn't there be news of his performances? You can't keep that hidden."

"Wait a minute..."

He heard Pim tapping on his computer keys. Then Pim's voice returned, slow and distracted, the sound of someone reading and talking at the same time.

"I'm not seeing anything on Baiss Channon since he performed with the Omaha Symphony in November of 2001—a memorial concert for those who died when the World Trade Center fell.

"Davidson got Baiss a spot onstage, a short piano solo between two other musicians doing larger works. Baiss played a song called *Lament*."

Pim was back to his usual conversation speed now. "I

remember Davidson telling me about that. He got choked up, could barely get the words out. It must have been a magical moment. This young guy playing what was in everyone's heart right there on the stage. After he finished, there were a few moments of hushed silence. Then a roar of applause, applause like gratitude, because Baiss had put into music what their hearts needed to know. Davidson said it went on for a long time. The audience didn't want to let Baiss go. But that's all the boy had prepared, and others were waiting to perform."

Mark could imagine the moment. What it must have felt like to be in the concert hall, listening to music that healed your soul. He wished with all his might he could have been there.

Pim spoke again. "Want to know something else?"

"Please."

"This might just be gossip, but Davidson believes the father was jealous of the son. That he was subconsciously trying to destroy the son's career." Pim hesitated. "What's that noise?"

"Music, actually," Mark replied. "A homecoming parade. I think an elementary school band just went by. Anything else?"

"Just a piece of trivia, if you're interested, about Baiss Channon's real name."

"What do you mean? What real name?"

"His full name was meant to be an anagram of Johann Sebastian Bach. Here it is: Baiss J.A. Beath Channon." Pim spelled it out for him. "Beath rhyming with Heath of course."

"That's it? That's the best they could do?"

Pim laughed and hung up.

Mark tried to form a picture in his mind, something that would enable him to see the real Baiss. A child prodigy with a heart that matched his talent. Given a really odd name by a pugnacious, possibly jealous father. As rich as anyone could want to be. Surrounded by a competitive, vicious, grasping family. What had Todd said once? That Baiss was not a normal kid. But the Channons were not a normal family. Didn't have normal feeling for each other, the feeling that a family should. Except for Elizabeth. Elizabeth missed Baiss with all her heart, that was obvious.

Sean was waving for him to come back. Mark hurried to his place just in time to see a blue pick-up truck with a dozen students standing in the truck bed. All wore black sunglasses and snapped their fingers as they sang a light-hearted, energetic tune into their handheld microphones.

"Elizabeth's in the cab!" Sean cried. He waved vigorously and called out to her. "Elizabeth!"

Mark waved too. He could see a smile of recognition on Elizabeth's face, followed by a handful of candy, which flew out the truck window.

"I know that song. It's 'Blue Skies.'" Sean started humming along.

They listened until the jazz choir truck was far down the street, the sound of its song replaced by a song blaring from the freshman class float—an aqua blue depiction of life under the sea.

Sean poked his shoulder, while unwrapping a Tootsie Pop. "There's a man across the street staring at us."

"What do you mean 'staring at us'? He's got a whole

parade to watch." But Mark looked. "That's Will Channon. I wouldn't think him the parade-watching type."

The gray-haired man seemed oblivious to the commotion streaming down the road between them. His head did not move to right or left. He stayed fixed.

"He is either looking at us," said Mark, "or at the 1895 beauty behind us." Mark raised his hand and waved. Will flinched as if someone had struck him, then turned and ambled down the sidewalk, going the same direction as the parade.

Another float went by. Sophomores dressed as aliens sitting on what looked like a moonscape. The float passed on, and Mark saw Will go up the front walk of the next house down. He climbed the steps slowly, almost sadly.

A sign in the front yard announced "For Sale." Did Will live there? At the top of the steps, Will paused and patted the railing. Mark stared at the motion. It was like someone absentmindedly patting a beloved dog.

"Have you had enough of the parade?" asked Sean. "How much longer is it?"

"You can't leave before the high school marching band goes by. They're the grand finale. And I'm a sucker for a marching band."

"Think your brain can handle that much noise?"

"Don't know. We'll see."

Sean leaned back on his hands, a doubtful look on his face, when Mark's phone rang.

"The college again." He got up and went down the street as before. This time it was Jerry.

"I stole a little time this week to look up the Channons. I think you might find this interesting."

"Shoot."

"The big news at the moment is about their corporations. Channon World is the big one that owns the others, and it's had negative earnings five years running. A Dutch firm is looking into purchasing them, and according to this article at least, negotiations are struggling along. Seems they do not want to keep the current Channon anywhere near the driver's seat."

"Which Channon?"

"Wilhelm."

"That *is* interesing."

"And there are rumors that something is not right with the corporate accounting."

"What do you mean? Like money disappearing?"

"Something like that. But it's just a few news articles, so—"

"I know. Not enough known yet."

"I didn't find anything recent on Baiss Channon. Any news about him seems to have disappeared when he did. I'll keep looking for you, okay? Oh, and Mark?" Jerry's voice sounded awkward. Hesitant. "I wanted you to know that we hired Michael Kim for the Asian History slot."

Mark was completely surprised. He didn't know the hiring committee had met. And he should have known. He was on the committee.

Was.

How did he feel about not being a part of it?

He didn't know. But, Jerry was waiting for an answer.

"Well, that's good," Mark said. "I liked Kim. He would have gotten my vote."

Jerry sighed with what sounded like relief. "Glad to

have that wrapped up and done. You take care." And he hung up.

"WHAT'S UP?" said the ever-observant Sean when Mark returned.

"Just a lot going on at the college." It felt like another world. Far away from this one.

"We can check your email as soon as we get back," Sean said. "And look, the marching band is coming. Have a lollipop. Nurse's orders. But we're stepping back half a block for the sake of your head."

The thought came to him as the clarinet section marched by in perfect rows—tall, white plumes waving in the air. Will Channon definitely had a reason for needing Baiss to return. But only if the family's hopes were true, and Baiss would indeed bring big money with him.

Of course, if Baiss did not return, presumably the house could be sold and the money split up. Wasn't that what the first round of Channon arguments had been about?

Even though they had moved some distance from the parade, Mark still clapped with the rest of the crowd as the band went by. They walked back to the car, the parade over, but the whole Channon family was still marching through his mind.

AS THEY DROVE BACK to Riverview, Sean asked, "By the

way, when is this Channon party? Are they going to need the whole house? Will they kick us out?"

"Don't know. We'll have to ask."

Todd definitely did not want to kick them out. And he was very apologetic about the main hall of the house being off limits that night, but he could show them how to get to the basement elevator, which would take them up to their rooms.

"That will be just fine," Mark said. "We'll do our best to stay out of your way. When is the party?"

"October thirteenth. Just a few weeks away."

Once upstairs they both sat down on the blue-gray carpet, and Sean dutifully opened the laptop and started tapping at the keys. The sight reminded Mark that he needed to say something, to address a subject that hadn't been discussed since it had made its presence known. It was his own doing, and, therefore, his to clean up.

"Look, about the research. I deleted it all one night. Maybe I should be upset, but for some reason I haven't regretted it. Not for one moment. So you don't have to worry about it either. All right?"

Sean nodded. "All right, sir." And there was that in his tone which said it truly was all right.

Mark felt relieved, something tight inside of him letting go. "Okay then. Let's get to the emails."

They had answered the usual ones—from the college, from his parents, and Patti—when Sean stared awkwardly at the screen.

"What is it?" Mark asked.

"A Theodore Monument Company." Sean said the words slowly.

"What?" Then he remembered. "Oh."

"They want you to approve the final lettering and spacing for the marker for Amy Marie Newlin."

The words hit him in the gut like a fist. Instantly, the tears flowed.

He didn't want to see her name in such a final form. Couldn't. He stared across the room at the legs of the ridiculously carved nightstand.

Sean went on gently. "Apparently, they have already been back and forth with your sister several times and have made all the spacing corrections she requested. She approved this one, so it just needs your final word for them to start work on it."

He vaguely remembered Patti saying something about it during the summer.

There was a dustball behind the nightstand that the maid had missed.

Sean spoke again, apologetically, as he turned the screen toward him. "I think it looks nice."

Mark took a deep breath, forcing himself to be resolute.

Amy Marie Newlin
Dearest

He stood up abruptly and went to the tower windows to look at the river. It hurt as much as he thought it would.

"It's fine," he said shortly. "Tell them it's fine."

Sean tapped away. When he finished, Mark was still watching the river. "Are you okay?" Sean asked.

Mark couldn't answer.

"You will make it. You will. For Amy's sake. Your wife is just like my mom. They didn't give us all that love, all those years, just to see us destroy ourselves because they're gone."

Sean shut the laptop and kept talking. His voice, the voice of remembering.

"That's what kept me going after my mom died. For a long time I thought of throwing myself off a bridge somewhere, but I kept seeing her face in my mind. Her eyes telling me how she felt. How she didn't want me to waste the love she had given me. So I stopped looking for bridges."

Mark wiped his face with his hand, and stared at the water through the thinning leaves. "No," he said quietly. "It's never good to look for bridges."

He took a deep breath. "You remind me of a Jewish custom that I heard about."

"Sir?"

"On the seventh day after a burial, the mourner's friends come get him, take him by the arms, and, no matter what he feels like, walk with him out of his house and around the block. It's supposed to be a sign of life for the future. That life will keep on going. That they are there to help walk the life of the future with him."

Sean looked thoughtful. "That's a good custom. So where were you seven days later?"

"In the hospital, flat on my back with a cracked pelvis. Broken ribs. Healing from surgery. Nurses making me breathe into machines to keep pneumonia at bay." He turned and smiled ruefully at Sean. "A medical custom, I suppose."

Sean's eyes were filled with understanding. "That's really rough."

Mark looked back toward the river. "That was the easy part."

He hated talking about these things. Hated remembering. Hated the flood of pain and the fearsome ache that always came with the remembering.

"Riverview House isn't actually on a block," said Sean, "but we could walk around it."

"Riverview House is a block all by itself," he replied, watching a bird swoop out of a tree on the riverbank. "And you've done enough."

MARK THOUGHT about all these things in bed, studying the shadowy ceiling. Tonight, the sadness, instead of keeping him awake, made him horribly tired. He had spent so many days stumbling in the fog of grief. He was weary to the bone.

Amy would want him to push back into life. She would not want to see him defeated by such great sorrow. She had known how much he loved her. There was nothing to prove to her by—as Sean put it—destroying himself. That would actually deny her love for him.

She had taught him so many things about love and about acceptance. Accepting their infertility, not seeing it as failure as he was apt to do. Instead she had poured her love for children into their nephews, into the college students that came over for cake.

But how he missed her voice. Her laughter.

Tears ran down his face, and he barely noticed them.

It was just how things were now. He didn't act like himself anymore. Not with Sean. Not in the emails he had Sean write to others.

The history professor that Sean had brought Sorenson to hear—well, that man didn't exist anymore either.

He had no more energy to think. He rolled onto his side and let the sadness push his eyelids shut.

THE SOUND of a scream pierced the night. Rising in pitch, driven by anguish. A soul-rending, desolate cry. Mark jolted awake and grabbed for his glasses. He was on his feet in an instant and flung open Sean's door.

A snore stopped mid-breath. The unmistakable sound of broken sleep. "What?"

"Did you hear that? A boy is screaming!"

"*What?*" Sean tossed back the covers and followed right behind as Mark went back into the main bedroom.

Nothing but dark silence greeted them. They both stood still in the middle of the floor. Mark turned his head from side to side listening intently.

A short, high-pitched squeal sounded outside. Mark went to the tower window and pulled back the curtain. Several cars were still in the lot, a group of four or five people clustered around them talking, though the restaurant must have closed a while ago. A woman laughed, a silly, tipsy, shriek of a laugh.

"That wasn't it," Mark said. "That wasn't the sound. It was—it was terrible." He glanced at Sean. It was hard to read his expression in the dark.

"Let's check the hall." Sean opened the door slowly.

Dim light came from the small lamps in the hallway. Everything was quiet. A slumbering house. He could hear the loud ticks of the grandfather clock in the main hall downstairs.

A car engine started up. Then another. Car doors slammed. The outside party was breaking up. Indoors, all was still.

Mark didn't know what to do. He couldn't very well prowl the halls of Riverview House this time of night. And where to search? He didn't remember seeing a child among the recent guests. He closed the door and turned on a light.

Sean rubbed his shaved head. He was in his usual nighttime gear, a torn ISU T-shirt and navy basketball shorts. "What do you want to do now?"

Mark ran his hand roughly through his own hair. "I don't know. I know I heard something. I don't remember dreaming anything at all. But, that awful scream." He could still hear it. The memory alone made his heart pick up speed.

"Maybe the house is telling its stories?" Sean offered.

"It can only do that in a manner of speaking." Mark sat down in the tower chair, frustrated and feeling foolish. He looked up at Sean. "You don't really believe that the house is using a physical voice."

"I wouldn't usually. I don't go in for the spooky stuff. But, knowing you, and knowing this place, I bet you heard something. Maybe even a fox or an owl."

"Maybe. It could be."

They listened awhile longer.

Nothing.

Sean went back to bed. Mark stayed in the tower chair with his number puzzle book, gazing out, trying to shake the last of the bewildered feeling. He must have been dreaming of something. Or, like Sean said, must have heard an animal.

Rebecca Powell came into view, walking slowly up the drive, just as when he had first seen her. Now she wore long sleeves against the chill of the autumn air. But the impression of trying to carry an intolerable weight was still there. She stopped under a streetlight, eyeing the house, as if the remaining slope was too great for her.

For some reason, he found himself silently hoping. *You can make it, Rebecca. You've got the strength.*

She began to move again toward the house. A few moments after, he heard the door downstairs open and shut. Then nothing. No other sounds. If the house had been speaking, it was not going to say anything more.

18

The Ritornello Game

MARK WALKED across the parking lot toward his car, keys in hand, ready for the doctor appointment that Matheson had made for him before he left Marlonburg. And he was going by himself.

The amusing thing about this outing was watching Sean hovering with concern, while trying *not* to hover with concern. They both knew Mark could do this—his first solo flight—and he wasn't worried in the least. His headaches had eased, and it would be good to hear what the doctor thought about things. Afterwards, there was something else Mark wanted to do, and he would rather do it alone.

"Call me if you need me, okay?" Sean had said, following him down the stairs and out the front door. "I'll run over to pick you up. Literally run. Don't worry about it."

"I won't. Because I won't need you to. Besides, what would I call you on? Have you kept up that prepaid phone of yours?"

Sean looked embarrassed. "It's out right now. I guess if you call the house, they'll find me. I'll just be with George cleaning the leaves out of the gardens."

Mark was surprised how much Sean loved to help with the gardening. Then again, Sean was a healthy guy, and in great shape. He probably needed to work with his hands or go crazy.

"I'll be fine," he replied. "You and George have fun."

Sean seemed to sense that enough was enough. He nodded and went around the side of the house to find George. Mark climbed in his car and headed out onto the now familiar streets of Ashington Mills. Whether he had ever expected to or not, he was healing. He was physically stronger.

The doctor seemed to think so too. Blood pressure, pulse, vital signs, and the physical exam were all declared satisfactory.

"You've lost some of your immunity with most of your spleen gone," he said. "So, if you find yourself getting sick, especially with a fever, give my office a call, and we'll prescribe antibiotics for you right away. All right? Otherwise, rest your eyes often as you increase your normal work, but overall you're doing very well.

"Oh, you don't need me to tell you this, but avoid any blows to the abdomen. And don't hit your head either."

"I'll do my best, sir," Mark replied.

"Healing can be a long road," the doctor added. "You're making great progress."

That was something.

Mark drove from the doctor's office to the visitors' parking section at Ashington College and made his way to the library's local history room. It was empty.

Several things puzzled him. How did Elizabeth fit into the family? Why was there such a difference between her and the rest of her siblings?

Also, what happened about thirteen or fourteen years ago, when, according to Pim Montgomery, Ernest Channon's career began to sour? Was that about the time Baiss ran away? Were they linked somehow?

And, what kind of picture could he find of Baiss Channon's life?

Mark was still haunted by that cry in the night. Odd though it sounded, even to himself, he connected that cry with the Channons. More specifically, Baiss. Even if it had been made by a screech owl.

He went right to the book the librarian had first found for him, and picked up where he had left off. Scanning and skimming. He didn't want to spend his limited reading power on anything that didn't pertain.

The word "scandal" caught his eye, and he slowed to look at the headline. *Secret Wedding Causes Scandal.* A gray-haired John Channon, Senior was pictured next to a much younger woman. From that background, it looked like the couple was honeymooning on some Caribbean island. The caption read, "Industrial Tycoon Marries Dead Wife's Maid."

According to the story, six months after John's first

wife Nora died, John slipped away and married Marie Allen, a younger woman who had been his wife's personal attendant for twelve years. John's five children avoided the couple on their return.

Five? Only five children? Where was the sixth?

Wait a minute. Mark looked closely at the picture of Marie Allen Channon. She had Elizabeth's hair.

He leaned back in his chair to rest his eyes again. That would explain many things. Why the older siblings had the air of entitlement about them while the youngest, the poor maid's daughter, did not. Why Fia and Juliane felt they could torment Elizabeth in front of anyone, as on the day he signed up for piano lessons. Why they could use her concert for their own purposes, to set up Ernie and strike him down. Why Elizabeth helped in the kitchen.

He flipped more pages and found an article on Baiss Channon's performance in Omaha, written by a Nebraska music critic, who had nothing but praise for the boy. "An unusual and prodigious talent whose heart-filled performance helped heal the people of Omaha after our nation's horrific tragedy."

Then, with one page turn, there it was. *Wealthy Channon Dies*. Mark checked the date. Barbara Channon, Baiss's mother, had died fifteen years ago.

Mark thought out loud. "He ran away after his mom died, then."

He flipped through the remaining pages, and the image of a car wreck caught his eye. He shuddered, but he had to check the date. John Christoph, or John Junior, had died five years after his wife. He had been drinking. The woman with him, a "Mrs. Channon hopeful," had died as well. But John's son Baiss had been long gone by then.

Mark sat back and rubbed his eyes gently. He stared at a piece of blank wall for a while, counting backwards by sevens. Then took a deep breath, closed the book, and stood up to stretch his legs.

What had Baiss's father done about his son's departure? The last entries of Channon history said absolutely nothing about a missing heir. Would news of a missing Baiss bring the wolves out? Put him in greater danger? Had the father's silence been for the son's protection? And not, as some thought, so his own star could shine alone?

A historian always needs original source documents. But any private papers would be kept somewhere else, perhaps at a lawyer's office. There's no way he would get access to any of that.

He had so much more to study, but his eyes were protesting and his brain was uneasy. He didn't want to undo all the physical healing of the past weeks. It had been hard enough to do the first time.

He scribbled in his notebook and slid it back into his pocket. Time to go. He had enough to chew on for awhile.

The biggest question remained. *Where was Baiss?* And, if he could come back, why wasn't he? Especially if he had a talent the world was waiting for?

A sudden urge made him go to one of the computers along the wall and poke it into life. He didn't dare look at the screen long, but a few glances could suffice.

He typed Baiss Channon's name into the search box, closed his eyes while the computer flickered, then looked at the dates on all the articles listed about him. He had to see for himself what Pim had pointed out. Sure enough, there was nothing more on Baiss Channon since the performance in Omaha and the subsequent reviews.

Nothing at all.

FOR JUST ONE moment he swelled with pride, like a grade-schooler who had run a race and come in first on Field Day. All because he had impressed his piano teacher and made her happy. He had worked hard on two extra pieces and begun memorizing the *Intrada.*

Elizabeth was smiling, a perfectly wonderful smile, and he was little-boy-cocky that he had brought it about. "I had the extra week, remember, because of homecoming." He was babbling.

She wrote some final notes on the side of Jeremiah Clarke's March and handed it back to him. "Very well done! Just tighten up the fingering in those measures, and look ahead for other pieces you would like to play."

She reached for her coat, and he said, "You're not working here tonight?" He had hoped for a few more minutes of conversation. He had been waiting all lesson long for a chance to ask about her father's memorial birthday party.

"No. Tonight's the fall play at the high school. I've already got a substitute."

As if on cue, the heavy oak door slid open from the outside, and a tall, sandy-haired man poked his head in. "I'm here to take your shift now, Elizabeth."

"Thanks so much, Jim!"

Jim hesitated, looking a bit anxious. "Wish me luck!" he said, before darting away.

"Wish him luck?" Mark asked.

Elizabeth picked up her purse and slid the strap over her shoulder. "Nick has been difficult lately. He's going to cater the birthday party and has the unfortunate habit of sharing his nerves with everyone."

Before Mark could comment, another head poked through the doorway. "Oh, good," said Sean, looking around the room. "You've finished. I'm not too early then. Hi there, Elizabeth. That was a great parade. Thanks for the candy. Hey, professor, I have a question. Have you heard of Simone Weil?"

"A French philosopher during wartime," he answered automatically. "Died young."

"I want to talk through some of her thoughts with you. They've got my mind stirring."

"Sounds good." Mark turned to Elizabeth. "We're leaving too. May we walk out with you?"

The three of them exited the house together, as comfortable and natural as three friends. It was a good feeling, and Mark wondered at it.

"What's this about Simone Weil?" Elizabeth asked.

Sean was his most engaging self. "I got a book on twentieth-century European philosophers from the library. I've only read the first chapter, but I've got enough material to keep the professor up all night."

She smiled at that and now it was Sean's turn to be little-boy-cocky at having been the cause.

Mark held open the door of her silver Passat as she got in, still wondering how to bring up the subject of the party. "Thanks so much for the lesson. I'm sorry there's tension in the kitchen. That must be rough."

Her smile vanished. "It's just going to be hard until the party's over." She looked back toward the house. Gray clouds were building behind it, promising rain in the evening.

"I don't think this birthday party tradition was a good idea of my father's."

"Why is that?" Mark asked.

"He was an old man when he wrote that into his will, and he only wanted something that he loved to continue on after his death."

Mark was confused. "What did he want to continue?"

She turned the key in the ignition and the motor came to life. "A game for music lovers. A game he invented for his children so we could learn about Bach and the Baroque. A game that meant more to him and certain members of his family than it ever could to any party-goer."

She lowered her window as he closed the door for her. "The Ritornello Game."

"It sounds interesting."

She put her car in reverse. "It is. To some. Others consider it a misery, which ruins the whole memory." She shrugged her shoulders. "In one week it will all be over." She waved at Sean. "Have fun with your philosophers."

They stood in the parking lot and watched the small silver car go down the drive. Mark could guess that Baiss and Elizabeth were two who had loved John Senior's game.

"What do you think the Ritornello Game is?" he asked Sean.

"Don't know. You want to go back in the house for anything?"

He was still holding his piano book. "Not really."

"One of the librarians at the college was talking about this great pizza place over on Nineteenth Street."

"Pizza and a French philosopher? Sounds good to me."

IT WASN'T A SPORTS BAR, which meant they'd be able to really talk. It was a light, happy restaurant with Italian folk music playing in the background, white tile floors, red tablecloths, green plants everywhere, and the rich smell of cheese, tomatoes, and garlic.

They gave their order at the counter, grabbed silverware and napkins, filled paper cups at the soda fountain, and chose a table. Sean automatically leaned back in his chair and stretched out his long legs. "This is living," he said.

"It definitely smells promising." Mark unwrapped his straw and inserted it into his raspberry iced tea. "And, I think I know which quote of Simone Weil's you wanted to discuss."

Sean sat up eagerly, long arms leaning on the table. "All right. Have a go."

"'Imaginary evil is romantic and varied,'" he quoted. "'Real evil is gloomy, monotonous, barren, boring.'"

Sean's mouth dropped open. "How did you guess?"

"It's a famous line, and very true. Plus, you've been

reading about the Medicis. Are you applying your newfound knowledge, Watson?"

"Trying to."

"Let me start you off. Thinking with Simone here: Real evil doesn't necessarily wear robot suits or fire laser bolts from the sky like in hero movies. It wears T-shirts, wool suits, or Renaissance gowns.

"Real evil is boringly resentful, keeping the same grudges year after monotonous year. It considers hatred its personal right. It burns with jealousy or envy of others, while producing nothing good, true, life-giving, or lasting. It is barren, just as Weil said. Is that enough for starters?"

"If it can produce nothing, then what is evil's point, Holmes?" Sean asked the question in total Watson character, which made Mark almost laugh. Yet Sean looked truly interested. And interest has a life-giving power of its own.

He could have been sitting on his back porch talking with Jerry and Luedders, working through ideas.

"The point is," he said, "that evil has an endgame. It reduces people, especially the people who wield it." He took a drink. "And then it destroys them."

"Like hatred," Sean put in.

"Exactly. Hatred takes over people, and then that is all they are, a mass of hatreds. Jealousy does the same." Mark found himself thinking of Ernie.

"I think that when we pretend evil doesn't exist," Sean said slowly, "we become an easy target for it."

There was vulnerability in the way Sean spoke the words. Some experience was in them. Mark waited a moment, hoping for more, but Sean didn't continue.

"Very good, Watson," he said lightly.

Sean looked right at him, all bantering gone. "You were talking about the Channons, weren't you?"

The swift change of emotion took Mark by surprise.

"Possibly," he said calmly.

Sean's only answer was a nod. He pulled the napkin in his hand into a long strip.

Mark waited, but Sean didn't say anything more.

Mark stirred the ice in his cup. "If we study their context, we see a family of achievers. Big achievers in both business and music. On a stage that is larger than what the average person stands on.

"Achievement of any sort brings its own kind of attention. And if you are born into a family with a high need for attention and achievement, and you are desperate for it, competing for it, well, it's too easy for humans to choose the lowest path."

"It's okay. We don't have to talk about this." Sean was picking at the tablecloth with his fingertips. "I don't think I *want* to understand the Channons."

"Understanding doesn't mean approval."

Sean looked up. "No?"

"Absolutely not, although people often make it sound that way."

"All right."

Mark wasn't sure if Sean wanted him to continue. Or if he had anything more to add to that thought, so he went down another avenue.

"I'd like to know what Baiss Channon is thinking now. He must be aware of this family party tradition. Perhaps he's even wondering if he should make an appearance this time."

"He hasn't come yet, has he?" said Sean. "If I were him, I wouldn't come."

"I don't know if I would either. If he did come, he'd have to have a compelling reason why. And he would have to come with strength, something that would mark his territory, so to speak."

"And protection," Sean added.

The pizza arrived and they both devoted themselves to taking large bites, trying not to burn their mouths.

Sean looked preoccupied, so Mark wasn't surprised when he said, "I have a particular question to ask you."

"Shoot." Mark took another swig of tea.

"Could I borrow your car tomorrow night? I have a date."

Mark wiped his hands on his napkin. Was Sean actually blushing? "It's not Kelly, is it?" For some reason, Mark found himself hoping it wasn't Kelly.

"Nope."

"Who then?"

"Felicitas. We've been meeting in the library some mornings. I really like her. I've already asked George."

Mark did not hide his delight. "Good choice. Take the car with my blessing."

As they finished their pizza, Mark thought about the Channon birthday party. It was sad that it was something Elizabeth dreaded. And he was glad that he and Sean would be miles away from Ashington Mills that day.

19

———

Rebecca's Request

THE DAY of the Channon party arrived. Mark awoke to a light gray sky. He was in the bathroom first and showered. Having a beard sure saved time most mornings. Today he was eager to clear out and have an adventure. It was good, so good, to feel some kind of energy again.

Back in his room, he pulled on jeans and a button-down shirt, then set out his satchel on the bed. After a moment, he put it back in the closet. Today was for looking outward, to new things. He and Sean were going exploring and wouldn't return until after midnight. He would only need his notebook and pocket pen. And a handkerchief.

He got clean socks from the dresser drawer, leaned on the edge of the bed, and pulled them on. They were planning to drive up the river as far as Galena, maybe even into Wisconsin, and he was going to drive part of it. He had set himself a twenty-mile minimum goal, and planned to accompany that with good, even breathing and a stream of thoughts telling his brain to stay calm.

It would be the first road trip he had driven on since the accident. He would probably have to count backwards by sevens from one million in order to keep his brain together, but he was going to do this. He was resolved.

A knock sounded on the door. When he opened it, he was astonished to find Rebecca Powell standing there.

"Rebecca! Is something wrong?"

"I have a favor to ask you—" She broke off, listening. A kind of howling noise came from the bathroom.

"Oh. That's Sean. He imitates jazz crooners in the shower when he thinks no one can hear him."

She almost smiled at this, but whatever her need, it did not allow for levity. "I have a favor to ask of you, Professor Newlin. One of our regular workers—Jim—is sick today. A high fever, maybe the flu, and Nick is real upset.

"We can cover Jim's kitchen duties, but Nick wants a man to stand at one end of the serving table to assist guests. You have such a distinguished presence that we'd like you to take his place there. Oh—"

She stopped as if she had just remembered something. "You won't have to lift anything. It's mostly standing and directing work, showing guests where things are. Making them feel well cared for. Most of them will think you're a detective or an undercover agent of some kind. I don't think it would be too hard for you, your health, I mean?"

Her words came to an end, and she stood watching him anxiously.

For a few moments he didn't know what to say. In the gap of silence, Sean's voice came clearly through. Mark recognized the sound of "Luck Be a Lady."

The moment was awkward. He really didn't want to do it, but he didn't want to add to the hidden burdens that Rebecca already carried. How often had he witnessed her nightly struggle just to make it. A thought came to him. This would give him the opportunity to witness the Ritornello Game.

He took a deep breath. "What will I wear?" he said.

"We keep a couple of black suits on hand. I'll bring them up and you can see which fits you." She darted down the hallway toward the back stairs.

Mark shut the door, and held still for a moment, absorbing the meaning of what he had just committed to. He reached into his pocket, took out his notebook and pen and set them on the dresser top. The shower water turned off. Sean was humming a tune Mark couldn't recognize.

Another knock at the door. Rebecca held up suits covered in dry cleaner's plastic. "Try them all on. Mix and match if you have to. Do you have a white shirt?"

Mark went to the closet, took one out, and held it up.

"I think that will work," she said. "Here's your tie." Long and black.

"I need to go. Come down to the kitchen to show us when you have it all on, okay? Oh, and Todd will refund part of your bill as payment. Thank you so much!" She hurried away.

Mark laid the suits out across the bed. He pulled the

plastic off the middle one and slipped the coat off the hanger.

"What's all this?" Sean appeared, ready to go, book bag over one shoulder. He eyed the suits on the bed suspiciously.

Mark told him, using the act of trying on a coat in front of the mirror to avoid seeing his reaction.

Sean lowered his book bag slowly to the floor. Disappointment lay heavy on him. "Man, I don't want to be anywhere near this house when all those people arrive."

"You don't have to be. You can still go."

Sean studied him for a moment. "I know. You don't really need a nurse. I'm more like a health coach and research assistant. Whenever you start a new project, I mean," he added hastily.

Mark buttoned the coat and studied its fit in the mirror. "I'm doing research tonight."

HE CAME DOWNSTAIRS for wardrobe approval and found himself in a fast-moving kitchen where Nick yelled orders at everyone. Rebecca took Mark out into the main hall, showed him the layout of the party, and explained what would be expected of him. She gave him a menu card to memorize, then left him alone.

Mark took the card and escaped out to the gardens for some relief. But here, also, activity prevailed. George had a small crew stringing lights on the porches and installing lanterns in the plantings and along the walkways. As Mark walked over to admire the work, George stepped toward him.

"Mr. Newlin, will you watch out for my daughter tonight? She does not understand how some men can behave." Concern was on his face.

"Yes, I'll be glad to watch out for her." He spoke with sincere confidence.

George studied Mark's face a few moments longer. He looked like he wanted to say more, but just nodded. "Thank you." He turned away to his work again.

Mark waved at Sean, who was draping lights around the gazebo, then went inside and up to his room for what he knew would be a much-needed, preparatory rest.

At seven fifty, Mark was at his post on the study side of the large fireplace's inglenook. Kelly was stationed opposite him on the dining room side, wearing an enthusiastic smile he had never seen before. Between them stretched a long, white-covered table filled with silver candelabras, glowing candles, and masses of heavy-headed autumnal flowers in crystal vases.

Mark felt like he was waiting for the opening act of a play—staring at the front door as if it were the curtain ready to go up. By a quirk of fate, he was not in the audience, but part of the production this time. Part of the stage crew, waiting for the Channons and their friends to make their entrances.

He felt the rush of anticipation. Mind alert. Ready.

At five minutes to eight, the string quartet took their places in front of the grandfather clock. Kitchen staff settled large silver platters of exquisitely designed appetizers on the table next to him. Nick stood in front of the table like an orchestra conductor, making sure everything was artistically perfect.

Rebecca Powell—in a long, midnight blue dress—stood near the front door with a tuxedoed Todd Channon. The official greeters to this party. Mark wondered where Stephanie was. Probably upstairs attending to the guests who were staying in the house.

Felicitas placed a serving scoop next to him. He tilted his head toward her and said quietly, "Remember. We make contact every fifteen minutes." He tapped his watch. "I promised."

She gave him a patient smile and a nod before turning back to the kitchen.

"Oh, it's the ailing professor," said a voice next to him. "And you are still wearing that unfortunate beard." Fia, dressed in long, shimmery silver with diamonds on her ears, already held a glass, which he guessed held her beloved gin and tonic.

Mark stood at attention, hands crossed and clasped in front of him. "It is necessary, ma'am. FBI. Undercover."

She stared at him, believing for just a moment, before letting out a single laugh.

Juliane joined their little group. She had chosen the color gold to shimmer in, and jealousy rose in Fia's eyes as she took in her sister's appearance.

"Baker's going to make an announcement tonight," Juliane said.

"He is? Of what? How do you know?" Fia's questions tumbled over each other.

Juliane looked annoyed. "What do you think he could

possibly announce, Fia?" She moved away, her older sister on her heels.

"Julie! Tell me! He found Baiss, didn't he! Didn't he?"

The front door swept open and a group of guests entered already talking, as if the party had begun on the front porch. At the same time, more descended the stairs from the guest rooms above, expensively dressed and tuxedo-clad. It was beginning to look like a night at the Oscars. The sound of voices rivaled the string quartet in volume. Guests approached the beautifully laid out food tables.

Mark practiced his "hospitable and welcoming smile" as Rebecca had termed it, arm extended toward the table. "Please. Enjoy."

Snatches of conversation swirled around him as guests filled their plates and moved away.

"I wasn't here the last time the Channons held a party. All together, I mean."

"I haven't been to one of these since, well, since before John died."

"Oh, further back, dear. Before Barbara died, surely!"

"You know, curiosity is the only thing that could drag Lou and me here."

"Do you see the cream in this? Just looking at it will make me fat."

"Look at that beautiful girl!"

"Such a natural."

Mark turned and caught Felicitas' eye. They nodded at each other, and she went back towards the kitchen, empty platter in hand. Talk continued to flow.

"How was Paris, darling? A trifle boring this time? I told you not to go."

"I never liked the color of all this paneling. I don't care how historical it is, it's overdone. I'd paint white all over it."

"Do you know why that front door is so wide? They had home funerals when this house was built, and the door had to be wide enough for a coffin to go through. Really. Isn't that ghastly?"

"Good to see you, Will. How's business?"

This was answered with a grunt. The head of Channon World stood nearby, drink in hand, looking morose.

"I hear Ernest is going to play for us tonight," a woman said, as she slid a stuffed mushroom onto her plate.

Ernie was standing at the entrance to the large parlor holding his hands away when people reached for them in greeting. Some looked slightly offended. Others appeared familiar with this eccentricity. Mark glanced around to find the one Channon he hadn't seen yet: Elizabeth.

She was standing by the quartet, speaking to the cellist. Her dark hair was not swept up like the other women's, but tumbled long and curly down her back. She wore a dark red evening gown and looked truly lovely. He felt proud of his piano teacher.

The women filling their plates with stuffed shrimp and melon batons caught sight of her at the same time. "Oh, look. That's Elizabeth!"

"So what? There's nothing exciting about the daughter of a maid, darling. Lowers the family prestige. Old John must have been off his head."

"When a man is grieving, he's likely to do any stupid thing. And what they say is true. Second marriages do produce differently from the first."

They seemed to realize that Mark was standing there listening.

"But she's such a nice person," one said a little too quickly.

"Oh, yes, and so kind of the older ones to let her come."

They picked up their wine glasses and plates, and moved away.

The daughter of a maid? Is that how they saw Elizabeth?

Todd Channon approached, escorting two gray-haired gentlemen to the food table, and he looked nervous, trying hard to please. The men, one tall, the other of average height, didn't look as though they would bite, but Mark detected an unmistakable air of authority about them.

Todd looked at him desperately, as a drowning man spies a rope. "Gentlemen, please allow me to introduce our professor to you. This is Dr. Mark Newlin, a professor of history at Gold College, popular teacher and author. He's spending his sabbatical with us this fall."

That sounded like more than Mark was worth.

"Dr. Newlin, this is Leal Baker, our lawyer, and Warren Egan, president of Ashington Bank. They are the brilliant men who watch over all things Channon." Todd gave an ingratiating smile, then glanced over his shoulder in the direction of the grandfather clock. "I must attend to something. Please excuse me."

Mark held out his hand. Egan, the tall one, shook it first, then Baker.

"You're the lawyer?" Mark asked. "I've seen your office on the city square."

"Yes, that's mine." Baker looked at him, then at the table, and returned to him with a questioning glance. "You don't look to be engaged in typical professorial duties, Dr. Newlin." Baker had a shrewd look.

"Someone got sick at the last minute, and I stepped in," Mark replied. "Friend of the family of sorts." Wasn't sure why he said that. Friend of Elizabeth and Rebecca at least.

Baker still looked like he wanted to interrogate the witness. "And what are you doing during your sabbatical, sir?"

"Resting actually, while I enjoy this part of the state. Oh, and I have the privilege of taking piano lessons from Elizabeth."

At this, Baker's hardness softened. He glanced in her direction. "She's the real treasure of this family."

Egan put in. "She had a double tragedy the year John Channon died. Her fiancé died too."

"Yes, I heard that." said Mark. Todd's needy introduction had given him an unexpected conversational opening with these men. But it was his association with Elizabeth that had given him instant status. That was interesting, but somehow, not surprising.

Before he could say anything more, a loud glissando came from the large parlor's grand piano—a single, bold slide from the bass to the highest treble note that made Mark's head tingle.

"The performance is ready to begin," said Egan. "We better grab some food and get in there." This was said matter-of-factly, as someone familiar with what was expected.

Most of the guests moved in the direction of the large parlor. Not all could fit, of course. A thick circle of people stood at the doorway, just as Mark had done the first night he heard Ernie play. Some guests ignored the summons and wandered around the main hall, looking closely at the paintings, or the clock, or a porcelain vase on a table.

A young man in a tuxedo stood alone by the entrance to the small parlor, his back to the wall. He had a studious look to him, the kind that comes from a life shaped by the indoors. No one appeared to know him or talk to him, and the expression on his face suggested that he did not expect to be known by anyone.

Did he look to be about thirty? Did he have any physical resemblance to the Channon family? Mark couldn't answer either question. Amy had always been better at that sort of thing, noticing similarities in the shape of a nose or the spacing of the eyes. Whenever she pointed it out, he agreed with her, but he had never been good at coming up with it himself.

Sudden, energetic music poured from the large parlor, drawing everyone's attention. There was no mistaking that light, quick, complex music that was the Baroque era's gift to the world. Mark could hear gasps of appreciation. This was definitely Ernie's place to shine—a perfect fit of audience to performer.

Nick appeared from somewhere, studied the table, removed a piece of fuzz that had settled onto the cake—a cake shaped and iced in the perfect image of Riverview House—swore under his breath, and hurried back to the kitchen.

Mark looked around for the young man who had stood by himself along the wall, but he had gone. Elizabeth was part of the crowd that couldn't fit into the parlor. She caught Mark's eye and gave him a quizzical look before walking across the hall toward him.

"I'm doing an impersonation of Jim," he said.

"You're filling in? Why?"

"Jim has influenza."

She shook her head. "They never should have asked you to do this."

"Well, I am finding it all very interesting."

She looked concerned for a moment, and he hurried to say, "As a historian, not a gossip columnist."

"I know."

He opened his mouth to ask her about the young man by the wall, but didn't get the chance.

A tall blond man with an assured manner came striding toward them. "Elizabeth! There you are! Let's have a drink." Before she could answer, he took her arm and swept her in the direction of the dining room bar.

Mark watched them go, thinking of Elizabeth. A woman pressured and pulled by the members of her family, and now this stranger. Yet, Mark had seen her with her students at the concert in this very hall. It had been clear that they both respected and adored her. Perhaps it was with her students that she could truly be herself.

Egan came to the table again and scooped some shrimp onto his plate. He caught Mark's eye. "I'm starving.

Missed dinner to be here." He looked in the direction of the dining room door, where Elizabeth and the blond man had been a moment ago. "Ol' Dirk is after her money again. Baker's going to blow a gasket. Think I'll eavesdrop for him." He popped a shrimp in his mouth and went into the dining room.

Mark decided at that moment that he liked Warren Egan.

The front door opened to a late arrival—a man in his early sixties who looked familiar to Mark, though he could swear he had never met the man. The newcomer looked around, hesitant for just a moment, then strolled in boldly with a smooth confidence that made Mark wonder if he had imagined the hesitation. The man was heading for the food when a woman in a plum-colored gown intercepted him.

"Victor!" she cried. "What are you doing here? Don't tell me Fia invited you."

Victor reached for a china plate and surveyed the offerings. "No, Ernie did."

It came clear to Mark in an instant. The face from the newspaper. Victor Gaff. One of Fia's ex-husbands. The politician. Ernie was getting his revenge for his interrupted performance.

The woman began to exclaim at this revelation, but Victor cut her off with a sharp question. "Is Baiss here?"

She looked bewildered.

"Baiss? I have no idea. I haven't seen him in so long, I don't have a clue as to what he looks like. You'll have to reintroduce me!" She laughed at her own perceived wit.

Victor ignored her and turned to Mark, pointing at the

item he had just put on his plate. "Can you tell me what this is?"

"Lobster roll, sir."

Victor nodded. "Thanks." He made his way slowly down the food table, pausing to stare at the elaborate cake before continuing on. The woman prattled at his side the whole way. At the other end, Victor gave Kelly an appreciative look, and Kelly responded in kind.

Oh, Kelly, don't let your desire for money take you to Victor Gaff.

It felt like the end of a first act.

All the players assembled.

Except perhaps one.

The heart of the drama still to come.

20

The Hired Help

THOUGH MARK WAS proud of his hard-won stamina, he needed to sit down somewhere. The kitchen was the only place free from the scrutiny of guests.

He went over to Kelly. "Is it all right if I take a break now?"

"I think so. I've already had one. Who cares what Nick says?"

"I'll be back soon."

His plan was to find a chair in some corner of the kitchen, but there wasn't one. With an apologetic smile, Felicitas, filling a tray with crab-stuffed tomatoes, pointed outside.

The air was crisp and cold—refreshing after the heat and babble of the main hall. He brushed off a step, sat down, took a deep breath, and let himself relax. He needed to get the Channons and their guests out of his mind for awhile. The currents of tension running through the gathered crowd could power a city block. *Let it go, Mark.*

No light appeared on the river, but the lights nestled in the ornamental grasses set off the plantings beautifully. He checked his watch. Ten minutes. That's all he better allow himself.

An unexpected email from Jerry Waite had arrived while he was getting ready for the party. Here were a few moments to think about it.

Luedders would be taking a group of students to England next semester. But a good number more were petitioning to be let into an already full class. Jerry's request was simple. Would Mark like to go and be the second professor? He could teach two sections of history there, leaving half his sabbatical to use later as he wished.

At this point—breathing the cool air, smelling the rain in the clouds—it seemed like a good idea. Another place of transition to help him get used to a home without Amy.

He skipped over that last thought quickly.

He could go to England. He could go and think and write.

Of course, going with Luedders would mean that Luedders would insist that Mark do one of his favorite things.

Luedders told the story often. On one of his trips to London, he had sat inside the dome of St. Paul's Cathedral and written in a notebook for over an hour. "You'd be surprised at the thoughts you can think, the words that flow out of you, while you are perched in the dome of that magnificent cathedral." Luedders claimed it changed his life, and he made writing in the dome a regular event.

Mark could use that kind of discovery now. He felt lost at sea without Amy. Sitting outside the kitchen door of someone else's house wearing a borrowed suit didn't help. But it didn't hurt either.

Now that his health was truly improving, he was beginning to feel capable again. The outside Mark anyway. The inside Mark? He wasn't sure.

Voices came from the back of the house. Some guests had decided to brave the chill for a walk in the lantern-filled gardens. He could see two of them bending over a bush by the gazebo. A woman touched its leaves gently.

A few others clustered together, talking intently. Their tone—secretive and proud and eager—was the sound of gossips on the scent. Mark felt a wave of dismay.

A male voice raised itself, carrying across the lawn. An insistent voice. Rising and falling, forcefully. The kind of voice that didn't care who heard him. That actually *wanted* to be heard. Though what he was actually saying was hard to make out at this angle and distance.

The gossips went silent. Mark brushed off the seat of his trousers and followed the brick walkway around the back toward the central fountain and the sound of the voice. He could see only two people in the back garden, and by the lamppost he recognized the face of Dirk, the blond man Egan had gone to spy on. The woman was facing away from him and wore a dark red dress. Elizabeth.

Like banker, like professor. Except that professors who

worked on small college campuses were used to stepping into the fray.

Half-empty wine glasses had been left on the short stone wall rimming the fountain. Mark stepped nearer and picked up the glasses, assuming the role of a conscientious butler, scanning the grounds for anything out of place.

"No, *you* are the one who doesn't understand." Dirk was clearly angry. "You will regret this, Elizabeth!" He strode across the grass, mounted the back porch steps, pushed past the watchers, and entered the house with a bang of the door.

The garden gossips seated themselves at a bench under a tree, staring at the place where Elizabeth stood, whispering excitedly to each other. Mark set the glasses down on the face of a sundial.

ELIZABETH STEPPED DEEPER into the shadows and took a long, slow breath. She was angry at Dirk, but also at herself—that she had allowed herself to become part of Dirk's melodramatic scene. Why did he always hunt her up when she least expected it?

That was it. She should have realized that he would be here tonight. If only this would be the last time. If he would just leave her alone!

"Excuse me, ma'am, might I be of assistance?" a voice at her side said quietly.

She started, then, with relief, saw Mark. She shook her head and gave him a wry smile. "I really don't know."

He offered his arm, and she knew what he was doing. He was giving her the chance for a graceful exit.

"Where would you like to go, ma'am? London, Rome, or Capri?"

She tucked her arm through his. "I was thinking of Madrid, actually."

"An excellent choice. I hear Madrid is beautiful this time of year. We have travel agents standing by, ready to make your reservations."

He was waiting, politely, for her to set their real direction.

She dropped the banter. "Could you take me to my car, please? That's where I was trying to go."

"Certainly. Do you have a wrap or something? It's chilly."

It was like him to be considerate, and after Dirk's selfishness, the contrast of kindness was too much for her emotions. She spoke quickly, trying to keep her voice steady.

"I left it in the house. It's all right. I'll pick it up tomorrow. My car will get warm soon."

They walked away from all the watching eyes, down the far side of the house. And she knew that it would take only a few moments for word to get around that the maid's daughter had gone off with the hired help.

MARK RE-ENTERED THE MAIN HALL, his mind still on Elizabeth. Concerned for her. Concerned about what Dirk had said or done to make her leave her family's party.

When he reached his post, Ernie was standing on the landing of the grand staircase, hands on the railing in front of him, addressing the throng below as a preacher at a broad pulpit.

"It is only fitting that at this party—on the anniversary of my father's birthday—we all take part in what he called the Ritornello Game. Some of you good friends may remember this."

Laughter and a few elegant groans. Including a not-so-elegant one from Fia.

Undaunted, Ernie went on. "In many Baroque pieces, the main musical theme is played by all the instruments. Then, a solo instrument plays the next musical theme. The main theme returns, repeated by all instruments together. This recurring main theme is called the *ritornello*, from the Italian word meaning *return*."

Mark was amazed. Ernie spoke well and was easy to listen to. Each word carried a resonance that drew the ear.

"My father invented this game to teach his children about musical structure. We had to listen carefully to a piece. When the solo part would play, we scattered into all the rooms of the house. But when the *ritornello* theme began, played by the whole group, we raced back to this main hall. We had to return to the original theme just as the music did."

Mark couldn't help but stare at the pianist. He felt he was seeing glimpses of the Ernie that could have been. Enthusiastic. Almost warm.

The instructions continued. "Tonight the whole quartet will play the *ritornello*, with each solo instrument taking the parts in between. This is the *ritornello* theme, the one you will hear over and over tonight, the one that will call you to return. Pay attention to it!"

Ernie waved his hand at the quartet. The room hushed as the string players filled the air with a lively melody.

A woman in gray stepped next to Mark. She pointed toward the musicians with her half-empty wine glass. "I don't like this game. I don't like it at all." Her eyes darted from side to side nervously.

Mark tried his best "put-the-guest-at-ease" voice. "Why is that?"

"I've played this before. After his first wife died, John Senior became superstitious about it. He played the game every day after she died, and at the returning part he kept looking for her. Waiting for her to come back. It was creepy." She took a sip from her glass and it jerked a bit as she brought it to her lips.

The music stopped and Ernie's voice rang out again. "When you hear that theme, you must come back to where you are standing now. However, while a solo instrument plays, you may wander the lower level of the house, but keep your ears active! Listen and return!"

A babble of voices answered him, some trying to protest, but Ernie ignored them all and motioned to the musicians. The quartet struck up the melody again. The woman in gray turned to speak to someone else.

The game seemed tragic to Mark. Painful, as he thought of the man searching and waiting for his dead wife. The music could never bring her back, of course. But he could understand the man trying. He could imagine him looking over the heads of the children as they came running back, hoping to see the heart of his life again. Oh, yes, Mark could understand him trying.

He shook himself to change the direction of his thoughts. He was on duty. He had to stay alert.

The Channons, curiously, had somehow stationed themselves at the entrances to the main hall. Will was holding a drink leaning against the doorframe of the study. Juliane was at the entrance to the dining room, wearing her usual mischievous look. Fia was talking to another woman by the painting of John Channon, Senior, in the long foyer. Mark wondered if she had seen Victor yet.

Another tuxedo was talking to Ernie, yet Ernie was clearly ignoring what he said. Were they all watching for someone?

The music shifted. The violinist stood up and began to play alone.

"Go!" cried Ernie. "Go, go go!"

Guests look confused, annoyed, disgusted. They filed obediently into the study, into the the large living room parlor. Some went out the back door for the porch. Many made a big push for the dining room bar, Dirk's blond head among them. No sign of the quiet, young man Mark had seen earlier. Instead he saw what Elizabeth hadn't wanted to see—the destruction of her father's special game.

Warren Egan stopped by on his way to the study. "I should have started by the food. Then every time the music changed, I could return here for another plate."

Mark smiled. "The perfect strategy."

Felicitas collected an empty tray, nodding at Mark,

and took it back to the kitchen. She brought out another, and as she was settling it into its place Mark found himself accosted by Victor Gaff.

Gaff was staring at Felicitas in a way that would have made George Juarez reach for the nearest gardening implement. He pulled a bill from his wallet and, without looking at Mark's face, slid it into his hand. It was a one hundred dollar bill.

"Make sure she's in my car when I leave tonight." He turned away.

"No, sir," said Mark.

Victor turned back and eyed him, a bemused, but confident smile on his face. "Do you know who I am?" he said in a low voice.

"Yes, I do." Mark held the bill back out to him.

Victor stared at it. His face hardened, even while the smile stayed.

"Human beings are not for sale," said Mark.

All of a sudden, Victor grinned and reached for his wallet again.

"At any price," said Mark firmly. He tossed the bill at Victor's feet and resumed his official stance, hands crossed in front of him, standing at attention. Felicitas had disappeared. From the corner of his eye, Mark saw Kelly's jaw drop.

Victor picked up the bill slowly. "Are you trying to humiliate me?"

Mark gave him the look he reserved for students who demanded a high grade, yet refused to study.

Victor glared at him, reddening.

Mark did not flinch and stared right back. Showdown at high noon.

The quartet burst into life. "*Ritornello! Ritornello!*" voices cried out. People poured from the doors and filled the hall from every direction. In the commotion Victor moved away, still glaring.

Someone patted Mark's shoulder. It was Leal Baker. Baker opened his mouth to say something when a sharp cry sounded over the music and the voices.

"I believe Fia has seen Victor," said Mark.

Baker gave a rueful grimace. "I would say she has. Not the *ritornello* she was hoping for."

Mark seized the chance to voice his question. "But she *is* hoping for a *ritornello*, isn't she? Aren't they all hoping Baiss will return?"

"Possibly." The measured, cautious tones of a lawyer were back.

"Do you see any of Baiss's friends here, Mr. Baker? His personal friends?"

The lawyer looked around the room slowly. "I don't think so. But I'm not in a position to know who those friends might be. What is your point, Dr. Newlin?"

"Just that a man would be more likely to return if his friends were here." He had been too nosy in the lawyer's eyes, and he felt it.

"I apologize," he continued. "I have lived here several months and may be too caught up in the family's concerns."

"You need a research project," Baker said dryly.

Mark laughed. "I completely agree with you."

The lawyer gave him a smile; his sternness eased.

The viola player stood up and began to play a slower melody, the kind that called these listeners to be more thoughtful than they wanted to be. But this wasn't about listening, this was about playing a game, and the guests, some still protesting, left the hall again. Baker nodded a farewell and headed toward the study.

Mark caught sight of Juliane laughing. Juliane was one of the last to leave the hall, and Mark got the distinct impression she was enjoying a private joke.

"Psst! Psst! Professor?"

Mark turned to look at Kelly.

"What did he want?"

"Who, Baker?"

"No, the other one."

He had known she meant Victor all along.

"Nothing good," he said.

Nick emerged from the kitchen, followed by Felicitas and Stephanie Channon carrying trays. "Take a break, Kelly," he said. "Five minutes, no more. You too, Newlin."

Mark chose the back porch this time and stepped out into a small crowd of people, some who wore the obstinate expressions of those refusing to play the game. The minute the door was shut behind him, he realized that it was harder to tell when the music changed out here. On the far end of the porch, Will leaned against the railing nursing a drink.

A few women complained of the cold and made movements to gather their things and go inside. One handed Mark her glass as she walked by. He took it and went down the steps to the gardens. He planned to go to the railing that lined the river overlook, but Victor was in conversation with someone out there. So he turned and walked around the back of the house to the kitchen door and set the glass down by the sink.

Felicitas was at the refrigerator, digging through the shelves looking for something. He stopped next to her. "Don't go out to your car alone tonight, okay? I can walk you out, then I'll drive after you to make sure no one is following you."

She pulled her attention from the hidden food for a moment. "Is that necessary?"

"A man named Victor Gaff makes it necessary."

A concerned look crossed her face. "Oh, okay. Thanks."

He passed through the kitchen and stepped out into the back of the hall. The bows of all four musicians were in vigorous motion, and the main room was filling again. He had just taken his post when a woman screamed.

Sharp. Loud. Arresting.

It was the woman who had handed him the glass. She was pointing at the railing where Ernie had stood earlier.

"John! It was John! I saw him. He was looking at us! He came back!"

21

If Baiss Doesn't Return . . .

HER WORDS SENT an electric shock through the room. Gasps. Short, disbelieving laughs. Stunned silences. The music faltered, then stopped cold.

The lights had been dimmed for the evening party, but Mark saw no one on the stairs.

Guests, surprisingly, looked at him. *They will think you're a detective,* Rebecca had said. He was on official duty.

He pushed through the crowd and up the stairs, all the way to the second landing and the window seat, then on to the second floor. The lights were not dimmed up here. The corridor was empty.

He went up to the third floor, the top floor, where the stairs ended and looked down the hallway. Not a soul. No door closing. No signs of a quick escape.

Leal Baker and Warren Egan had climbed the stairs partway after him, Todd Channon following in their wake.

"I don't see anyone," said Mark, as he joined them on the second landing. "But have a look."

Baker and Egan went farther up the stairs. Todd, however, stayed by Mark, looking tense. Down below, a sea of faces stared up at them, waiting. Up above the two trustees stood in the hallway and looked around.

"There's no one here," said Egan.

Todd swore.

The four of them came back down the stairs. "We saw nothing," Egan announced.

"Mary," someone cried out, "you're seeing things."

"No, I'm not! And I'm not drunk either. John was there looking at me. At all of us!"

A shimmer of gold caught Mark's eye. Juliane had come out of the dining room. For the first time that evening, there was no laughter on her face.

As he made his way back to his post, a man caught his arm. "You're sure you saw nothing?"

"Nothing at all."

"Well, Baker will handle this. He always does."

As Mark took his position, Leal Baker stood at the landing where Ernie had been. The lawyer's hand was up, asking for silence. Then Baker leaned over the railing. "Mary, are you all right?"

Mary was crying openly now. A few women had gathered around her, patting her back, talking earnestly. Mary did not answer.

Baker nodded sympathetically in her direction, then

raised his head and looked out over the rest of them. "Well, it has been a full evening already and still is not over. Let me take this opportunity to thank the Channon family for their hospitality. It is a privilege to gather here again in memory of John Channon, Senior. He was a good man and a good friend."

Applause broke out. When it faded, Baker continued.

"At this point we have had our Ritornello Game and have used its music to explore the beautiful rooms of this lovely old house. Now we come to the farewell part of the evening and some of the saddest announcements I have had to make."

The room hushed. Ice cubes clinked in some nervously shaken glass.

"Tonight is a night of two farewells. The first is to the parties we have enjoyed over the years because of John Channon, Senior. The trust that provided for these parties is officially ending. Therefore this is the last party to honor that great man—a driving force for good in the business world, in the community of Ashington Mills, and the world of classical music. If our musicians would lead us, let us sing "Happy Birthday" to this man one last time."

The quartet obliged, and Baker's voice, a surprisingly good one, carried through the hall persuading all to join in. It must have been a bittersweet moment for some. Applause followed the last words of the song.

Baker held up his hands for attention again. "The second farewell we must say tonight is not to a person, but to Riverview House itself. You are here tonight because you are friends, business associates, and longtime acquaintances of the family. They wanted to make sure you had a chance to say goodbye to a home that has been a landmark of Ashington Mills, a landmark for this family, for 125 years."

Sounds of dismay rose from the crowd. Todd Channon leaned against the wall by the entrance to the large parlor, head down, staring at the floor.

"Because of your long association with the family, they felt you ought to know the facts of the case." Baker consulted a small card in his hand.

This was interesting. The Channons never shared their business with others, told no one of their private tragedies, yet they had been forced to open their family home and make it earn money, and now their hidden agony was going to be public.

Reluctance and sadness filled Baker's voice, though his professionalism stayed intact. "According to the will of the late John Christoph Channon—that is, John Junior—the house, funds, and estate were to be kept in trust for his son Baiss until his thirtieth birthday. Should the estate be without its heir at that time, the entire estate, including this house and grounds, is to be turned over to the county and be used as they see fit."

Murmurs of surprise, misgiving, anger, and some snide remarks drifted to Mark's ears. The lawyer kept on, speaking slowly.

"I share with you some of the family's sadness, and trust to your good hearts not to increase their pain. Baiss Channon has not been seen since he was sixteen years old. If he does not make his presence known and claim his inheritance by his thirtieth birthday, then, according to his father's will, Riverview House will become county property. I believe Victor Gaff, the head of the county board, is also here tonight."

Uproar. Everyone talking at once. Baker leaned over slightly, his ear to the crowd as if he were trying to hear their questions. Mark couldn't make out anything intelligible from his position, but could guess the questions based on Baker's answers.

"No, Baiss is not dead. He is alive. . . . Yes, a thorough search has been made. . . . By December eleventh. . . . DNA testing will, of course, confirm his identity, but there are the Channon proofs. . . . I cannot tell you what those are."

A woman standing near Fia, cried out. "Baiss? You mean *Baiss*? He was at my swimming party last year. Handsome as all get out."

Fia turned on her. "Why didn't you say something?"

"Why should I?" The response was defiant. "I didn't know he was missing. How am I to know your business?"

Baker's face looked reserved. Doubtful. "Would you speak with me afterwards, please, Betty?"

Another movement in the crowd got Baker's attention. Victor Gaff was making his way up the stairs to the landing. He nodded to Baker as the lawyer stepped back. Then he turned to the crowd.

"I don't need to tell any of you who I am." The professional smile could not mask the haughty look in his eyes. His gaze landed on Mark for a moment before sweeping the rest of the group. "I'm here to speak for the county.

"The county greatly appreciates John's generous gift and plans to use the house as the new county office building. The dining room will be turned into a conference room. Important visitors will be housed upstairs. And John's elegant study will become my own."

Muttering and groaning answered his announcement, rising into a tumult fueled by a sense of outrage. Of course. It was the ultimate power play. Victor Gaff would take over what the rich, proud family could not hold onto. It was triumph for him and defeat for his enemies.

Fia threw her glass at him, which missed, arced over the landing, and fell into Todd Channon's usual lair. There was a sound of glass shattering, and something more.

Victor held up his hands for quiet, but the crowd only gave him enough to yell over and be heard.

"Don't you get it?" Victor looked around at the Channons. "Don't you get it?" he repeated. "If John couldn't have his money, he was damn well going to make sure *you* couldn't have it!"

"Mr. Gaff, please!" Leal Baker attempted to stop the man. "You have said more than enough."

"It's true! Every word! And come December, we'll be the richest county in the state!" Victor blew a mock kiss to Fia, came down the stairs, and swaggered his way out the front door.

Exit the villain, with disaster in his wake.

Gaff, it appeared, was an expert at public humiliation. All these people, traveling some distance to come tonight, were definitely not part of his constituency. He needed no votes from any of them. The taking of the mansion was a coup, not really for the county, but for himself.

A number of people appeared to enjoy the spectacle of

Channon comeuppance. Others appeared genuinely horrified. Elizabeth, at least, was missing this.

Baker stepped forward again. "Ladies and gentlemen, ladies and gentlemen!" he cried.

The voices calmed.

"I will not pretend that it will be easy to recover a festive mood after what you have just heard. But let me remind you, there still is time. Baiss Channon may return and make the county's plans mere presumption. But for tonight, Nick Powell has made a special dessert. If he would like to cut the birthday cake now?" Baker was working to redeem the evening.

Rebecca Powell hurried toward the kitchen.

"And," said Baker motioning toward the quartet, "if we could enjoy your lovely music again?"

The musicians immediately took their seats.

The crowd seemed to shift and turn, not through any command of the music, but going where they wanted to go. A good number got their coats and left. But everyone was talking, stirred, shaken.

"Baiss *has* to come back. He could never let that crook take this lovely house!"

"Baiss will return and everything will be just fine."

"Did you get that Betty? She just had to have her moment. She would lie to steal attention from a drowning man."

"Didn't they try to break the will?"

"Honey, that was years ago. John set it up too carefully. And believe me, if Baker could break it, he would."

"I don't think Baiss knows. How could he know?"

"How could he *not* know?"

"He's got to be dead, do you think?"

"Gaff can't wait to get his hands on this place! Revenge for the divorce, I'm sure."

"So that's why the hotel is closing. My friend tried to get reservations in January, and they refused her. I told her they couldn't be that full up. Nothing happens in Ashington Mills in January!"

Meanwhile, pictures were quickly arranged and taken. Nick and the cake. Nick and Todd and the cake. All the Channons and the cake. But without Elizabeth. And without Baiss.

At last the cake was cut. Rebecca approached Mark. "You don't have to stay in position anymore. Just wander through the rooms, help the guests, and pick up anything left from the kitchen." She glanced at the diminished crowd. "I think this night will end sooner than any of us expected. One can only hope." The burden that always hounded Rebecca was in her eyes.

She pointed to the table. "Have some cake first. You've earned more than that. Thank you so much for all you've done for us."

"Are you having some too?" He picked up a plate and handed it to her.

She backed away. "No—no. I have things to do. But Todd and Nick say thanks, and Todd will refund some of your money as promised."

He picked up a fork and looked at his piece carefully. It was an outer piece, and the frosting on the side was meant to be one of the dining room windows, probably close to his usual table. He could be in this cake, looking out those frosting windows right now.

He took a bite, "listening for flavors" as Amy had coached him. Spice? Coffee? A hint of chocolate? Absolutely delicious.

"How can you eat through that thing on your face?" It was Fia. With fresh wounds from Gaff's humiliation, looking for trounce-able prey of her own.

"The beard you mean?" he said calmly, scooping another bite.

"I mean that unbecoming hair on your chin." She made it sound as if he had the two-foot beard of a mountain man instead of a one-inch Renaissance special.

He waved his fork at her. "For you, Fia, I will shave it off tomorrow."

She stared at him, trying to determine if he were teasing her.

"I promise," he said. "The whole thing comes off in the morning."

She still hadn't said anything, but in her eyes he could see the young girl, tied to a tree, vulnerable, humiliated, and weary.

"I'll do it. I mean it. Next time you see me, I'm clean-shaven. Okay?"

A shimmer of nervous silver movement. "Okay," she said, slowly.

As Rebecca had hoped, the evening ended earlier than planned. Still, it was after midnight when Mark walked an exhausted Felicitas to her car and followed her home, to a small house in a well-kept yard, where a light burned in the window, waiting for her.

Riverview House was almost completely dark by the time he returned. He let himself in the front door and climbed the stairs slowly, past the landing where both Baker and Gaff had made their shocking announcements, and where Mary had claimed to see the face of John Channon.

His own room was in shadow when he entered, except for a small bedside lamp left on by his faithful assistant. He could hear the sound of Sean's rumbling snores and wondered how his evening had been. How much he would have to tell him in the morning.

22

———

What Baiss Left Behind

MARK TOLD Sean about the entire evening, from the moment the musicians set the music on their stands, to Felicitas flicking the outside light of her house as a good-bye. All the while, Sean stood leaning against the bathroom door frame, arms crossed, a frown on his face, as Mark talked and shaved. In fact, Sean was so quiet that Mark paused several times, razor in hand, to see if Sean was still with him.

When he spoke of Victor Gaff and his hundred dollar insult, Sean's eyes blazed and his hands curled themselves into fists. He shook his head at Baker's announcement and the "appearance" of John Channon. When at last he spoke, he didn't say what Mark thought he would say.

"I'll help you find Baiss Channon."

Mark wiped his face with a towel and looked at the result, giving himself time to absorb what Sean had said. The scars from the accident were still there, but noticeably less. You had to look for them to see them now. That was encouraging.

He turned to Sean. "Why do you say that now? What changed your mind?"

"We're still dealing with a bunch of irrational people here—"

"Given."

"But I'm starting to think it might be better if Baiss came back. Maybe better for everyone."

"Better for Baiss?"

"Don't know. Probably not. But that's something he'd have to figure out."

"You're right. We can make sure he knows the stakes, then we let him figure out what he wants to do."

For a moment, Sean looked uncertain. "How do you plan to hunt for him?"

"There you have me. I have ideas, but I'm not sure. I'm a latecomer to this whole show, and I've never met the guy. And, as Matheson told Jerry, an injured brain is deficient in the long-range planning department."

Mark hung his towel back on the rack, put his glasses on and led the way out of the bathroom.

"Ah, the free wind on my face once more," he said.

"Just in time for winter," Sean said wryly.

"Well, I have my reasons. You can keep your dashing beard."

"I will. Not everyone can pull off this look."

Mark ignored the teasing jab. "Back to the main question. I'm learning more about the Channon family with every day that passes. But that's not enough. We have less than two months before his birthday. He's been gone about fourteen years, and we're down to the last weeks. What we really need is to learn more about Baiss. How do we figure out what *he* is thinking?"

"We could start with something of his."

"I've gone over every page of the music book, but that's a young Baiss. I need the teenage Baiss, the one who decided to leave. And there's no more music in the bench or on the shelves that's his."

"What about looking in his bedroom?"

Mark stared at him.

Sean went on. "If Baiss ever lived in this house, his bedroom has got to be here. Even though Todd and Stephanie redid the rooms, they seem to have kept an awful lot of old family stuff. Maybe we could get ideas somehow."

"We could look after checkout time, when the maids are cleaning."

"Sure," said Sean. He gave Mark an embarrassed look. "I'll run some errands while you're at it. This house creeps me out. Just looking up those stairs gives me chills. Sorry."

"It's okay." It felt so good to finally have Sean as partner in this search, he would happily take whatever Sean could give. "What if I just find out and let you know?"

TODD CHANNON WAS at his desk, but not alone, and not happy. A man from the computer store seemed to be telling him all the problems that could ensue in trying to get the data off his damaged machine. Not the time to ask about Baiss Channon's room.

Mark wandered in the direction of the kitchen. He neared the door just as Rebecca came out. She looked tired, but was as polite as ever. "Oh, Dr. Newlin. Did you want breakfast? We've closed, but I can try to get you something."

"No, thank you. Sean wants pancakes today. I just came to ask a question. Do you know which bedroom belonged to Baiss? I got curious after the party last night, that's all."

"I can ask Nick for you."

He waited in the main hall, looking around at the scene of last night's debacle, or triumph, depending on the point of view. The serving tables had been removed, and the flowers in the vases repositioned on shelves and tables throughout the hall. The floral arrangements looked a little overdone in the stark morning light, like an overdressed guest showing up for family breakfast.

The sound of a motor took his attention to a back window. George Juarez was blowing the leaves out from under an exuberant crabapple tree. Blue skies promised a nice autumn day and made Old Man River bluer than ever.

Rebecca returned looking slightly downcast. "He says it's the one right above yours." Without waiting for his thanks, she turned away and went through the study door toward the elevator. He looked after her, sorry that his simple question had somehow made her life harder.

AFTER FOUR PANCAKES APIECE, and a slow and steady three-mile walk, during which both of them were more apt to think than talk, Sean took the car to run errands, and Mark took the elevator to the third floor. The door to Baiss Channon's old room stood open. Stephanie crouched by the fireplace looking at something in its depths, while a maid tugged the used pillowcases off the pillows.

The room had the same footprint as his own, but the carpet was a beige tweed and the bedspread, folded over a chair, was a plain cream color. He fought down a sudden impulse. They would probably notice if he grabbed the bedspread and switched it for his hideous salmon one.

"Ms. Channon, you're wanted," said the maid in a dull, tired voice.

Stephanie raised her head from the hearth with a look that said the last thing on earth she needed right now was to be hounded by some guest.

Mark quickly stepped all the way into the room. "It's nothing, Stephanie, just me. What's wrong with the fireplace?"

"Bats. The guests complained this morning of hearing skittering in the chimney. We haven't used the fireplaces yet this year. I opened the flue and got this mess." She pointed to a pile of debris that looked like a pulverized blend of plant material and animal droppings. "We'll have to get the chimney cleaners in. I tell you what, Dr. Newlin, I'm about tired of all this."

"I can imagine." Even the house seemed to be working against the Channons now.

Stephanie got to her feet and brushed the dust off her knees. "I keep telling Todd we've got to be looking for a new position. We've got to be putting applications out. But he won't do it. He doesn't want to leave the house. He keeps thinking Baiss is going to come back and say, 'Oh sure. You keep the house. I don't mind.' Well, I'm looking for work even if Todd won't."

She took a deep breath, and Mark thought she was trying not to cry. "These are going to be the longest two months of my life." She shook her head, and resumed what she could of her professional manner. "Are you sure you don't need anything?"

"All I wanted was to see Baiss's old room," Mark replied. "Just historical curiosity."

Stephanie waved a hand. "Feel free. Nobody can stay here until we get the bats out."

"Thank you." He went over to the tower window area where a table and chair waited, just as they did in his room directly below. He moved the curtain aside and looked out.

Todd had been right that first day. The view was much better from here. Stunning. He looked across the front of the house, past a short iron hook that stuck unobtrusively out between the stones, to the gracious central balcony. Beyond that, he could pick out the tops of the buildings that lined the downtown square. A partial roof kept him from seeing his own windows below.

In the other direction, he could see over treetops, and, catching a break in the farther trees, could see a long way down the river. Which meant Baiss would have seen a long way down the river. And had the same bird's-eye view of the parking lot. But there wouldn't have been a parking lot then. Just a family home with the drive going right to the garage in the back. The rest of this would have been beautiful green lawn.

Someone new stepped into the room. "Stephanie!"

There was no mistaking the pitch and command of that voice. Mark turned around, and his movement drew Fia's eye. Her mouth gaped open and her eyes widened when she saw his clean-shaven face.

"Hello, Fia," he said, in a friendly tone.

She blinked hard several times and shook her head. Hand on her hip, she turned back toward the head of housekeeping, who was examining the interior of the closet. "Stephanie, I am moving into the back corner room now."

Stephanie shut the closet door. "No, you are not. You are going to stay in that smaller room and like it!"

She took a few steps toward Fia. "We're stuck with you for as long as you stay, but I tell you this. You will remain in the room Todd assigned you. And you will make your own bed and change your own sheets and take out your own trash. I'm not going to spend my maid service on you!"

Fia's face was the kind that went white with anger. "Look here, missy–"

But Stephanie had come to the end of herself. "No, *you* look here! You are going to behave yourself. And you are not going to throw or break a single thing in this house. Whenever you come, we lose guests. And now you've smashed Todd's computer and our guest records and reservations."

Her face reddened, and she pointed at Fia. "If you damage one more thing, you will wash dishes in the kitchen until you pay for it. Even if it takes you all the way to Christmas! You just try to move into that room, and I will throw all your luggage out on the lawn."

Fia wheeled around and disappeared down the hallway, muttering curses.

Stephanie turned toward Mark. Her eyes were wet. "Look around all you want." She left the room.

The maid gathered up the pile of used sheets. "I'm going on to my next room. If those chimney sweeps come, I'm going to have to clean the room all over again anyway, so I'm not going to do it now." She gave him a look as if he were the one responsible for the bats and went out the door.

MARK WAS FINALLY ALONE in Baiss's room. He looked around, wondering what the room had been like then. The bathroom was too modern to have been anything Baiss had used. There was no point in going through the drawers, but Mark did it anyway and found them all empty. Of course, nothing of Baiss's could still be here. But he also couldn't have taken everything he owned with him when he ran. Only the most important things.

He opened the closet door and looked around as Stephanie had done. The rod held a dozen empty hangers. On the shelf above, a folded blanket and slipcovered pillow. The anonymity of a hotel room.

What would Baiss have hung there? What would he have put on the shelf? He must have had interests other than music. What would fill a lonely boy's hours? Books, maybe. He would check the study library later. Movies? Computers? Music, definitely.

He went to the table near the bed. This one was larger than his and had a CD player sitting on it. A basket on the floor carried a selection of CDs for guest use. Mark fingered through them. They represented the predictable variety he would expect hotel owners to offer their guests' differing tastes. Classical, of course. Movie soundtracks, some country, classic rock, even pop. The movie soundtracks were from recent movies. They would not have belonged to Baiss. He looked at the classical CDs more closely, taking the time to read them front and back, checking the dates of the recorded performances.

One had a photograph of Chicago's skyline at night. The back showed the picture of an orchestra, a grand piano in front, and a boy in a black suit and white tie standing by the piano bench. The conductor was pointing to him, while the orchestra clapped. The fine print read: *Baiss Channon with the Chicago Symphony—Young Performer's Series.*

For a moment, Mark couldn't believe it. He had struck gold!

In Chicago, Baiss had performed Bach, Mozart, a

Schumann piano concerto, and two pieces by Leonard Channon.

Leonard Channon. The man who built this house, Baiss Channon's great-great-grandfather. That must have been a proud moment.

He looked at the boy closely. Baiss appeared to be somewhere around twelve years old. His head was tilted down, as if the camera had caught him at the start or finish of a bow, so his face wasn't visible.

Mark couldn't wait to hear his piano.

He stepped out into the hallway still holding the CD. The maid was pulling fresh soap bars from her cart.

"I found a CD in that basket I think I'd enjoy. Is it all right if I listen to it in my room?"

"Go ahead," she said. "You might be the only one in the house tonight. You can play it as loud as you want. They'll never hear it back there." She cocked her head in the direction of the staff bedrooms behind her.

"Thanks."

Sean was still out when Mark popped the CD in the player on the dresser and turned it on. The Bach came first in a glittering rush of joy. Mark sat down on the bed in awe.

A person couldn't manufacture joy like that. It was either in your fingers or it wasn't. It was definitely in Baiss.

Music had been Baiss's home. A home filled with joy.

When he ran away, he had left Riverview House and the family it represented—hateful aunts, jealous uncles, indifferent cousins, an egotistical father who had driven away his piano teacher. But he had also left the world of piano performance, a world he clearly loved. Why?

The door opened, and Sean came in with bags from the bookstore and drugstore. "I found more puzzle books than you could possibly complete in a year." He stopped speaking and looked quizzically at the CD player. "Did you get to see his room?"

"Yes. And found what you're hearing now." Mark held out the CD case.

Sean set the bags down on the bed and took the case, turning it over carefully in his hands. "That's him, huh?" He shuddered. "That music gives me chills."

"Me too," said Mark. "Ernie's good, but there's something different about this. Something Ernie can't touch."

Mark held quiet for a few moments, in order to listen to the next track on the CD, to hear the relationship between Baiss and Mozart. Sean dropped to the floor, cross-legged, listening too.

At the end of the piece, Mark got up and pressed the stop button. "I can hear him. I can hear his voice somehow, and it makes it all so much worse."

He took off his glasses and rubbed his face hard before he put them back on. "You know, he could be homeless right now, begging somewhere. Or playing piano for food in a Texas bar."

"I could see him doing that," said Sean. "A lot of places would just pay cash and ask no questions. He could still be doing that. Have you asked Elizabeth where he might have gone?"

Mark thought of the many questions he had troubled her with during his lessons, and the painful scene he had witnessed when she left the party. She probably didn't want to see him for awhile.

"I think I've asked Elizabeth all I dare."

Sean brushed this aside. "It's Friday, isn't it? She would be at the school today." He stood up at once. "School will be out soon. Let's go surprise her."

23

A Lawyer's Secret

Leal Baker had barely slept after the Channon party ended. He had come to the office at eight thirty this morning, his usual time, but he was feeling eighty years old instead of his physical sixty-three.

The morning held two client conferences, the kind he could do easily over material he had been through a hundred times with others. His secretary had brought in lunch for him, a bowl of soup, and he had eaten it dutifully. Mindlessly. Because the biggest risk he had ever taken in his career could blow up in his face.

The afternoon was lengthening as he stared out his office window at the marble and granite sign. *Baker and Stow.* He remembered when it had read *Lawrence S. Baker,* and he had polished it weekly for his dad.

After he graduated from law school and was admitted to the bar, the sign had been changed to *Baker and Baker*. Immediately, his father had shared with him the management of the Channon family's concerns. The Channons had shaped his life and career. And his fears.

At the beginning he had dealt mostly with Carl Channon, son of the famous Leonard, and Carl's son, who had been the first John. Both men were good with money. Both tended to manage their affairs well. Carl was in his eighties then, and John Senior in his fifties. And the exploits of John's children were enough to make the older men put every precaution in place.

Sadly, after generations of Bachen–Channon industry, John Senior raised a family that had no sense of wisdom in the financial arena whatsoever.

Baker had never encountered such a group of hellions in his life. His own wife was afraid of them, had refused to go to the party last night.

After Carl died, two of John Senior's sons—John and Will—came to work. They unsettled the operations of Channon World more in one day than it had been in the previous five years. The boys cared nothing for management, innovation, or production. Their concern had been for the money that would come to them: how much, why wasn't it more, and why wasn't it given to them yesterday.

The boys didn't stay in the office long that time. Their father sent them away, then started to sell off divisions of the Channon companies, putting the money in securities that Warren Egan and his crew watched over.

Channon World had its own fleet of corporate lawyers, of course. But the Bakers had always been entrusted with the personal side of things. And they knew too well that John Senior could not stand up to his children, especially to John Junior.

Then Baiss was born, the youngest of the grandchildren, and the older man knew that here was someone special. When he found that they shared the gift of music, and that both Baiss's ability and his heart proved to be exceptional, the relationship between grandfather and grandson had gone deep.

He remembered a concert he had been invited to in John Senior's large rooms at the Channon mansion. Baiss was about six years old then. The audience consisted of his grandfather, his step-grandmother, his mother Barbara, Elizabeth, and Baker himself.

Baker didn't remember the names of the pieces, just that one had been technically demanding, which Baiss played very well. The next was entirely lovely. The third piece had been a surprise. Baiss played the intro bars of *Rigoletto's* "Questa o quella," then looked right at him. "Would Mr. Baker care to join me?" he asked, an earnest expression on his face.

Someone must have told him that Baker had sung opera in college, and this piece in particular. Baker was flabbergasted, but took his place next to the piano. Baiss started again, and Baker sang the whole song through for their admiring audience of four, Baiss listening and carefully matching him measure for measure. Regrettably, it was the last time Baker had sung opera in front of anyone, but the memory of that special moment had stayed with him ever since.

A few months after that, John Senior had sat in this

very office and told him that he wanted to settle the bulk of his estate on Baiss. "But the others can't know. I want this to be a secret trust. Completely legal. Accounted appropriately. But protected for Baiss and Baiss alone."

John Senior had had the sense to tell his family about their inheritances before he died. The children of his first wife knew and expected their fifty million each along with various pieces of real estate scattered around the country. John Junior received an extra ten million as oldest and the addition of the original family mansion in Ashington Mills. John Senior's second wife, Marie, had received ten million; Elizabeth inherited five million.

Baker respected Marie. She hadn't married John for his money and knew that the first wife's children would get the lion's share. She hadn't minded. In fact, being practical and realistic, she had insisted on it.

"If you love me," she had told her much older husband, "and never want to cause me pain after you are gone, then don't leave me any amount of money that would make your children jealous." Yes, practical and realistic. And she had passed her attitudes on to Elizabeth.

But for Baiss, there had been millions more in secret trust—including the proceeds from the sale of two companies that had been finalized while John Junior was in France at the Grand Prix, Will was unsuccessfully wooing a Canadian heiress, and Ernie was performing throughout Brazil.

John Senior continued to add to the Baiss Fund, as he called it, every year. Until he died. Baker's dad had died the same year. A year of sorrow and upheaval.

Baker asked Stow, a trusted law school friend, to fill the other half of his law firm. They did not share the same legal specialties. But Stow's expertise and his understanding of human nature in general, helped ground Baker in his dealings with the volatile Channons. As lawyer, counselor, referee, and nursemaid.

Several years later, the unthinkable happened. Barbara died. After that, Baiss went to stay with friends in Europe for a while. Or so they were told. And John Junior set up a will with these odd clauses and could not be talked out of it.

Only then did he hint that he did not know where his son was. Later, he angrily denied saying it. At the same time, Egan reported a trail of financial transactions on Baiss's debit card in various places throughout Wisconsin, transactions that did not look like a thief, but like a young man surviving on his own.

Baker could still feel John Senior's last handshake in this office, and his parting words: "Whatever you do, protect Baiss. Protect my grandson from all the others." Leal Baker had walked a tightrope ever since.

Even now he wondered if he should have told Baiss's father about the debit card trail. And he would have. But for one important thing.

He had a gut feeling that John Junior was hoping Baiss would not return. John suspected his father's preference for Baiss—a preference that surely had money attached to it. And he was determined to find the money.

Baker sighed. His last conversation with John Junior had been acrimonious. It had happened about ten years ago when Baker had taken his wife and two daughters to

Italy. Walking the streets of Cinque Terre, he had received the one phone call he had been dreading. John Junior was calling from his office in Ashington Mills, at the helm of everything that was left to Channon World.

"Baker, I'm going through my father's records for years past and some numbers are missing. Like millions. What's been going on here?"

He answered calmly. "That's unsettling. You mean stolen? Did you talk to your accountants?"

"They are too stupid to know anything. They say everything is in order and bored me with a line-by-line bunch of nonsense."

"I'll look into it as soon as I return," he said, with a sinking feeling.

"That better be tomorrow."

"No, Mr. Channon, that will be two weeks from yesterday."

"That's not good enough, Baker."

His wife and daughters were looking in a coffee shop window, their sleeveless arms freshly tanned. Christy had graduated from college with honors and would head to med school in the fall. Kim had been accepted at Duke. And his wife had made this family as wise and loving as possible. How much he owed her! There was no way he was going to stop their vacation because John Junior wanted more money.

"It will have to be, Mr. Channon."

"I'll fire you."

He took a deep breath. "Go right ahead."

John Junior cursed him out thoroughly before hanging up. Baker put his phone back in his pocket and wandered across the street to stare out at the turquoise blue water.

But the confrontation he dreaded never came to pass. By the time the Bakers' return flight landed in Detroit, John Junior had been killed in a car accident, and his siblings were arguing over his estate. Baker could still feel their fury when they found out it was essentially frozen until Baiss's thirtieth birthday.

Baker turned from the window and sat in his desk chair again. What he predicted, had happened. The other siblings had gone through most or all of their money, and now were circling to see what they could get from what remained of John's. Yet, Baiss and the county were in their way.

Would they learn what he and Egan had done? That they had continued to fund the boy's account every month as if nothing had happened? Egan had even been able to make sure a very old debit card never expired. The boy hadn't spent much, never even a tenth of what they put in each month. But had they done the right thing?

Baiss, where are you?

A rap sounded on the door, and at his call, Stow poked his grizzled head in. "So, how was the party last night?"

Baker shook his head. "Not good." He waved Stow to a chair. "But parts of it you might find interesting."

Stow listened intently while Baker told him of Victor Gaff's performance, his claiming the mansion for the county. At the end, Stow shook his head. "One of these days, that man is going to get what's coming to him."

"He got a hint of it last night." Baker told of the interchange between Victor and Mark Newlin, and Gaff picking his money up off the floor.

Stow lifted his head and laughed out loud. "Oh, I wish I had been there to see it! What a shock for the old boy to have his money thrown back in his face! You know, Leal, we don't need more lawyers. We need more history professors."

24

———

Sean Joins the Hunt

MARK POINTED out to Sean that two grown men cannot drive up and down the aisles of a high school parking lot looking for people without drawing the attention of the security guard.

Sean ignored him. "Turn here. I think that's her car. The silver Passat. Pull in next to it."

Mark did so. "When she comes out, you'll have to lead. I think I've offended her somehow." He thought of how he had been the one to witness her mortification in the gardens, and a look he could not decipher when she got into her car.

"Offended? That doesn't sound like you."

"I mean distressed. Distressed her somehow."

"You're not practicing your piano?"

"I'm practicing my fingertips off. I already have my *Intrada* memorized."

"That's impressive."

"For me it is. For Baiss it would be a breeze. For me it's like moving the Grand Canyon."

"So how could you have distressed her?" Sean pulled a mock stern face. "Are you ignoring your sharps and flats?"

"Stop it. Here she comes."

Elizabeth was walking across the parking lot toward her car, a purse and oversize messenger bag over her shoulder, keys in hand, and looking end-of-the-week tired. He couldn't imagine having to teach a full day after a night like last night.

"She knows you better than she knows me," said Sean. "I'll probably scare her." Nevertheless, he opened the car door and got out, leaving the door open.

"Elizabeth!"

Mark could see the puzzled look on her face, but she came over to them. Of course, how could she help it? Her car was there. And Sean was turning on the charm.

"We've come to rescue you from Friday night sameness. The restaurant's closed tonight, right? Can we take you out for pizza then?"

"All right," she replied. "But I don't think I have the energy to be good company."

"You're always great company." Sean stood at attention by the open passenger door and waved her in.

Mark noticed the hesitation on her part when she saw him sitting in the driver's seat. He hadn't imagined it. She was avoiding his eyes, he could tell. But she got into the front seat anyway.

Sean climbed in the back, saying, "We will do our best to be especially cheering tonight."

Mark started the car. "I have to warn you though. Sean orders extra cheese and the sight of the night is watching him get all of that melted stuff from the pan to his mouth."

Elizabeth glanced over her shoulder with a slight smile. "I love extra cheese."

A half hour later they were in the small Italian restaurant where Mark and Sean had discussed Simone Weil. An extra large, extra cheese with pepperoni and mushrooms sat in front of Elizabeth and Sean, and a thin bacon, tomato, and onion sat in front of him.

Mark had not been sure how to proceed, but Sean drew Elizabeth out gently, letting the pace of the conversation match her available energy, touching on her week at school, the concert music they were working on, and even what her favorite season of the year was. Elizabeth relaxed, and even looked at Mark occasionally in the usual way.

At the right moment, Sean began to relate stories of the improvisation group at ISU, the student-directed comedic dramas at SIU, even the Impression Club at Gold College. Demonstrations followed, and Sean mimicked Jack Nicholson, Charlton Heston, Jerry Seinfeld. Then Professor Sorenson and even Todd Channon.

"You're so good at that!" Mark cried. "You couldn't claim acting as a profession?"

Sean took a long slurp of soda. "Acting's about someone else's life. Always about someone else's life. As you've pointed out, I need to find my own. Which brings us to Baiss Channon." Sean looked meaningfully at Mark. This was going to be Mark's lead.

Mark felt suddenly awkward. He hesitated a moment, then said, "I hope this doesn't sound foolish or presumptuous. But, we're concerned about Baiss too. Is there anything we could do to help? Help find him, I mean?"

Elizabeth's direct gaze was on him, and he couldn't read it. He tried to explain himself.

"I play from his piano book. I touch the piano keys he used to touch. I just listened to his Chicago performance . . ." He took a deep breath. "I can't stand that he's gone. That he's out there somewhere. Please. Can we do anything?"

Elizabeth toyed with her napkin for a moment, then dropped it on the table. She reached for her purse. "Let's not talk here. What if we go get my car and then the two of you come over to my house for coffee?"

MARK AND SEAN sat on stools around her white kitchen island, while she filled a kettle with water and set it on the stove. She could tell they were politely waiting for her to begin. That they weren't going to push her.

How could these two care so much about Baiss? Yet, from what she had seen of them, she believed they truly did. And their compassionate interest made her feel like she could just start crying at any moment.

"Can I help somehow, Elizabeth?" Sean asked.

She shook her head. "No, thank you. There's really not much to do, and I like doing it."

While pouring the hot water gently over the fresh grounds, she started her story, but kept her eyes carefully on the flask.

"I was in New York at grad school when Baiss left. He didn't come to me, though I wish he had. I *really* wish he had. When Baker asked, I told him that Baiss might have gone to his mother's sisters, two aunts of his that lived in Wisconsin. Baker inquired, but nothing came of it."

"Anywhere else he might have gone, Elizabeth?" Mark asked. "Favorite teachers, mentors, buddies?"

She shook her head. "I wasn't in a position to know. I had been away for college, then grad school. When my father died, my mother moved out immediately. So going home meant going to New York, not here. My brother John took over the house and made it clear that my mother and I were no longer welcome. We weren't allowed to come to Barbara's funeral. That hurt my mother terribly."

"Is your mother still alive?" Sean asked.

She nodded. "Living happily in upstate New York." The coffee was ready, and she poured it into the tall white mugs that were her favorites.

"How did you find out that Baiss was missing?" said Mark.

Elizabeth set the mugs in front of them, and slid onto a stool opposite. She scooped some sugar from a bowl into her own mug and stirred slowly, watching the swirls in the liquid.

"John told me himself. The afternoon of my graduate recital. He called and told me Baiss had run away. Baiss had already been gone for weeks, and no one could find him. He added that if I were hiding him, he would make sure I was thrown in jail.

"I was devastated when I heard Baiss had disappeared. Absolutely terrified for him. I performed badly, failed my performance class, and had to spend a year with an artistic counselor in order to be able to perform in public again."

She paused for a deep breath. When she looked up, they were still there listening, real concern in their eyes. She didn't know if she could take it.

"Losing Baiss was like losing my little brother. We didn't live near each other anymore, but he would call. Or I would call. He'd tell me about the music he was working on, and I'd tell him about mine.

"He had amazing intelligence—cognitive, emotional, artistic—depths of it. And a joy that seemed miraculous." She sighed. "But it was so hard for him. John took an excellent piano teacher away from him and refused to get another. For Baiss, taking away music was like taking away his soul."

"Was there anyone close to him, supporting him on the home front? Classmates?" Mark asked. "Teachers at school?"

Elizabeth shook her head. "Baiss didn't go to school. He had tutors instead. So nothing would interfere with the hours he needed to practice." She took a sip of coffee. "The privileged life is a very lonely one."

They all sat in silence for awhile. Sean stirred more sugar and cream into his coffee.

Mark tapped the table. "Elizabeth, did Baiss ever play the Ritornello Game?"

"All the time. It was a birthday tradition."

"Last night it sounded like there was some sort of superstition around the game."

She frowned.

"I'm sorry," Mark said quickly. "Perhaps I shouldn't ask."

"No, I'd rather you knew the truth."

And she told them the story that she hadn't told anyone since David. About her mother's service to the rich, neglected, ill Nora Channon. How her mother tried to get John Channon to pay attention to his wife, to give her the healing love and concern she needed. But he was too busy with his own life at the time, his own achievements. And the woman died.

"They were both there at her deathbed. My mother on one side. John Channon on the other. After Nora took her last breath, her husband broke down completely. My mother's heart broke for both of them. She said that was one of the hardest moments of her life.

"The guilt he felt at neglecting Nora overwhelmed John. My mother still worked there, immersed in the job of going through Nora's things and cataloguing them. The head housekeeper would wake my mother in the middle of the night and say, "Mr. Channon is going off his head again, miss.""

The words were hard to say. It was hard to think of her father like that, even though that was long before he had become her father.

"What would he be doing?" Mark asked gently.

"Walking through the house, humming a Baroque tune, supposedly looking for Nora. My mother would go after him and speak to him. Would be sympathetic but also practical. Even reprimand him.

"She pulled him back to himself again and again. After months went by, my father realized that the one person he could trust completely was my mother.

"They got married in private, came back to announce it, and were received horribly. His children treated her as if she were still a maid. So, my father refused them the house. But when John married Barbara, she and my mother became friends right away, and John and Barbara moved into the mansion with us."

Elizabeth looked at each of them. "I know from what you've seen of the Channons that this might be hard to imagine. But we were a happy family, of sorts. Around the dining room table, there would be Father, Mother, Barbara, little Baiss, and me. Even John, when he was there, could be charming. For the most part, I loved our home life."

And she had. How grateful she was for the memories! Of that time, at least.

"I want you to know that John Channon was a different father to me than he had been to my older siblings. As they grew up, their behavior often humiliated him. He didn't understand it or where it had come from. He had lived for his business and a musical life of his own, and when he came home he felt he lived among strangers. So he retreated into music even more.

"Nora's death changed him, and I think he was ready to be guided by my mother's good sense. As a result, I was very much a part of my father's life. I actually feel sorry for his older children. I think I had the best childhood of any of them."

"Do you have any pictures?" Mark asked. "So we could see what Baiss really looked like? The back of the CD doesn't have a very good picture."

She got the large photo album out and showed them every picture of Baiss that she had. Baiss at the piano. At many pianos. At his birthday. In the stands watching the circus that he liked so much. And the one she loved—little Baiss on the piano bench next to her. Her arm tight around him. She wiped her face with the heel of her hand.

As they pored over the pictures, Mark realized that Fia and Juliane and Ernie and Todd had all been describing the Baiss who wasn't. They had been giving their own judgment, their own perception of him, which meant they were describing their inner thoughts and not Baiss at all. It seemed that only Elizabeth could describe the Baiss who truly was.

"If only we knew what Baiss had been thinking right before he left," Mark said. "If there was something in his own words that could give a clue to what was going on in his mind."

Elizabeth shook her head. "I don't have anything like that. We mostly talked on the phone. I left some messages on his, telling him about my recital and things, but he never answered. He couldn't have taken his phone with him, because John must have used it to track me down."

"So, nothing in original voice?" Mark asked.

Elizabeth gave a sad smile that twisted Mark's heart. "I have his music."

She led them into her living room and seated herself at the piano while they sat in the armchairs. "This is something Baiss wrote when he was thirteen. It was in memory of his grandfather. He wrote it out and sent it to me."

She touched the keys, and the notes flowed out. Lyrical. Moving. Tender.

Mark closed his eyes so he could listen more closely. He had the impression of a person alone, searching through a dark forest. Of white doves answering a hidden call and moving high into the sky. Of a gentling lullaby.

This was Baiss's original voice, a first person source. The music was telling him something, but he couldn't understand the language.

The piece was over too soon. He opened his eyes.

Elizabeth sat at the piano looking thoughtfully at the keyboard. The sound of running water told Mark that Sean had chosen the worst possible time to go to the bathroom.

"THAT WAS HARD FOR ELIZABETH," Sean said, as they drove back to Riverview House.

Mark agreed. "Very hard. I hope we didn't make it more difficult for her. She's got a lot on her right now, so I understood when she said she had to stop the piano lessons."

"When did she do that?"

"When you were in the bathroom."

They fell into silence, not saying anything more all the way back. When they were turning into the drive, Sean said, "It's really great that Elizabeth has those pictures."

"Yes, it is. I think I understand Baiss a little better." Mark put the car in park and shut off the engine. "But, I still have no idea where he would have gone."

MARK SAT in his tower room looking toward the river, watching for the lights of a barge through the leafless trees. It was late and completely dark outside. Sean was out with Felicitas, had left an hour ago with a big smile on his face. Mark welcomed the time alone.

He took a deep breath and let it out slowly. All the exhausting emotions of other people's difficulties washed over him.

Last night's party. Dirk and Elizabeth. Victor and Fia. Ernie and Juliane. The hysterical Mary and the invisible John Channon. Tonight's new insights into Baiss. Pictures of his youth. The closeness he had with Elizabeth. And that piano piece that wove its way through your heart with every note.

A pinpoint of distant light appeared downriver.

He wondered what Amy would think of his life now, what she would make of his dealings with all these volatile, hurting Channons.

It's like living on a soap opera set, Mark, but without a commercial break.

Right, Amy, he'd answer. And the show's never over for them.

She would love Sean. Adopt him like a son.

Maybe we're supposed to be part of the life he is looking for.

She would know why he was afraid to go back home again, why he had emailed Jerry Waite a little while ago and told him he would go with Luedders and the students to the UK.

But he wouldn't go to France. Ever.

Someday you will, Mark. Someday you will.

No, Amy. I won't. Some wounds are too deep.

She would be silent and twist her mouth slightly—her thoughtful look.

What would she think of his piano lessons? He could see her making one of her amazing dinners while he played piano in the background. She would light candles, and he . . .

No.

The barge passed out of sight, a slight flash of red as its stern light slid out of view.

Well, he wasn't taking piano anymore anyway. He realized he would miss it, and that he was disappointed with Elizabeth for canceling them.

She's probably falling in love with you, Mark.

What?

He sat bolt upright in the dark.

Amy could always spot them, the students who came too eagerly to his office, the graduate assistant who over-explained and over-lingered. She always helped him put up gentle but firm barriers to their misplaced emotions before anyone could be foolishly hurt.

He whispered into the dark. "I can't love anyone but you, Amy."

She knows that. She would be the one to understand that.

That's why she's pulling away?

What else could she do?

That unexplained look on Elizabeth's face when he held the door of her car for her after the party. Her restraint around him this afternoon, even at her home, all the avoiding eye contact, yet her easy openness in speaking with Sean.

That explained it. Reason and rationale.

If Luedders said you could discover things while sitting in the dome of St. Paul's, what would he say to sitting in a tower room having imaginary conversations with your wife?

Mark wouldn't suggest the piano lessons again, but he would still practice through Baiss's book as far as he could before Riverview House closed.

He was sad though. It was hard to lose a friendship for any reason, and he valued Elizabeth's insight, her steadiness. He got up from the chair and stretched himself. The river was empty and dark now. He turned to look at the parking lot.

Someone was coming up the drive alone, coat pulled tight against the chill wind. It was Rebecca, of course. Mark rubbed his face roughly with his hand and turned away.

25

I Could Never Do It Again

THE TROUBLE with having a mind is that it will go spinning on and on.

Elizabeth's was spinning in the same circles.

She needed it to make linear progress.

From one place to another, like a Bach Invention.

And finally finish.

She had tried to pull her thoughts out of spin, to at least slow the spin, but had not been successful.

A Saturday morning meant the gentle ritual she looked forward to all week. Putting the breakfast casserole into the oven. Grinding coffee beans for the French press. Slicing strawberries into Grandmother Allen's blue china dish—the Allen dish a necessary reminder that there was more to her than Channon. Adding mandarin oranges.

Setting the table with a seat that faced the back window where she could see the last color of the leaves.

Then, into the living room for a date with her piano while her breakfast baked.

The piano room was her favorite. She had done it all in white—white walls, white curtains, white cabinetry—all warmed by the glow of the honey-colored wood floor. And in the center, her matte black baby grand Steinway. She felt a deep sense of happiness every time she stepped into the room.

After such a trying week, she needed that today.

She cleared away the books and papers from the piano's music stand, all the paraphernalia of her school-work, and stowed them on a shelf. Then opened the piano all the way, sat down, breathed deeply, and rested her hands on the keys.

Today, she needed to let the piano talk, saying what-ever it wished to say, while her fingers moved across the keyboard. It was a time she could just be herself. Not a teacher, or a restaurant helper, or a choir director, or a half-sister, or a Channon.

Just to be Elizabeth. To remember that when she was born, the piano had been born in her heart.

Baiss had known this. Baiss had always understood this. The prickling in the fingers at the sight of a piano. The yearning to touch the keyboard at the sound of a beautiful piece of music. That ache to be *in* the music, to be part of it, which nothing but playing would relieve.

Today, she decided to start with E-minor, a thoughtful key, and explore modulating paths in order to find a satisfying way to end triumphantly in E-flat major.

She would let the melody emerge in whatever way it wished.

Her mind, however, wanted to keep spinning.

E-minor brought Baiss to mind and the constant fear she felt for him, the continual grief at his absence.

D-major brought up Mark Newlin.

She went back to E-minor's mourning. Unfortunately, she liked the melodic movement from E-minor to D-major. Well, she wouldn't have to stay there long. Back to D-major.

She was a private person, naturally preferring to let other people talk about themselves in any social gathering. So what was it about Mark Newlin that just made her open her mouth and tell him things?

She didn't understand it. She felt embarrassed by how freely she had spoken last night. About her family, about Baiss, about her struggles.

The melodic movement led her to B-minor.

Mark Newlin was still there.

With the look he had given her when he was concerned for her at the party. And the look in his eyes last night when she finished playing Baiss's piece. Yes, B-minor was a good key for heart-wringing.

She was despairing of ever making it to E-flat when the phone on the side table rang. Her mother was the only one who called that number. This would be a welcome interruption. Elizabeth lifted the phone from its holder and sat down in the white armchair next to it, tucking her feet under her.

"I thought I would wait for the weekend to ask you how the party went this year." The tinkle of dishes in the background sounded as if her mother were having a late breakfast of her own. "You told me about the rumors. I take it Baiss didn't come after all?"

"No, he didn't, but I heard that after I left, a woman thought she had seen Father."

"You are joking!"

"No, I'm not. Remember, anything can happen with Channons in Ashington Mills."

"Yes, I remember." A sigh. "I don't know *how* you stay in that town."

"I don't think I will stay much longer. Baker made an announcement at the party. Do you recall anything about John's will?"

"I heard there was something unexpected about it, so I pushed it from my mind. I want you to know that everything I have is yours when I die. Simple and straightforward."

"Same goes from me to you."

"Well, I don't want to think about that," her mother said adamantly.

"I don't want to think about yours either," replied Elizabeth.

Her mother returned to the point. "So, what did Baker say?"

"I left before that part, but he left a message on my phone the next day. John left his money and our mansion by the river to the county, unless Baiss comes to claim it by his next birthday. The county will turn it into their own offices. I don't think I want to be here to see that."

"I smell Victor Gaff."

"I think so." Elizabeth stretched her legs out. "I'm a bit

tired of Ashington Mills right now. Tell me about New York. Did your latest group graduate?"

"Their naturalization ceremony was held on Tuesday. I was very proud of them. I'm proud of every group, but the discussions in this one were so interesting. There was this doctor who told me all about what Budapest is really like in such detail that I could actually smell it!"

The aroma of baking eggs, cheese, and sausage wafted into the living room. Elizabeth relaxed as her mother spoke of each of her students with enthusiasm. The passion for teaching—something her mother had discovered late in life—was something they shared.

"But you haven't told me why you left the party early."

Elizabeth hesitated for a moment. "Dirk Attalar was there."

Her mother was a clean-speaking woman. The only time she ever swore was at the mention of Dirk's name. She did so now.

"And?"

"He proposed again with such a *deep* outpouring of love it was hard to resist. Let's see, how did he put it? With his genius and my money, we could do great things together. And if I don't see that, I'm a fool." She forced herself to say the words lightly. "Oh, and he's sure I'm his last chance at marriage."

The words on the other end of the line came thick and fast. "He's up to his same tricks again! Dirk is a man who only has enough money to fly from state to state in an attempt to pry women from theirs."

"A robber in plain sight."

"Exactly. If he has such genius, where is *his* money?"

"Of course nothing would tempt me to spend more than five minutes with him," Elizabeth said. "But he has a way of stirring up fears." She wished her voice didn't shake as she said the words.

Her mother snorted. "So does the devil."

"True."

"You say you may not stay long in Ashington Mills. So where will you go? To New York City? Or maybe even upstate near me? The leaves are so beautiful this autumn. I spend hours every day under the trees."

"I'll think about it. It's hard to be a Channon in this town, especially lately."

"I promise I will not force you to stay, but do consider New York as an in-between."

"I like New York, Mother. I wouldn't feel forced. It's just, I don't know."

She was not sure what to say. Or how to say it. She was allowing herself to form the words for the first time. Would be telling her mother as she told herself.

"Mother, have you ever looked in a man's eyes and seen such a heart there you were almost frightened?"

Her mother took a long, slow breath. "Yes," she replied softly, "but not since your father died." There was a pause. "I know we're not talking about Dirk. Who is it then?"

"He's a history professor staying at the house. He's healing from a car accident, and I ended up giving him piano lessons until recently."

"What happened?"

"I—I couldn't do it anymore. That is, his wife died in the same accident, and he's grieving."

"Ohh."

She knew what her mother's next question would be. Her mother had asked it before. And even as she knew, she also knew what her answer would be, and it made her hold her breath.

"Is he like David?" Of course, her mother meant more than physical appearance or any outward characteristic.

"I'm very afraid he is more than David."

"Ohh." Another pause. "Oh, Elizabeth." There was understanding in her voice.

"I loved David very much, but we had to work to get a real sense of togetherness. I mean, I always hoped David and I would fit together better than we did in reality. With Mark … I feel it could just happen."

"If you feel that, there's a good chance he feels it too. Give him time."

"No, I don't think I can."

"Why ever not?"

"Because even if he started to think of me, I would always and forever be his number two."

"Elizabeth—" Her mother's voice was filled with gentle coaxing.

"No. Listen, Mother. I can't. I just can't." She was trying not to cry. "All my life, it has been beat into my head that I am the second, the lesser. The one who has to get by with leftovers. And just once I would like to be someone's first choice."

"Elizabeth, it's not like that."

"It is for me. You and Daddy were just great. I know you were happy. But you have to admit that your happiness was completely surrounded by storms.

"I don't know how you did it. I'm grateful that you did,

for my sake. But I grew up always being the second family, and I know I could never do it again."

There. She had said it. It was a creed of sorts. And the words hung firmly, but sadly, in the air.

"I could never do it again," she repeated.

"But you'd be asking someone else to do it, wouldn't you?"

"What?"

"If you consider your David as number one, wouldn't anyone else be your number two?"

"That's different."

"*Is* it?"

Elizabeth took a deep breath and changed the subject. "So why don't you tell me what Budapest is really like. Maybe I'll go there next summer."

26

―――――

A Flash of Fear

AFTER THE PUBLIC announcement of the closing of Riverview House, hope seemed to evaporate. Clouds of fear, distrust, and anger billowed everywhere. What had Churchill named his first volume on the Second World War? *The Gathering Storm.* And Mark had a front row seat.

Todd and Stephanie argued openly in the hallways. Stephanie had found a job that would wait for her, one that Todd was tight-lipped about. Todd planned to go down with the ship, hoping beyond hope that the house he was so proud of would not be turned over to the county.

Kelly told Mark that a restaurant in Chicago was considering taking Nick on as partner. The waitstaff bustled about like scared rabbits the night the offer fell through. Rebecca had dark circles under her eyes. Only Juliane was laughing.

Juliane and Fia continued to inhabit the third floor. Will Channon moved in also, perhaps because his house had sold. Ernie came frequently for dinner and to use the large parlor piano. Mark had no idea where he came from. Elizabeth stayed away except for helping in the restaurant during busy times. Mark rarely saw her.

Because of Jerry's guilty generosity, Mark was here for the duration. So, he continued on, working out his healing as best he could.

He played the piano daily, missing Elizabeth's vision for the pieces. But kept at it doggedly. Stubbornly.

He and Sean had left their early dare behind weeks ago. Sean had already read more than five books—he was reading about the Tudors now—and Mark walked miles at a time.

Sean ran every morning, a knit cap on his shaved head against the cold. If Felicitas was working, he would join Mark for dinner at Riverview House. If not, they would get dinner out somewhere. Once when Sean had the car for a date, Mark walked to the diner and had a bacon, lettuce, and tomato sandwich with no ill effects. He kept this secret from Sean. And did it again.

More and more, Felicitas joined them in the college library. Sean and Felicitas sat side by side—his book on the table, her laptop open and papers spread out—smiling at each other during every break in their study.

Mark couldn't help remembering that Thursday afternoon so many years ago, when a certain lovely undergrad had happened to choose the table next to this graduate student in the library at the University of Illinois. It had become a habit until they just started sharing a table, then going somewhere to talk or get dinner together afterwards. Bittersweet memories.

Mark put down his own reading, left Sean and Felicitas to their conversations and smiles, and went to walk laps around the college lake. Around and around. Whatever the weather. Forcing himself to look at the geese, to watch the effects of the wind on the lake, the color changing on the trees.

He missed Amy so badly. He thought he caught a glimpse of her one day at the mall, and it almost brought him to his knees.

How long does it take for a wound to heal? For the bleeding to stop?

Luedders sent him a list of things he needed to know and do in order to get ready for the trip to Britain. But he dreaded going back to Marlonburg to pack. Dreaded the empty house. Didn't want to re-live the pain the last returning had brought him. Strangely enough, the Ritornello Game had given him words to describe it.

"I returned to my place," he told the geese as they swam by on the lake. "But the music was wrong. It was supposed to be *tutti*—the players all together. But it was only me, the soloist, and out of part."

And over it all was the haunting puzzle of Baiss Channon.

Mark had this feeling that if he could just understand what Baiss had been thinking, what the boy had thought and acted like before he left, he could somehow know what he would have done and where he would have gone.

After the evening at Elizabeth's house, he had looked through the books on the study shelves at Riverview. He found three with Baiss's name printed in the front. A kid's mystery book. A book on electricity. And a biography of J.S. Bach.

ON ANOTHER NIGHT when Sean was out with Felicitas, Mark decided to poke through the study shelves again. To understand anyone, you had to look at what they read. Guests brought books in and out of their rooms, so maybe something else had turned up.

The restaurant was filled to capacity, and through the open study door he saw well-dressed diners out in the main hall, waiting their turn to be seated. He had planned on getting his own dinner out somewhere.

The study, with its dark wood furniture and comfortable leather sofas, felt like a safe haven compared to the bustle out in the hall. A place that invited you to read and think.

He was scanning the book titles for new arrivals, when Rebecca Powell entered, carrying two glasses, a menu card, and silverware rolled up in a linen napkin. Evidently the study was going to be used for overflow dining tonight. Overflow dining for a Channon, he would guess.

"How are you tonight, Rebecca?" he asked, as she swiftly arranged the items on the large desk.

"Fine, Mr. Newlin," she replied, polite as always,

opening up the napkin and laying out the silverware with quick hands.

Something behind her caught his eye. A row of bookshelves underneath the window seat. One he had never noticed before. After she hurried out, Mark knelt down by the shelves and took the books out, one at a time, checking for any that might have Baiss Channon's name inside.

Luck was with him. Three more books carried Baiss Channon's name. *The Hobbit, Hatchet,* and *A Complete History of the Circus.* Two were adventure books about survival against great odds. The last one—of the circus— was unexpected. But hadn't one of Elizabeth's pictures shown Baiss under a "big top" somewhere?

Mark thought back to the night of the Channon party, to the young man who had stood alone near the clock. According to the pictures Elizabeth showed them, the man could have been Baiss Channon. And, honestly, could just as easily not have been.

He got to his feet, still holding the circus book, when Ernest Channon entered the study, followed by Rebecca. Ernie went straight to the desk, sat down, took the cloth napkin with a flourish, and laid it across his lap. He glanced at the menu card.

"I'll have the sautéed shrimp and the swordfish."

Rebecca nodded, took the card, and left the room.

Mark stepped around to the front of the desk and stood in front of the sofa. He wanted to go through the rest of the books, but he couldn't very well crawl around on the floor behind Ernie's back while he ate. The circus book was still in Mark's hand. He wondered if he should take it to his room, if it would have anything new to tell him.

"Good evening, Ernie. And how are you tonight?"

Ernie did not reply. Instead, he eyed Mark as one who had escaped the fishhook. "I heard you practicing earlier, Newlin. You'll never make it as a piano player."

Ernie needed someone to support his ego tonight, and Mark did not feel like taking on the job.

"I'm a professor of history, Ernie, not a musician."

"Pffft. What's history?" said Ernie, picking a piece of lint off the desk and dropping it onto the carpet.

Well, this was fun.

Mark purposely ignored Ernie's meaning. "You don't know the definition of that, at your age?"

Ernie gave him a patronizing smile. "You have chosen a morass of a field to specialize in. Something no one can master. A discipline made for mediocrity. But one man can completely master the piano, above all others."

If Amy were here, she would have shot Mark a warning look. Even grabbed his arm to give him pause. But she wasn't here. And Mark couldn't help himself.

"And you are that man?"

Unbelievably, ridiculously, Ernie said, "Yes."

Ernie leaned back in his chair, his carefully guarded hands folded protectively in his lap. "Each of my hands can play fifteen notes per second. Fifteen—at the same time. Yes, I am that man."

Perhaps being raised as a Channon, Ernie's view of himself felt natural. But Mark almost choked on the arrogance. He made himself answer.

"Impressive."

He decided to keep Ernie talking. Any man who would freely admit a belief in his own greatness, could inadvertently admit other things. He sat down on the sofa and asked another question.

"Do you believe that a man's skill in one area makes him surpass all other men in quality and in importance, no matter what their field?"

Ernie adjusted the napkin on his lap. "It qualifies a man for celebrity, for success, and for the adulation that is his right."

Yes, there was something a little scary about Ernie.

"How fast could Baiss play? Do you remember?" Mark had a feeling that Baiss would care more about the notes themselves than about how fast he could play them.

Ernie looked startled for a moment, but didn't answer.

Kelly entered and plopped a plate down on the desk in front of Ernie. She left the study without saying a word. Ernie picked up his fork and stabbed a piece of shrimp.

Mark was fascinated to see Ernie actually using his hands, but frustrated with himself. He had to keep Ernie talking about things, and one sure way to do it, though he hated it, was to give a sop to his conceit.

"Were you ever a teacher for Baiss? I mean, did you ever show him what you know? It would be a natural thing to do."

Ernie could not have looked more uninterested. "He had his own teachers."

Mark thought quickly and tried again. "You know the world of professional piano more than anyone else here. Could Baiss be lost in a crevice of it somewhere?"

Ernie's face hardened even more and the words he spoke were cold. "I do not know, nor do I care."

But, hadn't Ernie been behind one of the searches for Baiss? Perhaps with a different reason than the others. A horrid thought came to him. Perhaps Ernie tried to make sure Baiss stayed away.

What should he say now? What question could possibly bring more information out of Ernie? Mark's brain searched wildly, but only found a variant of the over-worn question.

"You don't expect him to come back? Or do you *know* he won't come back? Then, do you know *why* he left?" Mark gestured with the book in his hand.

Ernie's demeanor changed abruptly, like something had stung him. Was that fear? Whatever it was, anger swiftly followed.

"My business is not with that overgrown adolescent. He can stay gone if he wishes. I have no need to beg his charity like Fia. I'm not the kind to lose my townhouse in one night's gambling. But there are more important things to do with the Channon money than give it to Baiss, whether he comes back or not."

"Wait. The *Channon* money? It's *his* money. It belongs to Baiss. You already got your inheritance, and now you want his?"

"I am the senior member of this family, and he is the most junior. And besides, I have the greatest gifts."

"What does the legal transfer of money have to do with that?"

Ernie scowled. "Look, Mr. Newlin. I do not have to discuss anything with you. You are merely a paying customer who has long outstayed your welcome in my family home. But understand this: Baiss will not return. And Victor Gaff will not get the money.

"My brother tried to be too clever when he wrote his will, but he made some mistakes. In the end, the money will return to the head of the family, as is only reasonable. So you see, where Baiss is at the moment has no bearing on the Channon money."

Mark leaned forward. "You intend to take it."

Self-satisfaction showed on Ernie's face. "I intend to make sure I receive it." He picked up his knife and calmly cut another piece of the fish. "My brother John always knew I was his superior. And from somewhere beyond the grave, he's going to learn that I still am."

"But you're talking about theft. That's what this is, isn't it? Theft."

Ernie gave all his attention to the swordfish. "Mr. Newlin, you are boring me."

"What did Baiss ever do to you, Ernie?"

Ernie did not answer. He reached for his glass, yet his eyes, almost against their will, glanced at the book in Mark's hand. As he took a drink, dots of moisture broke out on his forehead, one by one.

Mark set the circus book carefully down on the coffee table in front of him. A memento of the missing man's boyhood interest. Baiss loved the circus, it seemed, but he had loved the piano so much more.

Yet, he had an uncle, a jealous uncle. Jealous of his money, jealous of his skill. And that was disturbing.

Mark got to his feet and looked at the man sitting at

the desk, who was showing all the signs of being completely engrossed in eating.

"Do you ever wonder, Mr. Channon," he said, quietly, "why skill, however great, has no power to make men moral?"

MARK LEFT THE STUDY, his mind racing through all that Ernie had said. Why had Ernie immediately shifted the conversation from Baiss's whereabouts to the Channon money? For the opportunity of bragging? Ernie had no need to brag in front of a college professor he barely knew. And, what was behind that flash of fear? Mark needed the answers to those questions, and they wouldn't be coming from Ernie.

JULIANE CAME in the front door as Mark was heading for the stairs. She was wearing her black boots and coat, and looking as much like a dark curse as when he had first seen her. On impulse he said, "Juliane, what if I buy you a drink somewhere?"

She gazed at him. Perhaps amused. "All right."

"We'll have to walk, so it's the Bar on the Square if you're up to slumming tonight."

"I can slum. I'm not like Ernie. This sounds interesting, Mr. Newlin."

He went upstairs to get his coat, and when he came down she was still waiting for him. She must be hard up for excitement tonight.

They walked down the drive. It was a still night, but

cold enough to see one's breath. "If you haven't eaten, I can get you something. I hear they have good burgers at the Square, and I'll be getting one."

"Just a drink, Mr. Newlin."

They were waiting at the traffic light to cross the street by the square when she turned and looked at him. "You want me to tell you something, don't you?" This clearly in the tone of someone who was really saying, *you're not getting anything out of me.*

"I have a question to ask you, yes, but whatever else you'd like to talk about is completely up to you."

The light changed and they crossed the street. Juliane was a brisk walker. Adrenaline made it easy to keep pace with her.

They were passing Baker's office when she said, "What makes you think I'll answer you?"

"Absolutely nothing," he replied. "If we were different people, I'd tell you how beautiful you looked on the night of the party. I would compliment your talent for mischief. You would laugh and be so flattered that you'd gush and tell me anything. But since both of those hypothetical people would make us gag, I'm not going to do that."

He held the bar door open for her, then followed her in.

27

———

Under a Streetlight

Loud, yes. More country music than he could stand, yes. Though on a good day, he didn't mind it so much.

The bar restaurant was long and narrow, with tables scattered down its length. Juliane chose a small round barrel of a table near a black-curtained window, a spot where the music wasn't so loud. A battery-powered candle flickered in a lantern in the center of the table. She ordered a Manhattan, and he the burger and a beer.

Juliane looked coolly at him. "So what question do you have for me?"

There would be no reason to gently ease into the topic. Juliane wasn't that kind of person. It would be direct and fast. He dove in.

"You have a brother who took something from you

that you cared about very much, who tore up the beautiful plants you had nurtured. I want to know what Ernie took from Baiss."

The slight shift. A blink. She hadn't expected this question.

He went on. "You told Fia of a prank. Something that Ernie had done to him, maybe the year he ran away. A prank you wouldn't even tell her about. What was it? He destroyed something of Baiss's, just like he destroyed something of yours, didn't he?"

She set a trim black purse on the table, and smoothed her dark hair with one hand. "I think Ernie regrets telling me."

"But he needed someone to brag to. Someone in the family."

She smirked. "And I kept his secret so I could use it against him."

"Waiting for the opportune moment?"

She smiled like a cat. "I make every moment an opportunity."

"I just spoke with Ernie, and I get the feeling he has a plan afoot to get Baiss's money."

"Of course he does. Ernie hasn't been able to get along with any of his agents or managers for years. And if you can't get performances or recordings, you don't get paid. Yes, he definitely needs the money. They all do."

"Not you?"

"I don't need it. If you don't need something, you can't be controlled by it."

"True."

"So I can control you by not giving you the answer you want right now."

"Frustrate, yes. Control, no."

The waitress set their drinks in front of them. "Burger'll be up in a minute."

Juliane was not the kind who needed things sugar-coated, so he spoke truthfully as he saw it. "It's your own type of game, tormenting your siblings, isn't it? You took after your older brothers and learned their ways well. I take it John was as heartless as Ernie. Did they have competitions to see who was worse?"

"They did. It terrified Barbara."

"It would terrify any sane person. Was it fun for you to watch them?"

She actually smiled at this. "It made life exciting."

"That's why you do it now?"

She laughed out loud.

"You haven't told me who was better at this game. John, Ernie, or Will? Of the three, who would you bet on?"

"You've forgotten me, Mr. Newlin." She leaned back in her chair. "When Nick was a boy, his father was invited to dine with the mayor of New York City. How carefully he prepared for it—buying a new suit, studying protocol, having his hair cut, a new cologne even. And he told me several dozen times how bad he felt that I hadn't been invited too."

There was sarcasm in her voice. "So off he went in the taxi and showed up at the door of Gracie Mansion with his invitation, only to find—"

"That he hadn't been invited after all. The invitation was forged."

Juliane's eyebrows lifted slightly. "You're clever, Mr. Newlin. He wasn't. He was angry for weeks, roiling in fury. Then Nick told him I had done it. The divorce followed soon after, of course. And Nick learned the hard way that he sided with the wrong parent."

Juliane, like Ernie, needed someone to boast in front of.

"All right, you've convinced me of your talent. Then you're in a good position to give an opinion on your brothers. Who was worse? Who would you put your money on?"

Juliane eyed the tables behind him thoughtfully. He hoped she was deciding to talk. He was finding her company as nauseating as Ernie's. Yet he had to be patient.

"Ernie," she said at last.

"What makes you say Ernie?"

"Because he could take two people out in one stroke. All John could manage was one at a time."

"Like tying up Fia. Or ruining Elizabeth's recital."

Her eyes actually widened. "You know about that?"

So the timing of John's phone call *had* been purposefully done. He felt sick, but kept the act going. He cocked his head and looked directly at her. "I'm not sure I'd bet on Ernie. He's too smug for this kind of work, and he doesn't like to use his hands."

"Ernie used friends."

"No." *Ernie had friends?*

"Of course he did. How else could he get Baiss out the window?"

He tried not to react. Years of listening to students talk

about their shocking lives stood him in good stead. He kept his voice calm. "I don't know. How did he do it, and why did he want to?"

The waitress brought his burger and fries, each stuffed in short, brown bags and nestled in a red plastic basket, indoor-picnic style.

After she left, Juliane stared cockily into space, then rested her hand on Mark's arm. He had reached out to sample a french fry, but changed his mind. The touch made him remember how still and frightened Elizabeth had looked when Juliane reached for her hair. He pulled back.

"I think I better go." He needed to know what Ernie had done, but he'd be hanged if he'd play mouse to Juliane's cat.

All of a sudden her demeanor changed. Her eyes brightened and she leaned in as if he were the most important person in the world. "All right, professor. You wanted a story."

Juliane was finally telling her secret, and she was getting all the enjoyment out of it she could. She told him the whole story and more with as much élan as if she were flirting with the president. And he knew that some of her laughter was due to the sick horror on his face. When she had finished, she stood up and slurped the last of her drink in one gulp.

"Don't walk me back. I see a friend." She rested a hand on his shoulder—too long—then sauntered off down the length of the bar. Like the villainess of a noir film.

He turned to watch her go—struck dumb by what she had told him—and saw Elizabeth sitting at a table farther down. She held his gaze for just a moment, pain in her eyes, before she turned away.

Mark was on his feet in an instant, grabbing his burger sacks, shoving some bills into the hand of a passing waitress. He went over to Elizabeth's table and muttered a quick "excuse me" to the brown-haired woman sharing the table with her. The hurt had not completely left Elizabeth's face. He reached for her arm.

"Elizabeth, could I talk to you for a minute? Outside? Please? It's very important."

The hurt changed to flustered alarm. "Certainly, Dr. Newlin."

He stepped back while she got her coat and made some explanation to her friend, then he took her arm again. It was like holding onto sanity in a world filled with madness.

They left the bar and the twanging guitar and turned east, away from the river and deeper into the square. He was wondering how to begin when he saw a man sitting alone in the doorway of a closed travel bureau.

"Here," he said, releasing Elizabeth's arm and going up to him. He handed the man his dinner. "Here's a hot meal for you."

The man looked surprised, then nodded, and took it from him, looking curiously into the bags.

They crossed the streets to the next leg of the square, walking side by side. Elizabeth was being patient, silently waiting for his explanation. Finally, the words formed themselves in his mind.

"I want to thank you for your help back there. Because of you, Juliane told me what happened the year Baiss ran away. What must have made him run."

"Because of me?" She sounded as if she wasn't ready to believe him.

"It's true. Juliane knew what Ernie had done, but dodged telling me, in her usual style. It was more than I could stand. I told her I had to go, when she saw a chance to antagonize you. But she wanted to use me to do it, and the only way to keep me was to tell me what I wanted to know."

Understanding replaced some of the hurt in her eyes. She glanced away. "You really think she told you the truth?"

He nodded slowly. "Yes. Because the secret might be losing its value to her. And because what she said fits with what we know about John, Ernie, and Baiss. And it explains things, Elizabeth. Explains a lot of things."

He stopped under a streetlight and turned to face her. Tears filled his eyes and constricted his throat as he tried to find the words to tell her. She watched him with increasing concern on her face.

He thought of the joy he had heard on that old CD. Baiss's heart and talent. His gift for the world. How it had helped the people of Omaha heal. How it had brought joy to Chicago. How he had been moved by it in the middle of his own grief.

A group of teenagers walked by. One called out, "Hi, Ms. Channon!" Probably a choir student. Elizabeth called out a response, but kept her eyes on Mark.

"Elizabeth, Ernie made sure Baiss would never play the piano again."

Her eyes widened with horror. She covered her mouth with both hands.

"According to Juliane, Ernie couldn't tell John what he had done because John would have found a way to kill him. But he had to brag, so he told Juliane."

He told her the story under the street lamp while the chill wind sprang up. While the darkness deepened. While the door to the bar across the square opened and closed, leaking country music out into the cold, autumn night.

While tears streamed down both their faces, and their hearts bled and writhed with fury and agony for the boy who had made a continual search for the four most beautiful notes.

The boy who had beauty flow from his fingertips. Who had played joy and healing for the people who heard him.

And who had finally disappeared, stripped of his gift, grieving and alone.

28

———

A Startling Accusation

Mark sat on his bed thinking and not wanting to think at the same time. It was late—after midnight—and he couldn't sleep.

Knowledge always has implications. Truth has its own demands. You couldn't study as long and as deeply in his profession and fail to realize that. He missed Amy terribly, wanting to talk with her about this, wanting to discuss with her what he should do.

The doorknob clicked, and Sean walked in quietly, then stopped. "You're still up?"

"Not for much longer. What time is it?"

Sean shut the door. "Around one."

Mark nodded, just to show he heard. "How was your night?"

Sean dropped to the floor as was his habit. Those historical chairs were too small for his restless height. "Wonderful."

His tone carried a hidden message that made Mark look closely at him.

"I think I love Felicitas," said Sean. "Really." There was an unmistakable glow on his face. More was lighting up the room than the bedside lamp.

"I think I can understand that."

Sean was looking at him. "You all right?"

Mark got up and went to his closet, unbuckling his belt and pulling it from his waist. "Going to bed now." He hung it on a hook on the closet wall.

Sean looked too happy. Anything Mark would say —*anything*—would destroy that. Now was not the time. Sean was in love. Let him enjoy it.

Sean got up and headed for his own room. He paused at the door. "Pancakes for breakfast, or are we eating here?"

"Is Felicitas working?"

"No."

"How about that coffee shop at the college? We're working there tomorrow, right?"

"Yeah. Sure. Let's do that." Sean was happy. Agreeable to anything tonight. "Oh, and we have an invitation to Thanksgiving dinner—you and me—with the Juarez family. George told me to be sure to ask you."

"Tell him yes. Can't think of any place I would rather be." He meant it sincerely.

Sean grinned. The bathroom light made his teeth even brighter. "Great. Thanks."

Mark crawled in bed, listening to the muffled sounds from Sean's room, and waited for sleep. Then he got out again and turned the CD player on. *Baiss Channon with the Chicago Symphony.* He wanted to concentrate on each note. But the horror of Juliane's story permeated every phrase.

AFTER A FEW HOURS at Ashington College, during which both Mark and Sean had trouble concentrating, for completely different reasons, they returned to Riverview House to complete a regular duty. Laundry.

A new orange and brown wreath decorated the front door, greeting them with holiday spirit. This dissipated a few feet into the entryway, and completely disappeared in a circle of scowling Channons staring at their hotel manager.

Todd was in his lair, frantically searching through desk drawers.

Mark stepped toward them. "Is something wrong?"

Stephanie answered him without taking her eyes from Todd's activity. "We've been robbed. Several thousand dollars." She glared at her husband. "Why wasn't it in the safe? It always goes in the safe. How could you leave it out?"

Fia spoke up. "Because this hotel thing has always been a joke."

"Shut up!" Stephanie screamed at her.

Mark turned to Todd. "Look, can we help somehow? Is there anything we can do?"

Before Todd could open his mouth, Will spoke up.

"You just back away, professor. You and your little buddy." He looked over Mark's shoulder at Sean. "You know, I think we may have the culprit right here." Will stepped around Stephanie and came towards them.

"A guy like you sneaking around in the middle of the night, waiting for my boy to make a mistake, watching for the chance to fill your pockets." He stared at Sean's worn jean pockets as if he saw hundred dollar bills hanging out of them.

"You must be out of your mind." Sean's voice was level. Controlled.

"You were sneaking around after midnight last night. I saw you." Will, red-faced, narrow-eyed, inched closer. Mark didn't move out of his way. "The money was there when Todd locked the door last night. It's gone today."

Sean wasn't moving either. "I got back around one in the morning like I often do. But if you saw me, then you must have been sneaking around too."

Will's face flushed even redder at this. He took a step closer. "Don't you *dare* try to accuse me. Todd, let's get up there and search his room."

"Only with a police warrant," said Sean quietly.

Todd's head jerked up. "What?"

"The only way my room will be searched is by the police and that with a warrant. Not by you, or anyone else in the hotel." Sean could look hard and intimidating too.

"Dad, stop." Todd was pleading.

Will faltered like a rhino mid-charge who just had a small bird fly into his ear. "What? Why?"

"I don't want to call the police. We don't do that."

"We don't have to," Will answered. "This is our house. We can go into any room we like."

"This is Baiss Channon's house. Run, by the agreement of his trust, as a public hotel," said Mark. "If you disagree about the bounds of your authority, perhaps you should ask the trust. Warren Egan or Leal Baker would know the answer for you."

"Stop mouthing off, Will," said Fia. "Call Baker, and leave the boy alone."

Will's eyes narrowed even more. The look on his face showed he wasn't going to let it go. And he was going to stay on his course, allies or no allies.

"I saw him open your drawers, Todd," Will said. "He was going through your papers."

"What papers?" asked Sean calmly.

"The ones in the top—" Will suddenly looked bewildered. Mark wondered if he had a drink or three in him.

"Papers or money? What's missing?"

Mark admired Sean's control.

"I didn't think of checking for papers," said Todd, pulling open the drawers again.

It was turning into a farce once more, and the key players didn't realize it. Fia rolled her eyes and stomped off toward the restaurant.

"Look, Todd," said Mark. "Sean and I are just going to get our laundry and head to the laundromat. You can call us there or ask us any questions you wish. We're getting pizza tonight, but we'll be back. We'll cooperate with anything you ask within reason. All right?"

Todd looked from Mark to Sean, to his father Will,

and back again. Stephanie stood motionless, watching all of them.

"Sean, did you go through my desk?" Todd asked.

"I did not. I have not touched your desk the whole time we have been here."

"Okay, then. Thanks." Todd shot a nervous glance at his dad, and bent over the computer.

"May we get our laundry now?" Mark asked.

"Yeah. Sure. Go ahead." Todd didn't meet his eye.

Will was breathing hard when they walked past him and up the stairs.

Sean's control evaporated as soon as they were in their room, the door shut behind them. He threw his backpack against the wall. "What the heck is going on down there?"

"You recognize it." Mark kept his voice light. "This is called Dealing with Misfortune, Channon-Style. This is the first lead performance I've seen from Will. He has his own charm, don't you think?"

He turned serious. "However, you earned my highest admiration. That was difficult."

"Will almost swung at me!"

"I know."

Sean let out a loud, exasperated groan, picked up his backpack, and went to his room. Mark gathered his laundry bag from the closet. Took some books out of his own satchel and replaced them with puzzle books. He was trembling, shaking with the adrenaline that was now washing through him looking for something to do.

Will's fist would never have found any part of Sean.

Not as long as he was there. He stretched his fingers and shook his arms, trying to let some of the tension go. He took a deep breath and let it out slowly.

Amy, this is worse *than a soap opera nightmare.*

Sean came back through, his backpack and laundry bag packed full. "I'm not leaving anything behind. I don't trust them. You know they'll go through our rooms while we're gone."

Mark zipped up his satchel. "Should we leave a note? Write a big 'HI, TODD' and paste it on the bathroom door?"

Sean almost smiled.

Mark punched his arm. "Aw, Felicitas picked a good guy. Let's go."

Todd was on the phone at his desk when they came down. He waved them over. "It's Baker. He wants to know if the two of you will stay close until all this is resolved. Strictly on your own honor, of course."

"Of course," said Mark.

"And will you vouch for Mr. Merritt?"

Sean let out a forceful breath.

"He does not need any vouching for," Mark replied, "but since you seem to need to hear those words—yes, I will."

"Thank you. Uh, that's it."

ONCE OUTSIDE MARK couldn't get to the car fast enough, but he forced himself to walk slowly. All they needed was to be seen running for their car, clutching overstuffed bags. He felt like doing that on purpose. But it wouldn't help Sean any.

Sean didn't say much for a long while. Not until they found open machines, threw their clothes in, and put in enough quarters to start them running. Mark settled himself in the most comfortable chair he could find, which meant one that didn't wobble, and opened his puzzle book. He wanted to think about something almost pointless instead of that disgusting drama. He found the page and creased it open, making himself focus on how many different combinations of seven numbers could add up to thirty-one.

Sean stood next to him. "I'm hungry. Is it okay if I go get some real food?"

Mark glanced over at the large, ugly vending machine. "You mean outdated candy bars and stale chips don't appeal to you?"

Sean didn't answer. Then Mark realized what he had heard in Sean's voice. The parolee asking permission of his parole officer. The vouch-ee asking the vouch-er for trust.

Mark handed him the car keys. "Get out of here."

He was deep into his third puzzle, trying hard not to think about a single Channon, when Sean returned and thrust a burger sack at him.

"I thought we were having pizza."

"This is an appetizer."

"For you maybe, wire-weight."

"You've got nothing to worry about. Dr. Waite is going to be so impressed when he sees you again." Sean unwrapped his sandwich and took a big bite.

Mark peeled back the paper from his. "And this is your healthy choice for me, Nurse Merritt? You mean I've wasted all that time sneaking these behind your back?"

Sean feigned horror then did the professional act. "All in balance, sir. If you've noticed, I skipped the fries this time, made sure it was cooked well-done, and added extra tomato and lettuce to yours."

THEY TRIED to be light-hearted and enjoy a Friday night, but Will's accusation weighed on them. After the trunk was filled with folded laundry, they went for their customary pizza at the sports bar and watched part of an ice hockey game on the large screen. But Mark felt worn and dull.

Sean said it was because the baseball season was over. Because they were running out of things to do in this town. Because it was getting too cold. Mark saw him rubbing his hands together as they walked back to the car and made a mental note to buy him some gloves.

Sean suggested they get Elizabeth again, then changed his mind, looking questioningly at Mark.

"She and I are okay now," Mark said. "I ran into her yesterday and we talked like old friends." He still couldn't bear to tell Sean what it was they had talked about.

Sean watched him closely, with the look of someone trying not to be obvious about it. "What about a movie then? If it's too loud for your head, we can leave."

They went and saw a movie.

It was eleven thirty when they came back to Riverview

House with their bags of folded laundry. They pretended to see nothing unusual in the sight of Todd Channon sitting alone on a couch in the main hall, reading a newspaper. Or that he folded his paper, flicked off the light, and followed them upstairs.

29

A Man in the Doorway

MORE DAYS WENT by as November worked its slow way toward Thanksgiving. They were oppressive days for Mark.

The accusation of theft tainted the air at Riverview. Baker came for several closed door sessions with Todd, but beyond those, Mark saw no other evidence that something was being done about the disappearance of those thousands.

Of course, the theft was a minor thing compared to the imminent loss of John Channon's money and property to the county. On top of that, Mark's own struggle with grief and the horrible secret surrounding Baiss Channon made Riverview House virtually unbearable.

Sean was too much in love to think about Baiss now. As his love for Felicitas grew, his interest in the Baiss question waned. He spent much of his time with Felicitas, so Mark was often on his own. And he didn't want to spend any more time in the Channon home than he had to. When Sean was out on a date, Mark walked the downtown streets, rotating through the few dinner places that were open near Riverview House.

He spent his thoughts on Amy. On preparing for London. But often as he walked, he wondered about Baiss. Prayed about Baiss. And stared down the twilit streets, imagining Baiss walking somewhere nearby. With his crushing secret.

On a night when Mark was roaming downtown again, trying to decide on a dinner place, he had the feeling someone was following him. A quick glance over his shoulder showed a man, bundled against the chill, walking about a third of a block behind him.

Mark decided to turn down the street before the square to see if the man might be purposefully following him. It was silly, of course, but nevertheless, he did it. This street showed the back side of businesses, most now closed, with Dumpsters and scattered parking places punctuating the sidewalk. The un-pretty behind-the-scenes of the square.

Mark walked briskly, then allowed himself another quick glance. The man had turned down the street after him.

Mark went to the end of the block, and took a left, heading toward the brighter lights of the square. Another left and Mark would know for certain. No reason the man's path should double back on itself. Unless he truly were following him.

He came out onto the square, made his turn, and was going back towards the river, past the doors of closed shops with their security lights glowing through their windows. He was almost to the Bar on the Square when he looked back one more time.

The man was still following.

Mark hadn't planned on eating at the Bar, didn't want to set foot in it since Juliane's performance. But there it was, and he was tired of being followed. He pulled open the door and went in.

The place was less than half full. It was too early for the night crowd. Small groups of customers were sprinkled about the row of tables lining the walls. There were the same black curtains. Same fake lanterns on the tables. A few patrons sat at the bar itself. At the end, two tired-looking policemen chewed their way through the house burger on a pretzel bun.

Mark gave them a nod, then walked down the aisle to get a table. He chose the table Elizabeth and her friend had been sitting at the night Juliane spilled her secret, and took a seat that gave him a view of the door.

"The house burger, fries, and a small Blue Moon," he told the waitress.

"I'll have it out in about ten minutes, luv," she replied, in a lilting voice.

The accent surprised him, and took his mind away from his follower for a moment. "Are you British?"

"I wish," she said. The lilt slid away. "Spent the first

part of this year in London and loved it. When I miss it, I put the voice on."

"Ah. I'll be taking a group of students to London next semester with another professor. Did you ever go up in the dome of St. Paul's?"

She shook her head. "Too high for me. The others wanted to, so I went to the Tate and hung out there instead."

She brought his beer. "Burger will be out in five minutes."

He took a swallow and looked around the bar. No one had entered after him, but from where he sat he could see a hand resting on the handle of the glass entry door. Perhaps the hand of a man wondering what to do next.

Mark decided to just get busy. He took his notebook from his pocket, fished out a pen, and forced himself to think of the classes he would teach in London. Classes he had taught many times before. He planned to bring something different to them, use the uniqueness of London. That was the whole point of going there. He needed a few books from his office, but maybe Luedders could pick those up for him. One thing for sure, he would lead the first session of his class sitting down.

The waitress plunked a basket down on the table, hamburger and fries tucked in their thin brown picnic sacks. The burger smelled good. He was hungry. At least he'd get to try it this time. He slid his notebook back in his pocket and reached for the mustard.

The first bite told him he had spent his money well. The second was good enough to almost make him forget the man who still hovered in the doorway. While he was chewing the third, Will Channon entered the bar.

Before he could decide whether to be relieved or annoyed, Will started down the aisle toward him. Mark hoped Will would walk by, but Will pulled out the chair across the table from him and sat down.

What was it with the Channons? Did they never ask before joining someone at the table?

"Hello, Will," he said, as casually as he could. "How have you been doing? Are you out for a little exercise?"

Will scowled at him in reply, then reached out and picked up the salt shaker, spinning it in his hands. It had the look of a nervous habit.

Mark ate a french fry and took a sip of his beer. When Will still hadn't said anything, Mark offered, "Is there something on your mind?"

"You know what's on my mind."

This was clearly going to be an uphill conversation.

"I suppose I can guess. The theft of Todd's money."

The salt shaker stopped spinning. "And the thief."

Mark had no patience for this. "If you still have Sean in mind, I can assure you that you are completely wrong."

"I don't believe you."

Mark shrugged. "So what? I don't have to prove it to you. We're not in the courthouse. It's over there." He gave a vague gesture in its direction, and ate more fries.

Will stared at him. The salt shaker started up again between the fingers.

Will was clearly the most clumsy of the Channons. Clumsy in the way he pursued things. The way he thought and communicated. That might not always have been the case. Couldn't have been, if, once upon a time, he had been able to keep up with John and Ernie. But years of heavy drinking have a way of dulling anyone. And it was easy to see why the new buyers didn't want to keep Will at the head of Channon World.

Mark was losing patience. He considered leaving, but Will would probably follow him out. And it would be wiser to put up with his game here, in an open, public place.

"Look, Will, why are you sitting here?"

"I'm sitting here for your benefit."

"Really." He couldn't hold all the sarcasm back.

"What if I told the police what I saw the night the money was stolen?"

"All right. What if you did? Every responsible citizen is supposed to do that. There's some policemen at the bar right now. Go tell them."

Will faltered for just a moment, then put on the sneer. "It wouldn't go well for your little friend."

"I suppose you want me to ask you what it is that you saw."

The salt shaker stopped for a moment, then spun some more.

Mark waited. Will was clearly building up to something, and there was no getting rid of him until he had done whatever he had come to do. Mark leaned back in his chair and watched him.

Another twirl of the shaker.

"Okay, Will, since you want to be asked. What is it that you saw?"

"I saw Sean hanging over the upper railing, watching the front desk. Waiting for his moment."

"And when was this?"

"Just when I told you. Around one in the morning."

"I don't think you saw that." For one thing, Sean would never willingly look down from any kind of height.

Will reddened. "Are you calling me a liar?"

"You can call yourself whatever you want to, but you didn't see Sean do that."

"I will tell the police that I did, unless . . . "

Mark fell for it. "Unless what?"

Will smirked. An oily smirk. "Unless you give me a certain amount of money every month. Let's say, five thousand dollars." He put the salt shaker down in the center of the table. "Just to keep your friend out of jail, of course. Wouldn't want him to go there, would you?"

Mark felt incredulous and furious at the same time. Incredulous at the stupidity of Will Channon. And furious that this evil man would attack a humble assistant who had spent the last year or more babysitting grumpy, injured professors. Mark swallowed carefully and feigned naiveté.

"No, no, of course not. Out of curiosity, where were you standing when you thought you saw Sean?"

"Down below. I looked up and saw his face hanging over the railing."

Mark cleared his throat. "You know, Will, I don't think that's how it happened. I don't think that's how it happened at all."

Will's eyes narrowed. "What are you saying?"

"Because for you to look up and see Sean, you would

have to be standing by Todd's desk yourself. And, that would implicate *you*, not him. That would make *him* the witness against you." Mark leaned forward in his chair and gave Will a cold look. "So, are you sure you want to persist in this futile blackmail attempt?"

For a moment, Will Channon looked like someone had knocked the wind out of him. His planned performance wasn't going the way he had expected. Someone had changed the script.

But for his part, Mark had had enough. "Look, Will, you know what happened to Todd's money, don't you? Why don't you just give it back to him?"

Will stared at him. His mouth moved, but no words came out. Then his face flushed hideously. He dove across the table. Mark had barely a moment to move out of the way.

Not far enough.

The table, the lantern, the hamburger, mustard, beer, and a large, raving Channon came crashing down on top of him. His head landed on something soft, but his legs were pinned. And Will had the advantage.

Mark was outraged. He blocked Will's attempts to grab at his throat. "Get off of me!" he roared.

Will ignored him and wriggled to get at his throat again. Mark could hardly move his arm, but a jab got Will right in the eye. He was stunned, blinking. And in that moment, a long, dark blue, uniformed sleeve reached down from above and grabbed at Will's collar.

"So, what's happening here?" said a voice of calm authority.

Mark was not surprised when Will responded with the childish cry. "He started it!"

Mark got slowly, painfully, to his feet, as french fries and pieces of hamburger fell off of him. A woman darted forward and grabbed the bag he had landed on.

They had drawn the attention of everyone in the bar. He got a quick impression of staring faces—nervous, angry, curious, disappointed—turned their way.

The policeman looked at Mark. "And what do *you* say?"

Before he could answer, the waitress piped up. "He didn't start it. The big one did. The big one dove for him. I saw it!"

"That's a lie," cried Will. "I'm a Channon, and he was insulting me!"

"Very well," the officer said. "If you wish to press charges against this man, I will need to take you over to the city jail where you can both spend a pleasant night while we sort things out."

Will looked horrified. "What do you mean? It's *his* fault! I'm not going to jail because of him!" The man who had so happily threatened Sean with jail was absolutely terrified to go there himself.

The second policeman stood next to his partner, watching.

"That's the law for everyone," the first one went on. "Until the law can discover who was actually at fault, you both go to jail. Do you still want to press charges?"

Will pulled himself away from the policeman's grip and stood up straight. He cast Mark a malevolent look. "No."

The words came out quickly, and Mark didn't call them back.

"But I do," he said.

The policeman turned to him. "You understand that you will have to spend a night in jail also?"

"Yes, I do," Mark replied. "I will gladly spend a night in jail as long as you make sure he does too. Just don't put me in the same cell, that's all I ask."

Will blanched. "You can't do that! I'm not going! I refuse!"

The most satisfying sound Mark had heard in days was the snap of the handcuffs around Will's wrists.

30

A Message from Baiss

"You're lucky," the policeman said as he slid a section of the bars open, motioning for Mark to enter. "We've got a slow night. We can put the big guy farther down there."

Six cells faced each other, three on a side, the bars a pale green. One long bench lined the back of each cell.

"Am I allowed one phone call?" Mark asked. "You know, like in the movies?"

"Phone's right on the wall over there. You can call all you want. But only collect calls if they're long distance. The phone will refuse any other kind." He slid the bars closed and locked the cell. "I can get you a lawyer's name if you need one. Do you want to call a lawyer?"

"No." Mark went over to the wall and picked up the receiver. "My piano teacher."

The officer stared at him through the bars.

"It's okay," Mark went on. "I know her number."

The man shook his head and walked back up the stairs.

Mark pressed Elizabeth's number into the phone. It only made sense. Sean was pretty careless about putting minutes on his temporary phone. But Elizabeth knew Felicitas, and Felicitas would know where Sean was. No sense calling Jerry Waite unless things got real serious. And he didn't want to alarm Patti.

After the phone had rung for some time, Mark left a message, then sat down on the bench to wait. He took a long, slow, deep breath. It hurt. In fact, he hurt all over. How was his head? He couldn't remember it hitting the floor. Had it landed on someone's shoe or someone's purse? His head seemed to be okay, but the rest of him wasn't.

In the last hour he had been threatened with blackmail, physically assaulted, and now he was in jail. Furthermore, a pain in his side was slowly increasing.

Hang these Channons! Did he come up here to heal or be killed?

He leaned forward and rested his arms on his knees. His insides didn't hurt quite as much that way.

The corridor and cells of this basement jail were lit, but empty. Mark preferred that at the moment. Because it was a strange, unsettling experience to be on the wrong side of the bars.

He tried another deep breath. Ouch.

So why was he here? Was it his own stubbornness? His own insistence to teach someone a lesson? A lesson that he would have to pay for too? What would Patti think? What would the college say?

He put his face in his hands.

Mark, Mark, Mark. What are you doing?

No answer came to mind.

He felt like a fool.

He should have left Ashington Mills weeks ago. He could have made arrangements to pay Jerry back. Which, of course, Jerry would never agree to. And which would cause more trouble between them. Because Mark wasn't supposed to know that this was all on Jerry's dime.

The door opened above. Will Channon's voice came through it first.

"I'm not going down there! I'm a Channon, I tell you."

"Yes, you did. And I've spelled it correctly. You just take a deep breath and control yourself. If you decide to tell us what the fight was about, we can go see Detective Mitchell."

"I don't have to go see anyone. We built this court-house! Don't you understand that?"

"And we thank you very much. Now will you come along, or will you require some assistance?"

Will was too busy protesting to notice Mark as he passed the cell.

"But I tell you, I shouldn't be here!"

The policeman remained calm. "I agree with you completely."

The cell door slid shut with a clang. Will let out a bellow. It was still echoing off the walls when the upper door closed again and only the prisoners were left in the jail.

Will fell silent for awhile.

Mark held still. Making no noise.

"Newlin?" The voice wavered. "Newlin, are you in here?"

There was no point in answering. And his silence didn't matter anyway. Because Will called his name again and cursed it thoroughly with more language than Mark had ever heard in all his years on a college campus.

He rested his head in his hands and let the tide roll over him.

HALF AN HOUR PASSED before the upper door opened and the sound of footsteps came down the concrete stairs.

Elizabeth looked at him through the bars with the same look of worried compassion on her face as when he had first seen her peering out the kitchen doorway at Riverview House. But now, instead of embarrassing him, that look heartened him.

"You look awful, Mark. You must be hurt. *Are* you hurt?"

He stood up and walked stiffly over to the bars.

"We'll figure that out later. Did you tell Sean?"

"I called Felicitas. Sean's on his way. And Baker too."

"I'm not sure he'll be thrilled about this."

"Your face is smeared. Do you have a handkerchief or a tissue?"

"They have it all upstairs. Including my notebook, with things I'm adding to my history courses in England. My students, if they knew, would be rooting for the Ashington Mills Police Department, and hoping they impound my notebook forever. But look," he said, demonstrating, "classic use of a sleeve."

He buried his eyes in the bend of his elbow for a quick rub.

"Now you have more mustard on your face." She rooted through her purse and pulled out a tissue. She held it up in the air between two fingers and waved it at the watchful policeman at the end of the corridor. "It's only a tissue. Nothing else. So he can wipe his face?"

"I'm sorry, ma'am. Give nothing to the prisoner."

Elizabeth frowned and put the tissue back in her purse.

"It's okay, Elizabeth." Her sadness cut him to the heart. "It's okay, really. They're on our side. I used to use mustard for warpaint when I was a kid. Works so much better than ketchup."

She almost smiled. "I didn't really understand your phone message. Mark, why are you in here?"

"I stopped at the Bar on the Square for something to eat. Will followed me in." Mark spoke as quietly as he could.

"*Will?*"

"He tried to blackmail me with a lie about Sean taking Todd's money. I suggested what probably happened to the money, and he jumped me." He said it carefully, mindful that Elizabeth was Will's half-sister. "I'm sorry."

"You think Will—?"

There was a stir further down the hall. "Elizabeth? Is that you? Wait! Don't talk to Newlin! Whatever he said, he's lying!"

Elizabeth was spared more of this by the door opening

again and more footsteps. Baker came into view, followed by a policeman, and another lawyer-looking type. Mark couldn't remember seeing the third man before.

"You looked better the last time I saw you, Newlin," Baker said.

"I felt better then too. If you don't mind, I think I'll sit down."

"I've already read the statements upstairs, but more importantly, so has Stow. This is more in his line."

Stow turned to the policeman. "I assume you have read both these gentlemen their rights."

"Yes, sir. Officers Scott and Bristol have."

Stow went down the corridor. "Well, Will Channon. How have you been?" He had a pleasant voice. Firm and intelligent, speaking in a tone meant to bring equilibrium to a volatile situation.

Mark didn't hear the answer, because at that moment the door above opened again. And with relief, Mark looked up and saw Sean. All six foot and more of him, holding his black nurse bag, with fear all over his face.

"Professor, are you all right?" Sean turned to Baker. "I have to check him. I have to check his blood pressure. After his surgeries, something could have torn. He could be bleeding internally."

Baker turned to the policeman. "Could we check, Wayne? You can lock me in there with them. The professor is staying in our fair city for the sole purpose of healing, and this man is his nurse."

The policeman nodded, and soon Sean and Baker were sitting on the prisoner bench too, one on either side of him, Sean pumping away to inflate a blood pressure cuff, then listening intently, while Mark smiled at Elizabeth through the bars. She didn't smile back, but appeared to be listening as intently as Sean.

Sean released the cuff and pulled it off his arm. "That's definitely lower than normal. It could be dropping. Do you have pain in your abdomen, professor?"

"Some."

"He looks pale, Sean," said Elizabeth.

Sean responded by flashing a light in his eyes, taking his temperature and pulse, and looking in his nose and throat.

"Mr. Baker, the professor needs to go to a hospital. He needs to be checked out by a doctor. Something's going on inside of him, but I can't say for certain what it is."

Baker sat watching soberly from his spot on the bench to Mark's left.

"Please, Mr. Baker. Please," Sean said earnestly. "We have to get him to a hospital. Please."

Sean wore the look of the frightened child again. But Mark didn't have the strength to tease him out of it. He turned his head to see Baker.

The look on the lawyer's face was indescribable.

Baker didn't answer, but stared at Sean for several moments. Then blinked and assumed his professional manner again. He stood up and walked to the bars.

"Stow?" he called. "We could have an emergency here."

Then to the policeman. "How can I get him out of here?"

"Wait!" Will yelled out. "What about me? Where are you going?"

"Pipe down, Will!" This from Stow. "We're trying to save you from a manslaughter charge, all right?"

Well, that sounded serious.

All eyes were back on Mark. He had the vague feeling he had been in this position before. Now Elizabeth looked pale. And the expression on Sean's face unnerved him.

"I'll do whatever I have to do. Sure." He motioned toward Sean. "Just do whatever he says."

HE WENT TO THE HOSPITAL. In an ambulance. Again. Which put him right back in the horrific summer he had been trying to forget.

Sean insisted on staying with him every moment. But he was surprised that both Elizabeth and Baker came too. Sometime in the middle of the night, he underwent emergency exploratory surgery. Laparoscopic, they explained to him, using the records from the previous surgeon. He was blissfully asleep through it all, and spent the early hours dozing between pain pills.

He was trying to eat a few bites from a late breakfast tray, bits of scrambled eggs with no discernible taste to them, when Patti walked in.

"Don't be too surprised," she said, pulling up a chair by the bed. "Sean called us. We drove through the night. Zach's at the hotel sleeping now. But, oh, you look rough, Mark."

She tucked the straying strands of her long brown hair behind her ears, and her green-blue eyes looked tired. People used to think he and Patti were twins when they were growing up; they looked so similar. Mark recognized that funny squinched look on her face. She was trying not to cry.

"You broke your promise," she said. "You said you'd take care of yourself."

"I didn't break my promise. I've been eating well, sleeping better, exercising. Sean will give me a great report."

"Then what's this about being jumped in a bar? That doesn't sound like the brother I know."

"It's a long story." He pushed the tray away and took as deep a breath as the stitches would allow. "Patti, life has gotten really bizarre lately."

In the few words he had energy for, he told her about the missing money and Will's bullying, all of which did nothing to remove the worried look on her face.

"Gosh, Mark! I would be so angry! I'm furious! Aren't you?"

"Yes, actually. Though I don't have the spleen to show it."

She just looked at him. The creases in her forehead deepened.

"All right. Lousy attempt at humor. Truthfully, it's just a part of a bigger picture."

"What do you mean? What bigger picture?"

"The Channon family was a dynasty, a dynasty to be proud of once. Now I'm witnessing their collapse. The bar incident was just a piece of swirling debris caused by the fall."

"A piece of debris? Don't get all historical–philosophical on me, Mark. You're in a hospital bed, for pity's sake! That 'debris' could have killed you!"

"That's what Sean keeps saying. Once he got past the first fear, he had enough lightning bolts coming out of his eyes to be angry for all of us."

"Surely you don't have to stay here anymore. Can't you go home?"

He didn't want to tell her about Jerry's arrangements. Didn't really need to, because there was a more compelling reason to stay now.

Resting against the pillows, he slowly told her the story of Baiss Channon. Except for what must have been Baiss's reason for leaving. He couldn't bear to say those words again.

"Well, I don't know if I completely understand." She leaned back in her chair and looked at him for a few moments. "But it sounds just like something you and Amy would get involved in."

He gave a sad smile. "It does."

"So what happens now? How long will you be in here?"

"If all goes well, I can leave tomorrow. The surgeon said they found some tears near the previous surgical site, but she thinks they repaired them all."

"This is awful, Mark."

He tried to think of something encouraging or funny to say. He decided on honesty instead.

"It is." He glanced away, toward the window. "But it's been worse."

Elizabeth came by after school. A different Elizabeth. He was just waking up from a nap when she walked in with new energy. She sat down in the same chair Patti had used earlier, and smiled at him.

"Baker said I could share some news with you." She was watching him, anticipating his reaction.

"He's heard from Baiss."

"*What?*" He tried to sit up, then decided against it. "From Baiss? He's sure?"

"Absolutely."

"What? What has he heard?"

"He didn't tell me everything, but he said to make sure to tell you that Baiss has been watching the affairs of the household, and Baker is to release Sean Merritt from all suspicion."

"About the stolen money?"

She nodded.

He took a slow breath. "Well, that's good. I wish he would have said it a few days earlier and saved me all this."

The moment he said it, he regretted it. It's the thing he could have freely said to Sean or Patti. But Elizabeth was a Channon, after all.

Some of the light in her eyes faded. "I'm so sorry, Mark."

"You didn't do it."

"But I'm still so sorry."

He changed the subject. "Did Baiss say anything else? Is he coming back? Does he know about the will, about the deadline?"

"I don't know. I don't think Baker knows either. He said

that all we can do at this point is to trust Baiss to do whatever he wants."

He looked at her for a moment in silence, and he thought he understood the questions in her eyes.

How had Baiss survived this long, and what condition would he be in if he returned?

31

Thanksgiving Night

LATE THE NEXT AFTERNOON, Mark was released from the hospital. Patti's family left for home, and Sean and Felicitas brought Mark back to Riverview House.

"No stairs for a while," Sean said, leading him slowly towards the elevator.

"And I'll bring your food up to you, Dr. Newlin," Felicitas said, before she went off to the kitchen. "You take it easy."

Mark lay down on his bed and stared at the ceiling where his imaginary map waited for him. "Back to square one, I suppose." He tried to say it lightly, but it fell flat.

Sean gathered a water glass, puzzle books, paper, pens, magazines, and brought them to his bedside. "At least your glasses survived."

"That they did."

Sean sat down on the floor in his usual spot. When minutes had gone by without talk, Mark turned his head to look at him.

"What? Are you going to watch me sleep now?"

Sean's face was serious. "You didn't tell me everything yet. Why did Will attack you?"

He looked back up at the ceiling. "Best way to cover a guilty conscience, I suppose."

"What do you mean?"

"Will was planning to lie to the police about seeing you the night of the theft. He wanted me to pay him to make sure he wouldn't. I told him it would be better if he just gave the money back."

"And that's when he jumped you?"

"Yep."

If he erased Europe, he could begin again on the ceiling with South America. First, find a good ridge for the Andes.

Sean was still sitting there when Mark fell asleep.

THE ATMOSPHERE of Riverview House changed again. Instead of being infused with fears of imminent closure and financial ruin, hope burgeoned. Hope centered around the possible return of Baiss Channon.

With it came a certainty of what Baiss would do when he returned. Various members of the family seemed to want to talk about it, and since no one in the family cared to listen to each other for very long, they needed an outside person to talk to. Mark realized he was filling that void. He was also a slow-moving target.

His third day back, while he sat on a sofa watching the large fire in the main hall, Fia joined him. She talked for thirty minutes straight—almost without breathing—during which she called Baiss a generous boy and said she was sure he would help her out of her debt. She would soon live freely again. And Victor wouldn't get the house.

Juliane, wearing a sly grin, caught him in the parlor while he was at the piano. She was looking forward to seeing the first tender greeting between uncle and nephew. She also told him with glee that the Bar on the Square was billing Will for damages.

Kelly was looking forward to the heir's arrival also, with extra makeup and a new haircut.

Ernie seemed ever-present and played the grand piano in the large parlor for hours. Mark avoided him. But Todd Channon, at his desk, was a close-at-hand prisoner to these concerts.

When Mark asked how things were going for him, Todd said that Stephanie had given up the job waiting for her. Todd himself was sure that Baiss would like the idea of the hotel continuing. He also said that by the strict orders of his lawyers, Will Channon was not allowed within fifteen feet of Mark. It wouldn't happen again, Todd assured him.

Then Ernie took the bench in the other room, crashed out a loud arpeggio, and Todd rolled his eyes.

Mark didn't forget the darker side of it for one moment. Ernie had stolen Baiss's gift from him and was now filling the house with his own music before the heir's return. The vicious, old dog marking his territory. Getting ready for the challenge.

Mark still hadn't brought himself to tell Sean what Ernie had done to Baiss. He would, of course. But the right moment never came.

And Will left every room Mark walked into.

ON THANKSGIVING MORNING, Mark awoke to such an unexpectedly heavy weight of sadness, he felt it would crush him.

"Amy," he whispered to the early light. "Amy. Come back. It's enough. It's been long enough. I can't do this."

He covered his face with the pillow. He didn't know how he made it this far without her. Today, he didn't think he could make it any farther.

After a long while, he forced himself to breathe deeply, to get up, to shave and shower, and get dressed for the day. Moving slowly, though only a slight soreness remained from his surgery. He chose casual pants—navy blue. Button-down shirt—light blue. Amy's favorite.

He picked up his puzzle book and mechanical pencil and went to the tower room area, automatically checking the river for traffic as he sat down. Most of the leaves on the trees were down—only the oaks clung to their wrinkled browns—and he could see a long way downriver. In the distance, a wheelhouse gleamed white in the morning. What did it feel like to have your world be a long highway of water on a bright, cold morning?

He took a deep breath and wrote numbers into the

puzzle—the easy ones, the ones you could do without thinking—while he made a decision. He would carry the pain of today's grief and feel it, without trying to escape or run from it. Just bear it, even if it killed him. Which today it felt like it could.

He heard the shower water running. Sean was up.

The four unique numbers that add up to eleven are one-two-three-five.

The group of barges was much closer now, being pushed upriver by a stubborn engine that wouldn't take backwards for an answer.

Sean started to sing "That's Amore" in the shower, with gusto.

Four cars came up the drive and swooped into their parking spaces. The first arrivals for a completely booked Thanksgiving brunch.

The shower water shut off. He could hear the squawking sound of the shower walls being rubbed dry. Sean's habit, even though they had maid service.

A group of six unique numbers that add up to twenty-three will never have a nine among them. The nine would have to go into the other square then.

A horn honk. More cars. Loud voices. The door of Riverview House opening and closing. Holiday bustle.

Sean was standing next to him, wearing his white shirt and freshly cleaned jeans. On his face was the look of a nurse who did not like the numbers he was seeing on the chart.

"Are you okay?" It was not a rhetorical question.

"No. Not really."

"Holidays are the worst. The very worst. I should have

warned you. You can be doing okay, and then a holiday comes and knocks you over. Grief is twice as bad on holidays."

"How long does it take?"

Sean knew what he meant. "Years."

He nodded slowly, then closed his puzzle book and set it on the table, the pencil at its side. He stood up. "All right then. In the meantime, let's go see Felicitas."

"You think Victor Gaff will come today?" Sean asked, his hand on the doorknob.

"I don't think so. I don't think he could top his October performance, and he knows it."

They took the elevator down and entered the main hall, stepping into a world of white-covered tables topped with candles and silver and bowls of cranberries. Their reserved table was in the small parlor, one of four placed there.

Nick surpassed everything Mark had seen presented so far. Steaming roast turkeys with citrus and onion, rosemary and herb, or apple and sage dominated the room. Carvers stood by cranberry-glazed ham and beef pepper roast. Other tables held potatoes—russet, sweet, and gold—alongside enough ingeniously done vegetable dishes to sing a savory chorus to heaven. The aroma of fresh baked bread wove through it all. And a dessert table in the distance promised even more.

None of the Channon siblings were there yet. Elizabeth wouldn't be. She had flown to New York to spend the holiday with her mother. Mark thought he recognized a few faces from the Channon party. He saw Warren Egan, who introduced his wife. Egan shook his hand heartily.

"So, they let you eat today? Good, very good! With this vicious flu going around, I was sure someone would be sick, and I'd come in and see you standing at your old post."

Mark felt numb and dull, but he tried to say the polite thing. "Today that post is held by Jim, and I think he does a better job than I could."

"I wouldn't know about that. Glad we had you on hand for the party though. Trickiest event I've been to in some time. I wonder where our ghost went." Egan laughed at these words and turned to get in line for the citrus turkey.

Mark met Leal Baker by the fresh cranberry salad and said something he had been wanting to say for days. "Thank you, sir, for helping us out of that horrible mess."

"Certainly." Baker smiled, a relaxed smile. A lawyer letting down. A hard-working man at ease. Mark wanted to ask him about Baiss's message, but he didn't have the authority to. That truly would be interfering in business not his own. Instead, he wished Baker a happy Thanksgiving and moved on.

Felicitas was in charge of the small parlor, bringing drinks, removing dirty plates, and making Sean's eyes glow. It occurred to Mark, in the middle of a bite of rosemary-encrusted turkey, that Sean may have found the life he was looking for.

Much later—in front of large dishes of *arroz con pollo* at the Juarez house, listening to George Juarez praise Sean's gardening help, and seeing the love in his daughter's eyes as she gazed on this nurse, assistant, health coach, and friend—Mark was sure of it.

· · ·

SEAN AND FELICITAS did the dishes afterwards, with direction from Mrs. Juarez. Everyone insisted that Mark do nothing but relax. George turned on the TV for a football game and invited Mark to join him.

"Does Gold College have a football team like this?"

"No. No football. Football teams are expensive. We have soccer instead."

"World-class?"

Mark smiled at this. "We hope so, George. We hope so."

"Next year, I'll come see a game of yours at Gold College."

Mark was surprised. "Really?"

"Yes." George said it with certainty.

"I'd be glad to have you there, George. You tell me when you can come, and I'll buy the tickets. We'll probably win with you in the stands."

During a commercial break, George asked how he was feeling after his surgery. Mark told him that he was healing nicely.

George looked grim. Perhaps thinking about the event that caused the surgery. After a few moments he said, "I worked hard to give my family a place in this country, Dr. Newlin. John Channon, Senior, was a good person, but his children are not. My business is growing. Soon, I will have enough accounts to replace the large Channon account. Felicitas will work for me and we can leave the Channons behind. Of course, if the county gets the building . . ." His face darkened. "I will not work for the county."

"I understand your feelings, George."

George waved the remote in the air, as if gathering

thoughts. "This Baiss," he said, returning to the Channons, "the one they all want to return. What if he has become like all the others?" He paused a moment, then added, "What if he is worse?"

"I don't think he would be. Elizabeth told me wonderful things about him."

George shook his head, doubtfully.

Mark saw his chance and took it. "Did you ever talk to Baiss? Did you ever see him, you know, out in the yard? Playing as a kid?"

"Only from a distance. Sometimes he would wave at me, and I would wave back. But, it was my job to stay out of the family's way. To be almost invisible as I did my work. I didn't mind. I kept my part of the work agreement, and Mr. John kept his."

A long touchdown pass drew their attention to the screen, and they didn't speak about the Channons any more.

It was past ten o'clock when they said goodbye. Heavy clouds filled the dark sky, promising snow.

"You know what I think?" Mark said, as Sean backed the car down the driveway. "I think you're going to transfer to Ashington College before Gold gets a fair chance. You'll be adding another college to your list soon."

"Don't need to," said Sean. "Felicitas graduates in May." He flashed his signature grin.

Mark adjusted the heater as Sean drove down the long street, aiming, as usual, back toward the river. The time at the Juarez home had been good. Reminding him that there was another world outside of grief, outside of the Channons.

Driving back in a cold car, Mark felt the simmering cauldron of unpleasant emotions bubble inside him again. Sadness, irritation, anger, fear. All of a sudden Riverview House seemed intolerable.

"Let's go get a drink somewhere," he said.

"The sports bar?"

"Too loud. It doesn't have to be that kind of drink."

"All the coffee shops are closed by now."

Sean turned onto the main road that ran along the river, the one that would take them back to Riverview House. He glanced at Mark, thinking out loud.

"Most things are closed today. Bars are too loud. Fast food places are too, well, fast."

Mark pointed. "Turn there."

"Not the diner. You can't be serious! Not the diner. After all you've been through, you really can't eat here."

"Turn in!"

Sean pulled into a parking spot, but kept the engine running.

"I have a confession to make," Mark said. "I have eaten here exactly six times when you were out with Felicitas, and I never got sick. Not once."

He opened the car door and got out. Sean turned off the engine and opened his, reluctance clear on his face.

"Look, we just ate," Mark told him. "So you won't be tempted to get that big cow burger again with half the farm on it. But you should be able to get a soda or something without losing your insides." Mark changed his tone. "You don't have to go in, but I will."

Sean was watching him. His face in the streetlight sober, cautious. "I'll go in. It's okay."

Mark caught himself and shook his head. "I'm sorry. I feel like I've got a bear inside me, but it doesn't need to growl at you."

"It's okay, really. I'll find something in there that's nontoxic. It's gotta be warmer in there than out here."

It was. Steam fogged the windows. Rows of turquoise vinyl booths lined the walls, some with torn and taped upholstery. The grill was concealed by a half wall behind the long counter fronted with stools. The diner was mostly empty. A few scattered, expressionless faces, chewing on a late night patty melt. Or slurping a bowl of chili. Alone on Thanksgiving night.

Like he would have been. Except for the people who cared about him. His tether to life was still there.

Sean bent to whisper in his ear. "Professor, look down there."

At the end of the long counter, on the last stool by the big black clock, sat Rebecca Powell.

Mark led the way down the aisle toward her. Just as they arrived at her side, the cook behind the half wall perched a plate on the ledge and slapped a small bell. The waitress took the plate and shoved it in front of Rebecca. Mark couldn't keep from staring at it. A tuna sandwich on toasted grocery store bread, faded lettuce, and some greasy-looking fries.

He spoke without thinking. "You're eating that?"

Rebecca shrugged and reached for the ketchup bottle. "Late dinners are what I'm used to."

Mark felt stupefied. Speechless.

Sean leaned in. "But everyone else—Jim, Felicitas, Kelly, the extras—they all eat in the kitchen. You don't?"

Mark found his voice. "You prefer diner food to what Nick makes?"

She looked at both of their faces in turn. "No and yes."

Mark stared, disbelieving. She put down the ketchup bottle and pivoted on her stool so she could face them. The heavy weariness was on her now, and Mark knew he must be adding to her burdens.

"I'm sorry. I didn't mean—"

"It's okay. You might as well know. I'm not allowed to eat in the kitchen. I'm not allowed to eat anything Nick makes."

She glanced at her plate for a moment, looking embarrassed. "I disagreed with him about the flavor of a sauce. I thought it had too much lemon. He got cold angry and told me I was never to eat any of his food again." She gave a wan smile. "So I haven't."

"But if you apologize?" said Sean. "Smooth it over? Surely that would make things all right again."

"I have and it didn't." She turned back to her plate and stabbed a french fry with her fork.

Mark thought of all the nights he had seen Rebecca toil up the long driveway. The nights she had stood in the drive staring at the house.

"How long ago was this?" he asked.

"Over a year." She took a bite of tuna fish sandwich.

He remembered how she had backed away when he had offered her a piece of cake the night of the Channon party. He thought of the tables this morning weighted down with exquisite food.

She had eaten none of it.

And it had all been made by a man who refused to feed his own wife.

Mark pulled out his wallet and fished out several twenties. He put them down on the counter next to her plate.

"What's this?" she asked.

"A Thanksgiving Day treat. Call it the tip that you deserve."

She looked hesitant. Unsure.

"Please, keep it. I'd be glad if I could buy you a week of dinners at least."

Sean pulled out his wallet and threw a couple of tens on the pile. "Me too."

Her eyes filled with tears. She nodded silently, not looking at them, and slid the bills into her purse.

"Hey, Rebecca," Sean said, his voice friendly and gentle. "Sorry the Brewers didn't make it to the playoffs."

She tried to smile at this, "Well, they say there's always next year."

32

What Wound Did Ever Heal But by Degrees

THEY LEFT without ordering and stepped outside into a cold wind. "I feel sick," said Sean. "And it wasn't the diner."

The bear in Mark was fully awake and snarling. In the middle of the parking lot, he wheeled around. "What kind of man doesn't feed his own wife? How can he feed everyone else so lavishly, and refuse her a crumb? It's—it's evil!"

He glared at Sean and was glad to see the anger in his eyes also.

Mark pointed at the diner. "Every night she's had a sandwich alone at a greasy spoon. How has she kept on? Day after day, smiling at all of us, working for Nick, then being turned out to eat alone?

"When I think of Amy—" His voice broke. "I'd give her anything."

He glared in the direction of Riverview House. The turrets and roof were easily seen over the intervening buildings. Snow swirled around its security lights. As he stared at it, he felt heartsick for Rebecca, heartsick for Amy, and heartsick for Baiss.

His head hurt in that too-familiar way. His body ached. But standing there as the snow flurried across the parking lot, he finally told Sean what Ernie had done to Baiss.

Angry tears streamed down his face as he told the awful story of how cruelty, how jealousy had stopped the music. Proving the barrenness of real evil, just as Simone Weil had written. Sean watched him closely, an inscrutable expression on his face.

Mark wiped his eyes with his bare hands, his energy spent. "On their courthouse they have those words, remember? The courthouse the Channons built? *I, the Lord, love justice.* It's a good thing *He* does because men surely don't."

"Some men," Sean said quietly.

Mark stared down at the snow swirling around his shoes. He felt weak and useless. His injuries, both old and new, drained him. And grief had not slowed its ceaseless ravage.

"Let's get you inside," said Sean.

Mark reached for the car door and climbed in.

~

WATER.

His limbs were on fire.

He opened his eyes. The room was still dark. The clock by the bed glowed in blue digital numbers. 4:27.

He sat up slowly. Every part of him throbbed.

Water. There would be clean glasses in the bathroom. The maid always put them there.

He stood up. Legs unsteady. Weak. Unreliable. He made his way to the bathroom, keeping a hand out for the wall, and turned on the light.

The light stabbed at his eyes. Ouch.

He picked up a glass from the tray, filled it from the tap, and drank the whole thing down. His lips felt hot as they touched the glass. The water hurt his throat.

He reached to put the glass back on the tray, blinking against the light, and missed. The glass fell onto the counter, rolled toward the sink, and fell in. Loudly. Had he broken it?

He stood there stupidly trying to think of what to do. Sean appeared in the mirror behind him. Sleepy. In his worn T-shirt and basketball shorts.

"What's up?"

"Got a drink. Dropped the glass. Sorry."

Sean picked up the glass and squinted at it. "It's not broken." He put it on the counter. "But the heat is just radiating off of you. You get back in bed and let me take your temperature."

Sean made sure he was safely in, before leaving to get the thermometer.

The sheets felt cold. Mark pulled the blanket up to his chin and shivered.

Sean turned on the lamp by the bed. Mark winced and turned away from it, eyes tightly closed.

Sean ran a small ball across his forehead.

A silence.

"102.8, Professor. Let me take a look in your throat."

Sean examined his throat, nose, eyes, ears, even the lymph nodes in his neck. He produced a stethoscope, made Mark sit up, and listened to his lungs. At last he was finished, and Mark sank back onto the pillows with relief. Sean tucked the covers around him, then got the spare blanket from the closet and spread that on top of him too.

"Thanks."

When Sean brought a glass of water and set it on the table by his bed, Mark noticed he was fully dressed. "Where are you going?"

"To the twenty-four-hour drugstore. You probably have the flu, and I'm going to assemble an arsenal to help you fight it. I already called the doc. He's ordered anti-flu meds and antibiotics. Since you are asplenic, we're not going to take any risks. I'm only going to be gone about fifteen minutes, then I'll come back and stay put, okay? Don't you try to do anything while I'm gone."

"What will you do if Will claims you're prowling around?"

"Bust him in the chops, just like any nurse would."

Mark managed a chuckle. "You do that."

The door closed softly, and Mark drifted off into an uncomfortable sleep. He woke to Sean handing him a glass of water and a small cup with two pills in it. "For the fever."

Mark swallowed them without question.

Sean took it back and handed him another cup with more pills in it. "Here's the anti-flu medicine." Mark swallowed that too.

"And the antibiotics."

He swallowed again.

Sean pulled a chair up to his bedside and sat down. "Okay. Here's the plan. We make sure you rest, stay hydrated, stay nourished, and then we give the body whatever it needs to fight this thing."

Mark nodded weakly. "Good plan."

"I called your sister. She said that flu is going around their area too. She told me to tell you that she never stops praying for you."

Mark mumbled a thanks and drifted off into sleep again.

The day passed, and Mark was oblivious to most of it. It seemed that every time he woke up Sean was there, taking his temperature, handing him another glass, more pills, more medicine. Somewhere in the afternoon Sean presented him with a large bowl of chicken soup. He felt a start of alarm.

"This isn't Nick's, is it? I'm not eating his stuff any more."

"Mrs. Juarez made it. George brought it up."

Mark drank it all and went to sleep again.

The day blurred into night to another day. Whenever Mark woke up, there was Sean, sitting by his bed reading, lying flat on the floor with a pillow sleeping, but he would always start awake at any movement from Mark.

Sean brought tissues. Cough syrup. Flu medicine. Fever reducers. Antibiotics. Water. Juice. Soup. Take-out food from the healthiest restaurants in town. Sean even emptied the trash can.

After several days Mark had to ask. "How are you not getting sick from me?"

Sean grinned at him. "Nurse tricks. I can sanitize surfaces with the best of them. Not to mention I have the immune system of an ox. I also think that chicken soup is magic. Mrs. Juarez makes enough for both of us."

One evening Sean presented him with a bowl of soup that he knew was Nick's. Nick's signature rolls were on the side with pats of butter, and the salad Mark always chose with the vanilla vinaigrette.

"I'm not eating this," he said.

"I didn't order it," Sean replied. "Rebecca brought it up for you herself."

He ate it.

The maid was afraid to clean the room, so Sean did. Sean even changed the sheets while Mark was propped up in a chair in the tower room. And when Mark got back in bed and was too restless to sleep, Sean picked up a book—a light-hearted Wodehouse novel—and read to him, doing all the character voices.

A week went by. Mark felt he was in a world apart again. A world where the only focus was rest and healing. That's what he had done so much of this year, waiting for healing.

He told Sean this, and Sean responded with Shakespeare.

"'How poor are they that have not patience! What wound did ever heal but by degrees?' That's *Othello*."

"Those acting classes," said Mark, "they can take you far."

"Yes, sir."

THE OUTER WORLD still remained and pushed in on theirs. Overnight guests came and went. He could hear car doors slam, footsteps on the stairs, voices in the hall, the thump of luggage, the rumble of the elevator, and Ernie playing the large grand in the parlor below.

One day when Ernie began an especially crashing, domineering performance, Mark groaned and buried his head in the pillows.

Sean darted out of the room in a flash. A few moments later the music stopped, then Sean re-entered their room quietly.

Mark pulled his head out from under the pillows. "What happened?"

"I told Ernie to stop playing," Sean said, dropping onto the floor. "It was wonderful!"

"And he did?"

"He snarled at me, but I told him I would get movers to take the piano out if he couldn't play quietly. And guess what? Todd backed me up!"

Mark was surprised at this, and grateful. Talking made his throat hurt, but he had another question. "Did they ever find the money?"

Sean shook his head. "I haven't heard."

Mark rearranged his pillows and sank back into them. He still agreed with his original instincts, that Will had taken it. Will had been too eager to accuse someone else.

If Baiss knew Sean hadn't done it, did Baiss know who had? Had it been an overnight guest? And how could Baiss possibly have known?

Mark couldn't keep these thoughts going for long. He felt too weak to even think about the Channon mess. Too weak to hold a pencil for number puzzles. Back to sleep.

Once when Sean was in the bathroom, Mark got up to turn the CD player on and set it to repeat. He wanted to hear Baiss Channon play, over and over again. He got back in bed and stared at the ridges of plaster on the ceiling, listening.

Sean came back in. "What's up?"

"The music. It's like magic. I don't ever want it to stop."

But it had.

Mark stared through blurry eyes at the map of Europe —or was it South America now—that he had imagined on the plaster ceiling, and tried to distinguish every single note of the Schumann concerto Baiss was playing, tried to take every single note into his soul, until sleep came again.

Mostly, he tried not to think. But when he thought, it was of Amy and Sean, Baiss and Elizabeth. The days on the calendar crawled slowly by. It was already the fifth of December. Only six days remained and Baiss had not yet come.

Finally a day dawned when Mark showered, shaved, and put on fresh clothes. He would keep to his room still, but sit up and count the boats on the river again.

Then it struck him. In less than a week, his stay at Riverview House would be over. Either Baiss would come and claim his inheritance or Victor Gaff would claim it for the county.

"What if he's not who everyone is hoping for?" Sean asked, from his familiar spot stretched out on the floor.

Mark gazed out at the Mississippi. "It's rare when humans get what they hope for. I wonder what *Baiss* is hoping for." No boats were in sight along the river. "And I wonder about something else now."

"What?"

"I wonder if he's healed enough to come back."

They both were silent for a moment, until Sean spoke.

"That would depend on a number of things, wouldn't it?"

Mark nodded. "And if there's one thing I've realized in all this, it's that no one can do your healing for you."

Sean leaned back on his hands. "Well, it's about time for us to make our exit, isn't it? When should we start packing? Todd said we're paid up through checkout time on the twelfth. Apparently, the family is allowed a few transition days before the house goes to the county."

"How about the night before then? We don't have much to pack. Beyond several dozen number puzzle books that is." Mark went back to watching the barges on the river.

A LITTLE LATER HE thought of something else. "You shouldn't be babysitting me. You haven't seen Felicitas in a long time. I'll be all right. You get out of here."

"She's got finals this week."

"In my experience that has never kept two lovebirds apart. Just don't bring her grades down, okay?"

Sean was gone for the rest of the afternoon, and Mark

had time to let his thoughts go back to the young man he had seen standing quietly against the wall on the night of the Channon party. That man would have been the right age for the returning Baiss. The right height, too. And he had had just that sense of watchful aloneness that Mark expected Baiss would have. Standing in the middle of all the noise, hidden in plain sight, as the saying went. And he had disappeared that night so easily and quietly.

Had Baiss healed enough? Had he healed at all? If he decided to return, would his old life destroy him? Would he come back only to embrace his ultimate ruin?

Mark mentally shook himself. Words like "ultimate" and "ruin" sounded rather dramatic. Until he thought of the family that waited for Baiss Channon. Of everyone who wanted a piece of him, or, rather, a piece of his wealth. And Mark feared that Leal Baker and Elizabeth together would not be strong enough to protect Baiss from all the rest.

WHEN SEAN RETURNED, his arms were full. Take-out pizzas from the sports bar. More soup from Mrs. Juarez. Home-made penuche from Felicitas. And Christmas cookies from Elizabeth.

Mark stared at all of it. It was evidence that they had made a type of home here, and though he would be glad to see the last of the Channons, some goodbyes were coming that would be hard to say. As he watched his able companion pulling a slice out from the first pizza, the cheese stretching long, he knew that the toughest would be saying goodbye to Sean.

. . .

A FEW DAYS LATER, while Mark was reading the newspaper in the downstairs study, Fia walked in. She sank into the big chair with her gin and tonic in hand, and told him the news.

After a family meeting with Leal Baker, it had been decided that the restaurant would close after breakfast on the morning of the eleventh. No other guests would remain in the house that night except for Mark and Sean, and they would leave the next day.

Elizabeth wanted to have a birthday party ready for Baiss. She had asked Nick to bake a special cake. For the first time, or so it appeared to Mark, Elizabeth's older half-siblings went along with her ideas.

"You should be at the party too," Fia said.

Mark put down his newspaper and stared at her.

She took another sip from her glass, all her attention on the ice cubes clinking against its walls.

He realized in that moment that even Fia understood that Channons were safer when others were with them. And that Fia was afraid of the coming storm.

33

———————

A Birthday Gathering

THE WEATHER HAD no such fear. December eleventh arrived clear and cold. Mark watched from the tower room as the last of the overnight guests put suitcases in their cars and drove away. He went to his door and opened it and held still, listening to the growl of a vacuum cleaner on the floor above, the last time a maid would clean the guest rooms, unless Todd Channon's wildest dreams came true.

The maids and the kitchen staff had been looking for new work. Many had already left to take other positions. Mark hadn't seen much of Jim or Kelly to know what their plans would be. Felicitas would work for her dad, and George was glad of it. George had already worked on the grounds of Riverview House for the last time.

It was a sad day, and a sober one. Late in the morning, Mark walked through each floor of the house slowly, giving a mental farewell. He went outside and circled Riverview a number of times, staring up at the window to Baiss's old bedroom for a long while.

Back inside, he lingered in the small parlor, hoping the county would be gentle to this happy, elegant room. He lifted the lid of the piano bench and slid the worn teal green book inside. There it would await its owner.

If he came.

Perhaps the tragedies of his youth had overcome him. Perhaps he no longer cared about anything Channon. Perhaps the unreasonable expectations of the members of his family were just so much smoke in the wind.

Then why was he watching?

Mark went with Sean to the classic burger place one last time, and they had a quiet lunch. There didn't seem to be much to say.

Partway through their meal, Mark said, "We didn't do that big road trip out west yet."

"Maybe next summer?" But Sean said it wistfully. In the kind of tone that realizes it probably won't happen at all.

"What's next for you? Any college ideas yet?"

"Just another job offer. Don't have the details, so there's not much to say." Sean filled his mouth with another bite of burger, and Mark got the idea that he really didn't want to talk about it.

FOUR O'CLOCK WAS the appointed time at which they were all to gather in the large parlor and wait. No one had yet specified for how long.

At five minutes before the hour, Mark came down the stairs with Sean behind him and poked his head into the room. Most of the Channon siblings were already there.

Ernie, standing by the front bay window, stared down the drive as if daring the heir to come up it. Will stood by the side window, staring at nothing, a drink already in his hand.

Juliane was on a sofa, looking through a magazine as if she had not a concern in the world. Fia sat on another sofa, noisily swirling the ice in her glass.

Kelly and Rebecca were setting out plates and forks at a small table on one wall. Another table held Nick's offering for the event, what looked like a three-layer cake covered with chocolate ganache. The sight of it made Mark feel sick.

Elizabeth had not yet arrived.

Fia saw Mark and Sean at the doorway and waved them in. The reaction to their entrance was instantaneous.

"What are you doing here?" Will was in combat mode. Those were the first words he had spoken to Mark since that night in the jail.

"Mr. Newlin," Ernie said angrily, "you presume you are wanted. You're not."

"Shut up, Ernie," said Fia. "I asked him to come."

Juliane kept her eyes on her magazine. Ernie was glaring at her, waiting for her to say something.

"I think they should stay," she said lightly. "It will be fun."

"Even if we have the professor, we don't have to have *him*." Will stabbed a finger in Sean's direction.

Todd came in then. "Dad, please," he begged.

There was finally room for Mark to speak. "If I am to stay, I'd like my assistant to stay also, but since this is a family gathering, it's your call."

"He's still healing up, Will. Leave him alone," said Fia. "It's your fault anyway."

"So why are you so compassionate now, sister?"

"We have no kitchen staff left," said Rebecca calmly. "If Sean stays, he can help Nick and me."

Before Will could protest further, Ernie's voice broke in. "Baker's here."

Mark went to the other side of the large window and looked out. More than Baker had arrived. Three black BMWs pulled into parking positions, one beside the other, and after them a silver Passat came up the drive.

"That's a lot of people," Ernie said, still looking.

"We'll need to get more chairs," said Todd. He scurried out. Sean gave Mark a pained glance and followed Todd.

Mark watched the men get out of their cars. Several of them carried serious-looking briefcases. Others wore the uniform of security guards, guns in holsters at their sides. Baker was not taking the potential return of the heir to the Channon millions lightly.

The lawyer led them all into the large parlor where they filled the center of the room. Elizabeth slid in quietly behind them and took a place next to Rebecca and the cake table. Todd and Sean reappeared with folding chairs in their hands.

Ernie looked indignant. "What is all this about, Baker? Theatrics? Who are all these people? Is this some kind of game?"

Baker smiled as Todd helped him off with his overcoat. "Of course it's a game, Ernest. The Ritornello Game, the game in which someone returns with the music. Didn't you describe it that way at your party?"

Todd looked nervous. "The room is pretty full, sir. Should we move out to the main hall?"

"Thank you, but no. I think it will be better in here near the piano."

His assured answer made Mark wonder, but Fia voiced the question for him.

"Do you know what is going to happen today?"

"I have no more idea than the rest of you, my dear. But let me make some introductions. First, are we all here?" He looked around the room. "Ah, Dr. Newlin. Glad to see you. It's always good to have a history professor up one's sleeve."

"I'm not sure why," answered Mark, "but I'll take the compliment for my profession."

Todd and Sean set up the folding chairs. Nick, still wearing his chef uniform, came in behind them and sat down.

"Now we're all here, sir," said Todd, as Stephanie walked in.

"Fine. Let me introduce these gentlemen, and then we can all get comfortable. I believe most of you know Warren Egan already. I present to you the remaining trustees for the Channon Trust—Tom Brown, Rick Flint, Don Belinsky, and this is Dr. Dill, a music professor at Ashington College."

Ernie frowned at this last, unexpected person, but said nothing as Baker went on. "Officers Brent and Chad are in the security division at the bank and have the duty of escorting the contents of the Trust's safe deposit box to this gathering and safely back again. They are also fellow witnesses that nothing that was in the box has been removed or damaged in any way, but was placed in this briefcase and brought here without any alteration whatsoever."

"What's in the briefcase?" asked Ernie.

"Proofs of the heir. The same proofs that John Channon's father left to him, as did his father before him."

"I don't know anything about this," Ernie cried.

"You wouldn't," said Fia. "You're not the firstborn. You're only trying to act like one."

"Sophia is partially correct," said Baker. "The contents have only been passed down from father to firstborn son through several generations of Channons. This is the only time the proofs have been legally required."

"Mr. Baker," Elizabeth asked. "What happens to the proofs if Baiss does not return?"

"There is a day specified on which they will be destroyed sight unseen."

Even Juliane looked sober at this news. She had put her magazine down and was watching Baker closely.

Baker looked back to Ernie. "So the other answer to your question, Ernest, one equally correct, is that this is not a game. Not a game at all. Now, shall we all find a seat and get a little more comfortable? Not there please, Miss O'Connell."

Kelly had perched on the piano bench, but immediately got up.

Mark sat in a folding chair along a far wall. He wanted to be a watcher, not a participant in this drama. Sean dropped down in a chair next to him.

"Aren't you glad you wore your best jeans and white shirt?" Mark whispered with a smile. "I told you this was formal."

"Man, this is making me crazy," Sean replied. "If I had hair, I'd run my fingers through it. Madly."

"You don't have to stay if you don't want to. I'm doing this for Fia and Elizabeth. And because I just need to see the Baiss chapter through to its end."

Sean thought a moment. "I'll stay. I'd be a lousy assistant if I left now."

"Lousy is one thing you've never been. I owe you so much for putting me back together three times that I'm going to have to surrender my retirement fund just to pay you back."

"You better stop talking like that. You're going to make me blush in front of this crowd."

Rebecca Powell stepped in front of them. "Coffee for you two?"

Sean started to get up. "I was supposed to help with that."

"Stay put. There's no room to move around in here. Black or cream?"

"Cream," said Sean. "This time."

"Black," said Mark. "This time."

She returned with two cups and moved on.

"What do we do now, Baker?" Fia called out.

"Now we wait."

"Hah," said Will. "For how long?"

"Baiss Channon's birthday ends at midnight."

"That's eight hours!" Fia cried. "I can't wait that long."

"You may leave if you wish," said the lawyer.

"Fia, you've been waiting for years," said Juliane. "What's eight more hours?"

"Let's eat the cake then," said Ernie.

"Not before the birthday boy arrives," said Elizabeth. Ernie glared at her, and Mark felt the urge to smack him. But Elizabeth met Ernie's look with one of her own and did not back down. Ernie was the first to look away.

Baker and Egan whispered together for a few moments, then Baker said, "Nick, you weren't expecting all of us, but do you have any light snacks? Something quick and easy? We don't mean to put you to work when the kitchen's shut down, but we could be here a while."

Nick called to Rebecca and Kelly, and they followed him out of the room. Kelly did not attempt to hide the frown on her face.

It was a strange gathering, full of unrelated yet related people. Mark considered each person, and automatically reviewed their history with Baiss Channon.

Todd resented Baiss, called him an abnormal person, yet wanted him to turn Riverview House into a larger hotel under Todd's command.

Fia had expressed nothing but disregard for the young Baiss. Now she wanted him to set her free from all her gambling debts.

Juliane was here to watch people squirm. More to the point, she wanted to see Ernie's face when Baiss walked in.

Will needed money so badly that he probably risked stealing from his son to protect his own hide. Mark suspected that he had stolen from his company too, and was going to be caught if he didn't pay it back in time. The purchase of Channon World had temporarily stalled; the buyers, too, were waiting for the heir. Baiss's return could reveal much, especially things Will wanted to keep hidden.

Ernie hated Baiss. Had been the cruelest of all to him. Yet he was determined to get the rest of what he called the Channon money. Baiss was only in his way. But so were John's will, the trustees, and Victor Gaff.

Nick badly wanted a restaurant of his own. And Baiss had the money to fund it for him. Yet, Nick had recently blasted Baiss's absent ownership in a newspaper interview, blaming Baiss for the closing of the restaurant.

The chef appeared just then and set down a meat and cheese tray on the low coffee table in front of the sofas where Fia, Juliane, and the trustees sat. Rebecca put another tray near the window seat, where Will and Ernie pounced on it right away. Kelly followed with baskets of crackers.

"You want anything?" Mark asked Sean. Sean had been quietly watching the whole room alongside him.

"No," said Sean. "I think for once I've lost my appetite."

"Twice," said Mark. "The diner."

"Then you'd have to make it three times."

"Three it is."

Mark glanced across the room to where Elizabeth sat listening to something Rick Flint was saying. She caught his eye and gave him a quick smile before turning all her attention back to the trustee.

Elizabeth was the only Channon who wanted Baiss to come back because she missed him. Because she cared about him. Because she loved him.

Baker too, seemed to care about the boy and what had happened to him. He was determined to discharge his trust well.

It was all up to Baiss now. Up to him to decide if he wanted his inheritance with all its complexities, or if he would stay anonymously in whatever new life he had carved out for himself, and let the Channon family fade out of Ashington Mills.

Mark set his cup down on the small table at his elbow and stood up. Sean looked alarmed. "Where are you going?"

"Upstairs for a minute. Coffee goes right through me, remember?"

THE REST of the house felt oddly silent as Mark climbed up to his room. He could easily imagine the house holding its breath, waiting with the others for the return of the heir.

On his way back downstairs he took the opportunity to do something he had wanted to do for a long time, and now no one was watching.

He stopped on the staircase and tried to remember where the woman Mary had been standing when she said she saw the face of John Channon. He tried to put himself on the stairs in the right position to be mostly hidden and couldn't do it. Because everyone would have seen someone on the staircase. Could Mary have been looking through the stairs, through the railings to the other alcove? He walked over that way. Sure. But guests were in *every* room in the house that night. Someone else would have seen John, or really, Baiss. Because Mark was sure that was who it really had been, and he bet Baker thought that too.

He walked over to where Mary had been standing—as close as he could remember—and looked toward the stairs. What did he see? The staircase. The far alcove. A bit of the porch window.

Baker said Baiss had been watching them. Had he looked in the window and frightened Mary?

Mark walked quickly to the alcove and pulled back the curtains. No one waited on the porch. Not a soul in sight now. But George and Sean had strung white lights all over the porch, and a face in the window would have been seen.

He saw something now, in December's darkening twilight. A small part of the roof of a police car, visible just over the curve of the driveway, invisible from the windows of the large parlor. It waited at the base of the drive.

Baker was taking no chances. He didn't trust anyone either. But wait. What if Baker hadn't asked for the police, but Baiss had?

The hands on the grandfather clock pointed to 5:09. Mark couldn't leave Sean alone in this agonizing mess any longer.

He went to stand where Mary had stood one more time. Looked in the direction that she had, then tried to follow the angle of her arm where she had pointed, and walked slowly toward the window. It framed nothing but an angle of the porch roof and a small hook, the kind used to hang decorative lights.

All at once, he knew.

He knew who Mary had seen.

Someone tall, who had been helping George with the lights. Who would have only needed a step stool to quickly replace a burnt-out bulb under the roof.

Baiss *had* been watching. Closely. He had come unlooked for, unrecognized, and seen his family for who they were now.

He had spent months watching his life from a type of distance, perhaps waiting for the courage to take it up again. Struggling to find out if he even should.

Mark felt baffled, completely bewildered. So many questions swirled in his mind, they felt like a physical force. He took a deep breath. The answers would come. But now, more than ever, he had to get back to the large parlor.

WHEN HE RE-ENTERED THE ROOM, half a dozen expectant faces looked up, then registered disappointment and irritation when they saw only him. He caught Baker's eye. A look of understanding passed between them. Baker was going to let Baiss lead. Well, then, so would he.

Elizabeth gave him a welcoming smile. He held her gaze for a moment, trying to put encouragement into his look. He saw a question appear in her eyes before he moved on.

Sean was sitting where he had left him, reading the magazine Juliane had discarded.

"*Coastal Living?*" Mark asked, as casually as he could, when he sat down.

"There's lots of coastline in this world."

"Did you study geography too?"

"I'll put it on my list. Maybe I'll double major at Gold. Have you ever been to the coast?"

"I've been to Florida. Clearwater."

"Really?"

The tension in the room felt so oppressive that these words of small talk felt like heavy weights on the tongue.

They both fell silent.

Todd was saying something to Baker while Stephanie listened. Will helped himself to another drink. Ernie held a newspaper open in the window seat. Juliane flirted with one of the trustees. Fia watched her sister's bright expression, a wistful look on her own face. Kelly showed Elizabeth her bracelets, and Elizabeth kindly listened to her tell about each one.

Mark leaned over and whispered in Sean's ear. "They may have just set a new record on how long they can all sit in a room without killing each other."

Sean looked up from his magazine. "No. No record. Look at that."

Mark followed the direction of his gaze. Rebecca was standing at the cake table, her back to the room. Nick was standing beside her, facing the same way, but speaking quietly and firmly into her ear. Her head drooped as he spoke. A swift movement of her hand. The motion of someone wiping tears away. She seemed to shrink more each moment, as if she were dying right in front of them.

Sean stood up quickly, tossed the magazine, and started across the room toward them, resolve on his face. But first, he stopped by the piano, leaned over the keyboard, and with one long finger began to pick out the melody of "Happy Birthday."

All the voices in the room silenced. Heads whipped around. Ernie threw his newspaper down. Nick stopped talking and turned toward the piano. Rebecca didn't move.

When they saw it was Sean, Ernie swore at him. Juliane started laughing.

Will bellowed, "For the last time, get that idiot out of here!"

Baker held up his hand for silence, his gaze intent on Sean.

Sean pulled out the bench and sat down. To Mark's utter amazement, and overwhelming relief, Sean began to play.

Ernie swore again and started toward the piano, but one of Baker's security guards intercepted him and stood stolidly in his path. Ernie backed up, his precious hands held carefully away.

Elizabeth's eyes were wide.

A frantic scrambling took place near one of the brief-cases. The music professor opened some papers and the trustees near him peered over his shoulders.

Mark's heart felt tight in his chest, thudding into his ears. He struggled to listen and watch and absorb what was happening, and longed for more senses than he possessed.

Sean played on, seemingly oblivious to the commotion around him, his heart in the music, his touch on the keys like that of an old friend, like restoration after a long parting.

Mark stared at the expression on Sean's face. For there was the boy with joy in his fingers. The music had not died completely after all.

The last chord sounded, and Sean lifted his hands from the piano gently, reluctantly. A hasty conference was going on around the briefcases. The rest of the room was silent, thunderstruck, waiting for Baker to tell them what, in God's name, this all meant.

And as Mark watched, Sean looked over at Elizabeth and smiled, then played four notes, one after the other. Four hauntingly beautiful notes.

34

Channel Markers in the Dark

Elizabeth couldn't breathe. She stared at the man sitting on the piano bench. A man with an imploring, pleading look—a scared look—in his eye.

"I remember you liked these even better." Sean played four more notes. Hauntingly beautiful.

Yes. She had liked those even better.

"Baiss?" she whispered.

Sean gave a small nod.

There he was. Baiss. Alive. Breathing. Reasonably okay? She wanted to see his hands, but the side of the piano blocked them from her view.

She looked at Mark. *Had he always known?* The wonderment on his face told her that he hadn't. That any realization must have just happened.

She turned back to the man at the piano. There was so much she needed to ask, to know. But not now. Not here. Baiss's greatest enemies sat in this very room.

Yet, in spite of that—here he was. And he had chosen to come home.

She gave him a smile, trying to tell him that she would understand. Whatever he would be able to tell her, she would understand.

Sean returned her smile, then glanced over his shoulder. "This one's for you, Mr. Baker." He played several energetic measures that she recognized instantly. *Rigoletto.*

"From the night when you sang for us," Elizabeth said. "Baiss had practiced your favorite song so he could surprise you."

Baker rose and cleared his throat with difficulty. "Ladies and gentlemen, I am happy to announce the return of Baiss Channon and the end of the Guardian Trust."

MARK WATCHED as the import of this news washed over the group. The Channon faces froze, caught for a moment in time—like a classic painting of the Renaissance multitudes, staring up at a sky with clouds parting and the Lord of Glory descending. Their faces showed every kind of human emotion.

The return of the Channon heir had always been a concept, vague and uncertain. Now here he was, a man in flesh and blood, who knew more about them than they wanted him to.

Fia's mouth opened and closed several times, but she said nothing. Todd put his head in his hands. Stephanie looked hopeful. Kelly reddened. Juliane's eyes danced.

Will lowered his drink to the table and stood blank-eyed, like a gaffed fish. The only one who had the money to bail him out of his difficulties was the very man he had threatened and accused of being a thief. Will blinked rapidly and fled the room.

Ernie held his ground. "This is some kind of a joke!" he cried.

"Come see the proofs for yourself," said Baker.

Ernie pushed past the security guard, glared at the young man on the piano bench, tried and failed to take the music from Dr. Dill's hand, and had to lean over the music professor's shoulder to see.

Sean played the whole thing again, while Ernie, Dr. Dill, and Elizabeth, who had picked her way across the room to stand at Dill's other side, followed the notes he was playing—Dr. Dill pointing at each measure with his finger while Ernie fumed. Mark tried to watch them and Sean at the same time.

When Sean finished playing, Dr. Dill called out, "That is *exactly* what is written on this sheet."

Elizabeth nodded agreement. Ernie stared at the music in silence, his face contorted into an angry scowl.

"I can understand your need for reassurance," Baker said, addressing the Channons, "so let me tell you this. No one has ever known of this secret manuscript except the Channon eldest. The secret was so well-protected that the key to the case carrying the music was itself locked away in a sealed box, and only opened this afternoon in the presence of all the trustees.

"I assure you all, there has been no fraud. We will run the usual DNA tests for the record, but, gentlemen," turning back to the trustees, "so they know this is not my verdict alone?"

The one Mark thought was Belinsky spoke up. "We have no doubt that this man is Baiss Channon."

Warren Egan went up to Sean and shook his hand warmly. "Welcome back, Baiss. It's so good to see you."

"Thank you, sir." It was said humbly, nervously.

Ernie took a step toward Sean. "I don't believe you. You don't play a thing like Baiss did."

Mark stood up, ready for anything, surging with anger at Ernie's audacity.

Sean faced his uncle and stayed calm. "You probably noticed that the leaps to the higher notes, especially with my right hand, slowed the tempo some. Tell me, do your friends Tray and Denis still do their rope tricks? Have they ever tried them on you?"

Ernie's face paled to stone. The whole room hushed. No one moved. Mark's heart pounded; the blood pulsed loudly in his ears.

Suddenly, Juliane began to howl with laughter. Yes, howl was the only way to put it.

Ernie's face went from white to red. "They—they got carried away. They went too far."

Juliane cried, "That's not what you told me!"

"Ernest," Baker asked, "is there something we need to know?"

Ernie ignored his question and turned on Juliane. "Why are you laughing, you damned cat? You'll get no more money out of me!" He darted from the room, the front door slammed, and a few moments later Ernie's car flew down the drive. A police siren sounded not long after.

"Well, since this is my birthday party of sorts," said Sean, surveying those left, "what if we cut into this cake right now?" He looked over to Nick, but Nick made no answer.

"Thanks, Nick." Sean went over to the cake, cut a large piece, put it on a plate with a fork, and handed it to Rebecca.

Rebecca stared at him, eyes wide.

"Please, take it," Sean said, "From me."

Rebecca lifted the fork to her mouth and ate a bite. Nick turned his back on all of them and walked out.

Then Sean brought a piece over to Mark, apology in his eyes. "I'm really sorry. I can explain everything," he said. The hand that held out the cake was shaking.

As SOON AS he decently could, Mark slipped out of the room and went upstairs. He closed the door to his darkened bedroom and stood staring at the knob for a few moments before going over to the tower area and lowering himself into the chair. A barge group was coming steadily upriver in the early winter night. The searchlight flashed to the bank then to the channel markers, back and forth, trying to pick out safe passage in the darkness.

"You and me both, fella," said Mark in the quiet room.

He didn't know why, but before today he had never considered that Sean was Baiss. Maybe because everyone's description of Baiss did not resemble at all the person Sean was now. Probably not even who he had been then. Except Elizabeth's. But even her pictures contained barely a clue.

In his years of living on his own, Baiss had grown into a man, added height, shaved his head, sprouted a beard, and become a runner. The boy could no longer be recognized.

Baiss was back home, one could say. Elizabeth was happy. Baker was happy. That was good. But Mark wasn't. He had too many worries.

He wished, oh, how he wished, that Baiss had been someone other than Sean.

Why couldn't he have been the stranger they had all been waiting to come up the drive? Why couldn't he have been the quiet man against the wall at the party? A man who had been another bored guest.

Mark wanted Sean to have a happier life than the one mapped out for Baiss. He couldn't forget the look on Ernie's face as he left the parlor. This whole blasted, vicious family!

Well, as he had told Sean just a few hours ago, he stayed because he had wanted to see the Baiss chapter through to its end. And he had. So, he might as well start packing.

He got up, turned on the lights, then went to the closet and pulled out his suitcase and satchel.

But he couldn't stop thinking. He had totally missed

the similarities between Baiss and Sean. The death of the parents. The Chicago connection. Mark had been just like the Channons. Looking for someone who fit their own perceptions, instead of seeing what was right in front of them.

He felt like a fool.

He was up to his elbows in folded shirts and socks, when Sean came in hesitantly, a nervous look on his face. "I think the party's over."

Sean glanced at the bed and said, "Here, let me help with that." He picked up a shirt from the pile on the chair and began to fold it.

Mark snatched it away from him. "You shouldn't be doing that! You're a multimillionaire now." Then his arm dropped, limp, with the realization. "But I guess you always have been, haven't you?"

"Please, may I help, sir? It would make things feel a bit more normal." Sean was clearly struggling too.

"All right." Mark tossed the shirt back at him.

They finished packing his suitcase in a strained silence that was rare between them. Finally, Sean broke it in a timid voice.

"Baker's asked us both to be his houseguests for a few nights. Are you up for that? He's waiting to drive you over."

Was he? He had to somehow get closure on all this mess.

"Sure."

Sean nodded. "Okay, sir. Thanks."

· · ·

MARK RODE in Baker's car down Green Avenue. They pulled into the drive of a beautiful, historic home, white with tall columns and black shutters. The very home that Mark and Sean had admired when they first came to Ashington Mills. The lawyer himself carried Mark's suitcase upstairs to a spacious bedroom, inviting him to make himself comfortable and rest for a few minutes.

Mark sat down in one of the armchairs clustered by the window, glad to be alone with his thoughts again. This room was definitely more comfortable than Riverview House. But of course, no view of the river. One light pole illuminated the center of the backyard and a swimming pool, now buttoned up for winter.

He sat there for some time, staring into the dark of the trees in the yard, when a knock sounded on the door. Elizabeth was there, a concerned look on her face.

"Mark, can I talk to you for a moment?"

He turned on another lamp and ushered her over to the comfortable window chairs.

She got right to the point. "Sean talked all the way over here in the car. The words poured out of him so fast he was almost babbling. I think I'm beginning to understand why he kept hidden. But he's terribly afraid you are angry at him. He knows you have good reason to be. The two of you had so many talks about Baiss, and he felt like such a liar keeping up the pretense."

"Well," Mark took a deep breath, "he never really wanted to talk about Baiss very much. I'm the one who kept dragging him into it. That is, until after the party when he heard about his father's will. I can imagine each discussion became a hypothetical testing of courses of action for him."

Elizabeth nodded thoughtfully. "I think they did. But, I have to tell you this. What really got through to him was you. You cared so much about Baiss. You worried about him. Thought about him constantly. And he saw that you were so angry about what happened to him.

"Sean found you listening to his Chicago performance when you were sick. He saw the look on your face, how you truly loved his music. He went back to his room and cried."

Elizabeth leaned forward, and he could see the sincerity in her eyes. "You're the one who healed him, Mark. Because of you, Baiss was able to return."

Mark shook his head slowly, staring out into the dark. He wanted to have an answer for this, but didn't. There was too much to think over. Too much to absorb.

Finally he said, "I don't know if I'm more angry at him or at myself for being such a blind fool."

"Don't forget. I was blind too."

"No, you can't blame yourself. You didn't have the constant opportunity I did to see what was right in front of my face. The Channon arguments took him completely apart. He was like a scared child, needing to leave, to run away again. He couldn't bear to go into his old bedroom when Todd first tried to assign us there, or after the party when I wanted to find something that had belonged to Baiss."

"But I had known Baiss," said Elizabeth. "The child Baiss, at least." She gave a short laugh. "You know, I liked

Sean the first time I met him. Liked him immediately. And I couldn't figure out why."

"He reminded you of someone you knew?" Mark couldn't help but give a wry smile.

"On some level, I'm sure he did."

"Sean's a likable guy. Decent. Loyal. Virtually selfless. When I think of all he's done for me, how can I be upset with him?"

They both gazed out the window, at the darkness softened by the distant city lights, and he posed another question to himself. A question that needed to be answered.

Hadn't he, Mark, been doing the same thing as Sean?

Hadn't he also been viewing his old life from a distance, trying to get the courage to return, wondering if he even should? Wasn't this upcoming semester in England part of his own search for that courage?

They had needed each other in the same quest. Unlikely partners, yet on the same internal road. He shook his head again, laughing at himself inside.

"What is it?" asked Elizabeth.

He took a deep breath and smiled at her. "I'm not going to be angry at all."

She smiled back, a relieved smile, like a burden had slipped away.

"What's going on downstairs?" he asked.

"No one's here except for Sean and Baker. Sean would like to talk to us. He wants to explain some things. Will you come?"

"I certainly will."

Mark followed her down the staircase to another comfortable room in the back of the house, where tall windows framed a brick fireplace, with a cheering fire behind the grate.

Sitting in a leather armchair by the fire was someone who looked like Sean, but wasn't. Something had changed, some facade had slipped away. The man who sat in the chair looked a bit unfamiliar to him now.

35

Making a Path

MARK HESITATED FOR A MOMENT, trying to determine what was different, then gave it up and came all the way into the room.

Sean stood up immediately. "Thanks for coming, Professor."

He heard it in the sound of the words. Saw it in the stiffness of manner. The usual camaraderie was absent. The ease of friendship gone. Sean looked at him with anxious eyes. Mark couldn't stand it.

"Can I get you something to drink, Dr. Newlin?" Baker asked. "I can offer you my wife's hot mulled cider. The best thing on a chilly night."

Mark nodded. "That would be great. Thank you."

Baker went toward the kitchen. Elizabeth, after a quick glance at Mark, followed.

Sean was still staring at Mark, a worried look in his eyes.

Mark looked right back at him. "Forgiven, okay?"

"Okay." A half-smile.

Mark held out his hand. "I've been wanting to meet you for some time, Baiss Channon."

The release of a held breath. Sean took his hand and shook it. "Thank you."

"And," Mark added, "before you get started answering all our questions, let me see those hands."

Sean held them out. Mark took them gently and turned them over, looking at them as carefully as a doctor. He hadn't noticed before but there was a bit of off-proportion in the shape of the right hand.

Baker and Elizabeth returned quietly, set mugs on the coffee table, and took their places on the sofa.

"Did they heal then?" Mark asked, releasing them.

"Not completely," Sean replied. "Enough for today. Enough for the kind of stuff you play in bars, where no one really cares much about technique. But I was working on the Goldberg Variations at the time. That's really hard stuff. I knew when I was hanging there that my career was over."

Sean said it in a low voice. But Mark could hear what was behind the words. The pain and fury and fear, and the desperate, desperate grief.

"Please, sit down," Baker urged them. "Let's settle in here. We have a lot to talk about. And, if you are ready,

Baiss, I think I'd like to know exactly what happened with Ernie."

Sean returned to the chair by the fire, while Mark sat in the next one. Across the coffee table from them, Elizabeth and Baker, sober expressions on their faces, waited to hear the story they had been waiting to hear for years.

Sean hunched forward, rested his elbows on his knees, and rubbed his hands together with a slow, deliberate motion. "I'm not sure how to begin."

"Fourteen years is a long time," Elizabeth said gently.

"Professor," Sean spoke without raising his head. "Remember when you saw that picture of my parents in the magazine in the library. And you wondered if they were a happy couple?"

"Yes."

"They weren't. My father was away much of the time—going to splashy places around the world with his friends—and Mom was sad. She would have good weeks, then slide into a depression for a while. I never saw any sign that my father loved her. Not one.

"I was miserable after she died. Grandpa was already gone. Grandma and Elizabeth had moved away. There was nothing but sadness and anger in the house.

"I was home alone one afternoon, in my room, when I heard laughter downstairs. Silly, infectious laughter. Nothing like that had been heard in our house for so long.

"I went downstairs and found Uncle Ernie with two characters, dressed in flashy exercise clothes. He said that they were acrobatic circus performers. He said he knew how much I liked the circus, so he brought them over to cheer me up."

Sean paused after this, staring at the carpet. Mark felt his own shoulders tighten.

"They were funny. Really engaging characters. They had done shows all across the country—Branson, Las Vegas, Los Angeles—and they had all sorts of stories to tell me, things that happened in performances, favorite stunts. I really enjoyed listening to them.

"They said they wanted to show me one, one I could help with. One that always got them standing ovations and yet it was so easy."

Sean shook his head slowly. "I've gone over this so many times in my mind. I think what caught me was the lure of fun, the relief that a few moments of happiness can bring after months—years—of heavy sadness. That's what made me willingly take part. I didn't know what the trick would be.

"We went up to my bedroom and climbed out onto the roof section there. One of them, Tray, explained the stunt. He was going to walk on the edge of the roof. He would wobble and sway, making audiences think he would fall. And then Denis would *actually* fall, but not far, and the crowds ate it up.

"The key was that they needed a third person's weight to pull it off. So they brought me in, to make it all work.

"Tray assured me it was safe, not to worry about him. The rope was looped around a hook in the outer wall, and around some roof pipe and then tied to all of our waists. Everyone would be safe. I could keep my hands on the rope to steady myself, and they would take care of the rest.

"It's all a blur to me now. Tray started prancing on the roof edge, pretending to fall, and then he really did go over the edge. Before I could see where Denis was, the rope pulled me over the edge too. It slid until I was hanging there, the rope tangled around my arms and hands. Tray was swinging back and forth from his end of the rope like a monkey. Both of us in midair.

"He was laughing. 'We fooled you. See? That was the *real* trick!'

"My hands were being pulled apart, and they hurt so bad. I knew what this meant to my music, my piano. Ernie knew it too. I looked around for him, calling frantically, and he stood on the lawn, watching. He looked at me for just a moment. Then he walked over to his car and drove away.

"It took an eternity for Tray and Denis to get me down. I could barely open the front door to go back into the house, so Denis opened it for me. Apologizing. My hands were bleeding. I filled the bathroom sink with cold water, put my hands in and just stared at them, trying not to know what I knew.

"After a while, I heard my father come home. I dried my hands and came out. He wasn't in a good mood. He asked me why I wasn't practicing. I told him I had hurt my hands, and he blew up."

Sean stared at the floor in silence for awhile before continuing. "I don't want to remember everything he said. But the main point was that without my hands working properly, I was worth nothing."

Elizabeth covered her mouth with her hand. Mark felt sick with anger.

Sean didn't raise his head. "He told me he didn't care what had happened, but I'd better be practicing before half an hour was up. So, I packed a bag, went out the side door, and to the bus station. I had a car, but I didn't dare take it. Instead, I took a bus to my aunt's house in Wisconsin. She hated my dad. She also had a chiropractor neighbor who came over and worked on my hands. I'll always be grateful to him."

Mark and the others listened closely as Baiss's story poured out at last. They learned how he had left his aunt's home to protect her from his dad. How, using the name Sean Merritt, he stayed in a women's and children's shelter in Madison. How a pizza place near the shelter had an old piano. How one night he played a simple jazz song with hurting hands and people began to clap. How the owner hired him to play, first in Madison, and later at his other pizza parlor near the university in Bloomington, Illinois.

Sean told the story he had told Mark months ago on the road—all his colleges and work adventures. "But, I had to keep moving, because I knew that my money transactions could easily be traced. I kept waiting for the money to run out, or be removed from my account, but every time I checked it was always there."

Baker cleared his throat. "Egan and I talked it over. Your money patterns were similar to what they had always been, and appropriate to someone your age. We could get a general idea of what you were doing and where you were. Egan made sure all your transactions went through data processing, and that your card stayed alive. And in September he burst into my office with the news that a few recent transactions had taken place in Ashington Mills."

"But," Mark had to speak up. "There were searches for

him." Mark looked to Baker. "That skip tracer too. And yet, you knew what Baiss was doing?"

The lawyer frowned. "The skip tracer was Ernie's idea. I didn't trust Ernie, so I had the Guardian Trust take over the search. We paid off the skip tracer and sent him away. He made more money not looking, than by looking."

Elizabeth looked accusingly at Baker, and Mark could see the shadow of hurt in her eyes. "But you had an idea of where Baiss was? All this time?"

The lawyer, too, had something to confess.

"Not *exactly* where he was, no. But there was something that kept me from pinning him down." Baker rubbed his forehead. "I was torn between two opposing forces—a promise I had given and questions that had been voiced, but never asked to me directly."

He turned to face Elizabeth. "Your father made me promise that no matter what happened to the rest of them, I would watch out for Baiss. Protect him. From his own father, if need be."

At this last, he gave Sean a look full of concern. "I hoped it would never come to that. Tried to believe it never would. You see, John never told me you had run away. I had to guess. He was hiding the truth for some reason. And until I knew exactly what had made you run, I felt that for your own safety we had to keep what we knew secret. And once you were of adult age, then the choice was yours.

"Meanwhile," Baker continued, "we were watching the money. You were auditing courses at colleges all over the state."

Mark leaned forward. "Wait. Auditing? Just auditing? You're kidding, right?"

Sean grinned sheepishly. "Confession: I don't have a real college credit to my name, Professor. I didn't dare settle anywhere." His face sobered. "If you're auditing, you can leave fast, if you need to. I was afraid of my father coming after me, but I should have known that he wouldn't."

Mark was drowning in that helpless anguish that comes from hearing of pain you can do nothing about. Problems you cannot fix.

"That piece you heard me play today?" Sean looked around at them. "It's called 'The Inheritance.' My great-great-grandfather wrote it as a way to guarantee that Channons would continue to value music for generations.

"He established that every eldest Channon would be taught the piece when they were thirteen years old. He taught it to my great-grandfather, who taught it to my grandfather, who taught it to my father. But my father didn't teach me.

"My grandfather was aging fast. He took me into his apartments at Riverview House, sat me down at his piano, and taught me the piece from memory, measure by measure. I was eleven, almost twelve then. I knew that my grandfather didn't trust my father, because he always told me, 'Don't worry about your father, Baiss. No matter what happens, *I'll* take care of you.'

"My grandfather died, and all through my thirteenth year I waited for my father to teach me 'The Inheritance.' On my fourteenth birthday, I realized that he never would, and that my grandfather had known this."

Silent tears streamed down Elizabeth's face.

Baker cleared his throat. "Your grandfather did more than that."

"Sir?"

"Your grandfather set aside some money for you as well. Money that no one knew about. Money that no one else could touch. He spent years selling off divisions and companies and putting the money away for you. My father helped him do it."

Now Sean's eyes filled with tears. "That was very kind of him."

"It was," Baker replied. "And wise. Egan's team managed it very well, and I am happy to tell you that you are now the richest man in the state of Illinois."

They all stared at the lawyer. Baker sipped his cider, a smug smile on his face. And also, Mark thought, a look of profound relief.

"That's wonderful!" cried Elizabeth.

"And to think I was worried that you didn't have enough money for gloves," Mark said.

Now Sean looked like a gaffed fish. Stunned. "I—I hope you'll guide me in all this, Mr. Baker."

"Your grandfather made me promise to. But I would have done it anyway. Would you like some more cider?"

Baker stood up and took Sean's mug into the kitchen. They all waited for the lawyer's return, and then Elizabeth asked, "What made you decide to return to Ashington Mills now?"

"I was so tired of running," Sean replied. "I wanted a real address, a home, a place to be. I needed to see what my family was now, but I didn't want to go alone. Then, an opportunity fell in my lap."

"Literally," Mark said. "Or should I say, you caught it before it hit the floor."

Sean did not smile. "You were more than opportunity, sir. It turned out we needed each other at the same time."

The story had finally come out. The context. The reasons. The rationale. Mark gave Sean a sympathetic look. "These past months must have been very hard for you."

Sean nodded slowly. "They *were* hard. Once here, I didn't want to stay. I wasn't sure what to do. I thought about just telling Mr. Baker who I was and walking away." He glanced at the lawyer. "But I didn't know how that would go down.

"When I heard about the will and the loss of the house, I thought I might have the power to do something good. And I thought of how Elizabeth had waited for me for so long."

He looked at her. "All these years, I wanted to contact you, but then you would have to tell someone that I did. You'd be forced to tell someone, and I—I couldn't—"

"It's okay," Elizabeth said softly, leaning forward. "You're here. You're all right. It's okay." She nodded at him to go on.

Sean took a deep breath. "So here I was, stuck in a mess that I had helped to make. I wasn't sure—even up to the last minute—that I would admit who I was. But every day I had seen the professor struggling to deal with what life had given him. Saw all the courage that took. And I saw much more—"

Mark protested. "What *can* you be talking about? Stumbling around weeping all the time? That doesn't feel like courage."

"It probably wouldn't, sir. But every interaction you had with my difficult family was making a path for me. Showing me how I could step in again."

Baker spoke up, "We can't thank you enough, Dr. Newlin."

Mark shook his head. "There's no need to thank me." He felt so embarrassed by this. So awkward. "I didn't do anything. You're looking at a man who can be taken apart by a simple holiday."

"Well, as it turns out," a smile stole over Sean's face, "I have an idea for the next holiday."

Elizabeth and Baker shared knowing looks, and Sean was wearing his quirky grin. Something had been discussed while Mark was upstairs. Something that Sean was planning. One of his first actions as Baiss Channon again.

"All right," Mark said. "Lead on."

"You don't want to know what it is first?" Sean was giving him the full raised-eyebrow look.

Mark leaned back in his chair. "Nope. I've learned to do whatever you say."

36

———

I Would Also Be Honored

SNOW WAS FALLING IN MARLONBURG, and Myra Waite watched through her living room window as the flakes floated to the ground. She missed Amy Newlin so much.

Somewhere over the years, she and Amy had fallen into the habit of planning their holidays together every year—sitting at the Waite's dining room table, or with coffee and cocoa in Mark and Amy's cozy living room. Not that they *spent* their holidays together each year; they were usually with their own families on the actual day. But the idea-sharing, the planning, had become its own special event.

Not this year.

Her own pain over Amy's death, she kept to herself. She didn't dare share how she felt with Jerry. It would only add to his burden of guilt. A burden he wouldn't let go. Maybe ever.

She heard footsteps upstairs, the thump of a file drawer sliding to a full stop inside its cabinet. Jerry at work in his office.

It had been a sad semester for him. The loss of Amy, and then Mark's absence too. He said he couldn't bear to look at Mark's office—the closed door, the dark glass window—every day. With the horrible knowledge that nothing would ever be right again.

A mail truck pulled up to their mailbox, the mail was shoved in, and the truck drove off into the graying afternoon, snowflakes swirling around it. Myra rubbed her arms. It was chilly standing by the window. Best to get the mail in and get started on dinner. A pot of stew would taste good tonight.

She pulled a coat from the closet, hurried out into the cold air, snatched the mail from the box, and ran back inside.

Catalogs, bills, and a short stack of Christmas cards. Perhaps some of the cards would be from former students. That would cheer Jerry some.

She climbed the stairs and poked her head into Jerry's office.

"The mail came, Jer."

She sorted it through her fingers as she entered.

"Oh, look! Here's a postcard from Josh Perkins. Isn't he at the History Museum in Chicago now?" She made her voice as bright as she could.

Jerry swiveled in his chair, an inquisitive look on his face, and took the card she held out to him.

"There are a few more cards too, and this one, which looks personal, but not very Christmas." She looked at the return address. "Do you know any Channons?"

Jerry looked up from the card he was reading. "Channons? Not personally." He took the envelope from her and reached for the letter opener.

"It could be one of those businesses that try to look unusual just to get you to open their mailing," she said. "I cleaned out the recycling bin earlier. It's over there."

Jerry unfolded the letter, and a check fell onto the desktop. Myra bent close to him, trying to see what was written on it.

"Jerry! It's a check for twenty-one thousand dollars! It *can't* be real! *Is* it real?"

She glanced at her husband. He had a dazed look on his face. She craned her neck to read the letter over his shoulder.

Dear Dr. Waite,

I don't think you could have realized when you sent Professor Mark Newlin to Riverview House the impact his presence would have on my life. While he was there, he discovered that his stay was due to your generosity. I'm glad he did, because now I can thank you properly for your gracious gift and return it, dollar for dollar.

Please accept my deepest gratitude. Best wishes to you and the entire History Department at Gold College.

Sincerely,

Baiss Channon

· · ·

"MYRA!" Jerry's face was suddenly animated. "Mark did it! He found Baiss! He found Baiss Channon! Oh, wait 'til I tell Pim!"

"Jerry, who is Baiss Channon? And what is he talking about, *your gracious gift*. You gave someone twenty-one thousand dollars?"

He looked sheepish. "I've been wanting to tell you about that ..."

But she couldn't hear what he was saying. She squealed and grabbed his shoulder.

"Oh my gosh! Jerry! Look, look!" She pointed to the postscript.

P.S. I WOULD ALSO BE HONORED to fund and sponsor a yearly group of history lectures at Gold College each January—The Amy Newlin Memorial Lecture Series. My lawyer will be contacting you soon to make all the arrangements.

MYRA FELL INTO A CHAIR. They both stared at each other for a full minute, not able to say a word.

37

———

A Ritornello for Mark

ON A COLD DECEMBER afternoon in London, Mark Newlin climbed the 157 steps to get to the interior of the dome of St. Paul's Cathedral. He took the breaks he needed to on the way up, but made it just fine. Sitting down on the outer bench, his back to the dome wall, he took a moment to breathe as he looked around.

From this angle, he could see a portion of the black and white tiles far below him. It was an odd, disorienting feeling, and he was glad for the bench to sit on, grounding him in midair, as it were, and for the other benches and railing in between.

Most of the people that passed in front of him were cautious of the great height. One man in a black shirt kept his hand tight to the railing as he inched by; he looked over the side just once and muttered something under his breath.

Mark opened his notebook and drew a pen from his pocket. He had planned to write a letter, of sorts, to Amy. The Amy in his mind, at least.

But the moment his pen touched the paper, all his intentions turned into something different. A small, closed door inside him swung open again.

DEAR LORD GOD,

Thank You for Amy.

Thank You for the beauty of her eyes, for the sound of her laughter—the way it would start, then catch, then come out stronger. The way she would fan the air with one hand when she couldn't stop laughing.

Thank You for the way she said my name.

THANK You for her love of old movies and popcorn, and for the funny duck voice she used whenever something was ironic.

Thank You for how we read aloud to each other at any time, all the time, everywhere we went, and how she loved people with food.

IT WAS A LITANY, of sorts.

A litany from this side of death.

Time passed and he wrote on, saying everything he could think of.

• • •

THANK *You for the way she curled up on the sofa to listen whenever I was thinking through an idea, and for her wisdom about things.*

Thank You for the way she believed in me.

Thank You that her love made me a better person, in so many ways.

PEOPLE WALKED BY HIM, climbed to the higher dome, and came back down, while he still wrote.

Pages.

Filling the notebook.

Thank You for the way she felt, lying by my side each night.

Thank You for the feel of her hand in mine, for our together life. Every moment of it.

I know that it was You who made her, You who made us.

She was Your gift. Thank You. Thank You so very much.

HE CAPPED HIS PEN, took a deep breath, and covered his face with his hands. He felt empty. Spent.

Somewhere far below him, voices started singing.

The music rose from the cathedral floor high into the dome, soaring and echoing around him. He looked up to where the dome narrowed in a ring of arches far above his head, and listened in awe. The music seemed to never stop, and he had the strange sense that it was calling to him.

. . .

No more let sins and sorrows grow,
  Nor thorns infest the ground;
  He comes to make His blessings flow
  Far as the curse is found, Far as the curse is found . . .

THOSE FAMILIAR WORDS. Had he ever really heard them before? They were written by a human writer, and sung by human voices, yes. But suddenly he could see the Someone present in them. So clearly.

Someone who wanted him to heal.

Someone who would make it happen.

He slid his notebook and pen back into his coat pocket, and leaned back on the bench, listening to the music that surrounded him.

There was a real *ritornello*. There was.

Not one of superstition or of man's contrivance.

Not an eccentric man's educational game, or grief's delusion.

But the *real* music of mercy, of Someone always calling.

His grandfather had told him years ago, on a summer night at his midwestern farm, that love heals life. And Mark had believed it, up until he needed healing for himself. Then, it had seemed absolutely impossible.

But in this moment, sitting in the dome high above the cathedral floor, he saw that it was the music of Christ's eternal love that called you to life—and back to life—again and again and again.

It had called him through Patti and her family,

through Jerry and Tulia and Luedders, even George, Felicitas, and Baker. Through Elizabeth and Sean.

And it was calling him directly now.

WHEN HE STEPPED DOWN onto the black and white tiles, Sean was standing nearby, reading through a brochure. He folded it quickly and gave Mark the old analyzing look.

"You make the stairs okay?"

"Every one." Mark smiled. "Did you hear that music? That singing? It's too early for evensong with all the tourists around, isn't it? Where did it come from?"

"A wandering choir came through a little while ago. The brochure says it's from Perth, Australia. Seems like a special Christmastime thing."

Then Sean leaned closer, a puzzled look on his face. "You look different."

"How different?"

"Better."

"I feel better. How long was I up there?"

"About an hour and a half."

"Thanks for waiting. Any word from Felicitas yet?"

"No, but that's all right. It took me months to get used to the idea of being Baiss Channon again. I can give her more than a few weeks."

"Good man. Where is everyone now?"

They walked as they talked, exiting the huge cathedral, heading down the Strand toward their hotel. Their eyes were drawn by the light displays in store windows and coffee shops, the festive greenery adorning historic London.

"Patti and Zach took the kids back to the hotel to get ready for dinner. And Grandma and Elizabeth were able to charter a minibus, so later we can see all the Christmas lights of London."

"My nephews will be talking about this for weeks, months, years! I know you don't want me to keep saying 'Thank you,' but, well, thank you."

"Then it's my turn." Sean looked serious. "Thank you."

"For what?"

"For insisting on looking for me, even when I was a pill and didn't want you to."

Mark laughed, then looked closely at him. "No regrets?"

Sean thought a moment and shook his head. "It will be hard. And challenging. And right."

"Good. Then, officially, and for the last time—you're welcome."

"You're welcome too, Professor."

"You know, you're going to have to stop calling me 'Professor.' As someone once said, you could actually be my little brother."

"*Pesky* little brother, I think he said."

Mark laughed again. "No, not pesky. Definitely not pesky."

They stopped outside a brightly lit storefront. By invisible means, an enormous red Christmas cracker turned slowly, each end of it flaring out like the ends of a shiny candy wrapper.

"Okay, big brother, what about this? I think I'm going

to officially change my name. I promised Baker I'd wait until all the paperwork settles. What do you think of Baiss Sean Channon?"

"Sounds good." It was another sign of strength. Sean was choosing the name he would use for his new life. "Sounds really good."

"By the way, that Professor Luedders is a really funny guy," said Sean, his eyes on the slowly-turning cracker. "I'm glad he came over early with us. Grandma keeps talking about how witty he is."

"He brings the house down at faculty meetings." Mark zipped up his coat against the cold. "Which reminds me, were you the one who gave Stanwick and Jerry the brochure for Riverview House this summer?"

A look of uncertainty passed over Sean's face. "Yes, sir. I—"

"It's fine," Mark said quickly. "Everything's just fine. I'm putting all the pieces together, that's all." He stuck out his hand. "We're like brothers, remember?"

Sean grinned, clearly relieved. "Yes, Mark. Brothers." He grasped the hand firmly.

ACKNOWLEDGMENTS

To the following people, my deepest, heartfelt thanks:

My preliminary test readers, for your generous time and enthusiasm: Adam Connor, Bjorn Olson, Hannah Olson, Bonita Krupp, Caleb Eckhardt, and Laura Eckhardt. I can't do this without you.

My expert test readers: Adam Connor (law enforcement), Caleb Eckhardt (academia), Julie Buchner (medicine). Any errors in the manuscript are most definitely mine alone.

Rick Kolbe and Darcia Narvaez, for thoughtfully answering my questions and giving me additional insights into the world of academia.

Ralph and Mitzi Montgomery, for insights into the world of musicianship and performance.

Jamie Moldenhauer, for being a second pair of eyes for me in London and the dome of St. Paul's.

My brother Rodney, for bringing me a sack of college courses to listen to while I was healing from a brain injury

—a sack which contained *Bach and the High Baroque*, and the seed for this book.

My own college history professors: Robert Fiala (in memoriam), Larry Grothaus, Jerrald Pfabe, and James Pragman, for planting the conversation of history and humanity so deeply in my life.

Kristen, my graphic designer, for another amazing book cover. Somehow you always know the perfect thing to do.

Jenn—every author dreams of an editor who loves a book as if it were her own. I have one. Thank you so very much.

My husband Dale, for absolutely everything.

To the Lord Jesus Christ, for Your outrageous love for the people of this world. May this humble work bring You honor.

ABOUT THE AUTHOR

Rhonda Chandler was born in California and spent her childhood traveling with her family in Asia Minor, Europe, and all across the United States. In 1979, she graduated from Concordia College, Nebraska (now Concordia University) with degrees in education and history.

After teaching at the high school level for several years, she left to devote her time to her husband and daughters, and to writing.

She now lives with her family in southern Illinois, where on Saturday mornings they make breakfast, brew coffee, and talk for hours about all the important things in life.

Rhonda writes historical, contemporary, and fantasy fiction with spiritual and historical overtones. To find out what's new, visit her at rhondachandler.com and subscribe to her mailing list.

If you enjoyed this book and found it valuable, please leave a review on Goodreads and on Amazon, Barnes & Noble, Kobo, or wherever else you purchased it. In today's world, reviews are very important in helping people like you find this book. Thank you so much.